PRAISE FOR LINDA WINDSOR'S HISTORICAL

THE FIRES OF GLEANNMARA

"Linda Windsor deftly weaves a tapestry... the glory of knowing Christ, creating a masterpiece of medieval... *Riona* is more than a novel, it's an experience—a journey to a faraway time and place where honor and faith are lived out amid the clamor of swords. A glorious read!"

LIZ CURTIS HIGGS, BESTSELLING AUTHOR OF *BOOKENDS*

"With a lyrical voice worthy of the Isle of Erin, Linda Windsor's *Riona* is a wonderful novel, peopled with memorable characters who will lay claim to your heart. I believe I could see the green hills and feel the kiss of mist upon my cheeks with every page I read."

ROBIN LEE HATCHER, CHRISTY AWARD-WINNING AUTHOR OF
RIBBON OF YEARS

THE FIRES OF GLEANNMARA #1: *MAIRE*

"This story has it all: spiritual inspiration, history, and love…. Ms. Windsor's voice is crisp, vibrant, and professional in its delivery, providing readers with characters who will live long after the last page. Linda Windsor provides readers with a lush Celtic saga sure to touch their spiritual soul with a promise of love both secular and religious. *Maire* is a breakout book sure to find its way to many a bestseller and reader's keeper lists, creating a whole new sub-genre where a Windsor book is going to be the classic standard to achieve."

ROMANCING THE CELTIC SOUL

"Linda Windsor's talent for creating a faraway land and time is flawless."

ROMANTIC TIMES MAGAZINE

"A captivating fictional chronicle of Christianity's dawn in Ireland. Remarkable for its appeal as both a historical saga and inspirational novel, *Maire* achieves success that few other books can boast."

SUITE101.COM

—◦◦◦—

NOVELS BY LINDA WINDSOR

THE FIRES OF GLEANNMARA SERIES
Book 1: *Maire*
Book 2: *Riona*
Book 3: *Dierdre* (Available April 2002)
It Had to Be You
Not Exactly Eden
Hi Honey, I'm Home

RIONA

BOOK TWO OF THE FIRES OF
GLEANNMARA SERIES

LINDA WINDSOR

Multnomah® Publishers *Sisters, Oregon*

RIONA
published by Multnomah Publishers, Inc.
Published in association with the literary agency of Ethan Ellenberg Agency.

International Standard Book Number: 1-57673-752-7
© 2001 by Linda Windsor

Cover image by Bord Failte, the Irish Tour Board
Cover design by Uttley DouPonce DesignWorks

Scripture quotations taken from: *The Holy Bible,* King James Version

Multnomah is a trademark of Multnomah Publishers, Inc.,
and is registered in the U.S. Patent and Trademark Office.
The colophon is a trademark of Multnomah Publishers, Inc.

Printed in the United States of America

For information:
MULTNOMAH PUBLISHERS, INC.•Post Office Box 1720•Sisters, Oregon 97759

LIBRARY OF CONGRESS CATALOGING-IN-PUBLICATION DATA:
Windsor, Linda.
    Riona / by Linda Windsor.
        p. cm. – (Book two of the fires of Gleannmara series)
    ISBN 1-57673-752-7 (pbk.)
    1. Knights and knighthood–Fiction. I. Title.
    PS3573.I519 R5 2001   813'.54–dc21   2001002100

01 02 03 04 05 06 07 08—10 9 8 7 6 5 4 3 2 1 0

Once again, to my family—Jim, Jeff, Kelly, and Mom— without whom I could not possibly have dedicated the time needed to complete Riona.

Dear readers,

In an effort to maintain historical accuracy, I've used several terms or mentioned historical figures that may be unfamiliar to you. You will find these explained in the glossary at the end of the story.

Speaking of the glossary, the earthy speech with which I have Erin present the foreword, the glossary, and the bibliography is not reflective of the educated Irish, either by past standards or by those of today. It is intended to effect the earthy speech of an old storyteller or *seanchus*, and is reminiscent of that which filtered down through my grandmother from her grandmother, an uneducated mother of eleven. This lady supported her children as a laundress, surviving three husbands. I am proud to claim her as an ancestor. Like those who fled to Ireland in the dark ages of western Europe, she was a brave, devout, and honest soul who came to America with a dream: building a better life for her children.

Linda Windsor

I greet you a free soul, good friend! Sure, it's been a long time and ye're a joyful sight for these sore eyes. All the while I've been collectin' me memories of me sixth century after the death of our Lord Jesus, and the second hundred years of me children's enlightenment of God's Word. My heart leaps like a mountain spring over a fall with excitement and pride, for them seeds of knowledge the good Lord planted the century before took root and grew beyond the ken of the angels themselves.

I am none other than Erin—the blessed Green Isle to the North of history and legend alike; Thomas Cahill's savior of civilization; motherland to warriors and bards, kings and saints, magic and miracle. Ye read as much, did ye not, in the first of me series of stories, *Maire, Fires of Gleannmara*? Aye, 'twas there ye saw the first flame of Christianity kindled in me heart.

Now, in the wake of Patrick and his likes, a new Erin emerges, where secular and clerical schools have grown to quench me children's thirst for knowledge while churches multiply to nourish their souls. I'm proud to say that public education began right here on me shores.

But what would ye expect in a place where literacy was near a religion in itself? Why in one generation me children mastered Greek, Latin, and some Hebrew. And their own Irish was so pure there was no dialect, no matter where 'twas spoken. When they weren't mastering a language, they was inventin' one, like that secret one, Hisperica Famina, made up as it were of bits o' Latin. And books, my heart, they were turnin' 'em out the likes of which was unheard of. Sure, I lay claim to bein' the world's first publisher. What with libraries fallin' to barbarian flames all over the continent and in Rome itself, there were me priests and druidic bards preservin' history and culture alike on pages for all time. And, I might add, fit as I am to bust me britches, that in the process of savin' such masterpieces of the past, their whimsical doodles and witty commentaries jotted in the margins come to be admired as an art form in itself.

Alls I can say is it's time, well enough, for the world to recognize me Celtic forefathers as far more civilized than their pompous Greek and Roman counterparts gave 'em credit for. No culture copycats among us! Our poems and tales, preserved by word of mouth, are purely our own dear Irish—a delight to the eye as well as the ear.

Plagiarism was not tolerated, as demonstrated when our precocious, but no less dear, Saint Columcille copied a rare and coveted psalter that his teacher, Ninian of Moville, had just brought back from Rome. High King Diarmait decreed "to each cow, it's own calf," and the disgruntled student had to give back his copy. By me mother's own milk, 'tis true!

Meanwhile, me feisty lads o' the cloth made a few o' their own rules, like confession. Ye see, Rome would have a body confess his transgressions afore all, public-like. Instead me saints adopted their ancestral custom o' sharing a soul's innermost fears and secrets with an *anmchara* or soul friend. In Patrick's time and afore 'twas said, "Anyone without a soul friend is like a body without a head." Me children looked for the likes of wisdom, holiness, generosity, loyalty, and courage in an anmchara, and in Columcille's time, me saints took to this private confession like fleas to a plump, hairy hound.

Aye, lads and lasses, whilst the rest of Europe was plunged into darkness by the barbaric hordes, I glowed like a lamp to the world, drawing seekers of truth from the black-hearted throes of destruction. Offerin' men and women alike refuge from oppression. I was an America o' the Dark Ages, there to share mercy and light, both within and beyond me shores.

Unlike elsewhere in the world, me daughters held social, political, and spiritual sway as queens, entrepreneurs, and abbesses. Me saintly sons gave up their greatest earthly love—the love of their mother country and people—to take God's Light and Word into the barbarous blackness beyond me surroundin' waters. Evidence o' their travels as far away as Iceland and the Americas exists to this day. Just take a gander at St. Brendan and the Milesians in the back o' this book if ye've a notion to see their wonderful accounts. Blessed so, how on God's green earth could I not turn out more missionaries for Christ than any other nation in time? Shame on the soul who takes such a gift as the gospel and doesn't use it to the glory of Him who gave it.

Yet, for all their best intentions and piety, me children were still troubled by temptation. They took the bounty for granted, no different than God's chosen in Scripture. If something went awry, like spoilt prodigals, they blamed God for their failin' faith, not themselves. Greed for power and wealth turned clan against clan and, sad to say, clergy against clergy at times. Such, ye see, is the power of worldly corruption. Aye, me children have their faith, thanks to the fifth-century saints, but hanging on to it will require all their courage and stubbornness, heart and spirit. Thankfully among the Irish there's no lack of such virtues.

So against this illustrious settin' I give ye me second Gleannmara story, that of Kieran, the great-great-grandson of Queen Maire and King Rowan, whose faith has fallen more on his sword than his God, and of the gentle Riona O'Cuillin of Dromin, the lady he's sworn a blood oath to protect.

So, I pray ye, sit back and savor each word as a tempting morsel of a grand feast for yer heart, yer mind, and yer soul.

May the good Lord take a likin' to ye.

ONE

The mist over the loch was so thick a body could walk on it. It permeated the tunics and cloaks of the warriors on the bloodied banks at the lake's edge. Kieran of Gleannmara walked among the wounded and slain, his lean, muscled legs as heavy as those of the dead. It was wrong, all wrong, he thought, turning over this body and that, numbly searching their features, now waxed in the horror of their demise. What the devil had happened?

Their early morning raid took the enemy by surprise and routed the marauding pirates from their stronghold on the bank. Bold when striking a helpless trading vessel, the cowardly brigands had scattered like smoke in the wind in the face of Kieran's forces. They'd either taken to the water in whatever would float or disappeared into the thick air at the Dalraidi's charge. At least that's what was thought. The main of the Dalraidi forces, among them Kieran's mercenary warriors from Gleannmara, had turned to looting. The more for King Aidan, the more for them.

It wasn't the loot that attracted Kieran, a young lord from Erin's tuath by the Wicklows. It was the adventure, the prospect of putting the long years of training in warfare to use. For all the heath fruit of Brigh Leithe could not make enough beer to induce the euphoria of plunging into combat, weapon to shield, blade to flesh, and—if need be—brutish hand to brutish hand. The greatest challenge at home was an occasional cattle raid or petty clan squabble and scholastic pursuit. Aye, it was good exercise for the mind, and Kieran of Gleannmara's fine, muscled body and keen battle senses demanded testing.

Young, hot-blooded, and eager to put their training to practice, Kieran and his chiefs had left with the high king's blessing to join King

Aidan of the Dalraidi Scots on his campaigns against pirates who had been harassing his fleet and the trade routes along the coastal waters. The restless young warriors from the various clan lands of Gleannmara had rallied enthusiastically to Kieran's call for volunteers to help their Scottish cousins establish their domain across the sea.

Mayhap a year later Kieran hoped to return, richer and wiser, yet on this day, and at this hour, he would give his share of the sacks and carts filled with booty to see his men—men he'd grown up with, attended school with, and learned to fight with—rise up from their still-blooded sleep. What in the name of Gleannmara's useless God had gone wrong? What had happened to the rear guard?

The sight of the well-armed and fresh enemy pouring down from the same craggy hill that Kieran and his men had just descended had taken Kieran and his men off balance. Only sheer will and raw courage helped them prevail. Countless bodies later, the enemy was routed for the second time and chased down until none lived in the godless mingle of lethal rock and bog that nestled the loch.

Kieran climbed the rocky rise, his limbs burning from exhaustion, only faintly aware of the fresh streamlets of blood the effort opened on his cut and bruised flesh. Faith, he felt colder than the dead surrounding him.

Kieran adjusted his cloak, securing it with a jeweled gold brooch worthy of his kingly station. All Gleannmara's royalty had worn it proudly. Its precious stones represented the union of Gleannmara's founding clans, placed in reverence around a silver inlaid Chi-Roh. As he fastened it, Kieran's staggered thoughts turned from instinct to reason. *If the rear guard had failed and let the enemy regroup behind them, then—*

"Kieran, God's mercy, hurry!"

At the top of the rise, Bran O'Cuillin—bard, would-be priest, and friend—waved at Kieran frantically. The young king's heart seized, run through by a terrible dread as logic came to conclusion. The rear guard was no more. And if that was so, then the O'Cuillins of Dromin, the clan who had raised Gleannmara's prince in fosterage and trained him under its champion, Murtagh, had been defeated. The image of his foster brother, the late Murtagh's son, flashed before him. *Heber!*

Kieran broke into a run, dodging and leaping over the bodies that lay in his path.

"It's Heber," Bran sobbed, confirming Kieran's worst fear.

Kieran mouthed the name and ran even harder after his foster brother's cousin. Heber was not Kieran's brother by blood. By law, Dromin's O'Cuillins were part of tuatha Gleannmara and owed allegiance to Kieran. But Heber was more than chief of a subkingdom. He was Kieran's *anmchara,* his soul mate. They shared life and all their secrets, their dreams. Heber's breath was Kieran's and vice versa since the day Kieran arrived at Dromin to be tutored in the art of war.

As Kieran broke over the ridge, his stomach turned at the sight of the carnage. The white leather tunics of Heber's men dotted the moss- and rock-covered plain, their bodies bleeding scarlet. Bran dropped to his knees beside one of the fallen and began crossing himself and pray- ing. The large warrior lying before the bard, drew up one leg unsteadily, as if trying to get up.

Relief nearly tripped Kieran. The chief of the O'Cuillin, the clan that had remained behind to guard the rear of their attacking force, was alive. *Thank God!* God had done little for Kieran since he'd lost the innocence of his youth. In truth, since Kieran's parents' death by the plague, he'd cursed the Christian God of his upbringing more times than he'd spoken to Him.

But for this, he had to give thanks.

He didn't deserve God's favor, but the faithful Heber certainly did. Heber's trials, of which there'd been many, never shook his faith. Kieran always said Heber had enough for the two of them.

"If God's not going to staunch his wounds," Kieran said to Bran, "then stop praying and at least help me."

Tearing his cloak from over his head, Kieran made a pillow of it and tucked it under Heber's head. The wounded warrior's black hair stood out in stark contrast to the cerulean blue of Gleannmara's col- ors—as did the blood soaking it.

"And how many brigands did Eimar help cross over before they learned that striking your head was for naught?"

Heber's hand tightened around the hilt of Eimar, his sword, as if to make certain it was still there and ready. He tried to laugh, but choked instead. Blood trickled out the side of his mouth, fresh and ominous. When at last he could speak, his voice gurgled. "Up."

Kieran hastened to help his broad-shouldered friend sit upright. Undoubtedly, he bled internally. Sitting upright would at least help him breathe.

It was then that Kieran saw the gnarled hilt of a dagger lying broken where Heber had lain. Instinctively, Kieran felt for its blade. As he feared, it was buried in the large warrior's back, just below the shoulder blade. His tunic must have twisted in the heat of the battle, leaving a seam exposed for one very lucky thrust. The tendons of Kieran's throat stretched fit to burst with the tortured cry of rage and agony he held back.

"Kieran." Bran glanced meaningfully as his elder cousin tried to find Kieran with his gaze.

Cradling Heber's head, Kieran eased him down like a babe and looked into his eyes. The ever-present twinkle was gone, replaced by a gripping desperation. No clever words of distraction came to Kieran's mind. His eyes stung so mightily it was hard to focus on Heber's face.

"P...promises." Heber let Eimar go, transferring his waning strength to Kieran's arm. "Remem...remember the promises."

Was it only last night Heber brought up the possibility that not all of Gleannmara's men would return to its precious soil? It felt like half a lifetime ago. Kieran had owned his friend's thought to Bran's musical rendition of an old tale of Irish warriors shipwrecked on a green island far to the north, beyond the ken of man. Had Heber had some forewarning of this fate instead?

"Aye, I remember." His blood curdled at what he must do, what he'd given his oath to do.

"T-tell me."

Kieran sensed more than heard Heber's words, for his lifelong friend was too weak to speak. His youthful strength soaked into the moss-covered ground beneath them.

"Though I can't carry you home, I'll not abandon you to heathen soil."

"Merciful Father!" Bran cared not who heard his cry or saw the tears streaking his face.

How Kieran envied the bard that freedom of manly constraint. His own pain longed to make itself known all the way to the halls of Gleannmara.

"*And—*" Kieran went on after a brace of breath—"I will take your sister into the protection of Gleannmara as my wife."

Heber convulsed and swallowed his own life's blood. "On your word."

"On my word as your brother in heart and soul, and as your king." Where the detached voice Kieran recognized as his own came from, he had no idea. Surely not from the black sea tossing his emotions on its crest like the remnants of a doomed wreck.

The reassurance was like a strengthening balm. Heber smiled and a familiar twinkle lighted in the depths of his gaze. "Then I shall see you and Bran on the other side. His tone was as light as when he'd teased his cousin Bran the night before for choosing a harp rather than a sword for his companion.

With that, the light went out in the lifeless blue of his eyes, and they stared not at Kieran, but past him, unfocused to all that was of this earth.

Bran helped Kieran lay their fallen comrade out. As Kieran took Eimar from Heber's side, he was aware that the septs and subsepts of Gleannmara had gathered around them, waiting, watching. The bard could not speak for crying, yet, when he crossed himself and took up the harp, which lay discarded nearby, his voice rang as clear as the strings with a song.

Part hymn, part eulogy, Bran's composition was worthy of the ancient poet Ossian himself. When honor was done to Heber and the bard's petition for the receipt of his soul into heaven by God and Creator of all things was ended, Kieran raised Eimar above his head with both fists.

Now he could scream. It increased the force of the blade he brought down with unfettered fury and anguish. Heber had known— as had they all—that the warriors could not carry back the bodies of their slain to the Dalraidi stronghold of Dunadd for proper Christian burial. Well they knew that the heathens would mutilate their fallen enemies, so all Heber asked of Kieran was to take the essence of a man, of all that he was…

His head.

TWO

Tuath of Gleannmara in Ireland, a few weeks later…

The morning sun emerged from the purple mist hovering over the eastern horizon, its thirsty rays lapping at the dew-kissed hillsides of Gleannmara. From the trees, birds as varied as the colors of green on Erin's landscape greeted the new day with song. Nearby, a brook, sprung from the bosom of its mother mountain, danced over a rock-studded path that wound down to a sibling river and on into Father Sea. The royal hill fort itself commanded the view over pastures dotted with brown, gray, and purple heathers and bright gorse and fields tilled in infant green rows straight as a warrior's sword. As if yawning at nature's wake-up song, Gleannmara's double-wide gate slowly swung open.

Kieran and Bran rode through, Kieran atop Gray Macha, a magnificent blue roan. With a streaming black mane and tail, the gray was a warrior's horse, strutting in a proud, eager gait. Taking three steps to the roan's every two was Bran's smaller steed, Bantan, a broad and sturdy creature with a shaggy coat still thick from the retreating winter. The animals moved in unison, making it clear to any watching that this was not the first time they'd traveled together, their nostrils flaring with frosty breath, the smaller deferring to a half-length behind the larger.

"Faith, good Kieran, 'twas a better plan last eve to depart at break of day," Bran reflected. He rubbed his hands together to warm them in the cool spring air.

"Hah!" Kieran snorted. "Just a fortnight away from the wet and chill of Dunadd and you're shivering like hound passing briars." Of course, he felt no warmer himself, but would not let on to his friend. What the bite of the early spring air didn't take out of him, the homecoming celebration the night before had. Still, he resisted the urge to pull his fringed cloak of blue and gold closer.

"Aye, and with each tremor, pain streaks lightning white across this mead-soaked blackness of a mind."

Kieran shook his head in wonder. Drunk—which they both had been more often of late—or sober, the poet in Bran could not be silenced. His gift of gab was part of the reason the young O'Cuillin had been turned out of monastic life. With the blood of the ancient bards running thick in his veins, Bran had not been content to leave Holy Scripture as it was. Embellishment came as naturally as breathing, so thus stifled, he left with the blessing of his ecclesiastical teachers. It was God's loss and Kieran's gain, for in Bran's company there was never a boring hour.

"Due penance, that's what this is. Moderation is a virtue—one that eluded me last night."

"One among many." Kieran reached over and plucked a long, flaxen hair from the bard's fringed cloak of scarlet and blue weave. It was no surprise, given the way the cook's daughter had curled at Bran's side like an expectant, ever-patient cat, waiting for his passionate rendition of their adventures in Scotia Minor to turn to a fervor more suited to her needs.

"Ah, Ailyss—"

"Alma." Kieran corrected.

"So it was." Bran agreed without seeming to suffer a single pang of conscience. He readily admitted he was born with a colt's tooth, and that weakness made him more suited to ply the feminine heart than her soul. After one year of clerical study, Bran abandoned the constricting life his priestly father had chosen and joined Kieran and Heber on their quest for adventure. At the memory of his foster brother, Kieran sobered. He chewed a curse till its bitterness paled the aftertaste of last night's celebration. He would have spat, but his mouth was too dry. Picking up a skin of weak ale, he uncorked it and shot it into his mouth. What spilled on his cheek he wiped away with his sleeve.

"Here, here, share, good fellow." Bran reached over and took the skin, helping himself. "I've yet to ken what quirk of nature it is that the sweet, overwetting of the pipes results in such acrid drought."

"Have you given any thought as to how I should tell Riona about her brother's death?"

Heber of Dromin was not the only warrior who did not return from the Dalraidi raids with the Gleannmara contingent, but it was his loss that pained Kieran the most.

A somber curtain fell over Bran's boyish, aristocratic features. He shook his head, his eloquence muted with a prolonged sigh.

As Kieran had been forced to inherit the kingship of Gleannmara, so Heber had been forced into leadership of one of its septs by the premature deaths of his parents. Built like his father, Murtagh, his great frame shook with his belly laugh, and the Sidhelike twinkle in his eyes could melt with earnestness or harden with fierce temper in a blink. With a wit sharp as his sword, the Dromin chief of the O'Cuillin clan had been a worthy ally and formidable foe. He was likewise the natural heir to his father's position as champion of the tuatha Gleannmara.

Or had been. Now his remains lay buried with his sword, Eimar, among the sleeping saints and fallen warriors of the Dalraidi royalty of Scotia Minor.

Bran had sung a final tribute to Heber's life and death, a piece worthy of such a kingly soul, while Kieran seethed. He was more bitter than ever at the God who took the good and left the lesser of His children unmolested.

"Better you send Colga with the news," Bran snapped in contempt. "'Tis that sniveling's fault."

"You speak ill of your cousin?" Kieran's tone was as dry as his tongue. Three strapping cousins born the same year, the sons of three brothers, left together to fight for glory and reward. Now there were two. The glory price was too high.

"Colga broke the rear guard and ran like a scalded pup for the trees. Faith, I saw it myself."

"Because he saw another band of Brits coming up the hill." Kieran repeated the O'Cuillin cousin's account as though trying to convince himself. "They were conjured by their druids, no doubt, to cover the real threat approaching from the other side. He and his men rushed to meet them and were lost in the bloody fog."

"It was as much a spell as you are a princess! I saw no one. Colga was trying to cover the fact that he'd wet himself in fear when the Scots charged. I shudder to think the same cowardly blood runs in my veins. My uncle is a fine smith, but his son has more ambition than courage to carry a battle out."

"Maybe not." Lost in thought, Kieran watched a small gold crest fly to a perch in an oak. Immediately it set upon some unsuspecting insect. Boldness might also be a prerequisite of manipulation. "Soon as he realized the trickery, he brought his men back to our aid."

Colga wasn't the sort to attack directly. The only time the young O'Cuillin bested Kieran in training, he'd taken weasel-like advantage of Murtagh's shout for the exercises to cease. Kieran didn't know what hit him until he regained consciousness with Colga bemoaning how he'd not heard the champion's bellow to quit.

"Colga will likely become the new chief." Kieran cast a speculative glance at Bran. "Unless you've a mind to challenge him."

"Me?" Bran burst into laughter. He almost sounded like Heber. "I'd rather cast my vote for Riona."

Kieran almost smiled. Heber had been as merry as he was large in stature. His younger sister was fiery. Heber would tease and laugh. Half his size, Riona would launch into him, eyes spitting blue fire, her wild raven hair a flying mantle over her face and shoulders. How the young men in Murtagh's charge loved to tease her. The heir to Gleannmara's throne was no exception. Kieran even took bets on how easily he could flush the flawless porcelain of her delicate face with color enough to shame the roses in her mother's garden.

If he were not king of the tuath and overlord of Gleannmara's various clan lands, Kieran would allow Riona to rule her clan holdings. Educated as well as her brother, O'Cuillin's daughter had the judicial, academic, and spiritual strength of an able ruler. Even now she increased her education and spirituality at the abbey of Kilmare, where she awaited Heber's return from war. But Dromin needed a strong-bodied chief as much as a wise one—one who could muster the clan warriors and lead them in battle as Heber had done.

The rule went by right to the nearest male kin of the same father or grandfather, according to the clan's vote. Their cousin Bran would be fine, if he'd apply himself. The only other choice was Colga, unless the O'Cuillin clan chose someone of a more distant relationship, thus breaking three generations of the O'Cuillin rule. It pained Kieran to return Gleannmara's debt to Murtagh and Heber with such a loss.

"Besides, I record acts of heroism. I don't perform them." Bran plucked at the velvet case containing Aingeal, his harp. The strings responded with muted indignation, straining to agree with their master.

"You could sing the heathen out of his paint with such a weapon," Kieran suggested wistfully. Much as the part of him nurtured by his Christian upbringing yearned to think otherwise, he knew now there was little difference in the druidic power of satire and the priestly power of prayer. Not believing in them rendered them useless. To Gleannmara's young king they were no more threat than that insect the gold crest had devoured earlier.

"As I recall, a blade was not an ill fit for your hands when you plied yourself to it. 'Twas you that taught us the sword song."

The sword song was something Kieran did believe in. Not every warrior performed the deadly orchestration to an unheard melody of weapon and limb. It was irony that a cleric's son heard the blade sing through the air, each movement making a different sound. Indeed, it was Bran who put the sounds together so that sword and body executed movement in a continuous, lethal harmony of aggression and defense.

"Aye, so I did. But that was desperation, friend."

Most of the warriors in training scoffed at the curious tune the bard hummed as he faced off with their seasoned tutor. But after an hour had passed and neither had gained more than a nick of the flesh, Murtagh called a truce, curious as to his poetic nephew's secret. Most agreed it was some sort of bardic spell, but Bran would not take credit for it. It was a gift from the Almighty he said, to protect those with willing ear to listen, faith to follow, and heart to praise Him for it. Something incredible, be it faith or bardic spell, allowed the cleric's son to remain a sword's length from Gleannmara's champion for an hour without a sound thrashing.

It was ironic that Heber, for all his piety, had tried his best to hear Eimar's song and succeeded only now and then, while Kieran, a prodigal if there ever was one, picked it up at once, amazed at what his ears reported. Even in the thick of battle, the haunting song of Melchior— the sword his late father bestowed upon the prince in his thirteenth year—rang and sang. The vengeful hymn of steel was not unlike the monks' bells accompanying their melodic chants. One invoked death; the other, life. Both claimed victory.

But when Eimar ceased to sing, Heber ceased to live. Eimar's last sound was a scream, or had that been Kieran's own voice slicing through the air as he severed Heber's head in Celtic tradition. After he wrapped it with the tenderest of care in his own blood-stained cloak, Kieran turned and carried it past his men, no longer able to hold back the tears streaming down his unshaven, battle-weary face.

Faith, he still bled from the raw memory. Through the haze that stung his eyes afresh, Kieran glanced over at his companion. He couldn't make out Bran's face, but he knew he'd not revisited the past alone. He heard the bard's whispered words—shapeless, at least to the human ear.

Kieran swallowed the gall that rose to the back of his throat, certain it contained shards of glass razing him from stem to gullet. "Best speak to that nag of yours, friend, for all the good your prayers will do. I wager that silver brooch you admired among Gleannmara's reward that Gray and I will be waiting for you at the ford."

With a click of the tongue, Kieran signaled the roan to the race. The warhorse, a breed for which Gleannmara was renowned, plunged ahead with a mighty leap that would have unseated any but the most skilled equestrian. That horse and rider had been inseparable since the first was foaled showed, for they were bonded—poetry of motion. Living up to his namesake—Gray Macha, the loyal steed of the Tain's warrior hero Cuchulain—the stallion plowed up clods of soft earth with his hooves and cast them in his wake.

This was more like it. Give him the fingers of the wind through his hair to soothe his tortured mind…give him the response of the powerful horse at the slightest pressure of his knees and the jar of the earth beneath them over the hopes that a fickle God might grace him with favor. Young and naive, Kieran had given God a chance once, and for all his earnest submission and belief, he'd watched his mother and father die of the plague that made him a king at twenty. Heber's faith rewarded him with becoming a corpse, run through with wounds, his life's blood soaking a foreign soil.

Nay, Kieran swore silently, give him the sword song for victory today, not a chant reserved for the next life. Today was for the living. Tomorrow was for dreamers.

True to Kieran's prediction, he and Gray Macha were waiting by the ford when Bran and his smaller steed caught up with them.

"If you keep this up, Kieran, I'll be looking for yet another mount before we reach Kilmare," Bran complained. "Mayhap another friend as well."

Slinging one leg over the short neck of the smaller horse, the poet slid to the ground. Taking up the reins, he led it over to the water's edge, where Kieran let Gray graze on the new grass.

"He's bred to these hills, sure of foot," Kieran consoled, letting Bran's latter remark slide. His companion would not.

"And you're baptized in the church, though painfully short of faith."

Kieran rolled his eyes. "So it's St. Bran now, is it?"

"Far from it, sir. I am not the son I should be and I may not agree with all God permits, like any child with any father, but I don't take kindly to others ridiculing Him. If you've no regard for the Father, then at least have regard for my right to revere Him."

Kieran met Bran's solemn gaze and nodded as guilt warmed his face. Heber had had a way of making him feel the same with regard to his faith—or lack of it. It vexed Kieran how Heber had accepted the death of his father in battle—and the resulting suicide of his mother—as the will of a loving God. It was beyond him

"You have my sincere apology, bard, so long as you don't start telling me how He's my father, too. I've said it before—" Kieran increased the volume in his voice in warning when Bran started to speak—"a father wouldn't treat His Son the way I've been treated."

"Are you better than His own Son, who also prayed to be spared an unthinkable death, yet was denied?"

Kieran shook his head. "No, as far as I see it, He let His own Son down, too."

"No, it was all part—" Bran broke off at the sharp look Kieran gave him.

Good. Heber hadn't been so easily dissuaded when he'd felt the urge to preach God's goodness.

"But if you keep on this track—" clearly Bran was not finished after all—"you'll make no headway with Riona."

Riona. Back to the second of Heber's last wishes. Kieran exhaled a long, weary breath.

"Riona will have no choice in the matter. I gave Heber my word as his anmchara in life and death."

"It will take more than a promise to a soul mate to make Riona change her mind about you. She turned you down once when she had no reason."

Kieran winced at the reminder. Was there anything harder to tolerate than a smug poet? The new king of Gleannmara needed to take a wife to provide heirs. Any lass in the kingdom and more would leap at the chance to become the bride of such a prosperous tuath, and Riona was not only the choice of logic, but of his heart as well. Kieran had always adored her as his precocious foster sister, but when she returned from her schooling at Kilmare for his parents' funeral, he'd fallen in love with the woman she'd become. At least he thought it was love. No beauty before or since consumed his mind day and night. Especially the nights.

I cannot give you my heart, dear brother, for it belongs to God.

Kieran's mouth tightened and his teeth clenched until the tide of anger, hurt, and humiliation from the past ebbed. Jerking Gray's head up with the reins, he sprang up on the startled stallion's back.

It took a moment to calm the horse. Once Gray stood statue still and ready for his command, Kieran spoke his mind. "Aye, *then* she had no reason," he conceded with ominous overtone. "*Now* she has no choice."

THREE

It was the busiest time of year in the dairy, but Riona loved it. Spring was a time of rebirth. The sun, allotted more time by the changing season, coaxed seedlings bullied into hiding by winter's chill out of the ground with the promise of even more light and warmth to come. New life flourished all around. Calves, lambs, and piglets suckled their mothers, growing stronger and sturdier of foot by the day. And here she was, a lady by birthright, performing a dairy-maid's chores in their midst.

Still, Riona would far rather be outside than closed within the walls of the abbey. Her energies were too ambitious to be satisfied closeted with needlework and prayer. While her banishment to the dairy wasn't intentional on her part, penance proved a blessing in disguise. At least if mischief sneaked up on her again and she found herself absently humming a bawdy bardic tune she'd learned from cousin Bran, neither cow nor calf would mind.

"Leila wants you to tell us that story again."

Startled from her milking, Riona realized the rascal Mischief had used her own reflections to its end. She crossed herself in remorse. Truly she'd intended to repeat the morning prayers that had been so abruptly interrupted when her six-year-old bedmate wet the bed. And there were thanks to offer that the orphan's regressions happened less and less, now that she and her homeless siblings were growing used to the abbey.

"Does she now?" she asked, looking past Liex, Leila's six-year-old twin brother, to his feminine version.

The only time Leila spoke it was in a childish tongue to her twin and an imaginary friend named Seargal. Only Liex understood her. The children belonged to gleemen, entertainers who traveled the country performing in the markets and courts for their livelihood. At her parents' death, they'd been run out of the village for carrying the dreaded disease into its midst, the wagon that had been their home torched.

They wandered into the abbey, trusting neither God nor man. It was Riona's hope to teach them faith for comfort and the skills to provide for themselves with hard work rather than the thievery they'd been reduced to. Even now, their elder brother, Fynn, worked with Brother Clemens, learning that knives, in addition to being thrown to amuse an audience, could be used to create useful items, such as trenchers and cups.

"I think that somewhere behind those twitching lips there lies the voice of an angel who longs to sing and speak. Do you think she'd sing with us? Or mayhap Seargal. Do you think he'd sing?"

Leila cast her pale, gray gaze toward the loft of the milking shed.

"So he's up there today, is he?"

Ignoring Riona, Leila murmured something to her brother.

"Seargal wants to listen," Liex translated. He stood the shovel he'd been cleaning the stalls with against the barrow of manure he'd collected.

Clearly, he wanted to tease Leila, but Riona had chided both him and Fynn for antagonizing their sister. There was something special about Leila, she told them, something God would reveal to them when the time was right. When a calf was crippled at birth and Domnall, one of the abbey's brothers, was going to kill it as was the custom, Leila refused to leave the animal. She rubbed its twisted leg and prayed ceaselessly, so that even crusty Brother Domnall was reluctant to intervene. He gave her one night for her miracle—and that was all it took. The following morning, the calf was walking like the others.

"Bring Nessa over for a drink," Riona offered, smiling at the pink-nosed calfling that had become Leila's shadow.

"Don't forget the song," Liex reminded her.

Riona cleared the dust from her throat. Would that it would clear from her skirts as easily as Nessa greedily suckled the milk cow. "Remember, if you or Seargal can chime in, I'd be glad for help."

Riona opened her mouth to sing a ballad when a voice chortled from the loft, more startling than melodic.

Fourteen-year-old Fynn jumped down to the dirt floor and rolled into Liex. The twin went down with a howl and in a flash entangled in a brawl with his dark-haired sibling. Nessa darted beneath the milk cow, which, with a bellow, bolted as far as its rope tie would allow.

"Boys, enough!" Riona snatched up the teetering pail of milk before wide-eyed Nessa plowed over it. The milk was saved, but the calf struck Riona with such force as to send her sprawling backward into the burrow—which was nicely mounded with manure.

"Ach, Father save us," she cried as the milk sloshed up on her face and chest.

The words, as close to an oath as the three siblings ever heard uttered from their benefactress's lips, separated the boys and sent Leila scrambling up the stick ladder to safety with her imaginary friend. Further embellishment of Riona's ire was checked by the voice of Brother Domnall.

"Like as not, the good Lord'll have nothing to do with this lot of ragmullions, much less a lady wallowing in cattle dung." The bent cleric peered at Riona and her charges from beneath the gray hedges of his eyebrows in utter contempt. "Mayhap 'tis penance for glorifying that heathen lore."

"Mayhap Brother Domnall will share a story then, while I rid myself of stench and filth." Riona shook out her dress in dismay.

Domnall started. "Oh, what with all the commotion, I near forgot. His Holiness, the Abbot, and Bishop Senan wish to see you at once in the hall. Them as well. All of them," he added, casting a glance at the top of the ladder where Leila watched.

"Why would the holy fathers wish to see the children?" Riona was fearful of the answer. Homes had been found for most of the orphans in her care. These three were the last, afterthoughts of the plague that had swept across Erin two years earlier.

"There's a couple from Dinwiddy who'd have a look at them." Brother Domnall's answer was sympathetic. So, the little ones had gotten to him, just as they had Riona.

"You mean we'll have a look at them," Fynn said, squaring a mulish chin. "We won't go with them if we don't like their looks."

"Of course you won't." Riona brushed off her clothing as best she could, stewing inside with dread.

There was so much she wanted to do with these foundlings.

Oh, Lord, show me Thy will. If this couple is truly needy of this little family, then so be it. I know I can accept the role of a sister in Christ to these foundlings with as much joy as that of a mother.

"Brother Clemens says I'm a fast learner," Fynn spoke up. "Maybe it won't be long before I can provide for the twins and we won't need parents."

Riona smiled. He wanted so to be a man, when most of his tall, lanky frame was still boy. "That well may be, but for now let's see what God provides for us."

I want the best for them, Lord, I truly do. Riona herded her brood like a mother hen across the short plank bridge over the fosse. A gray-robed brother opened the door to the reception hall as Riona and her entourage approached.

Gathering a twin under each arm, Riona stepped inside. It took a moment for her eyes to adjust to the inside lighting of the hall after being in the afternoon sun. She focused on a humbly dressed couple, neither of whom looked to have gone more than a few hours without food. Freemen, perhaps?

"Ah, Lady Riona, I—" Abbot Fintan stumbled over his greeting upon seeing her—"*we* welcome you and your charges into our presence."

"My lord brother," Bishop Senan exclaimed in equal shock. "What malady has befallen the Lady O'Cuillin since I was away?"

"None of consequence, your holiness."

Riona rushed forward to kneel before the abbot's elaborately carved chair, the only furniture in the room, save the desk and stool where Brother Ninian recorded the hearings. The paved floor was cold to her knees. Bishop Senan, the abbot's younger half brother, offered her a hand in rising so that she could return to where Leila, Liex, and Fynn held back in wary silence.

"My Lord Abbot," Riona ventured, "may I ask what this is about?"

Senan motioned toward the children with a grandiose sweep of the arm. "It is about placing these foundlings in a good home with Tadgh here and his good wife Mebh."

"Only the little ones, milord bishop," the man of the couple stipulated quickly.

Riona's heart sank, but there was no time to indulge it, for a veritable outcry ensued.

"We're not leavin' Fynn!" Liex grabbed at his elder brother's hand and pulled him closer to Riona as if she could protect them all.

"And I'm not handing the twins over to anyone," Fynn declared.

Leila practically disappeared in the fold of Riona's dress, nearly knocking her over.

"I...I must protest, Father Abbot," she stammered, regaining her footing. Fintan was a good-hearted man, and Riona was one of his favorites. He had to listen to her. "These children should not be separated on any account. Their family has been broken enough."

The abbot stared at Riona again as if he still could not believe it was his sister's noble granddaughter. Self-conscious, she lowered her gaze and took a step back. Humility might prevail where her ladylike demeanor did not. Only a bath would rid her of the stable stench.

"I must agree with Lady Riona. I can't believe it is in the children's interest to separate them. However—" the abbot raised his voice, cutting off Bishop Senan's rising objection—"perhaps this couple would reconsider taking the older lad as well. He's healthy and strong, certainly a boon to any freeman who works the land."

"If ye let me finish out this year with Brother Clemens, I'll be able to take care of myself and the twins, making wares for the table," Fynn announced. "Ask 'im! He says I learn fast and have a keen way with a blade."

"Look at the little dears, Taddy." The farmer's wife rushed over to Leila and fingered her long, straight hair. "So much like the babes we lost, e'en tho they was both lads. But I always wanted a girl. Surely we can take the eldest, too." She cast a pleading look at her husband.

"'E's a gleeman's son, born to steal. The little ones aren't old enough to be tainted with their parents' way, but 'e is. I can see it in them eyes."

If looks were blades, Fynn would have slain Tadgh then and there.

Instead, the lad heeded the subtle warning in Riona's gaze and stood, neck muscles strained red with his effort to remain silent.

"But I want the babies. I'll have no peace without 'em." From the stand taken in Mebh's voice, neither would Tadgh.

All eyes went to the freeman, who looked to Senan as if for help. Clearly uncertain as to which stand best benefited him, the bishop offered him neither support nor condemnation.

"Surely young Fynn will more than earn his keep," the abbot suggested hopefully. "What say you, lad? Would you go with your brother and sister as son of these good people?"

The stubborn set of Fynn's chin said it all. He wanted nothing to do with them. His respect for the man who'd welcomed him and his siblings into the abbey and given them food and shelter was all that held his tongue.

"Three mouths to feed, is that what you want, woman?" Tadgh exclaimed. "Three, when we could barely feed the two we had."

"But look at her," Mebh pleaded, turning Leila toward him. "Like a little angel, she is."

Apparently, were the decision left to Tadgh, none of the children would be taken. His aversion to Fynn, indeed, his wife's failure to make a whit of fuss over Liex did not bode well at all.

Riona started forward. "Father Fintan—"

"All right then," Tadgh conceded, cutting her off. "We'll take the lot."

Fynn could hold back no longer. "What makes you think *you* have the final say? We're not slaves. We needn't go with you if we don't want, and *I* don't want."

"Me, neither," Liex declared, digging in beside his brother.

Leila tugged away from Riona and marched to stand on Fynn's other side, arms crossed, leaving no doubt as to what she thought of the proposition.

Tadgh turned on Senan. "Ye said they was ours for the claimin'. I paid ye well enough for their findin'."

"They are," the bishop assured him hastily. "We are not an orphanage, your holiness," he reminded his superior. "We've carried these children through the winter."

"Paid?" The abbot's question riveted Senan to the spot.

"A donation to the abbey, nothing more."

"Ah." The slight upward curl of the senior priest's mouth betrayed the same doubt that Riona felt. Had it not been mentioned, Senan's pocket would hold the money rather than the church coffers.

Do it. The conviction came to Riona as sure as the compassion she felt for the frightened orphans. "My lord abbot, if I may be so bold…"

The abbot turned to Riona, clearly relieved to have another opinion. "By all means, milady, share your thoughts. You have invested too much time and affection in this matter to be ignored."

She took the step off the precipice into thin air, praying she would not fall and take the little ones with her. "I ask my lord abbot to consider allowing me to take the children to Dromin."

Her brother would not turn away three orphans. Heber's was a tender heart.

"But you've no husband," Senan pointed out, taken aback. "And what of your pledge to the church? Why on the way home from Kells, I pondered how well you've adapted to life here in God's service. I intended to discuss it with my brother, but this matter has preempted it."

Riona foundered. It was her heart's desire to serve God at the abbey, but these children needed a mother, which was exactly what she'd been to them since their coming. She loved each of them for his or her own special way.

"Perhaps the abbey's particular service to God is not Lady Riona's calling. The call of motherhood is a noble pursuit as well. Teaching children God's way is its own ministry."

Fintan smiled at Riona. Her mother's favorite uncle had come to know her well since she came to Kilmare. Unlike Senan, who coveted Riona's property more than her happiness, the abbot encouraged her to explore all her options before making a lasting commitment.

"Her own children, yes," the bishop agreed, "but what man of property, much less of noble blood, would have another's foundlings to keep?"

Fintan frowned. "Aye, taking in children in her brother's home without his permission could be a problem."

"An' I already paid 'im the worth of two cumals for the brats," Tadgh argued.

Beside him, Mebh began to wail, dropping to her knees. "Holy Father, have a heart for a mother what's lost her own babes!"

"You mean it?" Fynn's dark brown eyes were as bright as Riona had ever seen them, filled with hope. Never had she seen a more welcome sight.

"Aye," she answered softly. "You and your siblings have a knack for working your way into the heart." Maybe this was all part of God's plan. Heaven knew it hadn't been in hers, yet it felt so right.

"Then it's settled." Fynn gave a joyous whoop. "Between us, Liex and Leila will have a fine home."

Riona hugged the little ones as they rushed up to her and looked over their heads at the abbot. "Holy Father?" Surely the abbot could see this was right. Indeed, it was all she could do to keep from shouting with glee herself.

Bishop Senan was not as easily swayed by sentimentality. "Brother, how can you compare the love *two* parents can offer, albeit in humble hearth, to that of a maid without even the prospect of a husband and hearth to call her own? And again I ask, what worthy lord would take the offspring of another man, a gleeman no less?" Senan argued. "He'd want his own heirs."

"It does sound more than your cup can hold, given the circumstances," Fintan reluctantly admitted to Riona. "We must think it through."

Senan seized upon his half brother's indecision. "You know our cousin's daughter. Her heart overrules her reason. She has made it clear her first love is the church, and it's only her charitable nature that clouds her mind."

Hope began to crumble as Fintan nodded in agreement. "The bishop makes good points, Lady Riona. A husband in hand...even your brother's permission, would give me more peace in favoring your request."

A man. No matter the consequence, in church or home, a woman's measure was judged by the man in her life, be it father, brother, or husband. Humility banished by the blood rising to her face, Riona bristled.

"I have some means of my own, with or without a husband's or brother's indulgence." She may have no land, but her dowry was not easily dismissed. "I know my brother's good heart, regardless. Heber of Dromin would not turn these children away."

The abbot's troubled expression held her breath at bay.

"And I've enough love for *two* parents," she added, infected by a desperation beyond her ken. "Surely you can see that the children and I—"

The abbot held up his hand, silencing her. Slowly he rose from the elaborate chair of his station, his embroidered robes falling around a frame lean and bent from prayer and fasting. His strength drained from a winter-long affliction of the lung, he attempted to speak above Mebh's mournful protest and Tadgh's indignant one.

"I should like the evening to think and pray on this matter. I have to admit, I have my concerns with either proposition."

"But this lady is young and can still bear babes," Mebh cried. "The midwife says I'll have no more. For God's love, have mercy on a childless mother." With a body-riddling sob, she began to rock back and forth as though cradling her lost infants.

Normally gracious under the worst of circumstances, the abbot's patience snapped. "Have mercy on my *ears*, woman! Either curb her tongue or remove her," he warned Tadgh.

At the threat of removal, Mebh scooted back to Tadgh's side, her wails reduced to a whimper. Was it fear that restored her composure so quickly, or was her display, snuffed as easily as a lamp, an act? Riona stared at the woman. What was it about her that would not stir the same pity as others who'd lost their children to the Blefed? The matches of grief-stricken parents and homeless children that Riona had seen made in that room were joyful ones of broken families made whole. This bore no resemblance to such instances at all.

"Bishop Senan, show our guests to the hospitium. I shall ponder this decision till the morrow, upon which time I will announce my decision."

"There is no decision to be made," Fynn protested. "We go—"

Riona clamped her hand over the impertinent's mouth. "The abbot is a godly man. His decision will surely reflect heaven's wishes."

As the abbot took his leave, Riona hurried Fynn and his siblings toward the door. *Heavenly Father, I beseech You to do what is best for these children. Send a sign, if You will, something to make Your will known, and I shall abide by it.*

A parting glance over her shoulder revealed Senan closeted in a corner with the hopeful adoptive parents. She'd prayed about her instinctive dislike for the bishop to no avail. He reminded her of a wolf cloaked in lamb's wool, ready to pounce on any opportunity that presented itself for his gain. She didn't mean to judge, he just—

"Look there!" Liex pulled away from Riona's hand.

She lifted her gaze to follow Liex's stare as two warriors rode through the gate.

"By my mother's eyes, I never saw a finer horse." Fynn chased after Liex, easily catching up with and passing the smaller boy to greet the men who dismounted.

Just short of the great blue roan, Fynn stopped and gawked. "Can I tend him, sir? I swear, he'll have nothin' but the finest grain and fodder we have to offer."

Riona stood still with Leila, as if her feet had rooted in the ground. Disbelief warred in vain with recognition of the horse and its rider. It could be no one else but Kieran, her foster brother, and Gray Macha, a steed as bred to combat and command as its master. And where Kieran of Gleannmara rode, Heber would not be far behind.

God had answered her prayer!

Now the abbot would have no reason to deny her the children. Heber would never turn them away.

Hope lifted Riona from the spot and sped her toward Gleannmara's king. She was nearly breathless with excitement upon reaching the unexpected guests.

"*This,* you say is the Lady Riona?" Kieran arched a dubious golden brow at her. "She looks to be scullery…nay, a stable maid." He waved the air in front of his face, staring with disdain at her dress.

Color flamed in her cheeks. She'd been so thrilled to see her foster brother returned from the Dalraidi campaign, she'd forgotten herself. Too late to slink away before he recognized her, Riona lifted a regal chin.

"Aye, *this* is she. And she welcomes both you and cousin Bran from your journey. It has been many months, Kieran." She looked around the broad expanse of his cloaked shoulders and through the gate, to the outer walls of the circular enclosure for a sign of her brother. "And is the O'Cuillin putting his own mount to bed at the stable yard?" It would be like Heber to put his horse ahead of his reunion with his sister. Kieran and Bran, on the other hand, would put their own bellies first.

"Faith, is mucking stables part of God's service?" Bran exclaimed. "I wouldn't have known you, Riona, had you not spoken." He grabbed her hand and started to lift it to his lips, then apparently thought better of it, for he squeezed it instead. "You are a sight for these sore eyes."

"And a sore to the nose," Kieran put in wryly. "What in the devil happened to you?"

Riona bridled. "Not that it's any of your concern, but I fell in a barrow of manure."

"I believe it." Kieran's short laugh was like a burr to an already injured pride.

"Your gallantry takes my breath away, milord."

"As does your perfume."

"If you came to insult me, the task is done, Kieran. You may leave anon. You, Bran, are welcome to stay, as is my lagabout brother."

Riona marched to the gate and scanned the outer rath again. "Where *is* Heber?" she demanded with a stamp of impatience. Kieran had that effect on her. He'd try the patience of the Apostles themselves! Spinning on the ball of her foot, Riona waited expectantly.

"Well, Heber, he…" Bran cleared his throat and looked away.

Alarm seeped into Riona's blood, curdling cold. "He what?"

"He sends his love," Kieran spoke up. "I'll explain as soon as Bran and I have a chance to wash some of the dirt from our throats with the brothers' good ale."

Riona shifted her uncertain gaze from Kieran. "Bran?"

"And our eyes," her cousin agreed, rubbing his eyes until they were red. "'Tis something in the air. They've itched all the day."

"An overabundance of heath fruit last eve, more likely," Kieran whispered aside to Riona. "'Twill redden the eye and dry the throat of the stoutest man."

Something was amiss. She sensed it as sure as she'd sensed the same inconsistency with the children's prospective parents.

"Lady Riona, perhaps I should show these gentlemen inside, so that you may refresh yourself before entertaining them for supper."

"What?"

Turning, Riona saw Brother Domnall had taken charge of the boys and the horses. Indeed, Bran had lifted Leila to the back of his steed. His legs were almost as long as the horse's. She supposed Kieran's impatience negated the bardic choice of chariot or curricle for travel.

"I will entertain our guests until you are prepared to take over," Domnall said, his words penetrating the fog of distraction in her mind.

"Yes. That would be good." It was the path of least resistance, at least for the moment. She was so delighted by Kieran's appearance so shortly after her prayer that she could not imagine it to carry bad news.

Perhaps Heber was put out that she'd abandoned Dromin to Ringan, their most capable steward, so that she could serve at the abbey. Her brother had told her to wait until his return, but the plague waited for no one. She was needed more at Kilmare. Riona would explain it all, and her brother would see she'd made the right choice, both then and now.

Aware that all eyes rested on her, she emerged from the steady churn of her thoughts. "I'll join you after vespers." *And a bath,* she thought, dropping in a slight curtsy before taking her leave.

Nothing was wrong. It could not be.

Four

In the privacy of a corbeled stone dwelling assigned to them for the night's lodging, Bran paced back and forth like a hound in a cage. *"He sends his love?"*

Kieran ignored his friend's incredulity. He swished his razor in the shallow stone washbowl and applied it to his stubbled jaw again, staring at the smooth plaster of the wall as if a mirror hung there. Amenities were few, as were decorations. A few crosses carved in the headers and doorframes were all that graced the slanted walls.

Sparsely furnished as it was, the room was luxurious compared to most of the places they'd slept in the past year. It was paved and well drained, and the small fire in the round, sunken hearth filled it with a welcome warmth now that the sun reposed for the night.

"He sends his love?" Bran threw his hands up and dropped on one of the two stuffed pallets in the room.

"S'bones, you are more worrisome than a gnat." Kieran skimmed the water surface with his hand, sending it sloshing at the bard. "What would you have me say before curious monks and children? 'Oh, Heber couldn't come with us because he's dead'?"

Bran wiped the droplets off his tunic, unabashed. "You've only postponed her grief."

"Well, *you* could have confounded told her then." Wiping his face with the hem of his cloak, Kieran turned to the light of the single candle in the room. "There, am I fit for a lady's eyes?"

"If it's the sweet brush of Riona's lips you're preparing for, you've wasted your time."

"Ach, 'tis this very kind of thing that threatens the existence of the bards. You wear out your welcome with your barbed words."

"Given your temperament of late, your tongue has plied the same sharpening stone."

Kieran looked at Bran in surprise. The most timid of the O'Cuillin cousins was growing a backbone as fearsome as his wit and tongue. He was a maker of love, not war, he claimed, but the journey across the sea had changed the young man. There was less of the romantic and more of the realist in him. But then, the same could be said of himself, Kieran supposed.

Bran slapped him on the back. "You have my forgiveness for your churlish humor, for mine is by choice. Yours is by nature."

Kieran laughed, in spite of himself. The dart was well thrown. That's what he got for waging wits with one of druidic lineage. "Come friend, let's join the Lady Riona."

He offered his hand to Bran and hauled him up from the pallet.

"Are you certain you want me present? After all, we've chosen the right speech, and as many times as you've repeated it, I see no reason—"

Kieran held up his other hand. "I would consider it a favor. Truth, I'd rather face a horde of blade-wielding cutthroats armed with nothing but my teeth than see this matter done."

Bran looked over at the belongings on Kieran's pallet. "What about your mother's ring? Won't you give it to your bride-to-be?"

Kieran hesitated in the open door, then shook his head. "One battle at a time, my friend. One battle at a time."

Having rested after their arrival and subsequent request for a private audience with Riona once her duty to prayer was done, Kieran and Bran entered the refectory. The oak plank building with its receding gables and shingled roof of yew was abandoned for the evening vespers. The fires smoking in the kitchen, which adjoined to the dining hall by a covered arbor, held the evening meal for the praying servants of God. The melodic prayers and hymns of the worship filtered throughout the grounds of the stone-enclosed inner rath, weaving in and out of the stone, timber, and wattled structures scattered within, as if to bind them to the bosom of its chapel with praise and song.

A modest portion of porridge and a two-fisted length of bread had been set out at the end of the table for each of them. A bottle of wine—no doubt from the vineyards beyond the abbey—and two wooden cups were provided for their thirst. While not elaborate, the meal was filling and welcome to bellies empty since high noon.

As Kieran reached for the bread to break it in half, Bran admonished him in a sharp whisper. "Use the knife. We're not among the heathens now."

"'Tis too little to cut, but too big to swallow whole." Despite his complaint, Kieran took the blade and did as his more genteel companion suggested.

Without comment, Bran took the first slice and drizzled honey on it from a stone jar.

"I *am* the king," Kieran reminded him as he took a huge bite.

With a grin as laconic as the jibe, Bran handed the half-eaten piece back.

"Now who's the heathen?" Kieran brushed it away in disgust. Discarding the knife, he broke his own portion away with his fingers. "The handle's fit to come off anyway."

The rest of the meal progressed in silence, as if speaking were irreverent given the holy strains filtering in. The softer voices from the women's side of the divided place of worship were as distinct as the men's, yet all blended in ethereal harmony. Kieran could not help but picture Riona—not the muck maid of their earlier meeting, but the vision of their last parting—kneeling in the chapel at Dromin to pray for God's speed and protection on their journey.

If there were such beings as angels, none had looked more radiant or innocent than she. Her raven hair fell like a silken mantle about her shoulders, as if to worship them. Lashes just as dark fanned upon cheeks rouged by mother nature. And her lips, ripe as cherries, moved over the words of her prayer, mesmerizing Kieran so that tasting them was all he could think of, never mind that they'd dealt him rejection earlier.

"I'm sorry I've kept you. I came straightaway from the chapel."

Kieran started as Riona's voice pulled him back to the present. He hadn't heard the door open. Pivoting on the wooden bench, he rose with Bran.

"Now there's the beautiful cousin of my memory," Bran said, taking her hand to his lips.

Riona dispensed with etiquette and threw her arms about the bard in a grand hug. "Polished words, all, but I treasure each of them as jewels in my mind. You both look hale from your adventure. It must have agreed with you." She turned to Kieran. "And you, brother. Is your treasury fat enough now that you can turn your energy to Gleannmara rather than the sword?"

"Gleannmara's peaceful appeal grows by the day," Kieran admitted. "I've had my fill of adventure. It's time to think of family and heirs."

Surprise rendered the lady speechless, but only for a moment. "Well, before I ask whom you fancy to mother your sons, tell me about Heber. He's angry, isn't he?"

Kieran shook his head. "Ach, he could never be angry at you."

"Then why didn't he come?" Her eyes widened.

What glorious pools of sapphire they were, inviting enough for a man to drown in. "He's not hurt!"

The material of her wine red dress gathered beneath his fingers as Kieran took her by the shoulders. "No, not hurt."

The healthy glow he'd just admired seeped from her face. All the words he'd practiced fled his mind, and panic chased them beyond retrieval. Kieran cursed his rattled brain as he mumbled flatly, "Heber's dead."

Riona shook her head, refusing to accept what she heard. She looked to her cousin. "Bran?"

"On my life, I'm sorry, Riona. 'Twas done before any of us knew what happened."

"We were lured into a trap," Kieran explained, sharing the anguish tearing at Riona's delicate features. He eased her down on the bench he'd just vacated. "Would God that it was me."

She stared, not at him, but through him, her face a mirror of conflicting emotions. Putting her hands to her temples, she moaned. He watched, waiting to catch her should she swoon or embrace her if the pain grazing her gaze erupted in an outburst of tears.

"B…but you said he sent his love."

Her lips trembled with the denial as she lifted her gaze to him. A crystalline droplet broke from the grief welling in her eyes and trickled down her cheek. Kieran caught it with his finger.

"He did. His spirit had not got away when we found him," Bran informed her solemnly.

Riona inhaled shakily, bracing her shoulders as if to shrug away Kieran's comfort, to rely on her own strength. "Then tell me," she said softly. "Tell me all. Spare me nothing."

Where should he start? Kieran forced the replay of the battle, but his mind was as fogged as the day had been. He didn't want to remember. Bran was born to record detail the warrior forgot. Hapless and in desperation, he looked at his friend.

"'Twas Colga's fault," the bard said, abandoning his usual eloquence. "The O'Cuillin was our rear guard, with Colga as lookout. Our cousin saw the pirates sneaking up on us from behind and ran, leaving Heber to their surprise and mercy. By the time Kieran's and Aidan's force regained control of the fray, it was too late to help your brother."

"Colga said he'd rushed away to fend off another force, an illusion conjured by the enemy's druid to lead him away from the real approach of the enemy." Kieran ignored Bran's snort of disbelief. A man deserved to have his side told, whether or nay it was credible.

"And what of Heber?"

She had the look of a bewildered child hearing but disbelieving an outrageous story. The more Bran and Kieran shared with her of Heber's death, the less she seemed to hear. Yet neither of them could bring themselves to the details of his last wishes. Bran waited for Kieran, making him feel all the more burdened with shame. He'd face the fiercest of enemies without hesitation, but there were no words to tell Riona how he'd severed her brother's head and left his body to the carrion. She wouldn't understand. Hers was too gentle a world.

In truth, the memory still sickened Kieran.

"We buried his remains in Dunadd, among the royal and sainted dead," Bran finished. "I have commemorated the detail of his story to parchment if you wish to see it."

Riona held up her hand as if to say, "Later." For now, she had more than she could cope with.

"Colga." Riona repeated the name as if she committed it to memory for the first time. Kieran allowed her to digest it, having nothing else to add. Suddenly the water in her gaze iced, turning on him. "Colga will be the new O'Cuillin."

"If the clan votes to his favor." Kieran knew one vote the man would not receive. "Unless Bran will challenge him."

"I was born to poetic and spiritual pursuits, not war."

"And God has blessed you for it," Riona assured her cousin. "Just as He's cursed our king with the guilt of his foster brother's death." She swung her attention to Kieran. "Chasing after adventure and gold!"

Her chin quivered with emotion, and much as Kieran wanted to cup it in his fingers—nay, kiss away her pain—he dared not, lest he come away bitten by the teeth she now bared at him.

"And you asking me to marry *you* less than a season before you left on your folly! For what? Thank God I had the good sense to tell you nay. I'd seen my mother suffer too long married to a steel-worshiping champion. All of you, you thirst for blood." She sneered, accusing Kieran with a gaze harder and colder than any sword he'd ever wielded. "Well, I hope you drank your fill of it, including Heber's! I hope you drown in it!"

"Have a heart, Riona; Heber was his brother, too."

Riona shrugged Bran's hand from her shoulder and lurched to her feet. Although the crown of her head brushed just below his chin, Kieran felt the singe of her growing anger, for ice had now turned to steam with its rise.

"Would that it was me instead, grá," Kieran vowed in all earnest. It was not the first time, nor would his conscience make it his last.

"*Love?*" Riona slapped him soundly on the cheek, jarring his head to the side with a force that would have done her father, Murtagh, proud. "I am *not* your love. My brother's blood stains your sword as if it were the blade that spilled his life upon that bog. I warned you not to take up a fight that was not your own. I begged you not to take Heber. A curse on you and your sword…and your horse!" She swore hysterically. "May that kingly torque choke the breath from your black soul."

She flew at his chest as if to pummel out his heart, and Kieran seized her shoulders, pulling her close, trapping her fists between them.

Deprived of action, her rage and grief escaped in body-wrenching sobs. Kieran envied her that relief as much as he commiserated with her grief. His jaw clenched, trapping his own grief. He rested his chin on the crown of her head, shakily inhaling the sweet fragrance of the soap she'd used upon her hair.

Hours passed, or so it seemed, before Riona's emotions were spent. Her small frame, drained of strength as well, conformed in soft surrender to his braced one. Awareness of the woman Riona was registered with his male senses, despite the daze of his misery. Would that he could say that the brush of his lips upon the top of her head was offered purely out of the desire to comfort and not sullied by a baser motive.

"I'm best off," Bran announced to no one in particular. He backed awkwardly toward the door until he finally caught Kieran's eye.

Kieran blinked in grateful acknowledgment. It wasn't that he intended to take advantage of the lady and wished to be free of Bran's company. His motive was of the purest intent, simply to share his grief with the next closest heart to his own besides the late O'Cuillin chief. While he could not separate his feelings as a man for her, he would master them. If the lady would ever have him as a man, let it be of her desire, not her vulnerability.

At the drop of the wooden bar into its keeper, Riona stirred, backing only slightly away from the comfort she derived in Kieran's strong embrace.

"Bran?"

"Gone," Kieran whispered.

She exhaled a long, shaky breath and closed her eyes, struggling with its successor. "I still cannot believe it. Tell me this is a horrible dream."

He wished he could assuage the plea in her voice, but that was impossible…as impossible as finding the right time to tell Riona of Heber's second request. Now, when her rage and pain was at its ebb, seemed the best alternative.

"Your brother had one last request, Riona," Kieran said huskily.

She looked up at him.

"That I become your protector and husband. I gave him my word I would see this done."

The beast of blue fire Kieran had thought spent rallied with a spellbinding resilience before his very eyes. Its breath restored the flesh and bone of Riona's body so that Kieran instinctively tightened his embrace for his own protection. It grew, filling her until it demanded release.

"How *dare* you!" Arms pinned, her indignation found its mark with a sharp stomp to the top of his foot.

Kieran yowled in surprise and let her go, grabbing at his loudly protesting instep.

"How d-dare you!" Clearly she lacked words to match her brimming emotion. And well Kieran knew with Riona—when words failed, action prevailed.

He hopped back on his uninjured foot in anticipation but was not quick enough. She struck his chest with both fists, sending him sprawling to the floor. His elbow struck one of the benches in his attempt to catch himself, overturning it and sending fire darts up his arm as hot as those flying from his irate companion's glare.

"I will *never* marry a man I cannot respect, and I do not respect the likes of you or any other warmonger!"

A dainty, slippered foot shot out from the fullness of her dress. Kieran gathered his throbbing elbow to his side to take the blow. "S'bones, woman, 'tis Heber's wish, not mine!"

He rolled away, his own temper gathering momentum. Seeing her coming after him, he shoved the bench in her way and vaulted to his feet. "And no church would have a wench with a temper worse than God's own thunder."

The beast of blue fire roared as Riona seized upon the empty trencher and flung it at Kieran with an aim that would earn the envy of any warrior. What manner of madness made him think Riona of Dromin might be rendered impotent by feminine tears? He dodged Bran's trencher as well, but the cup that followed struck his ear straight on, emptying the remnant of wine down his neck.

With an explosive oath, Kieran charged as Riona drew back her arm with the second cup. He smacked it off course in midflight and seized the hand that launched it, wrestling it behind her back. He knocked the bread knife beyond her reach and pinned her at arm's length, facedown against the table. "I'm not asking you to warm my bed, woman! I'm offering my protection, nothing more."

"I need no man's protection," Riona mumbled against the smooth, worn wood crushing her cheek. "I have God's."

"And mine!" came a voice from behind.

Kieran bolted upright as its owner leapt upon his back and not-quite-man-sized fingers went for his eyes. Letting Riona go, Kieran caught the attacker's wrists and, with a practice twist, flipped the light figure across the table, where he rolled to the other side.

It was the lad who took Gray Macha to the stables earlier. But as the boy came to his feet, it was not a lad's weapon that flashed in his hand.

"Fynn!" Riona threw herself in front of Kieran, but reflexes of the youth were quicker.

Kieran grabbed her and dragged her to the floor with him as the knife nicked his shoulder. A moment's delay and the blade intended for his heart would have struck the lady a deadly blow.

Oblivious to the narrow miss, Riona scrambled to her feet and blocked Fynn from retrieving the knife for another attack.

"Have you lost your mind, lad? Haven't I gotten it through that mop head of yours that violence is the devil's work?"

"He was hurting you! No man, warrior, or king will lay a hand on my lady."

"*Your* lady?" Kieran nearly laughed at the idea of Riona and this wet-eared pup, except that experience had just shown him neither were to be easily dismissed.

Riona put her hands to her temples where the blood flooding her face pounded fiercest.

"Oh, Fynn," she said in exasperation. "Kieran would never hurt me. He is my foster brother. The truth is, I provoked him. Faith, I'm sorry, but I did." She walked toward the boy and drew him to her gently. "It seems we are both orphans now. My brother is dead, and I turned on Kieran in my pain and grief, just as you raged at us so often when you first came here."

Fynn glowered at Kieran, not nearly as sure of him as Riona seemed to be. "I'm not leaving you alone with him."

Riona kissed the crown of the lad's wild brown hair. He was just a boy, but that did not lessen the sting to Kieran's pride.

"I'm indebted to your valor, sir," she told the lad, "but it's not needed with Kieran of Gleannmara. I must tell you, as I've told him, that when God is my protector, I need no earthly one. This was all of my own making, and I go to do penance for it right now."

"Who is this young rooster anyway?" Kieran demanded.

"This is Fynn, the elder brother to the twins, Liex and Leila, whom you saw earlier with me. They are a gleeman's children, orphaned by the plague last summer. These last months we've grown close, so I decided to take them as my own."

"What?" Had his hearing been knocked awry by that well-aimed cup? "A lady of your station doesn't take common children to foster, even if she has the means, which you do not."

"Where there is a will to do God's work, He will provide the means."

"God's work," Kieran mocked with derision. "This is the work of a gleeman, as light of hand as of foot and as cunning as a fox."

"At least I know better than to force my attentions on a lady," Fynn retorted in kind.

"But for that lady, whelp—" A growl infected Kieran's voice, betraying his waning patience—"I'd have you skinned and hung to dry."

"But for the lady, your heart would be skewered by my dagger."

Kieran started forward. "You nearly *killed* her, you insolent little—"

"Enough!" Riona's voice was as large as her brother's when she desired it. Or soft as a babe's cheek, as it was when she continued. "I am to blame for all of this. I apologize to you both. I go to apologize to my God."

She steered Fynn through the door, stopping long enough to glance over her shoulder. "I apologize, my lord, for my behavior, but not for my answer. By that I stand. Good night."

FIVE

"Y ou could have killed Kieran," Riona scolded as she and Fynn
walked toward the mean lodgings assigned to her and the
children. Leila shared Riona's quarters, while the boys slept
in an enclosure off the back.

"I meant to! Why did ye leap in front of him like that? My heart
stopped soon as the blade left my fingers, but there was no callin' it
back."

"Because mad as I was with Kieran, I still love him. He's the only
brother I have left, even if he isn't my blood." A sob crept up on Riona
and her step faltered. She meant it. She did love Kieran. He was as
much a brother as Heber, even though they were not blood kin.

*Father, help me. I know well I don't deserve it after losing my temper as I
did, but I could bear no more this day. 'Tis as if the same weapon that took
my brother's life had run me through, making me mad with pain. I'm claiming Your promise of forgiveness. And forgive this child, for he was only trying
to protect me.*

"How was it you knew I needed protection?" Riona asked suddenly.
She turned the prodigal toward her, spinning him off balance with surprise.

Unwavering, Fynn met her gaze. "I was looking for you, and it was
there I found you."

"Why, Fynn? You should have been abed with Liex at this hour.
Father Clemens will expect an early start on the morrow."

"Because Tadgh intends to sell us to a slaver who will sell us in
Bristol."

Shock clutched Riona with fresh claws. Heber, Kieran, and now
this. "Whatever makes you say this?" Her thoughts tumbled afresh.
She'd heard of the Britons selling off their young, but surely no God-
fearing Irishman would do such a thing. Still, there was something not
quite right...

"Seargal told Leila. She and Liex are hiding in the milking stalls."

Riona rolled her eyes heavenward at Fynn's explanation. "Her imaginary friend?" Changing direction, Riona started toward the gate to the outer rath.

Fynn shifted in step with her, shaking his head. "No, that's not all of it. 'Tis that what made me look closer at the man. Then I recognized him for myself. We saw 'im in Dublin, leadin' orphans of the dead to a slaver bound for Bristol. They call him Silver Tooth." Fynn grabbed Riona's arm, stopping her, a plea in his voice. "I saw his tooth when I carried food from the kitchen to him and that hag he calls his wife. Her I've not seen, but him I know. I'd swear it on my life."

"Heavenly Father, spare us!" Riona crossed herself so horrible was the idea. "Tell me again that you're certain, beyond all doubt."

Fynn crossed his heart. "God take my breath now if I'm not speakin' the truth."

"He very well may," Riona warned him, still wary. While the lad had a good heart, there was much about Fynn's ways that gave her cause to be cautious. He'd been caught in so many lies told to suit his whim when he first came to the abbey. She prayed that was a thing of the past now that he'd spent the winter months here among the brethren. At least he hadn't been caught in a lie of late. Whatever the case, Fynn and the twins genuinely appeared to think it was so.

"So be it, then."

"So I was lookin' for ye to tell ye and came upon that bully forcing his attention on ye."

Riona closed her eyes, wishing that would erase the last hour as it did the moonlit yard, but that wasn't to be. "Kieran was only protecting himself from me, Fynn. Shame to say, I lost my temper and fell upon him."

Fynn's snort underscored the dubious arch of his brow.

"It's true. I've a fearsome temper, which I prayed was put to rest by faith. My foster brother has a knack for resurrecting it to its full-blown most. Sure, temper is the devil's own work, for you nearly spilled an innocent man's blood on my behalf, and I'd have been as much at fault as you." Riona grabbed the lad's face between her hands. "Do you understand what I'm saying?"

Fynn nodded, but from the stubborn set of his chin Riona knew he was not convinced. Still, that was a mission for another time. Seargal might be imaginary, but Leila had obviously recognized Tadgh or Silver Tooth. It was her curious way of warning them. Riona couldn't dismiss it with Fynn's added testimony. Her penitent prayers would have to wait. She needed to see the abbot immediately.

"I'll seek an audience with Fintan now. I don't think he's finished with his Scripture for the night."

The abbot read a chapter of the Word each evening in his office before retiring. On his better days, he allowed Riona to read it aloud to him, indulging her love of books and the Lord. Her mother's relation had baptized her a child of the church as an infant, and she'd hoped that in the near future he'd welcome her as a bride of the church as well. With the recent turn of events, that would be impossible. Faith, she needed to speak to her mentor as much for herself as for the children.

"You get Leila and Liex and put them *and yourself* to bed. The morning always comes too early for you as it is," she warned her stalwart protector.

Fynn would not be diverted from accompanying her to Fintan's private quarters. Too overwrought to argue, Riona left him in the courtyard garden where the elder churchman often meditated on warm days and stepped inside the cozy apartment of rooms near the chapel. Brother Ninian's desk was vacant, cleared of its ever-present books and logs. He must be preparing the abbot's bedchamber, Riona surmised, walking beyond to Fintan's private retreat. Riona knocked softly at the door.

"Who goes?"

"It's Lady Riona, Father."

"Come in, child."

Upon entering the inner sanctum, Riona found Abbot Fintan seated at his desk. Instead of the Holy Scriptures spread before him, an open, ornately carved casket sat on his desk. Surrounding it were letters, much like the one on which Fintan dripped molten wax.

"Father Fintan—"

"My answer to Drumceatt's call," he said, placing his seal on the missive before him. He sighed heavily and placed it in the box. "I fear that, like many of the bards, I've outlived my usefulness."

Stricken by the melancholy in the elder churchman's voice, Riona protested. "Oh no, Father. That could never be. Your devotion to God's service is a testimony to us all." Fintan's frame was bent with age, but the fires of his faith kept him involved in all the abbey's work and worship.

"Nonetheless, I shall send Bishop Senan in my stead with commentary on the fate of the bards and other issues at hand. Change is in the air, child. Like myself, the bards have outgrown their usefulness, at least by today's standards." A melancholy grazed the gray of his gaze. "Many have grown demanding and spiteful. They sow dismay rather than joy."

Or enough of that learned class did so, earning contempt for their innocent brethren, Riona added silently. It was a travesty the way they imposed upon people's hospitality and paid them with biting satire and curses, as if immune to God Himself. "I do not envy the high king in deciding their fate, for the nobles scream banishment."

"And how do you feel about them, Riona?"

Unlike many of the brethren, Fintan never acted as though a woman's opinion was of no import. Many was the night he'd challenge her as to what a particular reading meant to her. Usually she rallied with enthusiasm, but this night was not one of them. She thought a moment.

"I should hate to see them banished, for indeed they preserve our past and present with their gift of words, but some means of restraint should be enacted upon them for their brash misuse of rank and privilege."

"Hm." Her answer pleased him. It showed in the tilt of his mouth as he reached into the casket and drew out something. As he held it before the lamp, she saw it was a jeweled, silver-encased vial strung on a silk cord. "Holy water from the well at Kildare," he explained, "intended for the high king to drink for wisdom in his decisions." He cocked a bushy gray brow at her. "Think it will help?"

She wanted to say "the devil take the water," but she reined in her impatience to tell him about Tadgh. She'd enough to repent for as it was.

"It is God's creation," she answered thoughtfully. "The saints have blessed it. I think it's time man gave God credit for His wonderful works rather than devil's spawn."

"So you think it has power." It was a statement, not a question.

"If God intends it to, aye. But only the heavenly Father knows that for certain. Like the power of prayer, the result may not be what we expect, but God can make the best of it if we accept and believe He makes no mistakes."

Riona tried to think of a way to tie this strand of conversation to her purpose for coming without being rude or stepping out of her place. "For instance, I've prayed tonight for an answer to my quandary regarding the children and—"

"God sent you a husband."

Riona's jaw dropped, leaving her mouth agape in stupor. A husband! How could Abbot Fintan possibly—

"I met your cousin Bran at the chapel, where he was giving thanks for the safe arrival of himself and Gleannmara's king." Fintan leaned forward, compassion kindling in his gaze. "I know of our Heber's loss, child. I know why you're here."

"Th...the children?" she stammered, beginning to wonder herself. This wasn't at all what she intended to discuss.

"A husband may not be what you prayed for, Riona, but it's what God sent you, and just in time."

This was too much. Riona shook her head. "No, not a husband. That isn't why I'm here."

"But you have my blessing and, even in death, your brother's as well," Fintan pointed out. "That God can take such a terrible tragedy and turn it to good use—" the abbot clasped his frail, palsied hands around the vial—"I never cease to marvel at His goodness. I've been much concerned over you, you know."

Her brain was as shaken by the abbot's words as the water in the jeweled casing. It couldn't be as he said. How could she—?

"How could I marry the man who led Heber to his death?" she

blurted out. "Heber would not have gone if Kieran had not. It wasn't even their war."

The abbot's smile faded. "Surely you don't mean that! Heber was a man of his own mind. It was his choice to go to battle, to fight another man's enemies."

"But it was Kieran's idea." Riona threw up her hands. "He's always full of war talk, war games...sure, he dreams of war at night! How could I wed such a man when I seek God's peace, not war?" Her chin trembled with emotion. "You know what my mother went through with my father. Would you wish that upon me?"

"Riona, child—"

A knock on the door cut the elderly man off. At Fintan's acknowledgment, Brother Ninian peeked inside. "I heard raised voices," he said with an apologetic look at Riona. "I thought something might be wrong."

"I'm sorry, Brother Ninian," Riona apologized. "I've had the most tragic news and fear I became overly agitated."

"We are fine, Ninian. Thank you for your concern," the father added with genuine affection. His venerated station demanded such attentions, yet Fintan accepted them with a humility that endeared him even more to his junior clergy. "I will not need you any more this evening."

"Very well. I'll be retiring then. Good night, Father. Lady Riona."

As Ninian closed the door, Fintan pushed up from his desk and hobbled around to where Riona struggled with her despair. He opened his arms, and she walked into them. Pain in all its wretchedness was wrung from her throat in hiccups. Where did such depth of emotion come from? How much more was left to tear her apart so mercilessly? Heber was lost, buried in a godforsaken land, and with him a part of her childhood. As for Kieran...

"You are not only your mother's child, Riona, but your father's, too. There is a restlessness in you that will never be content here. I've waited for you to see it, for I believe you sense it as well as I. Listen for God's calling. He will show you the way."

Riona backed away. "But not with a man who has turned away

from God Himself! Kieran believed once, long ago. But now…now he has contempt for faith in an unseen God."

"The tree is barren now, child, but dig around it as the gardener did in Christ's parable and nourish it with love." Fintan curled his ringed finger beneath her chin, lifting it. "The gleeman's offspring were as void of faith as yon Kieran when they first came here. Like them, Kieran's faith was laid barren by loss of all dear to him, save one, and that is you. But under your loving care the young ones grow like seedlings toward the sun. Your stalwart love for the Father and His children is your gift. The king needs it as much as the pauper's children do. But for the grace of second chance, we'd all be lost."

"But…"

"Pray on it this night. God will show you what you must do."

Riona let her shoulders drop along with her resistance. She was so weary, too weary to think clearly. Heber's death, Kieran's proposal, the children's fate…and now Father Fintan's suggestion that she might not be suited to a life at the abbey. It was all too much too fast to take in, much less fathom, God's part in this horrible muddle. Only one thing made sense, and that was that the children needed her.

The children!

"Father, that man Tadgh—"

"I'll not allow the children to go with the freeman and his wife when I see a good home for them with you and Gleannmara's king."

"The man intends to send the children to the Bristol slave market. He's a slaver from Dublin called Silver Tooth. The children recognized him."

Abbot Fintan drew back sharply. "Are you certain of this? That is a serious charge, milady."

"Fynn saw his silver tooth. He swears on his life."

The older man turned and made his way back to his desk, where he dropped heavily onto the bench. "This is too serious a claim to base on young Fynn's testimony. His mind is set on your taking him and his siblings to raise. How can we know if it's true or one of the lad's schemes? It wouldn't be the first time he's lied to his own end."

"Perhaps we might ask Bishop Senan how he came to meet the

couple. Perhaps he knows more about them. If these people are selling our orphans into slavery, they need to be dealt with."

"Aye, that they must." Fintan gathered up the pile of letters from other churches and put them back in the gilded casket, placing the silver-encased holy water on top. "But let us think on these things tonight. We've both more than a mind full to ponder. Tomorrow, if need be, I'll ask Kieran of Gleannmara and your cousin Bran to convey this man to the Maille tuath. The lord there can hear his case. For now, the children are safe."

Riona reached across the table and drew Abbot Fintan's gnarled, arthritic hands to her lips, kissing first one and then the other. "Good night, dearest anmchara."

Fintan's benevolent smile took years away from his wizened face. "Good night, child."

Drawing slowly away, Riona turned and lifted the latch to the outer chamber.

"And remember, Riona lass, when all else confounds you, follow your heart, for it is noble and good."

Follow her heart. The kindly abbot's words echoed in Riona's mind as she stepped through the outer door. At the moment, her heart pained her so that it offered no direction. She glanced up at the moon, as if some direction might be shining in the beautiful night sky, then turned the corner of the building, and she plowed into a familiar robed figure.

"Lady Riona!"

"Bishop Senan!" She clutched at her chest where her heart skipped to a halt.

"Now I know the reason my brother's light burns so late. The two of you have been solving the problems of heaven and earth again," he accused gently.

"More discussing them than solving, I fear," Riona hesitated, wondering if she should broach the subject of Tadgh tonight or wait as Abbot Fintan suggested until the morning.

Wait.

She obeyed the inner voice. "We gave out before arriving at any solution."

"Then I shall see if the father would like his warm milk and honey. Seems to rest his bones in the damp of the night." Almost as an afterthought, he added. "And you have my deepest sympathies regarding your brother's death. Such a tragedy."

Riona swallowed hard, refusing to let her grief well again. Faith, there was no end to it.

Instead, she nodded and rushed around the side of the building toward the garden where Fynn waited. Except he was nowhere to be seen among the moonlit trellises and arbors. Straining to see, she caught a movement in the shadow of the abbot's lodgings. As a tall, lanky frame moved out into the clearing, she let her frozen breath go.

"You were eavesdropping," she said as the boy walked toward her.

"Aye, as much as I could."

How could she scold him when he was honest? "Well, it's impolite and smacks of deceit, but I appreciate your honesty." Slipping an arm behind the lad's back, she ushered him along with her toward the sleeping quarters. "Fynn, you *are* absolutely certain about Tadgh and his silver tooth, aren't you?"

"On my life, I swear it."

Riona nodded. "Then I believe you. We'll confront them in the morning after the abbot speaks to Bishop Senan."

"Now *he's* a sneak."

"Oh?" She stopped, waiting for her companion to go on.

"I saw 'im with his head against the door like his ear had been nailed there. When he heard you coming, he stepped around the corner so's to look as if he'd just arrived."

Frowning, Riona started forward again. Her confession had been a personal thing between her and Abbot Fintan, but she supposed there was no harm in Senan's hearing it. It was more annoying than anything.

"Even bishops have their faults, I suppose," Riona mumbled as much to herself as to her companion. "Let's get the twins in their beds before they take a chill." It wasn't particularly cold; Riona just felt that way.

They found Liex and Leila curled in the fresh hay next to Nessa.

Riona managed to lift Leila, amazed at how a child so little could weigh so much when dead with sleep. At first she opened her eyes wide with fright, but upon seeing it was Riona who held her, she laid her head against Riona's chest and closed her eyes in complete trust. Meanwhile, Fynn hauled Liex over his shoulder like a sack, but the little boy slept so soundly that he did little more than grunt. With a few grunts of effort of their own, they managed to carry the little ones back into the main compound to Riona's lodging.

Riona whispered good-night to Fynn, leaving him to take Liex to the enclosed stall attached to the back of her lodge. Carefully, she sidled through the door to the small, wattle-and-daub dwelling and put Leila down on the stuffed mattress.

Fynn cried out like a whipped hound.

"Stay here!" She tossed a blanket over the groggy child in haste as an unholy commotion ensued outside, fierce with growling and shouting, topped with Liex's hysterical shriek. Armed with nothing but motherly instinct, Riona raced around the stall behind her shelter, only to be bowled over by a body tossed from its dark entrance.

Down she went, the body on top of her. In the frantic scramble to untangle, she realized it was Fynn. Before she could ask what was amiss, a towering mass of warrior appeared over them, reaching for the boy.

"All right, you thieving cur, where is the ring?"

Riona knew that voice. She grabbed at Fynn's waist, adding her weight to the boy's as Kieran of Gleannmara hauled them both up. "Kieran, let him go!"

"Not till he gives me back the ring."

"I dunno what he's talkin' about," Fynn bellowed. "He grabbed me in the dark, causin' me to drop Liex."

"Ssshhh!" she hissed loudly. "You'll wake the entire abbey."

But it was too late. The clapper of the handbell used to sound alarm clanged loudly through the quiet compound. Riona used the advantage of the surprise to insert herself between Kieran and Fynn. With a sound stomp on his instep, she sent the larger man hopping backward. She'd learned long ago that Gleannmara's prince had a tender foot.

Within moments, the inner grounds filled with sleepy and confused monks from one side and women clucking like riled hens from the other. In the senseless babble, no one paid heed to Riona and her companions. The ceaseless ringing bell called them elsewhere. Relatively certain that the fray had abated, at least for the moment, Liex bolted out of the darkness of the enclosure straight to Riona.

"It's all right, little one," she assured him, as he tried to hide himself from Kieran in the folds of her dress. Leila peeped sheepishly around the corner, a blanket clutched to her small bosom, so Riona motioned her over as well. It appeared no one was going to sleep after all.

Loud whispers and shouts relayed a ripple of rumor over the gathering throng until it reached the spot where Riona and her companions stood.

The abbot is dead!

Murder!

Father Fintan's dead.

Oh, foulest of foul!

Dead!

They echoed over and over, punctuated by cries of despair and woe. The dreadful message hammered and hammered against Riona's disbelief. It couldn't be! She'd just left him. She placed her hands hard against her ears, refusing to hear, but the horrible pounding continued driving in the horror of it all until there was but one escape.

Oblivion.

Six

With the break of the soft gray dawn, sounds of mourning burdened the prayers and hymns of the abbey. Abbot Fintan lay dead in his bedchamber, his body awaiting preparation for burial. Riona trudged from the chapel, oblivious to the gentle rain. Mud grabbed at her hem and stuck to her slippered feet despite the fresh-cut wattling laid to make the walkway passable. A hearing had been scheduled in the refectory, which would hold more people than the reception area the abbot used for private audiences. It was hoped that some sense might be made of last night's murder and mayhem.

"Don't worry about the children, milady," one of the sisters assured her. "They're fresh scrubbed and with Brother Domnall at the dairy. When I left, he was telling them Jonah's story, though I fear he's having a hard time convincing them that a fish so large as to swallow a man can exist."

"Sea dragon."

The gray-clad sister gave Riona a quizzical look. "Milady?"

"He could call it a sea dragon. They'd understand that."

Riona's voice held as much life as she felt, which was none. She was moving. She felt her blood pulsing through her veins. She heard herself speak. Yet it was as if she wasn't really there inside her body but somewhere apart, watching this woman who was acting on her behalf. Maybe when she came back to herself, she would find this was all some terrible nightmare.

A stoop-mouthed man-at-arms stepped out to meet her as she approached the entrance to the refectory. "I'm sorry, milady—" he twisted the sharp upturn of his moustache self-consciously—"but only them witnesses involved in the abbot's death can go in."

Men-at-arms from the Maille chief of the neighboring tuath were at the outer gates before the sun rose. Riona assumed Senan had sent straight for the leather tunics last evening. Before breakfast, the lord Gadra Mac Maille himself arrived with more men. To see armed soldiers milling about the abbey grounds was a contradiction of the senses. But then, so was Fintan's death.

"I was with the Father Abbot last night just before he was...murdered." The word curdled in Riona's mouth so that she was hard pressed to get it out.

"Oh, all right then. In with ye." The soldier stepped back to let her in.

"Would you have me come with you, sister?" her companion asked. "You're pale as a bled goose. I've salts in my apron—"

"I will not faint. Last night..." Riona couldn't say she slept well. Sleep visited elsewhere while she tossed and turned. "I'm much more collected today after a good breakfast." It had gone down like the mud clinging to her feet, but Riona had forced herself to eat rather than argue with her kindly benefactress. "Just keep an eye on the children. They sometimes are overmuch for Brother Domnall."

The lamps inside the refectory made a vain effort to offset the darkness accentuated by the dreary day. Their tallow scent and the smoke from the fire in the hearth lay heavy in the damp air. The small table near the fire where the abbot and his immediate order usually dined was filled today with those presiding over the hearing. Bishop Senan and Gadra of Maille sat at the center. Brother Ninian sat at the bishop's side, and a brehon, clad in the somber robe of the law scholars, sat next to the lord.

Like Fintan and his half brother, Senan, Gadra of Maille was distant kin to Riona's mother. He'd fought with Murtagh and Kyle of Gleannmara with the northern Niall at Culdreime. Later he married a sister of King Baetan, king of the Uliad, a Niall cousin who also fought with them. Because the Maille had given land for the abbey and offered protection, Father Fintan was obliged to Gadra.

Gadra's political interests, however, gave the elder churchman cause for concern. The lord's marriage allied him with the Uliad's Baetan, who made no pretense about not coveting the role of the high king. One winter night, Fintan and Riona had discussed how, less than a decade before, the Maille, the Niall, and the Uliad fought as one against Diarmait. "Allies and enemies change with the wind," Fintan remarked, "but God never does." He tapped his finger on the table and winked at her as she pondered his words.

Faith, it seemed like just a few days ago…

"Lady Riona, if you wish to rest," Bishop Senan spoke up, "I feel certain this court would not object. We all know how difficult this last day has been for you, and I can vouch for your innocence in this matter."

"Your kindness is appreciated, Bishop Senan, but I wish to be here."

As she took a seat near the door, she caught sight of Kieran and Bran at the table nearest the dais. Kieran gave her a tender, questioning look that kindled the first warmth she'd felt that day.

She sent him an appreciative smile.

Last night when Riona regained her wits, she was in her bed, tucked in like a babe. She opened her eyes to the soft brush of Kieran's lips upon her brow. As she stirred, he drew back hastily, but his fingers were still entwined in her hair and would not let his tenderness escape detection so easily.

Leila babbled something to her brother and giggled as Kieran straightened as tall as the sloped ceiling would allow.

"She said you kissed the lady to life, just like a fairy prince," Liex translated.

Kieran scowled at the twins. The boy took a step back, but Leila, evidently undaunted by her measure of the warrior king, climbed on the foot of the pallet and made herself comfortable.

"Faith, woman, you frightened the life out of me."

For all the accusation in Kieran's voice, relief flooded his eyes. They seemed to gather warmth and light from the candle lamp on a shelf at the head of her bed. In them Riona saw the Kieran she loved, the youth who'd brought her a kitten from Gleannmara and gotten up early each morning to spend time playing with it before his training started; the one who'd risked losing a finger to take a wounded bird from her father's falcon thus keeping her from seeing its flesh pulled apart and then built it a cage so that she might nurse it to health. When the poor thing died, despite her efforts, it was Kieran who shrugged off the taunts of his fellow warriors-in-training to help her give it a Christian burial.

For an intangible moment, their gazes locked in a better time, a time for hearts to speak rather than tongues…until reality invaded. The door burst open, and Bran rushed in to tell them in breathless snatches the details of what had transpired.

Now Riona was snatched again from that sweet moment by Bishop Senan's voice. More nasal in quality than his half brother's, it lacked Fintan's resonance. It tended to lull a soul to rest rather than move it to action, but today she concentrated on every syllable.

"Let it be recorded that this hearing regarding the circumstances leading to the death of Abbot Fintan of Kilmare is now in session."

Brother Ninian scratched furiously on the clean parchment before him with a freshly trimmed quill. He was truly talented, never once splattering ink as Riona was sometimes prone to do. Fintan always asked Ninian to write letters for him, especially since age had stiffened the elderly man's fingers. Last night, however, the ink and quill had been on Fintan's desk. As Riona entered, she witnessed him sealing his statement regarding the synod issues. It had truly grieved the abbot that he was physically incapable of making the journey to Drumceatt to see his old friend Columcille once more.

Maybe writing in his own hand his support of the bards, and of the independence of Scotland from tribute to the Uliad king Baetan, was as close as he could get. The Uliad Dal Raidi owed tribute to Baetan as a subsept, but he greedily used their relationship to their Scotia Minor cousins to justify demanding as much from them. Fintan allowed Baetan to stew in his own broth when the provincial king had not been invited to Drumceatt, where the high king and council from church and state would decide the issue. The fire in Fintan's eye revealed that even the good abbot was given to temper on occasion. It had given her hopes that her own would not keep her from God's service, that in time it would mellow with the growth of the Holy Spirit within.

The memories faded as Riona heard the scene and evidence

reported for the record. She tried repeatedly to swallow the blade that kept forming in her throat. Bishop Senan told how he'd left Father Fintan to fetch the abbot's customary warm milk from the kitchen, and when he returned, the study chamber was dark. He assumed Fintan had gone to bed, but upon checking did not find his brother in his sleeping quarters. Alarmed, Senan called Ninian from bed, and the two returned to the abbot's study with a lamp.

There they found Fintan on the floor, a knife driven into his chest. His linen robe, so lovingly embroidered by the sisters of the abbey, was soaked with his blood. An overturned desk, spilled ink, and the courier chest and contents bound for Drumceatt were scattered about the paved floor of the chamber, as though there had been a struggle.

Diverting herself from the abomination, Riona searched the room, face after face, but those she sought were missing. There was no sign of Tadgh or his wife, Mebh. Had they somehow found out the abbot knew of their vile purpose and killed him? Had anyone given them any thought?

She rose to her feet, decorum an afterthought. Senan stopped giving his testimony, addressing her with consternation. "Lady Riona, are you ill?"

Riona felt color flood her face, but this was no time for humility or embarrassment. "Father Senan, I can't help but notice that the freeman Tadgh and his wife, Mebh, are not here, and I fear I know the reason."

"I do as well," Senan answered calmly. "They changed their minds about taking the children because of the older boy's hostility and took their leave at daybreak. But I fail to see what this has to do with my brother's murder."

Riona hesitated. If Fynn had lied to her, she'd wring his neck herself. Making up her mind, she seized the gauntlet of challenge.

"Father Senan, Tadgh is not a freeman. He's a man called Silver Tooth who gathers children orphaned by the Blefed and sells them into slavery through Bristol."

The ensuing gasp of astonishment threatened to suck all the breathable air in the room for a moment. Then murmurs spread like a wildfire over the gathering. Bishop Senan had to ring a bell to restore order. With his peppered white brow knitted in a solid hedgerow over his eyes, he frowned at Riona.

"That is a serious charge, milady, even though it has nothing to do with this hearing."

"But it does. Father Fintan knew about Tadgh. I told him as soon as the children identified the man. The abbot was going to confront him this morning. Now he's dead." She glanced around at the men who were staring at her as if she'd sprouted horns. "Don't you see? Tadgh must have somehow discovered Fintan knew and—"

"That is ridiculous, child!" Senan threw back his head, as if calling for reason from the rafters of the refectory. "My brother never mentioned it to me, and if he'd taken this seriously, trust me, he would have said something."

"But he did take it seriously, sir. I spoke to him myself. He assured me—"

"Exactly." Senan fixed her with a cold glare. "He *assured* you because you were in a hysterical state over your brother's death and he didn't want to distress you further."

Riona felt her cause sinking like swamped coracle. "But the children recognized this man from Dublin. They'd seen him selling orphans to a slaver."

"Milady," Senan warned sternly. "You cannot expect this court to take the word of a collective band of little liars, who would and have said anything to serve their own wishes over those of an honest working farmer and his wife." He rose to his feet and addressed Brother Ninian. "But for the record, Ninian, the freeman Tadgh and his wife spent the night in the sisters' hospitium and were abed, according to Sister Selia, before vespers were out. She herself was sharing the beauty of the night in the vallum until the alarm sounded and would have seen the guests had they departed the hospitium. Therefore," the bishop concluded smugly, "the freeman and his wife were dismissed this morning without suspicion. Is that agreeable and reasonable to you, milord?"

Gadra of Maille nodded. "Aye, most reasonable and agreeable. But we thank the lady for her concern, no matter how trivial." His patronizing smile was as yellow as the amber of the silver brooch he fingered thoughtfully.

"But if not a found-out slaver, then who would do such a loathsome thing?" Riona demanded of the head table.

"If milady would sit down, perhaps we might find out," Gadra suggested dourly.

With a proud tilt of her chin, Riona resumed her seat, back as stiff and straight as her glare. In the corner of her eye, she caught Kieran of Gleannmara wiping a smile from his face with a discreet hand and gave him an icy glance as well. Friend or foe among themselves, men belonged to the same league when it came to dealing with the opposite gender. Perhaps that was yet another reason she'd developed a bond with the children, for they suffered even less regard in the scheme of society than their mothers.

"Brother Ninian, if you will, please read the list of the evidence you and I found at the scene."

The scribe cleared his throat. Despite the authoritative demeanor he assumed, emotion cracked his first words. "Found in-in the body of Abbot F-Fintan—" he forced himself above it—"was a knife, which has been identified by the brothers in the kitchen as one set out in the refectory last evening for our visitor from Gleannmara."

All eyes, including Riona's, swiveled to where Kieran and Bran sat. It was clear from their expressions that they were as dumbfounded as anyone by the revelation. The only knife Riona remembered was the one Fynn threw at Kieran. The boy had retrieved it from the doorframe on their way out.

"Its singular identifying feature is a broken handle," Ninian said, adding aside, "which Brother Clemens was going to fix once—"

"Do the gentlemen from Gleannmara recall such a knife?" Senan interrupted.

"Aye, I do," Bran said.

All trace of humor banished from his angular features, Kieran nodded. But for that slight movement, he might have been carved from stone—a sitting statue, arms folded across the expanse of his chest, booted feet planted firmly on the floor.

"And was it still there when you left the refectory?"

Again the two acknowledged with a nod.

"When Brother Thaddeus came in after prayers, he said the table-ware was on the floor and a bench had been overturned…but the knife was gone." Senan glanced at the cook's assistant.

"So it was. So it was." The man's head bobbed. "Like a storm had blown through."

Riona cringed. She'd been so anxious to separate Fynn and Kieran, she'd not thought about tidying up. Heaven forbid her foster brother should stoop to such a lowly task.

"The bearer of bad news often incurs the brunt of the reception." Kieran turned an impeaching appraisal on Riona. "I've a sore ear to show for it." He swept back the shorter hair around his face to show a tiny scab where she'd bounced the cup off it and split the flesh. "But forgiveness is in order, as the lady *was* overcome with grief."

Humor rippled along the tables. Riona seethed through her narrowed gaze with a mixture of anger and humiliation. The murmuring abated, cut by the sharp finger Bishop Senan pointed at the young king of Gleannmara. No longer the impartial moderator, the older man bellowed with condemnation.

"Was it grief, Kieran of Gleannmara, or anger?"

Kieran met his gaze, a slight frown creasing his forehead. "Anger? Over what?"

Senan stood stiff and straight, his gaze accusing. "Over the fact that you sought to force your hand in marriage on a daughter of the church?"

SEVEN

The stonelike lord of Gleannmara suddenly erupted. "*That* matter lies between the lady and myself! It is not the business of some pious, robed windbag who'd like to see the lady's properties tucked neatly in his parish's pocket."

Senan wore the look of the cat with a belly full of kicking mouse. "It *does* matter if that is the reason you murdered my brother."

"*What?*" The idea was so preposterous, Gleannmara's lord laughed. "Tell me, Maille, if you were of a mind to kill someone, would you use a broken kitchen knife that would hardly cut bread—or something like *this?*" Kieran brandished a lethal-looking dagger from his waist and, in less than a gasp, was across the room, pressing it to Bishop Senan's throat.

"Mi…milord!" Positions switched, the mouse wailed beneath the cat's claw.

Gadra was pressed to hide his own disdain. "A well-made point, Gleannmara. A trifle overzealous, mayhap, but well made. Now kindly hand over your weapon before you provoke more suspicion than reason."

Kieran shifted his head, jaw jutting. Riona held her breath until he backed away, flipping the knife so that it dropped, blade-first, into the table in front of the Maille lord. Pivoting, Kieran returned to the bench and sat next to Bran, who looked as blanched as Riona felt.

Senan straightened his robe, gathering his composure. "Bran O'Cuillin, we've just a few questions of you, and then, since you were conspiring with Brother Ninian on rhyme at the time of my brother's murder, you may be dismissed."

Bran shifted, casting an uneasy glance at Kieran. "Aye, I left Kieran and Riona to their privacy in the refectory and came upon Ninian; he'd been ordained with my father at Clonnard. We collaborated to record an ancient rhyme."

"And were you aware of Kieran's intention to ask for the lady's hand in marriage?"

"Aye, it was her brother's last request…that Kieran take Riona into his protection as his wife."

"And Kieran was determined to do this?"

"Aye, if he could convince Riona."

"And did you not tell Brother Ninian that you wished Gleannmara's king luck, given the lady's dedication to the church and her previous rejection of his suit?"

"Aye, but—"

The bishop pressed on before the bard could finish his answer. "And did you not say the lady would have no choice in the matter?"

"I said that Kieran would give Riona no choi—" Bran saw the trap, but it was too late. It closed upon him.

"That *is* what Kieran said to you, is it not? That he'd give the lady no choice."

Bran shook his head. "In a manner of speaking, what with Heber making the request this time and not—" The bard glanced at his friend and was met with a shriveling glower.

He shook his head. "Kieran of Gleannmara would never force a lady to wed him against her will, much less kill a helpless old man. He is as noble a man as I've ever met. My lord bishop is leading me to say what I do not mean."

"I ply you only for truth, O'Cuillin. Nothing more, nor less." With a haughty flourish, the bishop withdrew a small, silken bag from within the folds of his robe. "And I would believe in milord Gleannmara's character and innocence as well, but for this." He shook the sack and produced a ring ablaze with sapphires. Lighter ones were arranged around a larger midnight sapphire, much like the brooch on Kieran's cloak.

Kieran was clearly taken aback as Senan held the ring up, a satisfied smile on his face.

"You know this ring, milord?"

"Aye, 'tis my mother's, the very one I intended to give Lady Riona *and* the very one that was stolen from my belongings while I spoke with the lady in the dining hall."

Confusion bled much of the credulity from Gleannmara's words. Riona could feel doubt's shadow drape across the room.

"You went to propose to a lady and left the ring behind?" The skeptical innuendo struck its mark.

Kieran bristled like a lanced boar. "Aye, for I knew she'd not say yes right away. For the love of heaven, man, she'd enough to bear with the news of her brother. I'd not force an answer from her on its heel. For all our differences, she is my foster sister, as beloved to me as was her brother."

A master of manipulation was playing her foster brother's pride, but the mule brayed too loudly to hear it. Riona could stand it no more.

"He speaks the truth!" Again, she leaped to her feet without the court's recognition rather than see this travesty go further. "Bishop Senan, while I may not offer him my hand, I would give my life for Kieran, and he for me. Truth, he was with me when the alarm sounded, in a snit because the ring was missing. He thought one of the children had taken it from his lodgings while he was away earlier. Kieran of Gleannmara could not possibly have murdered Father Fintan."

Silence grew loud over the crowd. Riona's word was well respected at the abbey, and the brethren awaited Senan's response. The bishop waited a full measure of time until undivided attention was focused on him, all the while staring at Riona. She sat down, feeling like a scolded child.

"If the Lady Riona's account is true, Lord Kieran—" Senan cast a patronizing glance Riona's way—"then how do you explain the ring finding its way to Fintan's murder scene?"

"The murderer was also a thief," Kieran answered readily. "He must have dropped the ring in his struggle with the abbot."

Senan nodded, as though considering the idea, but the consideration was short. "O'Cuillin, did *you* know the whereabouts of this ring?"

Bran jumped at the chance to redeem himself and Kieran. "Aye, Kieran left it behind on purpose. I saw him stow it among his things when we left to meet the lady. He felt the time wasn't right to infringe upon her grief with a proposal."

"Yet he did propose, did he not, milady?"

"He told me marriage to him was Heber's dying wish, Your Worship. He didn't actually ask."

"Because he intended to give you no choice!"

"No! It wasn't…"

"And when Father Fintan refused to bless the union, the same fierce temper demonstrated before our very eyes just moments ago drove Kieran of Gleannmara to kill him."

"The man's crazed on holy water!" Kieran matched the bishop volume for volume. With an oath not fit for the ears of man or beast, he started to his feet, but before they were square on the floor, six guards were upon him. The first two he shook off like lint from a cloak, but the remaining four soon had Gleannmara's king pinned to the floor as they chained his hands behind his back.

Yet another pair of guards stood by Bran lest the bard take up his friend's fight. Instead, Bran remained seated, judgment clearly the better part of his valor.

"I demand to be heard by the high king," Kieran shouted as the guards dragged him upright. "This is no court. This is a sham to cover one brother's greed for another's position!"

"How *dare* you, sir!" Bishop Senan left the table to stand before his accuser—and Riona allowed a sneer that he'd done so only when Kieran was in chains, with six men restraining him.

"How dare *you?*" Kieran shot back.

"This is a church matter, not an issue of state," the bishop snipped primly.

Kieran mocked him with equal priggishness. "'Tis a *greed* matter, and not an issue of justice."

"The bishop is right, Kieran of Gleannmara." For the first time the brehon accompanying Gadra spoke. "The crime, and hence the jurisdiction, belongs to the abbey. My lord Maille is only present as the lord bishop's enforcer and protector, while I am here at Maille's request."

"I'd have more justice from a court of Satan's own."

Riona winced. For all her temper, Kieran's was twice as explosive. Each time he opened his mouth, he forged another link in the chain of seeming guilt that bound him. A collection of outrage over Kieran's blasphemy and protest for justice filled the room.

"Bishop Senan!" Riona shouted above the discord. "Bishop Senan, please!"

Upon hearing her, he took up the small handbell and called for order.

"Your Worship, how can you discount my testimony that Kieran was with us searching for his stolen ring when the alarm sounded?" Riona charged. "Or Bran's account of the ring being left behind?"

Senan folded his hands in a show of indulgence. "If a lady would give her life for a man, would she not also try to protect him?" A few of the brethren nodded in agreement.

Smitten by her own words, Riona tried another tack. "But the lad Fynn and the twins, they all saw Gleannmara as well." Heads stopped, poised for an answer.

Gadra sneered. "The word of a friend and of three chronic liars?" He turned to his captain at arms. "Lock Gleannmara in the grainery. We'll take him back to the rath's dungeon tomorrow until we decide upon his punishment."

"Father Fintan gave his blessing on the marriage!" Desperate, Riona looked to her brethren, since it was clear that Senan's and the Maille lord's minds were made up. "He said it to me, and Bishop Senan heard it with his own ears because he was seen eavesdropping at the door."

"Clearly the words of a woman affected by her sympathies," Bishop Senan explained. In a grand show of compassion, he walked to Riona and embraced her. "Child, you are overwrought. 'Tis small wonder you are not reduced to hysterics given the news you've received of one loved one and now another. We all know the close relationship you shared with my brother. Your mother was his favorite of all our cousins."

"I'm not hysterical. I'm angry, you pompous toad!" Riona tore away. "Your brother lies dead, and you are squandering precious time with this mockery while the *real* murderer escapes."

Bran appeared at her side, clapping a restraining hand on her arm. "He's right, cousin. You are overwrought." There was more warning than consolation in his manner. "While it seems that justice is missing its mark here, we need to think how to steer it aright again. That cannot be accomplished with raised voices and hysteria."

The sound lashing headed his way halted on the tip of her tongue. Bran was right. She couldn't believe she'd called the lord bishop a toad. Why, she was as hotheaded as Kieran. Heaven help her, if last night had been hard to believe, this morning was even more so. Stunned by it all, including her erratic behavior, Riona accompanied Bran away from her antagonist. As they reached the door, Kieran shouted after them.

"Best get to Aedh with this."

"With all haste, friend, with all haste," Bran promised.

The stench of deceit followed them out into the fresh air. Even as they walked away from the refectory, Riona could hear the excited throng, still worked up by Senan's smooth ploy, clamoring for justice and Kieran's life. Others argued back, but the condemnation outcried the defense.

"These are men of God, of peace!" Riona's toe caught on one of the wattle branches laid down on the walk, and Bran steadied her. Faith, she could hardly see she was so disillusioned.

"There's something terribly amiss," Bran said. "Mayhap more than a brother's ambition to fill his elder sibling's chair. 'Tis not the work of the church, to be certain. Some in there saw it, if not all of them."

"But what?"

Bran shrugged his shoulders as if the weight of the world bore down upon them. "I've no idea, except that it somehow involves Maille. I don't know if Kieran was the unfortunate pigeon who walked in at the right time to be plucked or if it involves Gleannmara as well."

"His temper has only made things worse." Riona wrung her skirt with her fingers. Kieran's display was bad enough, but then *she* had to go and forget herself. Just being around Kieran of Gleannmara turned her into a different woman—one of unharnessed temper and tongue.

"He's been hard company since we left Dunadd," Bran agreed. "Half his heart was buried there, and you soundly stomped what's left."

"Have a care," Riona objected as they reached the small guest house where Bran and Kieran spent the night. "I'm as dismayed as any over this. If only they'd listen to me."

"I know, lass." Bran bent over and planted a kiss atop her head. "For all our good intentions, neither of us did Kieran a whit of good. Which is why I fly to Drumceatt."

The bard disappeared inside the low doorway and reappeared before Riona could follow him in. Slung on his back was his sack of belongings. "If the high king and Father Columcille can't help Kieran, no one can."

"God can."

Riona meant it with all her heart, although God's presence seemed sorely lacking in the hearing. She fell in step beside Bran as the bard started toward the gate to the outer vallum, where the livestock and dairy were kept. *Please, Father, make Your will known to me that I might make some sense of this.*

"It may well take God's help," Bran reflected aloud. "Much can happen to a man between here and my destination. Baetan's not likely to make passage through his lands easy for an ally of the high king."

"What are you trying to say? That the Uliad king is involved in the abbot's murder?"

Bran shrugged and lowered his voice. "After what I just saw, I wouldn't be surprised at anything. Baetan rules from Tara as though Rodanus never uttered a curse against it."

A decade ago, the hill of Tara was the home of the high king of Ireland, as it had been for centuries past. The same Diarmait, against whom Riona's and Kieran's fathers led the forces of Gleannmara at Culdreime a year before the king's demise, brought a curse upon the legendary capital with his violations of sanctuary and his inhospitality to God's own. Now a lesser king, Baetan of Ulster, occupied it with delusions of glory, while his cousin Aedh Ainmire ruled as high king from the Niall strongholds to the north.

Well Riona knew that no high king who hoped to rule with the blessing of church and God would ever choose the once-revered hill of ancestral rule for his court. Clearly the Uliad's Baetan flaunted his disregard for Tara's curse, as if he somehow hoped its spirit of the past might pass along to him its power and glory.

"But what is most important for you, my pretty cousin, is to keep Kieran from harm until I get back."

"Wouldn't it be faster to summon troops from Gleannmara?" After all, how could she protect her foster brother when Senan and Gadra would not take her words seriously?

Her cousin pulled an astonished face. "Why, Riona O'Cuillin, are you suggesting war?"

Riona bit her lip. Heavens, she was! If Gleannmara's troop clashed with Maille's, blood would spill for certain. For the first time, she knew how easily taking up the sword had come for Columcille when, a decade before, he too had acted in outrage at his kin being threatened in the sanctuary of the church. This time, though, it was the church itself—or rather its bishop—who championed injustice.

Father, keep us all from our human weaknesses. Do not allow Satan to use our love as a weapon against our souls. Let our love avoid bloodshed, not provoke it. Go with Bran—

"Hey you, bard!" Two of the men-at-arms ran after them from the gate in the stone embankment of the inner rath.

Bran and Riona stopped just outside the stables and waited for them to catch up. Fear congealed in her chest. Had something changed? Would the bishop or Gadra keep Bran from going for help?

"We'd have a look in that sack before you leave," the one in the lead huffed upon reaching them.

With grimace of impatience, Bran handed over his belongings. "Have a care for my harp. Aingeal is a gentle creature and sensitive to the touch of brute hands, e'en though they belong to such stouthearted men as she sings about."

Her cousin had a way of making words sting with the forehand and stroke with the back.

"Spare us your wily tongue. Given my vote, your likes and all their troublesome talk would be shipped off Erin's shores in a leaky boat."

The senior officer—a red-haired, mustached man—shook out the sack. The contents—a blanket, a spare leine and accessories, a razor, and the velvet case containing Aingeal—spilled to the wet ground. The harp strings shivered with dissonance at their careless treatment.

"Perhaps if I knew what it was you searched for, I might help you find it."

"Nothing here." The other soldier snapped the velvet that had encased the instrument. He tossed it aside and stood up as it sailed to the ground with the rest of Bran's things.

"Ye've no weapon at all?" the ranking soldier demanded.

A wicked glint settled in the bard's eye. "None but this." He stuck out his tongue. "Would you like me to demonstrate the power of a bard's word?"

The soldier shook his head. "Save it for talkin' down a hungry wolf. Come on, Oife."

For all his bravado, the man's retreat was nearly as hasty as his coming. It led one to think he was more leery of a bard's satire than he let on. Old superstitions died hard, Riona supposed, especially where faith was sown thin.

While Bran gathered his belongings and put them back in the sack, Brother Domnall came out of the stable with a bundle tucked under his arm. Next came Fynn, leading Bran's shaggy horse, with Liex and Leila skipping alongside.

"Well, this young man's either a gifted diviner or has the keenest ears in the abbey," Bran said, taking the reins from Fynn. "Either way, I thank you, sir."

"Good ears." Fynn gave him a sheepish grin. "I'd have brought the stallion, but he nearly blew me over the way he snorted through his nose. I'd half a mind to see fire comin' out of it."

"Hah!" Bran laughed. "If you'd managed him, then *you'd* be the man to ride to Drumceatt, not I. His temperament is as contrary as his master's, but like Kieran, he has a noble heart."

"I can believe it," the lad professed with whole heart.

Riona hadn't seen Fynn since she'd pulled him and Kieran apart. He'd vanished in the confusion and wasn't in his bed when she rose to dress for morning prayers. "And just where have you been, Fynn?"

"Around."

"He waked me up to see the soldiers this mornin'," his younger brother supplied helpfully. "An' then he was away. To mischief more likely."

Fynn started to give his younger brother a playful cuff on the back of the head, but Riona caught his wrist.

"I didn't think you cared what might happen to Kieran after last night. What's made you decide to help?"

Fynn scuffed his heel against his leg and tried to look indifferent. "He's innocent, even if I don't like him, which I don't, but I like even less me and the twins being called a little band of chronic liars." At Riona's sharp intake of breath, he went on, clearly pleased by her reaction. His ability to hide or blend into his surroundings undetected was a ceaseless source of delight to the lad. "Aye, I heard it all from my perch in the rafters. And that weasel-eyed Senan had no right to call you a liar. I wish the lord had peeled 'is bobbin' apple instead of handin' over his knife."

"The talk this lad has," Brother Domnall scolded. He handed Bran the linen bundle. "Take this, son. 'Tis some cheese and bread the twins gathered from the kitchen while Fynn and I readied your steed. God speed you to the high king and holy fathers at Drumceatt."

Riona gathered the little ones in her arms, sparing the elder Fynn such an embarrassment, and gave them a big hug.

"I don't know what Senan is up to, but I can see now he hasn't got a chance against the lot of you." After securing his belongings on the horse's back, Bran mounted up. But before he could ride off, Brother Ninian ran through the gate and shouted at him to wait.

"I begin to feel like Cuchulain, riding off to battle with this send-off. A fair lady, soldiers, brothers, children…"

Another time Riona might have cut him off with sarcastic wit, but Brother Ninian's approach bode ill. She felt it in her bones. Even the hair on her arms lifted, stroked by icy dread. As Ninian reached them, he took a moment to catch his breath. The exercise had forced more blood to the sedentary cleric's face than Riona had ever seen.

"You ride in vain, Bran," the brother told his friend. "Kieran of Gleannmara will be hanged before you reach Drumceatt."

"Hanged?" Riona ignored the way her knees turned to water, willing herself to remain upright.

Ninian nodded. "After the hearing was adjourned, I left with the others, when it occurred to me that I'd forgotten my quills. I returned through the back entrance from the kitchen and overheard Maille and the bishop in consult. The lord of Gleannmara is doomed and you are, too," he told Bran. "Men have been dispatched to see that you meet with some ill fate in the forests on the road to Tara."

"Then we'll have to do something on our own," Riona stated grimly. At least it sounded like her voice. Exactly what the resolute speaker had in mind was beyond her.

EIGHT

I've food for the lord of Gleannmara."

Riona tolerated the guard's examination of the basket prepared in the abbey kitchen with admirable restraint until the man stirred the porringer with his grimy finger. She snatched the basket away.

"I don't think a useful weapon can be hid in porridge and beans, but allow me to break the bread with my clean hands lest you contaminate it as well."

"Me and Oife is hungry, too," the guard said. He reached again for the food, but Riona sidestepped him. "You've two legs apiece and none of my sympathy. Get your own." She nodded at the bar of the grainery door. "Now open the door, or shall I advise Bishop Senan and my lord Maille that you offend me?"

Much as Riona was loathe to claim any relationship with the two connivers, distant or nay, it suited her purpose at the moment. Grudgingly, the man-at-arms opened the door and admitted her.

Kieran stood as she entered. There was no light, save that from the late afternoon sun streaming in through the open door. Instead of on her, Gleannmara's gaze was on the leather-clad men, taking their measure.

"It isn't lordly fare, but it's filling."

"Food is the last thing on my mind, milady," he growled sulkily.

"Then you'd best change your mind. This, at least, will keep you from tripping over that temper-fired tongue of yours."

Kieran winced as though she'd dealt him a physical blow. "Yours is its only match."

Riona smiled. "At least milord knows when he's well met." She took the linen cover off the food and spread it on the ground before placing the basket on top of it. "Sit. Eat."

With a scowl toward the door, Kieran dropped to a cross-legged position and took up the porringer. Despite his claim of no thought for food, he wolfed down the meal as though it were his last.

From all the rumors, that might not be far from the truth. The word of a bishop outmatched that of a tuath king—especially with the evidence that had been put out to indict Kieran. Even now those empowered to condemn him put their heads together over a feast of roast grouse hen in the late abbot's private chambers. Thankfully, Father Ninian kept a close ear to the goings-on from his station at his desk beyond the dividing wall.

"The way I see it, Bran should be at least three days getting to the high king and that much again and some in return," Kieran observed aloud. "If Senan doesn't have me hanged before."

"I'm certain the bishop will lend more time to this matter, once his shock over Fintan's death has abated. Reason and grief are a poor mix."

Kieran's brow shot up. "You should know well enough."

"Till then, you need to keep your strength up until Bran returns. Have some honeyed bread." Riona shoved the delicacy at him. "And take care not to drip it." The *drip* she referred to had nothing to do with the honey gathered by the abbey's beekeeper. It had to do with the note she had slipped beneath it.

"I don't—"

"Eat, fool!" She cut her gaze to the food to make the despondent lord look closer.

Riona suspected the guards would not allow them privacy. A note was the only way to let Kieran know what was going to happen—or what she *hoped* would happen. She made certain her back blocked the guards' view as Kieran secreted the note away in his belt and took a bite of the bread.

"Mmm…good," he garbled, mouth full. "Are you having second thoughts about wedding me now that I am a condemned man?"

"Wedding you, milord, is the very last thing on my mind. You may count my attention as Christian charity, nothing more."

Riona repacked the basket with prim efficiency, but as she made to rise, Kieran reached across the short distance between them and pulled her to him. The basket dropped, spilling the wooden tableware with a clatter. Her startled gasp received his lips and with them, a long, sound kiss. It smacked of honey and the wine she'd given him to wash down his meal, but the greatest distraction was the man himself. A curling warmth conveyed itself through the unsolicited union, the strength of which melted Riona's resistance.

It still worked its spell after the guards fell upon them and separated them.

"Unhand her, ye cur!" The senior officer knocked Kieran away from Riona with the butt of his sword, while the second steadied her from the plummet from her heightened senses.

"Milady, are ye all right?" the man Oife exclaimed.

"I...oh!" She cried out as the senior guard creased Kieran's forehead with the sword, laying open his skin. "Spare him, sir."

The guard stopped short of striking the dazed lord again, and Riona's mind raced. "Our court would rather he possess *all* his senses when his penance is handed out." She struggled to her feet on knees still wobbly from Kieran's unexpected assault. "Do help me gather these things. I must be off to the kitchen."

"What of our supper?"

"I'll see extra added to it for your gallantry, sirs. A good wine to soothe the troubled soul."

Oife grinned, revealing two good teeth. The rest were either rotted stubs or missing totally, no doubt the price of a drunken brawl. "That'd be more'n fine, milady, more'n fine."

"Unless you think it might impair your ability to stand guard over this ill-mannered buffoon," Riona said, feigning afterthought.

The senior guard sneered. "'Twould take more than a bottle made by clerics to dull a real man's senses, eh, Oife?"

"Sure as a pig stinks."

Riona masked her distaste and took the basket Oife handed to her. "Then I'll see to your meal at once, sirs." She tucked the linen coverlet around the contents and started for the door.

"I only sought to see if milady's lips were as sweet as her words," Kieran called after her.

She paused outside the grainery and glanced back in time to see him wipe his mouth in distaste.

"And sure one was as hard to stomach as another."

As if the fire flaming her cheeks scorched her heels as well, Riona stalked off toward the abbey kitchen. Once inside, she slammed the door behind her, rattling the utensils hanging on the wall. Father Domnall and the children looked up from their meals with widening eyes.

"Tell me once again *why* we are trying to save that wretched man's hide?"

Stomping to the table, she threw the basket, bouncing its contents out. Fynn grabbed the cup he'd helped carve as it rolled to the edge. Liex righted the porringer. Leila merely looked at Riona as if wondering where the gentle lady who had offered selfless love and care to three homeless children had gone. At length, the child rattled off something to Liex.

"Seargal says your husband made you angry."

"Well, he's half right," Riona fumed. "I *am* angry. Do you know what the ungrateful beggar had the nerve to—" She broke off. Father help her, she was addressing the child's imaginary companion. Abruptly, she turned to Domnall. "The note said for Kieran to create a diversion that would bring the guards to my rescue, and do you know what he did? He *kissed* me, that's what." She huffed like the bellows over a smith's forge. "Full on the mouth, no less."

"Shameful," the brother averred.

The nonexistent force of his disapproval was no more to Riona's liking than the twitch of his lips. As if to cover himself, he popped the remnant of his daily bread in and chewed without relent until it required washing down with a sip of diluted wine. With a grunt of satisfaction, he wiped his lips on the coarse linen of his sleeve and glanced up at her.

"It was successful, I hope. The diversion," he added hastily, "not the kiss. That was most ungentlemanly of him."

"He shoulda smashed his fist in your belly," Liex said, slamming his into the palm of his other hand. "That would get the guards' attention."

"If 'e was half as noble as he'd make one think, he'd 'ave just grabbed your wrist." Fynn's dark eyes fired with indignation. "An' I'll deal with him once we're away from here, milady, don't ye worry."

"I'll not have you going head-to-head with Kieran again, Fynn. I can take care of myself. I…well, it was just not what I expected him to do."

Riona took a calming breath and exhaled the last smoke of the fire Kieran and his disarming kiss had ignited. The last time she'd endured the lord of Gleannmara's affection, it had been a brutish, clumsy affair. He pursued romance like he plied an enemy: headlong, without regard for the sensibilities of his prey. Today's assault was no less forceful…yet it had been possessed of a play that taunted the senses rather than abused them. Had the guards not intervened, she might have been tempted to actually enjoy it.

The very idea made her shudder.

She put her fingers to her temples and massaged the ache there. This was not the time for discord of any nature. She put her fists on the table, ignoring all but what was most important. "We all need to work together, just as we've planned."

Liex slid off the bench, his blue eyes bright with excitement. "Is it time to go froggin'?"

At Riona's nod, Fynn was up and off, beating his younger sibling to the corner where the gig and sack lay. She and the children were to make their way to the outer fosse, which was filled with the earlier rainfall almost to the top of the earthen embankment surrounding the abbey. The closing twilight curtain afforded the perfect opportunity for catching frogs, which allowed Riona and the children to leave the confines without arousing suspicion. Once outside, they'd make their way to the forest where Bran waited in hiding after pretending to make off for Drumceatt. The rest was up to Brother Domnall, Kieran, Gray Macha…and God.

"But first, dear ones," Riona cautioned, motioning them into a small circle around Domnall, "let us pray."

"Rescue is at hand. Be prepared tonight. For now, make a diversion to summon the guards."

Kieran could not read the note he fingered in the darkness, but its words committed themselves to his memory—as did the sweet sampling of Riona's lips. When the guards pulled him away from her, he was fit to chew the beggars like raw fodder and spit them aside that his hunger for more might be satisfied.

Another place, another time…

Wiping his brow with the back of his hand, he tested the scabbed wound the guard had given him. The way Riona played the guards into taking an extra bottle of wine when she returned with their evening meal proved the church had not spoiled all the spice in her. The men fell asleep with dreams of the reward she promised Lord Maille would give them for their timely protection.

But what else was on Riona's mind, Kieran had yet to work out. Resourceful as his foster sister was, she was no match for the guards Maille placed at the gate.

Like the night before, the strains of the evening vespers haunted the air, straying from the inner vallum of the abbey to the grainery and outbuildings in the outer circle.

Kieran felt no reverence for the hymns and prayers. They were as false as the heart of the bishop leading them with hands folded and stained by his own brother's blood. That had to be the reason for this whirlwind condemnation. Senan killed his brother to attain the seat of power. Like the ascension of a clan chief, he'd need to be elected, but he was guaranteed first consideration because of bloodline.

Try as Kieran might, he could not fathom what had led Senan and Maille to fix the blame of Fintan's murder on him, save that Kieran was the unfortunate bullock who wandered too close to the sacrificer's knife at the right time. After all, the sooner Fintan's murder was solved and his murderer dealt with, the less between Senan and his coveted abbacy.

Kieran stopped his pacing at the sound of footsteps approaching the grainery and rushed to the door. The friction of the bar sliding from the keep grated in his ear. Stepping back, he saw it swing open. There were no Maille soldiers in sight—clearly they were staying close to the hut, which put them out of the line of sight of the grainery. But in the glow of their campfire stood a faceless monk, hooded and robed. He walked inside, drawing the door to behind him.

"Put on my robe, son, and hurry. There's no time to lose. You'll have to walk right by the soldiers to get to the stable."

Catching on instantly, Kieran threw off his cloak, waiting as the cleric pulled his dark robe over his head. It was a mean material compared to the lord's kingly cloak and scratched Kieran's arms as he shrugged it on. Smelling of cattle and hay, it skimmed the taller warrior's knees, while it had reached the ankles of its owner.

The monk chuckled. "You'll have to walk with bent knee, Gleannmara, if you hope to pass as this old man on his way to the stables with the armload of fodder outside."

His disparaging thoughts regarding God's servants still fresh, Kieran felt a pang of remorse as he clutched the brother's arm and shook his hand. "I owe you my thanks, Brother…"

"Domnall," the monk provided. He folded Kieran's cloak around his arm and handed it to him. "Now fetch that fine horse of yours from the barn. He should be able to clear the fosse beyond the rath, even though it's filled with rainwater."

"Aye, Gray could clear that as a weanling," Kieran allowed, peeping through the narrow crack of the open door. A monk's robe was poor protection, but his leather breastplate had been seized, along with his sword.

"Father, lend a hand."

Kieran grabbed the largest of the drugged guards and dragged him into the shelter, where he proceeded to strip him of his leather tunic. It wasn't quite as sturdy as Kieran's own, but 'twould serve. In a few minutes, he donned the robe again, this time over the leather.

"Just in case I'm discovered *before* I can reach my horse," he explained.

"Well done. Well done." Domnall patted him on the back with the same urgency in his voice. "Now ride west to the forest where the stream cuts through it. Your friends await you there."

Kieran hesitated at the door. "Friends?" He scratched his arms, where the rub of the sackcloth made his skin itch.

"Hurry, lad, there's no time for explanation now." Domnall shoved him through the door, then gathered up the fodder and handed it to him. "Keep your hood up, walk low and slow, and God's speed to you, Kieran of Gleannmara. Bring us back justice from Drumceatt."

"Drumceatt?" Kieran thought to head for Gleannmara and summon his clans. Bran was already on the road to the high king.

"The holy brothers will be praying that your safe journey and success will rout the evil from among us." The brother crossed himself. "Now go with the Lord. He will protect His own."

Kieran bit back his instinctive reply. Sarcasm was no way to repay a kindness, no matter what he thought of the man's God. Stripped of a weapon to fend for himself, he'd not mock help from any quarter.

Walking, or rather waddling on bent knee, toward the stables, Kieran took note of the whereabouts of Maille's soldiers. Most were gathered round the campfires, enjoying the fine wine and ale from the abbey stores. No matter what the brethren did, be it working the vines or fields, they did their best for God's glory, which made for superior products for export and sale. The profit benefited the poor, who were always at the gates of one rath or another.

"Ho, good brother. How about bringing our horses some food as well?"

The hair pricked at the nape of Kieran's neck. Ignoring the guard's request, he kept on shuffling toward the stable as if he hadn't heard at all.

"Ho, I say! What's the matter with you, dolt. Are ye deaf?"

Loping footsteps hastened toward Kieran. Still he moved toward the stable as though hearing naught. Suddenly a hand clamped on his shoulder, spinning him. With a loud gasp, Kieran threw up the fodder, as if he'd been startled out of his wits. Keeping the hood low over his eyes, he grunted and motioned wildly with his hands as he'd seen deaf mutes do at the fairs.

"Curse yer mother's milk, ye stupid oaf," the guard swore, picking up the cut and dried remnants of last year's harvest. "I'll take this." He pushed at Kieran, who stooped to help pick it up, and pointed first to the fodder and then to himself. "Mine," he growled.

Burning to make the man eat it, piece by piece, Kieran kept his head bowed and backed away. With a sign of the cross, he turned and hobbled off toward the stables, as though the soldier had frightened him. Behind him, the man laughed and made a derogatory remark regarding Kieran's lineage.

Once under the cover of the barn, Kieran straightened, pressing at the muscles cramping in his back from his hunched walk. "Gray!"

The stallion, hands above the oxen stabled next to him, stomped, dark tail swishing in anticipation. Kieran didn't need a light to remove the feedbag and slip tack over the animal's head and neck. After settling the riding cloth over its back, he led the stallion to the edge of the overhang farthest from the light cast by the campfires, and then outside. With a tap to the back of Gray's front hooves, he waited for the horse to stretch out as trained.

Hiking up the robe, he seized Gray's mane and swung up on the stallion's back, but fell short of his mark. With a curse, he stripped off the confining sackcloth and tried again. Once he was seen on Gray Macha no man with an ounce of wit would mistake him for a brother of the cloth, robe or nay.

Horse and master straightened simultaneously. Taking up the reins, Kieran leaned over the animal's neck and whispered in a low rumble, "All right, Gray Macha. 'Tis time to fly like the wind."

Kieran dug his heels into Gray's hard, muscled sides and clicked his tongue. The stallion lunged forward as if he'd been frozen in midgallop and just as suddenly thawed. Manes of horse and rider streamed in the wake of the rush. Within a few lengths, they drew the attention of the men at the edge of the encampment, including the guard who'd taken the fodder for the string of horses.

He ran toward Kieran, sword brandished over his head. Kieran had no weapon of his own, but he had Gray Macha. Snorting with the thrill of conflict, the magnificent warhorse plowed over the man as if he were made of smoke. Making a short circle, the animal carried its master back to their victim, pausing long enough for Kieran to reach down and snatch up the sword.

In the periphery of his vision, Kieran saw the gray's ears lay back and braced himself. He'd heard the footsteps racing up on them from the rear, too. Lowering its head, the horse kicked with its hind hooves and used the impact against the two men seeking to unseat its rider to spring forward.

The guards' warnings were knocked out of them, but shouts from others called more attention to the escapee. Hastily seized and launched, lances fell short as Kieran raced for the earthen rise that enclosed the outbuildings of the rath. Gray's pounding hooves echoed the pounding of the young lord's blood as they neared their goal.

A missile whistled over Kieran's head, and another grazed the leather covering his back as Gray Macha started up the embankment and plowed into the dark beyond. Clawing his way over the crest and throwing clumps of sod in his wake, the stallion seemed to pause just long enough for his mighty muscles to coil. Then, as if all that held his muscles snapped, the warhorse catapulted over the wide ditch. The tall rush parted beneath belly and hoof, whispering in deference to the stallion's speed.

As Gray struck the ground, the opposite bank cushioned the impact and, like a springboard, launched them away again, speeding horse and rider forward as if on the wind itself. Kieran glanced back. The astonished soldiers had not even collected themselves enough to open the abbey gates. He'd be well away before they readied their own steeds for the chase.

Freedom filled his lungs, which had felt contaminated by the damp, mold-infested enclosure. Kieran rid them of the cell's stench with a grateful and triumphant shout.

"Thank you, good brothers!"

He ran his hand along the powerful neck of his stallion and whispered into his mane. "And you, Gray Macha."

The warhorse may not have left as many fallen warriors in its wake as its legendary namesake, but there were three soldiers this night who'd remember Gray Macha well.

NINE

R iona washed the berries she'd collected in the stream, grateful that the moon had finally emerged from its cloak of clouds. Cleaning the berries not only helped pass the time, but would also provide some food for the children later. They'd have to travel through the night to put as much distance as possible between Maille's men and themselves. She only hoped Kieran's escape was as successful as the one she and the little ones had made.

They'd caught a few frogs near the main gate and handed them over to the bearded guards for their cook fires before moving farther away. The ruse worked perfectly. Within an hour, her party hastened along the road through the forest, ready to leap into the cover of the trees at the first hint of being followed.

Bran waited for them with his horse and a small pony he'd talked away from a local farmer with the promise of blessings from heaven and the high king. "Senan isn't as well loved as his brother," he explained at Riona's amazement on seeing the smaller version of the bard's own golden-maned dun. "Of course, I may have to marry the farmer's daughter," Bran reflected.

Her cousin's love of life, particularly the ladies inhabiting it, would be his undoing. At least now they had transport, even if it wasn't ideal. The pony's cart would have been perfect, but it limited the travelers to the road, which, by Ninian's account, would not be safe once it was discovered that they were headed for Drumceatt and not Gleannmara.

Somewhere a dove cooed above the hush of the running water and rustling trees swaying overhead. *Better that than a wolf*, Riona thought, recalling the guard's words to Bran of the dangers beyond the walls.

Father in heaven, what has brought so many innocents to this? What evil is about that Fintan lay dead and Kieran falsely accused?

"I'm going to check on the lads," Bran told her, tethering the pony nearby. He'd made certain that both horses were grazed and watered in readiness while Liex and Fynn kept a lookout on the road leading from the abbey.

Riona nodded and looked over where Leila chased fireflies by the stream. "Leila, come away from the water lest you slip on the bank and fall in."

Ever so slowly the little girl opened her clasped hands and the creature she'd captured flew away, unharmed. She watched until the firefly disappeared in the night and then cocked her head, as if she'd heard something.

Riona listened as well. Was that the pounding of hooves on the road or the beating of her heart?

Before she could discern the difference, a terrible commotion ensued. The shriek of a horse split the forest night. A man's curse was drowned by Liex and Fynn's excited shouts, then Bran's. Gathering up her skirts, Riona raced toward the place where the road crossed the stream, Leila in her wake.

Silhouetted against the moonlit ribbon of road that cut through the trees was a scramble of struggling figures. A short distance beyond, a stallion stood, quivering at attention, waiting for its master's command.

"Move an inch, and I'll slit your throat from ear to ear," Fynn threatened.

"Put the knife away, lad!" Bran snapped. "It's Kieran."

As Riona came closer, Fynn and Liex backed away. "But he's wearing a soldier's tunic," the youngest objected. "You're *supposed* to be in Brother Domnall's robe."

"These ragmullions nearly crippled my horse," Kieran roared as Bran hauled him to his feet. A hulk of a man in the darkness, he spun on Fynn. "You ever brandish that knife at me again, boy, and it'll be the *last* time."

Liex reached up and grabbed at Kieran's tunic. "Why don't you have Brother Domnall's robe?"

Kieran exploded. "What the blazes difference does it make, you towheaded wart?" The very force of his voice send Liex scampering toward Riona, while his sister hid in the folds of Riona's dress. "Another such *rescue,* and I'll have a broken neck."

"What happened?" Bran demanded of Fynn.

"We saw a soldier comin' down the road at full gallop and thought we might use the horse, so we—"

"They strung a line across the road and unseated me," Kieran grumbled.

Fynn held his ground. "You were supposed to wear a robe. We thought you were a soldier in Maille's tunic."

Bran stepped between the bristling boars and held up his hands, calling for quiet. "Are you being followed?"

Kieran nodded. "I imagine by now, yes. But I rode off toward Gleannmara, then doubled back, although I am pressed to understand why we didn't hie to Gleannmara and support rather than convene in the middle of the forest."

Riona tugged the twins toward the men. "Because going to Gleannmara would have resulted in a battle and loss of life. The best option is to present your case to the high king."

"Where is your head, woman? Gleannmara is a day's ride from here. Drumceatt is a good four." He glanced at the twins. "More with these troublesome mites in tow."

"I couldn't leave them at the mercy of Senan," she explained tersely, "and you are *very* welcome for your rescue from Senan's noose, milord." Riona turned from Kieran and motioned for Fynn. "Come along, children. We've a long journey ahead, with or without the protection of this bullish iarball." Her hand flew to her mouth, but it was too late. The spiteful name had slipped out.

Fynn draped his arm about her shoulders. "The Lord can't blame you for telling the truth. He *does* blow like the hole of a bull's backsid—"

Riona put her finger to Fynn's lips. "I'll not have you following my poor example." She crossed herself and gathered the twins.

"Better the iarball of a bull than a nagsome gnat," Kieran called after them, making a whining sound.

Fynn spun, his hand flying to his dagger's sheath, but Riona caught the lad's wrist, clearly astonishing him by the strength and ease with which she twisted it, bringing him to his knees.

"Enough! We need to be on our way, not exchanging insults."

"He started it," Fynn objected.

"*I* started it and I'm *finishing* it now! Understood?" The boy nodded, and Riona helped him back to his feet. "Now help me get the little ones on the pony."

Without so much as a backward glance at her cousin or the disgruntled lord collecting his horse, she herded her flock away. But Kieran's aside to Bran floated to her on the still night air.

"Look's like holy water hasn't washed all the tartness from the sauce."

"A drowning in St. Brigid's well wouldn't help you, ingrate," her cousin replied in disgust. "'Tis her and her God you owe your freedom to, not I."

Father, soften Kieran's heart and strengthen mine, she prayed, not the least proud of herself. Kieran of Gleannmara wasn't an evil person, but he could unravel the patience of a saint…which she, despite her best effort, was not.

Fynn lifted the twins onto the pony and vaulted up behind them. Riona handed them the bag of berries she'd collected during the long wait for Kieran's escape.

"Now if you get tired, let us know. We've a long night's ride ahead."

"We've a long journey ahead," Kieran corrected her, leading Gray Macha up behind them. "We'll need to travel by night and rest by day, at least till Dublin's behind us."

He paused, his hand patting the gray on its back without purpose. "And we've gotten off to a bad start," he admitted to Liex. "I should have kept the robes on. I didn't know the plan."

He extended his hand to the lad, and, at Riona's reassuring nod, Liex shook it.

In turn, Kieran did the same to Fynn, but the older boy met the gesture with a simmering glare.

The warrior shrugged and withdrew. "Keep that up, lad, and you'll wind up a puffing iarball, just like me."

Riona's pique wavered at her foster brother's awkward attempt to apologize. She held her breath as he took her hand and brushed her knuckles with his lips. "Milady, my apologies and gratitude. Will you show your forgiveness by riding my fine warhorse?"

He sounded sincere, but with his back to the moonlight Riona couldn't read the depths of his gaze any more than she could help the girlish flutter of her stomach at his gallantry. She'd fully intended to ride with Bran, but Kieran of Gleannmara had his measure and more of charm when he chose to use it. The end to which he did so was what troubled her. It wasn't like him to blow hot one breath and cold the next. What a fine trap he laid with that silver tongue of his. To refuse him would be a poor example for the little ones.

"Put that way, milord, how can I refuse? Not even I can hold a simpleminded beast's training against him." She petted Gray Macha's forehead and nuzzled his soft nose. "I'd be honored, noble Gray."

For the longest while, Riona sat erect, perched behind Kieran, trying not to touch him. But it was a struggle not to relax against the sinewy warmth of his back. She focused her attention on the little ones, who were so intoxicated with their adventure that they met her quiet queries as to their welfare with eyes wide and bright enough to challenge the sleeping music of Dhagda's harp.

The strain of the last twenty-four hours demanded its toll, and before long Riona felt the interplay of muscle in Kieran's shoulders beneath her cheek and the rippled board of his midriff within the circle of her arms as she held on. He was all she wasn't…hard to soft, warmonger to peace-maker, male to female. The differences were as confounding as they were beguiling, pitting the brace of reason against disarming senses.

She drifted in and out of sleep, listening vaguely to her foster brother and Bran speculate as to what lay at the base of their predica-ment. She tried to remain cognizant of the conversation, but their voices became a murmur, blending with the hush of the trees on either side of the way. Yet the moment her maternal ear picked up Leila whis-pering something excitedly to Liex, Riona was full alert.

"Do we need to stop?" she asked, recalling the little girl's inability to sleep through the night without wetting the bed.

"No, it's *soldiers*," Liex gasped, looking to Kieran for instruction.

Riona and the others looked behind them, but the slige, a road cleared extra wide by law so as not to afford cover for predators, be they human or animal, was as vacant as that before them.

"There's no one there," Kieran observed. "Now stop making up nonsense."

Leila gave Riona a pleading look and repeated her warning.

Liex shrugged. "She says Seargal sees soldiers coming."

"Who the devil is Seargal?" Kieran demanded.

"Perhaps we might take a moment to rest and tend to nature's needs," Riona suggested. She could well imagine Kieran's reaction to Leila's imaginary friend. More than likely, the little girl was embarrassed to ask to stop. "We ladies are not as suited to long journeys without stops as you men are."

Liex, however, had grown used to his sister's invisible friend's company and had no problem answering with childlike candor. "Seargal's Leila's friend. You can't see him, but he healed Nessa."

Riona couldn't help but smile at the skeptical look Kieran shot over his shoulder, as if he not only doubted what was said, but what he'd heard as well. "And who, I fear to ask, is Nessa?"

"A calf deformed at birth," Riona explained. "Leila begged it be spared and was given one night for it to recover, which it did. 'Twas most miraculous."

Kieran was not nearly as impressed as those at the abbey over what had happened. He scowled at Riona. "Do *you* need to stop?"

"I think it would be wise." She had no pressing need, but a respite could do no harm and might save another delay later. Besides, Leila did have a gift of some nature. Just what, no one knew, but Riona was hesitant to discount the child's warning.

Before Kieran could decide, Riona slid off the hindquarters of Gray Macha and straightened the fullness of her skirts. Leila, clearly distressed, again spoke to Riona in unintelligible syllables as she helped the child down from the pony's back.

"We'll slip into the cover of trees, little one," Riona assured her.

"She says we all must hide now. The soldiers are coming!"

Liex leapt off the pony to one side, while Fynn dismounted to the other. The elder boy dropped to his knees and pressed his ear to the ground. Riona's chest clenched when he straightened abruptly.

"There's horses coming this way, all right. I hear them. The earth doesn't lie, and neither does my sister." Without waiting for the men, he grabbed the pony's halter. "Stay here if ye want, but I'll not be taken with ye back to that child-sellin' rat."

"Let's move into the wood, then." Clearly Kieran was still not convinced. "At least for the ladies' privacy."

After dismounting, he handed his reins over to Bran and kneeled down to listen. His head shot up with a jerk of astonishment. "Horses!" he said to Bran. "A dozen or so."

With a curious glance at Leila, he took the lead. At the forest's edge, he cautiously cleared a way for the others to follow until the road was barely visible through the thick hazel underbrush. The fine hair of its leaves raked and clung to their clothing, but it was a perfect cover. Barring an unexpected noise, no one would find them.

"Ask Seargal if he thinks the fairies'll mind?" Liex whispered to his sister.

"Fairies," Kieran snorted under his breath.

Riona chuckled. "I don't think the fairies mind sharing the hazel brush with us. We're all God's creatures."

"And we need be *quiet* creatures," Kieran growled at them.

"Like cats waiting for a mouse," Bran suggested.

"But we'll let these mice go on, right?" Liex asked, not at all certain when Kieran took his sword from its sling.

Bran cuffed the boy on the head. "Right. Too many mice, not enough cats."

"Take the horses farther into the wood in case they make a noise, and stay till I call you," Kieran told Bran.

Driving the sword into the ground, he kneeled in the cover next to Riona. "If we are found, you and the children go with Bran. I'll divert Maille's men away. It's me they're after."

"We'll not be found," Riona said in quiet resolution.

"Oh?"

She turned her face to him. "God is with us. I know it in my heart. I can't say how, but I know we'll make it to Drumceatt."

"Faith is a noble thing," her companion acknowledged dourly, "but I'd as soon have this steel to back it up."

Always the warrior first, Riona thought, compassion battling with the urge to judge. "Did you kill a man for that weapon?"

"No, but I would have, just as he'd have killed me if he'd had a chance."

"Then let's pray you won't have to use it."

Riona measured off the wait in heartbeats so that when the mounted soldiers finally thundered past them, she felt as if she'd lived forever. After they were out of earshot, Kieran helped her up from her cramped position between the twins.

"You've done well," she told them. "Quiet as a mouse."

"We're very good at hiding. Da taught us," Liex announced proudly.

"Humph!" Kieran grunted. It wasn't much of a comment, but it was enough to bring Fynn about angrily.

"Go on, call us thieves. Everyone does. It's easy to look down your noble nose when ye've been born with a full belly. Me 'n' the twins have done what we've had to do to survive. That's nothin' more than even *you* would do."

Kieran stared at the boy for a moment and then nodded. "Aye, no doubt you're right. And thank your sister for the warning. She's got the ears of a good hound."

"You tell her," Fynn said. "She understands you just fine. She just doesn't talk right anymore. Not since our parents died."

"That's when Seargal came," Liex elaborated.

"Ah, I see." Kieran dropped to one knee in front of Leila. "Well then, milady, I thank you and your friend, wherever he may be."

Leila smiled at him, and Riona's heart melted. The little girl's smiles were rare.

"We'll have to walk the forest's edge from now on," Kieran announced. He gave a low whistle, signaling Bran to come forward. "That patrol may double back once they reach the hurdle ford. If they don't, they'll be waiting for us there."

"And if they are?" Fynn asked.

"Then we'll have to find another way over the river."

TEN

The leather tunics were stationed at the far side of the hurdle ford outside the port town, exactly as Kieran had predicted. Comfortably established in front of a riverfront hostelry, they watched the crossing with lazy eyes, more interested in the serving wench who filled their drinking cups. Judging from the steeds tethered nearby, they numbered a score or so.

"Faith, what a boil we're in now." Bran slung a stone into the brown river water. It was swallowed and carried off without a ripple.

"You and I could ford the river upstream, but it's running too high and fast with the recent rain to risk carrying Riona and the children," Kieran observed grimly.

He cut a glance at Riona, as if hoping she'd take the hint and allow him and Bran to go ahead to Drumceatt without them. Maybe she shouldn't have brought the children, but if she'd left them behind, they'd be at Senan's mercy. There had to be a way for her and the children to cross the river.

"We could ask Flora's father to help," Fynn suggested. "He could ferry us across on his boat."

Riona took heart. "Yes! I'd nearly forgotten." She turned to Kieran. "Flora was one of the orphans we placed in the home of a Dublin fisherman and his wife last fall." It had been truly a heavenly match, one of many that Riona and Fintan reflected upon with joy often during the winter months. "If we hurry, we might get there before he leaves."

"You think he'd take you?" Kieran asked.

"I'm almost certain of it."

"An' Fynn can get to see his sweetheart." Liex ducked as his elder brother took a swat at him, but in the close quarters of the pony's back, there was no escaping it. The twin yelped, but mischief danced in his eyes.

"She's a friend, nothin' more," Fynn declared to Kieran and Bran, color suffusing his freckled cheeks.

"Looks like the color of love to me," Bran quipped.

Kieran grinned. For the first time since they'd left Kilmare, he reminded Riona of the foster brother she loved rather than the haggard warrior of the last few days. "Then we'll see you safely reunited with your *friend*," he teased, vaulting up on Gray Macha's back. He turned to offer his hand to Riona. "Milady?"

A few questions later, asked of the early risers along the waterfront, Riona's group found Mully O'Laughlin and family repairing their nets. Mully not only agreed to ferry Riona and her charges across, but also fed the entire entourage with day-old porridge and fresh bread baked by young Flora.

"Somethin' told me to make extra for the market today," the young girl told Fynn. She smiled with pride as he bit into the loaf and chewed, nodding in approval.

Riona produced a coin from her purse. "And you shall profit by it still," she said, handing it to Flora.

The young girl shook her head, blond curls bouncing. "Faith no, milady. 'Tis small repayment for the kindness you showed me and my family. When the yellow blight took my parents, I gave up hope, but you promised that, with faith, God would send me a new family. I'm blessed to be sure," she said, hugging her mother. "And I'm tellin' Fynn here that the same will happen for him and the twins, if they have faith."

"It already has," Fynn informed her promptly. "We belong to Lady Riona now. O' course, I'm too old to be her son, but we're like as kin just the same, right?"

Riona hugged him ignoring Kieran's disparaging stare. "Right, you are." She didn't care if the lord of Gleannmara approved or not, the gleeman's children were her own. God called her to take them, of that she had no doubt.

"Is one of these gents to be your husband then, milady?" Nell, Flora's foster mother, asked innocently.

"Aye."

"No!"

Kieran and Riona's simultaneous declarations clashed, silencing the room save for the clink of Leila's cup as she placed it on the table. Her blue eyes grew wide in embarrassment as all gazes swung to her.

"There are many issues to be resolved before I could even consider marriage to Kieran," Riona explained. Always the husband issue! As if a woman could not live without one. Her ire spread its red heat from tip to toe.

Liex folded his arms across his chest and mimicked Bran's earlier observation. "Looks like the color of love to me."

There was nothing to do except join the laughter. Still, Riona was grateful when Mully entered and announced he was ready to set off. With good-byes and thank-yous, they followed the fisherman to his small boat, Kieran and Bran carrying the children. As Riona hiked her skirts to wade in, Kieran stopped her. Sweeping her up in his arms, he proceeded to the boat as if she weighed no more than Leila. On seeing her settled, he cupped his hand round the back of her head and pulled her to him, planting a kiss soundly upon her mouth. Hardly as mind-riddling as his last, it still left her speechless as he pulled away, a wicked twinkle alight in his eye.

"At least you're considering my offer, milady, which is more than you were yesterday." With a cocky smirk, he turned away.

Riona watched, slack-jawed, as he waded out of the river. Water ran off his tunic, gathering it to sturdy, well-formed limbs. She shifted her gaze to where Gray Macha awaited lest the sight conjure untoward fascination. What the devil ever gave the man the idea she was considering his marriage proposition? He was arrogant, bullish, and—

"Do you think he'll want us, too?"

Riona looked at Liex's hopeful face, and her indignation withered. "If he wants me, then he'll want you because you three have become a part of me."

Beside the lad, Leila giggled something.

"Seargal says that's our new da," he passed on.

"Tell that invisible lout to mind his own affairs," Riona snapped before she could stop herself. Heaven help her, she was arguing with an invisible man. Or worse yet…what if Seargal was one of God's messengers?

It wasn't the first time Riona considered the possibility.

As Kieran and Bran took off across the gorse-splashed moss on the shore leading the children's pony, she prayed aloud.

"Father, bear them safely across."

Liex and Leila crossed themselves as she did, but Fynn looked away sullenly. Riona wanted to say more but was at a loss as to what to pray for. Wearily, she closed her eyes as Mully shoved away from the shallows. There was only one thing to pray for, she realized. Surrendering, she added silently, *And Thy will be done.*

The current and a favorable wind carried the vessel toward the north shore of the town. The boat rocked gently under the steady hand of the fisherman while the cry of the gulls and the chatter of the children blended into a peace-giving lullaby. Riona fought sleep as they passed ships anchored off the coast and watched them load and offload trade goods. Wines, silks, and spices came in from the Mediterranean while hides, salted beef, and timber went out.

Mully put in on a strand of rock-strewn beach. Again Riona tried to pay the man, but he'd not hear of it. Providence had blessed him, he insisted, and this was his chance to pass it along. The son of a fellow fisherman offered to show Riona and her charges the way to the chapel by the holy well.

Nearly a hundred years before, St. Patrick himself had blessed the pagan inhabitants of the riverside community with a source of fresh drinking water after his hosts complained that the river water was too tainted for human consumption. With a tap of his staff, fresh water spouted up from the bog. Thus converted, they built a chapel by the well and marked the road with a stone cross in remembrance of the saint. Now pilgrims in need visited the place to partake of the holy waters in hopes of God's healing and blessing.

By the time they reached the ancient grove of oak nearby, their clothing was dry. Fynn gave it his best to keep moving, but the twins stumbled with exhaustion. Riona gently encouraged them to keep going until they were in the cover of the trees within sight of Slige

Culann, the road leading to legendary Tara.

Beneath a giant oak that was no doubt revered by druids of old, Riona unpacked the food Nell and Flora had prepared for them, but she was no different from her companions—too tired to eat more than a mouthful or two. The rest she wrapped for later. Then, sitting next to Fynn, she leaned against the towering tree and tucked her flowing brat over the twins, tucking the cloak close to protect them from the night's chill. There was nothing to do now but wait and rest. The latter came easiest, making the wait bearable.

How long she slept, Riona had no idea. It wasn't until she felt the touch of a hand upon her cheek that she opened her eyes to see Kieran smiling at her. He put his finger to her lips, silencing her.

"Sleep. We'll rest at least till nightfall."

Beyond him, Bran settled down by a tree and stretched out. Gray Macha, his horse Bantan, and the pony grazed on the undergrowth nearby. All was well, at least for the moment. Riona's eyelids fluttered closed again, a sigh of thanksgiving hovering on her lips.

What aroused her, Riona had no idea, unless it was the rumbling of her pillow. Bewildered, she sat up and instantly noticed the cool of the dark evening wedging between her and the warm shoulder she'd slept upon. Blinking to clear the fog of sleep from her brain, Riona made out Kieran's face, framed by the tumble of his fair hair.

A second golden head, smaller and more delicate, rested on his chest. Excluded from the ball of bodies formed by Fynn and Liex at Riona's one side, Leila had evidently sought out the warrior's warmth as well. The child lay curled in his lap under the cover of his brat.

He had to have tucked her in. There was no way she could have wormed her way beneath his cloak without his knowing. Was this really possible? Riona was warmed beyond measure at the sight. Or was she dreaming?

A loud snap from where the horses were tethered invaded the serenity of the makeshift camp. Kieran leaped to his feet, spilling a startled Leila onto the ground. No less bewildered, Riona stared into the darkness under the leafy canopy of the trees. The thin shafts of moonlight filtering through revealed movement among the animals.

Whether animal or human, it was enough to still both heart and breath.

"Who goes there?" Kieran challenged, brandishing his sword from its sheath.

Instead of answering, the figure broke away from the cover of the horses and ran deeper into the wood on two feet. Human. Riona found her breath, her pulse leaping to twice its normal rate.

Kieran started after the intruder when another figure sprang at the first, both tumbling down in a heap of leaves and crackling underbrush,

"I got him!" Bran shouted from the clamor of limbs. His declaration was followed promptly by a feminine shriek of outrage. "Faith, it's a gir—" The bard's astonishment broke with a pained yelp.

Kieran dropped his sword and reached down, plucking the female from the tangle of limbs and brush. "More like a horse thief to my notion."

"I wasn't stealing your horse. I don't even know how to ride the beasts." The female twisted and tugged to get away from Kieran's iron grasp to no avail.

"Then what were you stealing?"

Riona sat with the children, as befuddled as they by the commotion.

"My virility," Bran gasped, staggering to his feet unsteadily. "Sure, she's kicked it clear to Tara."

"I was hungry," the young woman growled, taking a shot at Kieran as well, but the warrior, forewarned by the hapless bard, dodged her foot and twisted her arms so that she faced away from him. "I thought there might be food in those sacks."

"A turn in Maille's dungeon might get the truth out of you."

At Kieran's threat, his captive dissolved in tears. "He took my brother, you cursed leather tunic. He might as well have me."

"And what did your brother steal?"

"Nothing, I swear it. He's only eight."

Riona scrambled to her feet and rushed over to where Kieran held the girl at bay. She was a young thing by the sound of her voice. "Calm down, child. We mean you no harm. What's your name?"

The captive ceased to struggle at Riona's assurance. "There's a woman with you?"

"And children."

"More for Silver Tooth, I'll wager."

"Silver Tooth?" Riona echoed in surprise. "He's here?"

"Like you wouldn't know it." The girl tossed her head toward Fynn and the twins. "I guess you'll be shipping them off as well."

"Heaven's, n—"

Kieran cut off Riona's denial. "This Silver Tooth is no friend of ours, and I'd be obliged to know where I might lay hands on him myself." He shook the girl, who still struggled to be set free. "Now I'll unhand you, lass, and you're welcome to share what food we have, but first tell us what you know about Lord Maille and Silver Tooth."

"I'll tell no leather tunic a thing," the girl railed in defiance.

Riona put a gentle hand on the frightened captive's arm. "What's your name?"

"Siony."

"Siony, I am Lady Riona of Dromin, and this is Kieran of Gleannmara. We've saved these children from Silver Tooth and suspect him of the murder of the abbot of Kilmare."

The girl shrank away as if afraid to accept her word.

Fynn stepped forward. "It's true, lass. And Gleannmara here took the leather tunic from Maille's guard so's he could escape. We're all runnin' for our lives."

"If we could capture Tadgh, we could prove your innocence," Riona exclaimed.

Kieran contemplated the girl. "I'm going to let you go if you give me your word you can act civilized."

"As civilized as the likes of you."

Riona wrapped her arm around the girl. "Come, Siony. Sit down and eat. We'll share our stories, for it seems we have all been wronged by Lord Maille and this Tadgh—"

"Silver Tooth," Fynn corrected.

"This murderer and slaver of children."

No one chose to improve upon Riona's final assessment. She led Siony to where the twins sat and made the introductions. Taking care to divide the food evenly, she handed out the loaves of bread and gave thanks for the many hands that delivered them safely thus far and made the meal possible. As she prayed, Riona felt even more certain that God was orchestrating all of this.

"And Father, we thank You for bringing Siony to us and pray that in Your all-seeing wisdom You will continue to guide us against this terrible evil plaguing our families."

At the chorus of amens, Siony hungrily began to devour her portion. Moved, Riona toyed with her own bread and gave their guest the rest.

"I'm too excited by all this to eat," Riona explained, avoiding Kieran's searching stare.

"I thank ye, milady. I haven't eaten since they took Naal."

"Ye'd never know it with that potbelly of yours," Bran accused grudgingly.

"Bran!" Riona gasped, shocked by her cousin's uncharacteristic malice. "Shame on you."

"Shame on her and that dastardly foot of hers."

"If you hadn't attacked me—"

"Attacked?" Bran stared at Siony as if she were demon possessed. *"Attacked?"* he echoed again. Riona's cousin always repeated himself when he was flustered. "My *dear* young lady, and I use that term most generously, I may never sit well on a horse again, much less carry on my father's line."

"Tell us about Silver Tooth," Kieran interrupted, bringing the subject back to its original purpose.

"And I'm *not* fat," Siony exclaimed. "I'm eating for two."

Kieran choked. "Two?"

Bran moved away to the other side of the circle, as if Siony's affliction were contagious.

No less shocked, Riona recovered first. "How old are you, Siony?"

"Eighteen come harvest."

"You speak as though you're more than a fisherman's wife," Riona observed.

Siony lowered her gaze. "My father was a merchant. He hoped I'd marry as well or better, but the heart cares not for the man's purse, but the man himself. I married a fisherman against my father's wishes. Then Rev and his boat were lost at sea November last, so Naal—he's Rev's younger brother really—and I came to the hurdle ford to find work and lodging. I help the cooks at the public house, but last night when I came home, Naal was gone. Silver Tooth and that woman of his are there, along with children they've collected." Siony wiped her eyes on her sleeve and sniffled loudly. "I know the brewy sold my brother to them."

"So Silver Tooth is at the ford with Maille's soldiers?" Kieran's tone was grim.

Siony nodded. "Aye, he's there, stuffing his barrel of a belly and bragging about how rich he'll be when the slaver arrives."

"And the children?" Riona inquired.

"Locked in a storage house and fed scraps." Siony spat the words, shuddering with contempt. "I was on my way to the monastery to see if the holy brothers might help when I came across your camp. I've been in such a stew, afraid the ship'll come in before I can get Naal away from the cur." Siony gave Riona a plaintive look. "No one cares about parentless children or a widow with child."

Riona gathered the distraught young woman to her. "We do, Siony, and we'll get Naal back for you...and the other children." She turned to Kieran. "Won't we, milord?"

Kieran stood up and made a grand sweep of a bow before her. "To be sure, milady. Yon Bran and I shall ride in and slay a score of Maille's soldiers, rescue the children, stop for a cup of ale, and then hie to Drumceatt on the morning." He ran his fingers through his hair and pivoted away with a growl. "The mighty Cuchulain himself wouldn't try such a feat. And even if we succeed, what the devil are we going to do, dragging a wench fit to burst with child and another gaggle of half-grown orphans?"

Bran wagged his head, staring at Siony as though she'd brought the entire weight of the world down upon his shoulders. "I say we steal the little beggars and run."

ELEVEN

The hour was past vespers, yet a song filled the air as the travelers approached the gate to the monastery. It was not a chant, but a single voice as sweet and pure as the first bird song of morning.

"Listen!" Riona seized Kieran's arm as they waited for Siony to enter the gates of the churchyard with Liex and Leila. Fynn would have no part of staying behind. With no possible way to escape with the freed orphans in tow, it was decided to leave the children to the sanctuary of the monastery. Siony would alert the brothers to be ready to receive both the rescued and the rescuers, provided their plan worked.

Father in heaven, it had to work. That had been Riona's prayer again and again since its conception, and now an answer came, almost from the heavens themselves.

Kieran cocked his head beside her. "What?"

Was it a lone pilgrim at the well just inside? Emotion surged in Riona's voice. "That song...it's..." The words raised the hairs on her arms, not with dread, but with wonder. It was as if God himself called out to her. Dared she trust her ears?

Behold, I am the Lord, the God of all flesh; is anything too hard for Me?

Their plight was no worse than that of saints past, their task no more formidable. Conviction filled her. "We're doing the right thing, Kieran. And we'll succeed."

"Because a priest is singing?"

"It's *what* he's singing, dolt," Bran snapped with impatience. "You would do well not to mock it. Words chosen wisely are easier to digest later."

"I don't doubt that your God can do anything. The question is *will* He?" Kieran patted the hilt of his sword. "*This* I can rely on, so spare me your flights of spiritual fancy."

Riona cringed at the bitterness in his words. Her foster brother was a good man, but thick-witted as a mule. "Aye, He will, and He'll even use a fool with a sword to accomplish His work."

The brewy by the hurdle ford was quiet when they reached it. From the main hall, smoke drifted up in shadowy wisps against a clear night sky from its three hearth fires. The scent breathed an invitation to the warmth and comfort within.

Two guards were left on duty while their comrades sought the comfort of the lodgings. Occasionally the two meandered from their posts by the bridge to the stables and back in an effort to remain alert. As if to assure them that all was well beneath the thatched roof of the open barn, an occasional whicker of contentment broke the sleepy hush.

Riona gave Fynn's shoulder a squeeze as the lad left the cover of the hedgerow that formed the northern wall of the brewy enclosure. Quiet as a mouse, and just as quick, the lad scooted toward the barn as the guards made their return trek toward the bridge. She didn't realize she'd held her breath until he reached the cover and disappeared within.

Inhaling deeply, she turned and edged her way around through the thick growth of scrub tree and briars to where Kieran and Bran waited. If they were discovered, the gleeman's son was to scatter the horses before the soldiers could assemble for a chase. She raised her hand to signal that Fynn was in place when a cord of briar caught her ankle and sent her sprawling into the undergrowth. Hurriedly, she tore away from its clutch, ignoring the petty slashes the mother bush made at her cheeks, and jumped to her feet. She waved, assuring the men who started toward her that she was fine.

Now it was her turn. She made straight for the kitchen end of the lodge and emerged from its shadow in a casual walk toward the building that Siony said held the children. Although no one could be seen guarding it, there might be someone inside who could sound a warning. Her heart beating three times to each step, Riona approached the door of the wattle-walled confine. Made of plank, it had a slide bolt with a dowel run through so that the wooden bar could be moved from inside or out.

She tapped lightly on the door and leaned her ear against it. There was a rustling from within, followed by a woman's voice.

"Whaddya be wantin' this hour o' the night?"

Riona instantly recognized the whining quality of the voice: Mebh.

"The cook's bankin' the fires and wants to know if them mites'd want some o' the bread scraps afore the dogs have their pick."

The bolt slid back from the keeper with a dull thud. Riona tugged the hood of her cloak further over her face. The chances Mebh would recognize her were unlikely, but she took no chance. The door opened just a crack, and Mebh's round face appeared, her uncombed hair, ratty with straw, framing her scowl.

"Got any gravy left?"

"I think so. If there is, I'll bring it." Riona rose on tiptoe, looking over the woman's shoulder. "And what about them?"

"Sleepin', the lot of 'em. Better we feed 'em good in the mornin', cause they'll be heavin' their bellies out through their gab once't shipboard." Mebh snorted. "An' bring me some ale." She smacked her lips together. "I'll wager ole Taddy Tooth's not half as dry as me and sleepin' in twice the comfort."

Riona's mind raced. Taddy Tooth. It sounded like a pet name. Perhaps there was a way to get rid of Mebh without knocking her lights out, as Kieran had suggested.

"Aye, as long as that redheaded wench keeps his cup filled and warms his lap."

The door flew wide open, and Mebh filled it with her swelling rage. "What's *that* ye say?"

"I only meant…" Riona stumbled back a step. Mebh looked bigger than she had in the abbot's quarters, and was nearly twice Riona's width. "It's like a man to take his pleasure and leave his woman to make do as she can."

The angry woman strong-armed her aside. "Shut the door and stay here till I come back, wench. I'll fetch me own vittles and drink."

Like a thundercloud on a blast of wind, Mebh marched toward the hall. Riona waited just long enough for her to disappear through the kitchen entrance before rushing in to wake the children.

"Naal? Naal, are you in here? I need your help," she whispered urgently.

"Here," came a sleepy voice from a corner.

"Siony sent me. Help me wake the others. We must hurry away before we're caught."

Riona counted seven children in all by the time she and the boy had roused them. They were bewildered at first but came to full alert on realizing that rescue was at hand.

Kieran appeared at the door. "What the devil possessed her? She moved too quick for me to take her."

"She'll give us all the distraction we need inside," Riona assured him. "Now, everyone hold hands and follow me. We're going to run to the church nearby, and we can't stop for anything. Understand?"

A childlike chorus of whispers carried affirmation. Taking a child by the hand, Riona paused by the open door as a shout erupted from inside the lodging. It was followed by the crash of furniture and more shouts of outrage. The two guards who'd been walking toward the stables doubled back in a run toward the hall to see the nature of the commotion. As soon as they were out of sight, Riona led the little ones out into the rear yard, straight for the hedgerow.

From the corner of her eye, she spied Kieran draw his sword but dared not stop. What was he doing? They'd agreed it was too risky to lure Tadgh out, that they'd leave the children at the monastery and move on to Drumceatt to seek a fair hearing. On reaching the trees, Riona looked back but saw no sign of Gleannmara's lord.

"Where did he go?" she asked Bran as he ushered the little ones toward the road leading to the holy well.

"Around the front of the hall. A plague on his stubborn hide." Her cousin swore under his breath. "Keep on with the children and stop for nothing. I'll signal the lad."

Riona nodded reluctantly. It was all going so smoothly...Mebh was making enough of an uproar to give them a window of time to escape. So help her, she'd kill Kieran herself—if someone didn't beat her to the task.

"Naal, take the lead. It's not a long way, children. Just keep running."

Riona brought up the rear of the small troop, stopping here and there to pick up some of the younger ones when they stumbled. She half expected them to cry, but even the youngest—a little girl she guessed to be about five years old—seemed to sense the need for silence as well as swiftness.

The third time the girl stumbled, Riona picked her up. Her own legs ached from the intensity of the run. She could imagine how the child's must feel. Perhaps the mile to the monastery was too much. Perhaps...

"Naal!"

At the outcry in the distance, Riona lifted her face and stared ahead in disbelief. There on the narrow road ahead, was a small cart drawn by the dun pony Bran had procured. A man in a robe rushed toward them, along with Siony. Half dragging, half pushing, they managed to get the seven children into the cart. Riona pulled herself up last and held on to the wickerwork sides as it jolted away.

"We're off to the shore," Siony told her breathlessly. "Maille's soldiers will not honor sanctuary, but the brothers know of a ship bound for Wicklow on the tide. They'll take us and the children to safety."

"But what about the men?" Riona cast a look over her shoulder, hoping she'd see Kieran, Bran, and Fynn riding through the narrow opening between the hedgerow surrounding the brewy. Nothing.

A commotion in the cart drew Riona's attention to a small, blond head bobbing through the menagerie. A second followed. In a moment, Liex and Leila were clinging to her, hugging her again and again.

"It's going to be all right, milady," Liex assured her. "Seargal is with them."

Riona kissed first the lad atop his head and then Leila. As she drew away, Leila smiled up at her, her eyes bright as the stars overhead. How Riona loved them! As for Seargal, more than ever she wanted to believe in the little girl's invisible friend.

The brothers' coracle, no more than a wicker frame with hides stretched over it, served to take the first half of the children with Siony and her brother toward the moored trade ship belonging to a cousin of the local bishop. They had been dining together when Siony arrived and informed them of their plight.

Riona paced the shingled shore, continually searching the rise of forest to the west for any sign of the men, while the remaining orphans huddled under a blanket one of the priests provided. From Wicklow they could make their way to safety at Dromin. It wasn't the answer to all their problems, of course, for Wicklow was a far cry from the high king and a fair hearing for Kieran, but at least the little ones would be safe. As for Kieran...

Riona shuddered, recalling his contempt. *Father, please spare him.*

"The tide's favoring you, milady," the captain remarked, drawing Riona from her quiet plea. "The prayers of the righteous have made it linger longer than I expected, but we must soon be away."

Before Riona could reply, she thought she caught movement among the shadows of the trees beyond the beachhead. Staring as if sheer will might produce Kieran and his company, she held her reply on the tip of her tongue. Whether the result of her will or a far more powerful one, a horse and rider broke free of the forest's cloak, followed by another. The steeds made short work of the distance, and before long, Gray Macha's hooves scattered clods of moss and sand on the shore as Kieran pulled the reins up short.

Riona rushed up to him and leaped into his arms. "Thank God you're safe! I'd begun to think the worst."

Kieran held her suspended, her toes brushing the damp earth, before lowering her with a reluctant sigh. "We rode to the church first. The brothers sent us here."

Bran swung a long leg over his horse's head and dismounted, while Fynn slid off the back. The lad rushed over to Riona, his voice filled with excitement.

"You should have seen it, milady!" He pointed at Kieran. "He was running in and amongst the soldiers shouting, 'There they go! No, there!' until they were running into each other. For all they knew he was one of their own, what with that tunic."

"Half their horses are on their way to Kilmare, and the other half will take the rest of the night to find them in the woods," Bran chimed in, face flushed with the excitement.

"An' Silver Tooth is swearin' and cursin' at all of them till he runs up on Gleannmara's sword."

Riona spun at Kieran, incredulous. "We agreed that taking Tadgh was too risky."

Kieran shrugged. "He ran right to me."

Weakness spiraled through her belly. "And you killed him?"

"Not exactly." Kieran sucked in his cheeks to check the smile pulling at his mouth. "'Twas his decision to swim in the river."

"I never seen a man his size run so fast." Fynn laughed. "An' milord here swattin' at 'is heels, with fat Mebh after him with a hay fork." The lad's estimation of Kieran had definitely escalated. He looked at the warrior as if the sun rode on one broad shoulder and the moon on the other. "The last we saw 'im, he was headed for sea."

Riona's lips thinned to a bloodless line. She'd escaped alone into the night with small children, her heart lodged in her throat with fear that they'd all wind up at Maille's mercy. She'd paced and fretted, worrying that the men had not been as lucky as she to get away unscathed. And all the while, they'd risked capture to make a great adventure out of the affair, having fun with the slaver and Maille's henchmen. It was more than her frazzled nerves would bear.

"Boils eat your worthless hide!" She stomped the instep of the unsuspecting warrior.

Startled by her outburst, Kieran grabbed his foot with a gasp, whereupon Riona shoved him soundly into the gentle lap of the tide. He landed with a bellow and splash.

"I *prayed* for you!" she shouted, kicking at him in her indignation. "I thought you and the lot were at the mercy of the soldiers." When that would not assuage her ire, she turned and unsheathed the sword from Gray Macha's tack.

"Milady!" Fynn exclaimed, reaching to stay her arm.

"And *you* think he's a hero?" Riona demanded, pulling away. "Well, here's what I think of your hero." She drew back the sword and swung it with all her might.

"Riona!" Kieran leaped backward, dodging the broadside of the blade.

"Gleannmara has met his match," Bran chortled. He danced away as the weight of the sword carried Riona about full circle.

She silenced the bard with a glare and wrenched the sword from where it was buried in the sand. With a grunt, she raised it again and turned to take up her chase, but Kieran wasn't there. Viselike fingers grasped her wrists from behind but not soon enough to offset the upswing of the blade over her head. Riona felt it strike and heard Kieran's cry of pain.

He stumbled backward, taking her and the sword with him. As they struck the beach, the impact knocked the wind out of her. Stunned, she rolled away and grasped the friendly hands Bran and Fynn offered. The seawater soaking her skirts seemed to add half again as much weight to sustain on legs already overtaxed. She swayed against Bran and looked over to where Fynn helped Kieran to his feet.

His hand laying across his forehead, the soaked lord of Gleannmara took the sword the lad fetched from the beach and leaned upon it. As he lowered his arm, a smear of dark blood streaked his furrowed brow.

"Faith, woman, you've wounded me!"

"I meant worse," Riona huffed. "But since God's seen fit to spare you, I will as well."

"I don't mean to interfere, good people, but I leave with the tide."

The captain's interruption fell upon Riona like a cooling shower.

"Them that will go, best come now," the man said. He held out his hand to Riona. "Milady?"

"I can't go to Wicklow, Riona." Kieran told her. "'Twill only invite my trouble to Gleannmara. My men are weary of war and have gone to their homes. I'm off to Drumceatt."

"Near Derry?" the captain asked.

"Aye, to the synod of the high king. It's my only chance to be heard fairly…and for that I'll be needing your testimony, milady. You know where I was when the abbot was murdered."

"And me," Fynn spoke up. "I've the knot on my head to prove it."

"And us." Liex stepped up, tugging a nodding Leila with him. "He's going to be our father. We have to save him."

Kieran shot a disconcerted look at the twins. "I never said I'd be *anyone's* father. I don't care what that invisible friend of hers says."

Liex's face fell.

If Riona had had the sword in her hands, she could have run him through. How could her foster brother be so heartless when the plague had inflicted the same loss on him?

"Who needs you anyways," Fynn said flippantly. "We belong to Lady Riona, and it's clear she has no intentions of taking you to husband." The lad tugged Liex and Leila over to where Riona stood, the pain of his disillusionment with his hero ringing bitter in his voice. "But the fact o' the matter is, 'tis *you* that needs us."

"And we'll go to Drumceatt to save your arrogant, insensitive skin, Kieran of Gleannmara, but then we're done with you." Riona turned her back to the disgruntled warrior to put a plaintive hand on Bran's sleeve. "But someone needs to take Siony and the youngsters to Dromin. They'll know no one there."

Looking as if a rogue wave had slapped him full in the face, Bran threw his hands up in protest. "Why me? I'm a bard, not a nursemaid."

"Bran, please. It's safe passage home—"

"Not with that kicking banshee."

"But they'll need a man with them. You're known—"

"What makes you think that anyone in Dromin will receive them with Heber gone?"

It was a valid point. There would be quarrel enough to elect a new lord. Riona could not count on Kieran as the overking to allow her sovereignty, even if she won the favor of her clan.

"Declare your interest in becoming chief. You've as much right as Colga and are far more well liked," Kieran put in. "'Twould save all a lot of grief."

"I wonder which of you is more daft." Bran shook his head. "I'm neither chief nor nursemaid."

"Take them to Gleannmara then," Kieran said impatiently.

Riona's eyes widened. "You'd take them?"

"We'll decide what to do with the lot after we return."

Bran spared the lord a dour look. "*If* you return. When those soldiers regroup, they'll be after blood."

"Which is why we need to be off." As if the decision were made for all, Kieran pointed to Riona's children. "And why it's safest for *them* to go with the others," he told her. "We'll discuss your keeping them later."

The three youngsters stepped closer to Riona. They'd not be separated without a fight, and, in her current humor, she was fully with them. The gall of the man. To think that for even the span of a breath she'd believed Kieran was softening when he offered safe harbor at Gleannmara. This was more of a plan to rid himself of what he considered excess baggage.

She put a reassuring hand on Fynn's shoulder. "They're *my* children, and *I'll* decide what's best for them, not a glory-seeking oaf with a sword sharp with folly." She plied her cousin again. "Bran, I am not thrilled with my present calling to help Gleannmara any more than you are to aid the orphans, but I am obliged by duty to do so. Kieran needs our testimony. The homeless need you. How could you, in good conscience, refuse?"

With a groan, Bran looked away and ran his fingers through his dark shock of hair. "I hate it when my conscience is thrown in my face. Mine is a free spirit. Faith, I might as well return to the monastery."

Riona stepped up and kissed her cousin on the cheek. For all his bluster, Bran had the tender heart of a poet. "God will reward you richly. You know it."

"We're off, all that's going," the captain impatiently called out from the coracle. Inside were the remaining orphans, bobbing with the tide.

Bran looked as if he would protest once more but then slapped Kieran on the back. "Well, my backside would delight in a break from the horse, that's certain. I know not which adventure will make the most fascinating rhyme, yours or mine." He fetched his sack from Bantan's back and blew a kiss to Riona before jogging toward the coracle. "God's speed to us all!"

Riona watched him wade into the water, where one of the brothers and the captain hauled the bard into the craft. For all his effort to look otherwise, he appeared as though he were off to an execution. In truth, she felt little better at the prospect of her own journey.

Second thought assailed her as the men rowed the coracle toward the moored ship. Kieran was right about the children being safer with Bran and the others. She'd allowed anger and defiance to override reason, not to mention composure. She flinched as her tempestuous outbreak replayed in her mind. Heaven help her, she'd turned into a madwoman, no kin to the lady she was raised to be, or the sister of faith to which she aspired.

"Mount your brood up," Kieran called over his back as he walked to Gray Macha. Still infused with the excitement of the evening, the horse stomped eagerly, ready to race again as Kieran sheathed the sword in its sling. "The journey's just begun for us. If the children can't keep up, we'll leave them at the next cloister."

"And to think, I was starting to admire him." With a cryptic grimace, Fynn led his younger siblings toward the cart.

TWELVE

The morning sun bullied its way through the leafy covering of the glen where Kieran elected to rest for a few hours at dawn. Another half-day's journey would take them to the main cross-road where they could procure provisions at a hostelry before moving on. If there was no sign of Maille's soldiers, which was unlikely now that they'd left his territorial land, he promised them a night under a dry roof rather than another in the damp outdoors.

Riona feared they'd all take a chill after a soft rain soaked them during the night's long ride. It came upon them in the wee hours of the morning before sunup, so they'd kept to the edge of the trees for cover. As Kieran pointed out, since they were to be soaked anyway, they might as well keep moving.

But these were children, not an army of hardened men, Riona thought, breaking off another tree branch to allow the warm, drying rays of the sun through the canopied fringe of trees. Everyone had stripped down to their leines and laid their outer garments out to dry in the small clearing. The three children slept in a huddle on a blanket Kieran had managed to keep dry in his travel sack. Next to them, he nodded off, his back to a stalwart oak.

For some reason, Riona had been unable to sleep. She'd heard Fintan say from time to time that he'd been too weary to sleep. Now she knew what he'd meant considering the lack of rest she'd had since Kieran's arrival—how long ago? Four, five days? It felt like months.

She stumbled through the thick grass to the clearing to check the brats and cloaks. The rising sun brought a sparkle to the surroundings, giving them an ethereal appearance. It's warmth felt good to her body, sore as she was from the hard travel.

Dry, she thought gratefully, fingering the rich woolen weave. She took Kieran's brat and spread it over the children, tucking it carefully round them. The instant relief of the warmth relaxed the huddle of small arms and limbs. Riona's mother had often warmed the blankets by the hearth on cold nights, making Riona and Heber feel extra special—safe and loved.

The thought of Heber and her mother acted like a vise upon her heart, closing painfully. At least he was with their parents. She was alone. Well, not quite. God had taken Heber, but He'd sent her three of His children as alone as she, and it did ease the pain. Their need for her left little time for grief and self-pity. They were her angels, delivering the message that life must go on, even if not as she had planned.

Throat constricting at God's overwhelming goodness in such a time of travail, Riona gently placed her palm against the children's cheeks and foreheads—no sign of fever. With a prayer of thanks, she again studied the fringe of branches overhead to make certain the sleeping figures had the maximum benefit of the climbing sun without it shining in their faces and then fetched her own cloak.

Kieran's rumble of a whisper startled her as she settled next to him by the tree. "If you'd care to share that, I'd be obliged."

Given that the children had both his blanket and his brat, she couldn't refuse, even if she were inclined. Warmth was warmth and needed to be shared. This was survival, not courtship. She'd do as much for anyone. Riona stopped the nagging voice of reason, annoyed that she felt obliged to justify herself. "It's nice and warm, thanks to the sun and its Creator."

With a noncommittal grunt, Kieran leaned forward so that Riona might spread a portion of the noble cloak with its five great folds representing the five provinces of Erin over his shoulders. He took up the majority, leaving her a portion of the fourth and the remaining fifth for herself. When he wrapped his arm as well as the cloak around her, Riona could not bring herself to object. But she felt the need again to reason out that this meant nothing, certainly not forgiveness for his arrogance and vexing ways. Aye, he was warm-blooded. So was a flea-bitten hound.

Not a single dream invaded the exhausted sleep that claimed Riona. All she knew was warmth and the comfort of Kieran's strength. She could remain like this forever…

Kieran roared and rolled away from her as if she'd bitten him in her sleep.

Robbed of his shoulder, Riona's head struck the tree trunk. With a cry, she sat bolt upright, instantly alert, certain Maille's entire army surrounded them.

Leila lay sprawled at Kieran's feet as well, staring up at him fearfully.

"What is wrong with you?" Riona demanded upon seeing nothing that offered threat in the sunlit glen. Nothing to explain a comfy shoulder being snatched from under her and the rough bark of a tree smacking her in its place. She brushed the annoying pain at the side of her head. It was wet, as if she'd sweated profusely. What in heaven…

It must have come from her *pillow,* for the other side of her head was dry.

A second shout distracted her. Kieran grabbed at the front of his leine and stared at Leila, mouth hanging open.

"I'm wet, that's what's wrong! And I suspect yon lapdog's the culprit." He pointed to Leila, and the child scrambled backward toward her brothers at the fierceness of his accusing glare.

Fynn and Liex unfolded from their huddle, grinning sleepily.

"It happens to us all the time," Liex consoled the glowering man.

"She wet on me, Riona," Kieran exclaimed. "She sneaked onto my lap like a mangy cur and *wet* on me."

Riona tried to master the humor tugging at the corners of her mouth. Poor Leila was terrified, and Kieran was in no mood to see the humor of the situation. "Come here, love," she said to the child. "Did you and Kieran have an accident?"

"*I* had no accident. 'Twas her."

Riona flashed a warning look at him. "Stop acting like a baby. Like Liex said, it happens."

Mortified, Leila mumbled something into Riona's skirt.

"What's that, little one?" Riona asked.

Liex giggled. "Seargal did it."

"Seargal?" Riona cast a dubious look at the little girl, but Leila wouldn't glance up at her. She glared at Kieran in disgust. "This child has never lied about this before. You've frightened her into lying with all that bellowing."

"The devil take him," Kieran swore.

"Who? An imaginary figure?" Riona chuckled wryly. "Faith, you become more childlike by the moment. Next I'll be wondering if you seek to blame this little one who cannot defend herself."

With a growl and a glower, Kieran snatched up the cloak and started to wrap it about him when he realized his mistake. Tossing it to Fynn, he pulled his brat from the boys and shivered as he covered himself. His golden hair was damp and clinging to his head, as if he'd been in a shower, and his face was flushed.

Riona frowned. Here was more than normal body warmth.

Without a word, she stepped up to him and placed her hand against his forehead. When he made to jerk away, she grabbed the folds of his brat and held him. "Be still." His skin was afire.

"We'd best be on our way," he muttered.

"*You'd* best go to the stream and bathe. Faith, you're soaked and burning with fever."

"I'm soaked from yon lapdog!"

"She wasn't sleeping on your head, ox."

"I'll be fine," Kieran insisted. "I took a chill during the rain. Now that I'm dry…" He cut his amber-shot gaze at Leila. "I'll be fine." He lowered his voice. "I thought they stopped such things at an earlier age than this."

Riona took Leila's leine off her and wrapped the little girl in her cloak. "Come, I'll join you by the water," she told him. "Why don't you children see if you can gather some kindling? I saw some spring roots nearby that would make a tasty soup."

"Shall I hunt?" Fynn asked, brightening. "I might bring back a squirrel or a rabbit…a bird at least."

"That would be lovely."

Riona waited, ready to do battle with Kieran if he did not change his plan to move out, but he offered no resistance to her taking charge. Instead, he ambled to the nearby stream, laid aside his brat, and dove in headlong, clothes and all.

Breaking into a run, Riona rushed to the water's edge. She breathed easier as she saw the warrior's blond head bob up, breaking the shimmering surface. As high as his temperature had been, she wondered the shock didn't kill him.

"I warn you, sir, if you feel faint, get yourself out of the water for I'll not be plunging in after you."

"This water's cold enough to wake a dead man. There'll be no swooning in here." A wicked curl tipped the corner of his mouth. "Although the company of a comely wench such as yourself would do wonders to warm me."

Riona kneeled on a rock extending into the stream and proceeded to rinse out Leila's shift. The sun was high in the sky, leaving plenty of time for it to dry before the night chill came upon them.

"She never did this until her parents died," she said in a low voice.

"Who?"

Riona cast a sideways glance to where Leila, swathed in the oversized cloak, hobbled around collecting small dead branches that had been cast off by the winter.

"She talked as well until she lost them. I suppose the shock has yet to wear off. She was particularly close to her father." Riona smiled at Kieran. "I think that's why she's taken to you."

Kieran waded out of the water, oblivious to his clinging clothes outlining every detail of his fine figure. Riona looked away. Gleannmara's king was entirely too attractive for his own good—or perhaps for *her* own good. She bent over the child's clothing and rubbed it all the harder on the rocks, determined not to look, much less admire.

But it was too late. The image had embedded itself in her mind like a stubborn seed, ready to sprout at the least provocation. One would think she'd never seen a man the way she warmed from the bone out. Were it dark, she'd glow like a dragonfly's tail.

"If you ever expect the child to wear that again, I'd ease my effort."

Kieran's wry observation struck Riona like a blast of north wind. Confound him, how could he possibly know what she was thinking— or rather, trying *not* to think? She swirled the garment in the water again, trying to destroy the perfect reflection of the man stripping off his leine behind her. Thankfully, he moved away before it became obvious what she was doing.

As she wrung out her wash, Kieran appeared beside her again, this time wrapped modestly in the blue and gold of Gleannmara. The sapphire brooch of his ancestors held the cloak draped over one shoulder, leaving the other muscle bare. He twisted the fine linen leine dry and shook it out before laying it over a rock. Riona smiled as she stretched Leila's smaller one out beside it.

Even if Riona were disposed to marry him, he was a strapping lord with a need for blood heirs. Few in his place would take on another man's lot as well. Her *little brood,* as he called the children, had hardly endeared themselves to Kieran.

Faith, they annoyed him at every turn.

Father, this cannot possibly be Your will. I'm so lost and confused that I cannot think straight, much less discern what You'd have me do. For this I beg pardon. See us through, Lord, give us—

A loud crack drew Riona from her prayer. Kieran leaned against the oak, the small branch that broke his fall, dangling from one hand. He shakily slid to a sitting position, his face a mirror of anguish as he struck the earth. Alarm seizing her, Riona gathered up her long skirts and rushed to him. She caught his face between her hands as he closed his eyes and shook it.

"Kieran! Kieran, what's wrong?"

His eyelids opened half way, as if leaden. "'Tis that wretched hag Mebh. She wounded me right enough with that stable fork. 'Twas just a scratch, but—"

"Where did she stick you?" He was still hot, despite his dip in the chilly spring water. "Like as not, it's infected."

Kieran winced as he dragged aside the folds of his cloak to reveal a sinewy thigh. Two gashes streaked with red and purple and oozing infection marred its swollen surface.

It served him right for taking excess risk, but Riona said nothing. He clearly suffered enough. Surely the night's ride had antagonized the wound even more. It should have been washed last night in the seawater. Many men lost limbs or died from the stab of the ignoble weapon as easily as from its nobler counterpart. For now, she'd have to hunt for herbs and pray she could stay the infection.

Or mayhap they should push for the crossroads. Could Kieran ride another half-day's journey?

"Milady!"

Liex darted out of a hawthorn thicket like one of the Sidh's own little people, his face as white as his eyes were wide. He half ran, half staggered into the small clearing, holding his stomach as if his haste pained it.

"Faith, what now?" Riona asked.

"It's Senan and Maille, paradin' big as ye please with company and flags flyin' back there on the road."

Panic jolted through her, striking a lump of fear in her throat. Forcing it down, she struggled to her feet, forcing herself to think. She glanced at Kieran, but he hadn't moved, as if he'd not heard Liex's pronouncement of approaching doom. Thank God they'd not lit a fire. Thank God Kieran insisted they rest away from the slige, out of its sight. She'd been so tired when they stopped, she'd have lain in her tracks.

"Where's Fynn?" she asked.

"Don't worry about him. He could snatch the fancy dillat right out from under Maille's backside and neither 'im nor 'is horse'd be the wiser."

With no time to correct the boy for his coarseness, Riona scanned the forested glen for Leila. The little girl stood near the water, watching her brother. At Riona's urgent wave, Leila dropped her armload of kindling and ran toward her, cloak half on and half dragging.

"Liex, get the clothes drying by the water in case Maille's men decide to water their horses upstream."

"We're hidden by the bend in the stream," Kieran told her, breaking his silence with effort as he tried to rise and failed. "Just secure the horses and stay put and quiet." If he felt alarm, it didn't show. Or was he too sick to care?

Riona checked the horses and moved the wash as an extra precaution, despite Kieran's assurance that it wasn't necessary. Once the garments were hung on the blind side of the hawthorn, there was nothing left to do but wait and hope the travelers would pass by without event. Leaving for the hostelry was out of the question now. Undoubtedly that's where Senan and Maille were headed. All lords, secular and ecclesiastical, would be on their way to the Drumceatt council at the high king's invitation.

By all rights, it should be Father Fintan making his way there. Riona's heart wrenched at the thought. Fintan dead, his murderer at large, Kieran falsely accused, the lot of them running for a fair hearing and the sanctuary of Drumceatt...

And now Kieran's fever. It was enough to make a grown woman cry. Except Riona had no time for such indulgence.

"Liex, you stay here with Leila and Kieran," she said, once she felt certain the party from Kilmare had passed them. "I want you and your sister to keep a cold cloth on his forehead and neck. He's quite ill, I think," she whispered, feeling as if she'd stumbled into a new nightmare.

Riona dug through the sack the brothers had packed for them, producing the linen napkin their bread had been wrapped in. She handed it to the twins.

"When Fynn comes back, tell him to build a small fire and pack its bed with stones." She thought a moment.

"Where are you going?" Liex inquired, a frown creasing his sun-pinkened brow.

"I need to gather some herbs for Kieran's wound and fever."

"Don't leave us!"

Riona put her finger to Liex's lips. Of course she couldn't leave them. *Father, I'm so confused.* The little ones were terrified—and why not? So was she. Riona took a calming breath.

"Let's eat and see if we can do so without making a sound."

It was a miserable failure at distraction. Riona munched on a small chunk of bread until it was tasteless mush, trying desperately to hear anything aside from the sound of her chewing. The sound of horses passing in the distance, the occasional whicker or rise of a man's voice, invaded the hush of the trees and the whisper of the moving water along the bank.

Judging from the trouble the twins had swallowing, they fared no better than Riona. Before they all choked, she put the bread aside and took their hands.

"We'll pray," she said in a conspiratorial whisper, "that Lord Maille and Senan keep right on moving."

Pale and saucer-eyed, the twins nodded. Even as Riona's words echoed again in her mind, a sense of relief came over her. The death-like grasp of the children's hands relaxed as they too received assurance. When she could think of nothing more to say, she just held their hands, listening for the enemy with her ears and God's word with her heart. She should have recommended this "distraction" first, she realized above her heartbeat and the heavy sound of Kieran's breath. Time seemed to stand, enveloping them in its stillness until a finch sang out in the tree directly over their heads, launching a conversation among the other birds. Like Noah's dove, it signaled that the danger was over. The party of men had passed.

Crossing her heart with thanksgiving, Riona struggled to her feet on legs that had been numbed by her immobility.

"I'm off to gather what I can find to treat Kieran's wound and fever," she told the little ones. "Keep his forehead cool with this cloth, and tell Fynn when he returns to start a fire."

"Should Fynn cook our supper?" Liex didn't question the fact that their brother would return with game for their meal. Given God's handiwork on their behalf thus far, neither did Riona.

"Just have him dig a small hole and heat some water with rocks. I'll be back before it's time to cook. Meanwhile, try to eat a little more bread and dip some in the ale to see if you can get Kieran to eat it. We must keep up our strength."

Liex saluted most seriously.

Riona pinched the lad on the cheek. "Everyone clear on their duties?"

The lad's head bobbed up and down. Leila gave Riona a somber nod and, leaning over, kissed Kieran's forehead. Then, snatching the cloth from Liex, she raced for the water, the bulk of Riona's cloak balled under one arm.

"And one last thing," she said, following the child with her gaze. Riona pointed to Liex's sack. "Could I borrow your sling and a few stones?"

Surprise widened the lad's eyes. "My sling? What will *you* do with my sling?"

Ignoring the slap of the child's incredulity, Riona replied, "I should like some semblance of protection out in the wood alone. Your sling will do nicely."

"An' pity the luckless soul that crosses it," Kieran murmured. So he was not totally unaware of his surroundings.

"Lady Riona is good with a sling?" This was clearly more than Liex could comprehend.

"If you think not, look at this." Kieran pointed to a scar on his brow.

"You did that, milady?"

Her small protégé was impressed, but Riona cringed inwardly. Her foster brother had earned it most heartily, teasing her to distraction, but when he'd taken her hair ribbon, she'd let him have it with her sling. Faith, she'd never seen so much blood. She thought she'd killed him, and Kieran, dramatic as he could be, did little to assure her otherwise. Still, all these years later, she regretted it.

"Aye, I'm sorry to say I did. David killed Goliath with little more, and where would we be without Gleannmara today?" If she'd intended to demean her feat, she failed. Clearly Liex thought she could fell a giant with a child's sling and a stone.

"Will you teach me?" the boy asked, handing it over with a tiny pouch of stones. "I'm not very good with it. Fynn is, but he never has time for me."

"I'd be delighted, provided you promise me never to use it in temper as I did, for I hurt a good friend."

Liex nodded eagerly.

"Be careful, lass. Don't wander beyond shouting distance." It was all Kieran could do to hold his eyes open. His words were rumbles of breath, little more.

At that moment, Leila caught back up with them and placed a wet cloth over his head, looking up at Riona with a bright smile. Somehow it bolstered Riona's moral.

They were going to make it. Riona didn't know how; she only knew that they would.

THIRTEEN

The proud hunter, Fynn turned the meat—a squirrel and a plump red grouse—on a green shaft of oak. While Riona hunted for herbs, he'd dressed his kill and prepared it with a skill that would make the ancient Fianna proud. When Riona returned and fretted as to how she was going to boil her herbs for Kieran, the lad produced from his travel sack a large cup he'd carved under Brother Clemen's supervision. By heating small stones in the fire and placing them in the water, they were able to bring it to a boil. They carefully added finely cut slivers of wild fennel root and, as much for flavor as its curative nature, bramble.

The brew cooled and steeped while Riona made a poultice of a few crushed mistletoe blossoms, which she'd knocked from a tree with stones, and some wood sage she'd found growing along the forest's edge downstream. Carefully, she wrapped it around Kieran's thigh. He flinched as she pressed it on and wrapped it, but made no sound.

"Hopefully this will draw out the infection. Would that I had salt," she lamented.

"Methinks the only remedy for this aching head is the slice of a sharp sword at the neck."

At Kieran's remark, Leila hopped dutifully to her feet and removed the cloth from his forehead. Riona watched the little girl make haste to the water to refresh it and wring it out. Skipping back, she laid it gently over his forehead, tender as a mother with her babe.

"Thank you, milady." The corner of Kieran's mouth tugged in an attempt to smile. "I'm a lucky man to have two such pretty maids tending me."

Leila's face lit at the compliment. Impulsively, she leaned over to kiss him, but was thwarted by the rag covering his forehead. Instead, she gave him a little peck on the tip of his nose.

"Now I know I shall improve."

"Fever improves your disposition, milord," Riona remarked as Leila returned to the fire with her brothers.

"A kiss on the lips from a full-grown maid would heal me entirely."

Faith, he could be charming when he chose. "That colt's tooth will win you no favor." She doubted his precocious yearnings had suffered overmuch of neglect, given the winsome manner in which he pursued them.

"'Twould take my mind off this pounding in my head."

"So will this." Riona picked up the tea and tasted it. It was palatable but no more, and considerably less. She strove to keep her features from contorting in distaste. "And this will help ease the fever and infection. 'Tis cool enough to take straight down, if you prefer." She lowered her voice mischievously. "Now drink it like a warrior, lest these children think you a ninny."

Three pairs of curious eyes rested on Kieran as he put the cup to his lips. He took a sip, lips thinning as he swallowed with manly composure. "I've wallowed through cattle mire that surely smelled and tasted better," he said aside to her. "You swear it will help?"

"I swear." It was all Riona could do to keep from snickering as he eyed her through narrowed golden lashes a woman would give her dowry to possess.

Kieran lifted the cup and drank it straight down so fast a sliver of root nearly went down with it. With a jerk forward he coughed it up and then fell back against the tree, exhausted. "I'd have a brace of ale, if you don't mind, to chase the foul stuff."

Riona handed him the skin. Most of its contents were gone. What was left she watered down to make it go farther. If he minded, he didn't let on. He merely swished it in his mouth, as if to be certain no taste of the herbal concoction lingered, and swallowed.

Leila scrambled over to him, digging in her apron pocket, and produced a green leaf. She put it under his nose.

"Mint," he observed in surprise. "Why, thank you again, milady." He popped the leaf in his mouth.

"Where did you find that?" Riona asked. She'd seen no mint on her search.

Leila shrugged and waved in a downstream direction before rejoining her siblings.

"Leila used to help Mother find herbs. She was good at it," Fynn informed them. "Mother said she has a nose for them keen as a hound's."

As if to demonstrate, Leila sniffed, twitching the little stub of her nose, and then giggled. Everyone laughed except Kieran.

"A fine quandary we're in," he complained, head laid back against the tree, eyes closed. "I'm laid up with this fever and leg wound and you and the children at the mercy of nature."

"*Mercy* is right," Riona agreed, but not in the sense her woeful patient meant. "Mercy has provided us with a fine hunter and cook, a good nurse, and the best wood scavenger I've ever seen."

"And a clear night," Fynn put in. "There must be a million stars out tonight. Better than last night's wet blanket."

"I think the meat is done," Liex announced, not the least interested in medicine, mercy, or stars. Of course, the lad had made the same observation every few moments since the smell started to fill the air and taunt the nostrils.

"I think you might be right this time, wort." With an air of authority, Fynn tested the leg of the hen with a tug. The meat pulled away without resistance. "Aye, you're right. Now hold on to this while I move the braces away from the fire."

He lifted the spit and handed it to the younger boy. With a short tug, he pulled up the Y-shaped branches he'd used to support the meat and, using a piece of firewood, drove them into the ground a short distance from the fire itself.

"Let it cool a bit, and then we'll have our feast. I'll have the king's choice since I killed and prepared it."

Kieran didn't protest. He just lay with his head back, eyes closed. Riona touched his cheek. Still warmer than normal.

"While the meat's cooling, what say we make up another concoction so that it will be ready for later?"

"I saved the stones," Liex told her, producing them from his pocket. "We can use Fynn's new cup, and Gleannmara will be back to his old pompous self in no time."

One of Kieran's eyes opened, peering half-lidded at the boy, but said nothing. She didn't know if he was too sick to take up the unwitting insult or was learning to temper his tongue, at least around the children. She feared it was the first; she prayed it was the last.

The finest fare ever spread on Dromin or Gleannmara's tables paled in comparison to the welcome taste of roast squirrel and fowl. Kieran nibbled a little, but aside from drinking down Riona's concoction and a little ale, he slept. With the energy of children, Fynn, Liex, and Leila were still high on their adventure as the twilight approached. They listened eagerly as Riona shared her memories of Dromin, as well as what she remembered of Gleannmara's hall.

"I don't ever recall having a home in one place," Fynn said, a faraway look in his eyes. "We traveled all the time, staying wherever we would be paid for performing. We juggled and sang. Even the twins were starting to take a place in our show."

"You'll have a home soon," Riona promised, her mind focusing on that goal.

With a new O'Cuillin chief elected, the lodge that had been her home would no longer be hers, but she had property, which was rented. She could have a lodge built for her and the children and live comfortably enough, if not in the luxury to which she'd been accustomed. Her tenants were good people and would make good neighbors. With her rightful share of their efforts combined with those of her own, she'd want for nothing of importance. To this end, her thoughts drifted and eventually faded in favor of sleep.

What seemed like moments later, Riona rolled away from Kieran at the intrusion of a stranger's voice.

"Well, if this isn't the picture of a fine family!"

"And food," chimed in another.

Fynn was up on his haunches in an instant, his knife drawn. Like Riona, he eyed the two men standing by the fire looking hungrily at what was left of the evening meal.

"Here now, who the devil are ye?" the lad demanded warily.

With a theatrical hop, the first man, clad in multicolored breeches and a tasseled shirt, announced, "I am none other than Dallan, gleeman extraordinaire, and this is my brother—"

"Marcus the Magnificent," the fairer of the two proclaimed. As if to punctuate his claim, he ran forward three steps and sprang into the air, doing a backward flip and landing squarely on his feet. "And this," he sang in a melodious voice, "is the Lady Finella, whose harp has no equal in all of Erin."

"A simple introduction will do, Marcus."

From out of the shadow of the trees, a woman entered the circle of firelight. She looked to be Riona's age, perhaps slightly older. A ruddy complexion confirmed she'd spent a good share of time in the weather. She looked past Riona at Kieran, who still slept, oblivious to their company.

"He has the look of a fevered man," she observed flatly. "What have you prepared for him?"

Marcus intervened. "Before you take to treating these people, good sister-in-law, perhaps we should confirm that we are welcome to share their fire." He glanced again at the food, now cold on the spit.

Riona recovered her startled wits and motioned to it. "By all means, you're welcome to what we have to share. And yes," she added to Finella, "he was wounded by a pitchfork and his leg is sorely infected. I've given him a tea of bramble and fennel root, as well as made a poultice of leaves. Now he sleeps."

"But you need salt."

At Riona's astonished look, Dallan spoke. "Get used to it. She does that all the time. My wife has a gift, sometimes timely, sometimes not. But always true."

"And she has a knowledge of herbs as unmatched as her harp music," Marcus informed them. "As luck would have it, she's prepared several for sale at Drumceatt this summer, so her supply is likely to include anything you need for yon warrior."

Finella walked over to Kieran and touched his forehead with her hand. "'Tis no luck at all, Marcus. Something told me to follow the river from the road."

"Something aside from the threat of being attacked by thieves and vagabonds?" her brother-in-law quipped.

"Don't argue with her, Marcus," Dallan warned him. "It's as useless as trying to fatten a greyhound."

"May I see your husband's wound, milady?" Finella asked.

"By all means." Riona didn't think to correct them. These people had come upon them so quickly and exchanged words like juggler's balls, and it took all she had to follow them at all so weary was she from the day and the worry over Kieran.

"May I taste some of that bird carcass? Merry, I could eat it bone and all." Marcus licked his lips expectantly, looking from Riona to Fynn and back again.

"Of course. Help yourself." Riona motioned toward the food.

"After you fetch the cart," Finella said without abandoning her examination of Kieran's leg.

"I'm away at your command, good lady." With a leap and a cart-wheel, Marcus disappeared into the darkness.

"We'll have nothin' for the mornin'," Fynn reminded Riona in a low voice.

"To turn these people away could be to turn God's angels away."

"Angels?" Dallan laughed at Riona's words. "We've been called many things, but never angels." He sobered, narrowing his gaze at Fynn. "And I'd vow I've seen you before, lad. Where are you from?"

"Everywhere." Fynn grinned. "Our father was one like yourself. Glasny was his name."

"Glasny." Dallan mulled the name over. "I met a Glasny in the south once. A fine voice he had. But that was years ago, before I met Finella. He had a son, and his wife was big with child." The gleeman traced a large invisible swell over his abdomen, illustrating that of a pregnant woman. He pointed at Fynn. "You do look like him…same reddish brown hair and dark eyes."

"Well, if he's the same Glasny," the lad answered, "then these are the cause of his wife's swelling." He pointed to his brother and sister. The two fair-haired children sat cross-legged on the blanket, blinking at the newcomers.

"His wife did have flaxen hair and eyes the color of a summer sky." Dallan leaned over Liex. "Here," he said, tugging the edge of a handkerchief out of his pocket. "Wipe the sleep from your eyes."

Liex eyed the man cautiously.

"Well, go on," Dallan insisted. "Give it a tug."

At Fynn's nod, Liex grabbed the kerchief and pulled it. To his astonishment, another was tied to its opposite corner. On tugging it free, another was attached, and another. The younger boy was in a fit of giggles when the final square of the many colored cloths came out. Dallan coaxed Leila into tucking it back into his shirt and carried on so, pretending to be ticklish, until tears of laughter streamed down the little girl's cheeks.

"Don't get them too excited, Dallan, or none will sleep tonight," Finella warned. She rose from her examination of Kieran's leg and straightened her dress. "I have just the thing for this," she told Riona.

"See, I told you she'd have something to fix up the man." Marcus entered the glen leading a shaggy black pony, which pulled a narrow cart enshrouded in a tent made from strips of various cloth. "Finella mixes potions for all manner of ills and matters."

"They burned our cart with mother's and father's bodies in it. We couldn't even give them a decent burial." Fynn stared hard at the vehicle and then, swallowing the bitterness in his voice, he turned away. "I'll go get more firewood."

Riona wanted to embrace the boy, but he was away too fast.

"Made a man before his time." Dallan shook his head at the unfairness and pulled the squirrel's carcass from the spit. "What happened to Glasny and Una? I think that was her name."

"Mama's name was Una," Liex confirmed. "She was pretty."

Dallan broke the carcass in half and handed one to his brother. "Aye, that she was, lad, and proud of her children, I'll wager."

"She said I was the best juggler that she'd ever seen, but our balls and everything was burned."

"Shame on the folk who'd destroy a man's means of support," Marcus exclaimed. He wiped his hand on his leg and reached into a bag he wore slung over his shoulder and across his chest. One. Two. Three red balls came out, and he tossed them at Liex, who caught them easily. "So entertain us. 'Twill be a delightful change, eh Dallan?"

His brother nodded. "Have at it, lad. Make your mother proud."

With less effort than it took Riona to toss one into the air and catch it, Liex tossed up the balls until all were making their own course up and down, weaving a wondrous spell for observing eyes. Dallan and Marcus cheered, and soon Leila joined in the three-ball toss.

Fynn returned and demonstrated his prowess with his knife, tossing it into the air and catching it by the handle. Riona couldn't help but feel a tug of jealousy, for the children took to the gleemen as if they were family. They were related, she supposed, by profession.

Finella, who'd been working off the back of the cart by the light of a small lamp, came around with a small copper kettle and what appeared to be a blanket roll.

"One of you, fill this up to here with water," she instructed.

Dallan rose to volunteer.

"We'll make enough concoction to last him for a few days," she told Riona, kneeling down beside Kieran. She untied the binding ribbons of the blanket and unrolled it, revealing many pockets on the inside of the cloth. With a flourish of her hands, she proclaimed, "Behold the fruit of Midach's grave."

Riona smiled graciously. The DeDanans of old may have been a real people, for there was always a seed of truth in most myths, but she attributed their reputed *powers* to knowledge of God's gifts to mankind, not power in itself. "You mean the fruit of God's earth."

"Aye," Finella agreed readily. "The same earth that Midach was buried in produced these herbs and was created by the One God, same as Midach himself. But the appeal of a little magic always sells well." Her lips tilted with the wry mischief of her remark. "And while we are clarifying matters, you are not married to this man, are you?"

"Well, I…" Riona stammered, taken aback by her companion's keen perception. "No. He's my foster brother." She wanted to know how the woman knew, but was too embarrassed at being caught in her inadvertent deception to ask.

"As I thought…a strange family indeed." Finella clasped her hands together. "Now let us conspire to make your foster brother well."

FOURTEEN

Morning came like a breath of relief, filling the sky with light just as Riona's heart was renewed with hope. Aid had come in the most unlikely form of the gleemen. Marcus—surely a child disguised as an adult given the way he carried on with the children—had provided a fine catch of fish for breakfast. Liex and Leila had the thrill of drawing in the net once he'd closed it around a school of brown trout and stickleback. They strutted about the campfire while the fish cooked, as proud as their older brother had been the night before.

Fynn tossed the bones of his portion into the fire and rolled away, holding his stomach. "Ach, I'm fit to bust."

"And you thought last night that we'd given away our last," Riona reminded him. "Remember the story of the starving widow using her last scrap of food to feed Elijah? What you give in God's name will be returned to you ten times over."

The boy nodded and then belched loudly. Liex joined Marcus and Dallan in a howl of laughter. Leila couldn't seem to make up her mind whether to join the men or hold back the amusement twitching at her lips.

Riona exchanged a mutual look of disgust with Finella. Such indulgence had to be a peculiarity confined to men and children, for neither of the women shared in the humor.

"So, you tell stories, do you?" Dallan asked, pulling a straight face.

"Aye, she does." Liex nodded eagerly. "And most wonderful stories at that."

"Then let's hear one. The one about the widow and this man Elijah," Marcus suggested. "We can always use a good story for skit."

"Drumceatt becomes no closer while we gab. Save the stories for the evening fire." Finella got up, brushing her hands together as if the matter was settled, and looked at her husband and brother-in-law. "If you think you can regain your adult composure, put yourselves to good use and carry our patient to the river for a bath."

Kieran had survived the night of body-riddling fevers and chills and now slept like the dead. The brothers carried him on a blanket to the water's edge. They'd already stripped him when his fever broke just before daylight, leaving his undergarment, a loincloth of soft linen, in place for modesty's sake. Riona washed out his leine and hung it to dry while breakfast was prepared.

Not even when the cool water was applied to his warm skin did Kieran stir. It was as if some dreamless sleep had claimed him, induced most likely by Finella's concoction. A mumble of protest when he was disturbed was the only sign that he was aware they were there at all. Had the woman used too much mandrake? Riona had agreed to the extra measure only because Kieran's head pounded so.

"What a fine specimen of a man your foster brother is," Finella remarked, glancing up from the wound she tended.

Riona wiped Kieran's brow and hair with a cloth and her scented soap to rid it of the sour smell of sweat. It was one of the few amenities she'd managed to smuggle out of the abbey. "I hadn't noticed."

"You're trying hard not to notice, you mean."

"I was raised in a rath of warriors, all strapping men, Finella." She lifted Kieran's head gently and wiped his neck, as wiry with muscle as the rest of him—and as thick as his brain. The gleeman's wife was imagining things, Riona told herself.

"But they do not possess your heart."

Riona froze for the blink of an eye before continuing on with her ministrations. "Aye, I love him, but not in the way you mean."

Finella smeared a paste on Kieran's thigh, the same as the plaster that had already drawn some of the swelling and poison from the wound.

Riona shook her head. "He's given to the folly of weapons and war. My mother loved such a man, and it plagued her all her life. I'll not do the same."

"She was never happy?"

"Of course she was. When father was there, her heart was so light she fairly walked on air." Riona sighed. "They were like two lovebirds, almost childlike at times. When I was older, it was embarrassing, but secretly it made me smile inside."

"Perhaps those happy times made the cost of her loneliness seem small. A man fierce in battle is as fierce in love, so I've heard said."

Kieran impassioned in love was more than Riona cared to contemplate. The very suggestion was enough to make her heart thud against her chest and her stomach roll over with weakness. She dropped his head unceremoniously and flinched with regret as he grunted. His eyes flew open, and, as if being attacked, he reared to an upright position, his hand flying to his waist, where nothing but a loincloth afforded him decency.

"By my mother's eyes, I'm naked!"

Assaulted by the toll of his effort, his upper body swayed unsteadily, so that he had to catch himself to keep from falling back with weakness.

"Who the devil are you, woman?" He glared at Finella. "And where are my clothes?" The brace of his arm held him for a moment; then that buckled as well.

"A friend, Kieran—"

Riona caught his broad shoulders and tried to ease him to the blanket, but his weight was such that he took her down with him. The very chest she'd painfully avoided staring at now smacked her square in the face. A crisp patch of chest hair tickled her nose.

Father, help us!

She scuttled away from the man as if he were a snake in the grass and rose to her feet so abruptly that she stumbled over her hem. Her face grew mottled with mortification's fire.

"So, the sleeping giant awakens," Marcus said, meandering over from the fire. "Still weak as a kitten, I see." The brown-haired man kneeled at Kieran's side and propped crossed arms upon his knee. "That torque, now. It's the torque of a king, solid gold."

Kieran said nothing. He rolled on his side to shove himself up.

Riona took his brat and tossed it over him. "Lie down, milord. This man means you no harm."

"He has an eye for another's property. That's harm in the making as far as I'm concerned."

"So you wish to be up and about, eh?" With a cynical twist of his mouth, Marcus stood and held out his hand. "Then by all means, allow me to help you, for your weight is too much for the lady when you fall, and fall you will."

"Besides, your lady said we're angels." Dallan approached from where he'd been harnessing the pony to the cart and stood cockily, arms folded, feet braced, over the wounded man.

Kieran assessed him in silence, his pale face a mask of stone.

Riona placed a reassuring hand on his shoulder. "They've been most helpful, Kieran."

"I'm Dallan, this is my wife, Finella, and my brother, Marcus. We make our way as entertainers, and our talents are such that we've not had to resort to thievery. Yet," he added, eyeing the brooch on Kieran's brat. "And because Lady Riona has been such a gracious hostess, we will overlook the aspersions you cast upon our character."

"And we won't call you an—" With a glance at where the children stood looking, Marcus mouthed the word so that only the adults could make it out.

Riona couldn't very well argue with the assessment, but in his defense, Kieran had been awakened abruptly.

"Finella had herbs, which have improved you more than my concoction. Marcus here caught us a fine breakfast this morning. And to be honest, I was relieved to have their company," Riona admitted.

Kieran acknowledged with a slight tip of his head. "Then you have my apologies and my thanks. And if one of you will kindly cut off my head, I should be even more obliged."

"'Tis the poison," Finella said sympathetically. She poured some of the herbal brew they'd made the night before from the skin it was stored in. "Young Leila insisted we put mint in it for you to make it taste better."

Kieran looked past the adults to where Leila nuzzled Gray Macha's velvet nose with her own, even though she had to stand on tiptoe to do so. "She's a strange little creature, that one, beguiling in her way."

"But she's lost without a father and will never speak until she has one who can match the love she offers." Finella left the medicinal goatskin with Kieran and rose, changing the subject abruptly. "My husband has cut two saplings. We hope to make a travois for you since you're too weak to ride. Your gray can pull it."

Kieran shook his head and then winced as though the pain shot from temple to temple with the movement. "Gray will pull nothing. He's a warhorse. The restraint of a harness would drive him wild. I'll ride."

"I'm not straining my back lifting your hide up on his back," Marcus claimed. "Finella is in charge, and if she says you don't ride, you don't ride."

Dallan agreed. "Aye, no one argues with Finella." He cut a sidewise glance at Riona and back to Kieran. "You'll learn a day is made easier by giving the fairer sex their way." He grinned. "They'll more than make it up to you."

"Leila says Gray Macha will pull Gleannmara, as long as she rides on the horse's back," Liex called out to them.

Kieran rolled his eyes and laid back on the blanket. "I know...my own...horse," he grated out with a stubborn set of his jaw.

An hour later, they were on the road. At first, the stallion acted exactly as Kieran predicted, tearing away from Marcus and Dallan as they tried to secure the trace lines, pawing at the air in front of him. Then Leila spoke to it in her strange language, her voice soft and assuaging. When the stallion ceased to balk, she walked straight up to it, unafraid, and took its halter in her small hand. At her nod, Dallan and Marcus were able to secure the travois to the gray's back.

Kieran was impressed, despite his effort to hide it. He asked Leila what her secret was, to which she replied through her youngest brother, "Seargal."

As imperious as its master, Gray Macha insisted on the lead. The stallion would allow no other horse ahead of it. Each time one of the other horses pulled ahead, the gray broke into a trot, nearly jolting Kieran off the travois. Perched atop the horse's back, Leila sat pixielike and played the tin whistle that Marcus found in the tented wagon. It

was an old tune, a favorite of mothers trying to coax precocious babes
to sleep.

Dressed again in his leine, thanks to the help of the men, Kieran
now slept under the influence of Finella's herbs and the sleeping music
the little girl played for him. Riona rode Bran's dun gelding behind
them, ever watchful for a change in her foster brother's condition.

The golden sprout of beard covering Kieran's jaw and chin made a
manly statement, yet there was something boyish about his face in
sleep. Perhaps it was because the pressures of adulthood no longer
weighed upon his brow so that worry's furrow hardly showed. Perhaps
it was the way his mouth puckered, full and tender, innocent of cynicism or oath. Surely, it was most charming at times…and warm…and
seductive…

Her mouth thinned as she banished the memory of his kiss from
her mind. Her body, alas, was less inclined to let it go. The clothes she
wore grew uncomfortably warm, due penance for allowing such things
in her mind, she told herself sternly.

At a rath belonging to a bóaire, the travelers were made welcome for
respite in the midday sun. Extending the hospitality for which Erin was
known, the cattle lord and his wife bade them stay the night, but Dallan
insisted they keep moving. The fairgrounds at Drumceatt would fill fast
with vendors and entertainers. He wanted his troupe situated among
the best, not only to compete for attention, but to learn.

Riona was relieved, for it was difficult to answer questions about
her company without telling the entire truth. Her host had to be satisfied with her story that her foster brother had fallen ill while escorting
her and her adopted children to Drumceatt. In truth, it was all the
gleemen knew as well. After the nunday repast, the bóaire and his wife
saw them off with a loaf of bread each, a cake of cheese, and an invitation to stop again if they returned that way.

For the next few days, the same pattern of hospitality followed.
Riona's companions were so gregarious and entertaining that they captured the most of their hosts' attentions, leaving Riona to quietly care
for Kieran. His fever rose and fell voraciously, yet the infection ceased
to spread and began to clear, heralding the triumph of prayer and

Finella's herbàl concoction. Meanwhile, the children offered an endless source of questions to distract Dallan and his company from prying too much—that and an instinctive discretion born of years upon the road traveling with strangers.

At sundown nearing the end of a full week of flight, a hostelry appeared around a bend in the road by a river ford. A sign with a red fox swung over the gate to the enclosure. Having been this way before, Dallan explained how this particular rath had once been held by a lesser lord and was hence fortified, until a hosteler was granted the land and cattle by the provincial king for public hospitality. The gates were open, and as they approached, a servant hung a lantern on the outside in keeping with the strict laws regarding his master's assignment. Hospitality was as much law as it was inclination for public and private landowners, guaranteeing the traveler three days of room and board before he was expected to travel on. All Riona hoped for was refuge from the elements.

"Welcome, good travelers," the man called out to them. "The master's lodge is full tonight, but ye're welcome to his table and to set up camp within the walls of the rath. Sure, all of Erin is bound for the high king's convention."

Riona's heart sank. The thought of a dry pallet in a lodge with a roof had heightened her anticipation of the day's end. But camping within civilized walls was still better than fending without against wolves and human predators.

"We thank you, sir. And does your master have need of entertainers this night?" Dallan asked him.

"We've princes and clergy, soldiers and merchants, but no entertainment save the master's own gray-bearded bard." The servant cast an appreciative eye at Riona and Finella. "And surely he can't compare to the beauty of your company."

Clergy and soldiers? Riona felt the blood drain from her face. She supposed she should expect as much, now that they were less than two day's from the synod. Travelers from all over Ireland were converging on the few roads leading to Drumceatt. Reason stayed the panic welling in her chest. Barring some unexpected delay, Senan and Maille were surely a day ahead of them. *Dear Father, don't let them be here.*

Marcus ran into a somersault, coming up before the astonished servant with theatrical finesse. "I pray your lord is a generous one?"

"He pays as good as he gets," the servant said flatly.

"Then have him bring out his large purse, good man," Dallan warned him, "for he and his guests shall be entertained in highest fashion tonight."

The servant's eyes grew round at the sweep of Dallan's hand. "*All* of you?"

"I feel I'm coming down with a touch of the same ague that has our friend indisposed," Riona spoke up. "So not *all* of us will participate."

Fynn started to protest, but Riona silenced him with a warning lift of her chin. "We'll discuss it once we walk out the stiffness of our journey."

"Ye sure it's just the ague?" Lifting the lantern off its hook, the servant started toward the travois where Kieran slept.

"He's not yellow, if that's what you mean," Riona responded sharply. Faith, she didn't want to start a panic. "But he's coughed himself into a stupor."

The man hesitated and rehung the light. "Then it's just as well you keep to the outer rath. I seen half a village drop dead from what they thought was the ague, till they turned yeller and died. Just follow me."

Dallan helped Finella out of the cart, while Marcus cautiously approached Gray Macha.

"If it would please his lordship, Gray Macha." He bowed lowly before the animal and motioned toward the inside of the rath.

Leila laughed and nudged the stallion forward after the servant. The rest of the troupe followed.

"'Tis a fine horse for such as yourselves. I can't make out 'is color."

"Gray," Fynn said.

"Dappled." Riona blurted out at the same time, not wanting Macha's true nature to raise suspicion as to their identities. "He's splotched. We came upon him easily because his hind hoof grazes his other leg in a run, ruining him for racing or battle. Since we've no need for a fast steed, he suited our purposes."

Thankfully the children did not contradict her. As for Dallan and his company, they were as good off-stage as on. They acted as if she told a story they'd heard many times before.

Riona couldn't explain why she felt compelled to lie about Gray Macha when it contradicted her nature and belief. Yet, the deceit was out, as if she'd rehearsed it. That being the case, she could only conclude one thing. The caution had been planted by Providence, for God could see beyond their present circumstance.

Her lips thinned. They shouldn't have come into the rath. Danger surely waited.

FIFTEEN

The hosteler sent out a servant with food for the troupe—boiled beef, parsnips, and bread, along with a small cask of honeyed beer. Thanks to the supplies Dallan and company carried in their wagon, Riona was able to heat water for a blood-bracing tea from Finella's dried herbs. Liex's warming stones, still in the little sack the child wore at his waist, and Fynn's cup had been a godsend the night before, but this way Riona could make enough for them all. The children had been exposed to dampness and fatigue enough to tax their health. A little chamomile to calm them, rosemary for a brewing sniffle, and the last of Leila's mint were just the thing to fortify them.

Yet with the excitement of watching the gleemen prepare for their night of entertainment, Riona feared it would take more than chamomile to calm the children. Leila followed Finella around, playing the whistle and fingering the silken material of her multicolored dress. Liex watched Marcus as if he juggled stars rather than hoops and balls. Fynn worried her most.

"If only I had my darts and knives, I could join you," he fretted, while Dallan practiced snapping off the heads of dandelions with the tip of his whip. "Mother stood with an apple on her head and one in each hand—"

"You must have been good then," Dallan observed, inventorying the various instruments he'd mastered.

Besides the harp there were three other stringed instruments, as well as pipes and horns. According to Finella, Dallan was master of all of them and had tutored both her and his brother to accompany him. She played bells and tabor, while the bagpipe, flute, and pipe were Marcus's accomplishments. When their skill as musicians wasn't needed among the nobility, they resorted to appealing to the peasantry with their acrobatic and juggling skills and Finella's herbal remedies.

"I've a set of knives and a board in the wagon. Let's see what you can do."

"No."

The gleeman and boy looked at Riona in sharp surprise. Riona could imagine what Dallan was thinking, and he was wrong. She did not look down on his profession.

"Why?" Fynn asked. "I'm very good."

What if someone recognized you? Riona wanted to say, but couldn't in front of Dallan. "I think that, given our situation, you need to rest with us. You're my son now and don't need to perform for your livelihood."

"It's a good life, milady," Dallan told her in a miffed voice. "One to which the lad was raised."

"I meant to imply nothing else, sir," Riona answered quickly. "But Fynn has chosen to live with me, and I would rather he not…" Heavens, what good reason could she give? Intuition, heightened by an ominous sense of danger, told her it could be foolish to admit to being fugitives to strangers, no matter how kindly they seemed.

Fynn was insistent. "After we leave Drumceatt and I'm properly adopted, I won't use the knives, so tonight may be my last chance to perform."

She wanted to grab the boy's ear and twist it, but he was so set on accompanying the troupe to the lodge that Riona gave in. Senan would know Fynn, but the bishop was a day ahead of them. At least she prayed so.

"Then do what you must," she relented, unable to make her case against it.

Liex was put out that he couldn't go with his older brother, but Riona's promise of a story eased his disappointment. The twins were so tired that they nearly fell asleep before she finished telling the story of how David was betrayed and fled to the wilderness. Riona knew how he felt. This miscarriage of justice against Kieran was a betrayal of the worst sort, orchestrated by one of God's own priests in the church to which she'd intended to pledge her life. How could she expect the children to respect the church and become God-fearing warriors of Christ when they saw such—

Was not Christ betrayed by His own church?

"You look as if you've seen a pooka."

Riona turned, startled to see Kieran watching her through half-lidded eyes.

"No, but I have discovered something most wonderful."

She hadn't been betrayed by the church any more than Christ had been. They'd been betrayed by people who professed to be one with God's will but by design or ignorance were not. Nay, she could not hold the church itself responsible for her plight any more than she could condemn an entire harvest over one rotten piece of fruit.

Seeing Kieran's intention to sit up, Riona broke from her contemplation and hastened to help him. He was stronger, for it was not nearly the struggle she'd had that morning to sit him upright.

He leaned against the wheel of the gleemen's cart. "Then share it, for I've had my stomach full of disaster."

And the bite was returning to his cynicism.

"Where are our light-fingered *deliverers?*" He fingered the torque at his neck to make certain it was still there.

"They entertain in the hosteler's lodge. Fynn is with them." She took a flat of bread with boiled beef and parsnips from a cloth and handed it to him. "The lodge is full of travelers bound for the synod, including soldiers."

Kieran stiffened. Riona saw the same concern she'd initially felt play upon his face. "Maille is a day ahead of us," he concluded aloud.

He pinched off a piece of the tender meat and popped it in his mouth, chewing thoughtfully. The amber warmth of his gaze suspended with wariness as he took in their surroundings—the closed gate with its lantern singling it out in the dark, the rise of the earthenwork enclosure, which had been allowed to grow over with brush except along swale that had been dug for drainage.

"Where is my sword?" Clearly, the warrior in him was returning.

"In the wagon." Riona fought becoming infected by his increasing apprehension. Had she leaned too heavily on faith and not enough on caution?

"Get it."

At least her foster brother was returning to his old self. Sooner than argue, she fetched the blade and lay it by his side, hidden beneath his blanket. Still, she couldn't resist saying something. "As long as you can fight sitting down, you'll do well, but if you have to stand...well, I'd try leaning a little more on prayer and less on the weapon."

"Hmm. Give me something I can hold in my hand, not something with the substance of air."

"Substance has nothing to do with power. Air provides substance for your next breath."

Kieran smirked. "Faith, 'tis like arguing with your cousin."

Riona poured a portion of honeyed beer into Fynn's cup for Kieran to chase down the food with. "You can't argue with truth. You may not like it, but you can't argue with it." She cocked her head as if listening for something, but the message came from within. "Take our situation, for instance. That was what I marveled over a moment ago."

One golden eyebrow shot up in a skeptical arch. "Then by all means, enlighten me, milady, for I am sore pressed to see what there is to marvel at aside from one malady heaped upon another."

"For which day, milord?" Riona countered, brightening by the moment as blessing after blessing came to her. They'd not been caught. Help came when they needed it most. No, the past few days had not been to her liking, but had they not survived thus far? The voice at the holy well near Dublin rang clear in her mind and on her lips.

"'I am the Lord, the God of all Flesh; is anything too hard for Me?'" Riona grabbed Kieran's arm in the thrill of her realization. Another time the maid in her would have noticed the bulge of a bicep so impressive that both her hands could not span it. For now, it was just a means of getting Kieran's attention. "We've been so busy, I've scarce had time to think of it until now."

"Methinks you've had more than your share of this beer. Am I not laid low by a pitchfork scratch and forced to rely on a would-be nun, three ragmullions, and now three more grown ones?" He grunted in dismay. "Faith, by traveling with them we have no more rights than they. We're naught but vagabonds with no country, no people, no family."

Riona touched the side of his face, caressing it until their gazes

locked. "When we are laid low, God is strongest. When we are unmolested, we take His love for granted."

Something kindled in her foster brother's gaze. Had she reached
Kieran or was it the reflection of the dancing campfire? Could anything
melt the rath of ice he'd erected around his soul?

"That's like saying the physician makes people ill so that he can
heal them."

"God doesn't cause our distress, Kieran. Sin does."

Her words seemed as futile as a gnat's charge of an oaken door, at
least at that moment. But then seeds did not sprout right away.

"Heber was no sinner. My parents were no sinners. They were
godly, all of them." Kieran slung the rest of his food away in the grass.
"Where was God when they died?" His bitterness was enough to sour
the sweet brew he swilled straight down.

"Crying." A blade of grief cracked her voice. Riona closed her eyes,
picturing an anguished Father looking down from heaven. How many
times had that same picture consoled her these recent years? She knew
in her heart the heavenly Father wept for Heber even now. "Just as He
cried when His own Son died."

"He could have stopped that, too, *if* He really cared or if He even
exists for that matter."

"Aye, He could have. But out of love He suffered from the choice of
sin-prone man, rather than take the easier way and leave mankind lost
and hopeless ever after."

It was a prospect Riona had discussed at length on those wintry
nights by Abbot Fintan's fire. "Why," she'd asked, "didn't He send the
angels to save Jesus?"

In her mind's eye, Riona saw Fintan's aged face crinkle with an
understanding smile.

"But that would have forced His will on the men who crucified
Christ. Our God is one who would have man do what is right out of
love for Him and righteousness, not out of fear or bondage to Him.
Satan would have us follow him as slaves, bound to his will alone.
Don't you see the difference?"

Moved by wisdom of the late abbot's words, she repeated them for

Kieran, praying that somehow they'd offer him comfort and insight—
that he might feel the all-encompassing love of God that she felt at that
moment.

When Riona of Dromin looked at a man that way, Kieran thought, he'd
agree to anything. And if there were angels, one even now placed her
hand upon his arm and looked imploringly into his eyes, bewitching
him. Maybe it was the herbs in that fiendish concoction the glee-
woman had given him, but the fire silhouetted Riona in an almost
mystical aura. Her eyes had never been more alive, as if the same flame
that burned without glowed within.

Kieran reached out and touched her cheek. "You are real, aren't
you? I'm not hallucinating?"

He wanted her. He needed her. She was the only light left for him in
this world. She was light, life, and love…and perhaps even liberty for his
shackled heart. He knew this in an even deeper place than the physical,
in a place without shape or form, one entrapped in heavy obscurity.

"Aye, I'm real."

He traced her temple, burying his fingers in her hair. An angel with
hair black as sin and soft as a breath, he thought, slipping his fingers
around to draw her closer, ever closer, until her faltering breath
warmed his lips. He leaned forward, brushing her mouth, tentative as a
butterfly lighting upon a rose, for that is what Riona reminded him of.
She was a winter rose that bloomed despite all that would make it
wither, while he who would protect it lay smitten by fate's twisted
humor. Trying to discern purpose in all this made his head ache as
much as the fever had.

"God has been so good to us, Kieran. Surely you must see it."

The words whispered upon his lips were sweeter than wine, soaking his brain so that the conflict of the heart and mind was lost in
intoxicating confusion. He pulled her to him so that all that stood
between them was her startled reticence. Even so, she was soft and pli-
able to his hard and unrelenting physique, as if custom-made to com-
plement him, to make him whole.

"If what I see and what I hold is from Him, then I cannot argue with you, sweetling." He cradled her head beneath his chin, inhaling the fragrance of her hair. "I would not want to."

The breath she'd held escaped her, leaving her body with joyful surrender. The fists balled against his chest opened, curling around his neck as she hugged him with a strength that belied her delicate build. Whatever muse dashed those words to his lips, he thanked it. Long had he dreamed of holding Riona this way, of being able to sample her lips at the mere dip of his head. Nay, not just sample, but devour—

Kieran's descent was checked by a demand of outrage.

"What do you think you're doing with *my* mother?"

Riona jerked, rolling away from him and staring as if she'd been bowled over by the question.

Fynn stood glaring at Kieran as if to slay him with the daggers in his eyes.

"That's between Riona and me, not some pug-nosed snot with a knack for annoying the fire out of me." Kieran shifted, wincing at the reminder of his wounded leg. With Riona so close, his senses had been riveted by the lady rather than by his malady. "And what do you think *you're* doing sneaking up on us like that?"

"There was no sneaking about it. I walked up here big as the high king himself, but you were so busy seducing my mother—"

"I was *not* being seduced," Riona exclaimed, casting an uncertain glance in Kieran's direction. "I was—" she thought a moment—"well…I was not being seduced, and I'll hear nothing more of it." She climbed to her feet and started toward the fire, then turned abruptly. "I thought you were entertaining with Dallan and his company."

Fynn tugged his resentful gaze away from Kieran. "I was and I did. I've coin to show for it, but that's not why I came ahead of the others. We've got trouble."

Riona put her hand to her chest.

"What kind of trouble, lad?" Kieran asked, touching the sword Riona had hidden beneath his makeshift pallet for reassurance. His fingers met with the cold hardness. It was willing, if his flesh was. The exertion of an innocent kiss had left him drained.

"Maille has offered a reward and posted his soldiers the entire way to Drumceatt. There's four here at the hostelry. I saw Dallan and Marcus speaking to them."

"*Blessings,* eh?" With a cryptic twist of his lips, he glanced at Riona. She'd almost made him believe. He'd certainly wanted to. Taking his sword out, he used it as a crutch to pull himself up. His leg ached to the bone with protest. "Then we'd best be away from here before these so-called friends turn us in for the reward."

The moment he was upright the stars above them began to whirl in slow motion before his eyes. His brain mimicked them within his skull. A black wind caught him behind the knees and laid him down with a breath-jarring crash. As he registered the pain of the impact, the clang of the sword against the wagon wheel rang in his ears.

"Kieran!"

He heard Riona call his name. That sweetness alone was the painful thread of light he clung to amid the anesthetic promise of darkness surrounding him. For her he'd fight to suffer rather than take the easier path to surrender.

It was for love He suffered...

Riona's explanation of love struck an awakening chord within.

"Here, let me help."

Kieran stiffened. There was no time to dwell on the revelation, for the second voice was not Riona's. As if appearing from thin air, the fairer haired of the two gleemen reached for him. Seizing him by the arms, Marcus held him until Riona drew Kieran's head to her lap.

"Kieran, be still," she cautioned, stroking his hair from his forehead. "Your wound is better, but you're weak from fighting the infection."

The stroke of Riona's fingers upon his scalp seemed to still the circling stars overhead.

"Why aren't you performing with your brother?" Kieran asked Marcus.

"Because, Kieran of Gleannmara, we have work to do if we are to see you safely delivered to Drumceatt."

Safely? Suspicion would not let the word settle rightly with him. "And why would you help us?"

Marcus shrugged. "Finella."

As if that explained it all, he rose to his feet and snapped his fingers at Fynn. "Wake your sister. We've a horse to paint by morning."

"A...horse?" Kieran repeated, disbelieving, when the gleeman nodded.

"Aye, the gray had best be another color by daylight or we've no chance of convincing anyone that Lady Riona is my wife and that the twins belong to us." He pointed to Fynn. "The older lad there can be Finella and Dallan's offspring."

"What about Kieran?" Riona asked. "How can we explain him?"

Marcus looked at Kieran. The gleeman's grin made the hair rise on the back of Kieran's neck. "Well, he'll need some painting, too. But that's Finella's job. She and Dallan will be along once their sleeping music takes effect."

"Sleeping music," Kieran sneered, no longer certain if he was dreaming or if he was at the mercy of lunatics.

SIXTEEN

"W e beg your indulgence that Dragon's Breath is unable to astound you with his feats of fire and strength," Dallan announced to the gathering of guests the following morning, "but neither skill nor muscle availeth against the inner fire of fever."

An uneasy ripple of amusement wafted through the guests and staff gathered in the outer rath of the hostelry where the troupe of entertainers prepared for a final show before departure.

"I'd have a look at 'im still." A soldier dressed in a leather tunic like that Kieran had stolen walked within a few paces of the bed where Kieran lay swathed in blankets. Stepping just close enough to see the warrior's face, he grunted and backed away. "Looks like one o' them Picts. His whole face is tattooed and hair straight up with lime."

Curiosity stricken, another guard ambled over. Riona prayed that Finella's efforts with paint would work again. The woman had spent the better part of the night drawing designs on Kieran's face while the men worked up a batch of dye for Gray Macha. She'd seen small animals dyed on their owner's whim, but Gray Macha was more than a notion to undertake, particularly in the light of a fire. Much to Kieran's horror, the magnificent warhorse was now a shade of bright blue, stylish enough for the noblest fancy. His black mane and tail were plaited and beribboned.

"Crikes, 'em red eyes'll make ye bones brittle up."

Kieran shifted beneath his blankets with a low growl, and the man backed away hastily. It was as much a reflection of his genuine humor as it was playing his assigned role.

"The Dragon's Breath is relatively harmless...more man there than wit, I fear," Marcus assured the guard. "But when he's well, he makes a wondrous spectacle, swallowing his sword and breathing fire. Perhaps those traveling to Drumceatt will see him."

Those travelers who waited while their servants prepared for the day's journey nodded, intrigued by a wild man who could swallow fire and sword.

"I wouldn't mind seein' it meself," the first guard laughed. "I kin see 'im astride that blue horse, blue face and all, like a matched pair."

It was an amusing thing to picture, but Riona was too distracted to appreciate it—or the seething frustration of her foster brother at being caught in such a predicament.

"And now for the skit we promised you, now that my wife is rested." Marcus slipped his arm about Riona's waist. "Fiona's to be a mother again and I a father, and as such I continue to do my utmost to assure there be two more like these." He pointed to the twins, and then, without warning, the gleeman leaned around and kissed Riona full on the lips.

Liex and Leila erupted in a spontaneous giggle, but it was Kieran's low growl that sent the curious guard yet another pace away.

Now that the shoe had fallen on her foot, it wasn't nearly as engaging. "That is a skit I prefer to perform in private, good husband." Riona walked to a table provided by the hosteler for the promised departing show. The raucous amusement sweeping through the crowd made her wish for the ground to open up and consume her, but that was not to be the case. "Let us begin."

With great reluctance, Riona had agreed the night before to act out the story of the scriptural widow who offered her last food to the prophet Elijah, played by Dallan. Finella narrated the story, drawing in the crowd with her artful play of words. Mischief-maker that he was, Marcus insisted on embellishing the story as the widow's brother, who had a taste for wine. Once the miracle of the oil jar that could not be emptied had taken place, earning a grand huzzah of approval from the audience, Marcus stole the show. He ran after the prophet to offer him the last of his wine in hopes of a source that would never empty. Elijah drank the small remnant and told him that he'd be blessed by the spirit in which it was given. After the prophet exited, the onlookers howled as comical Marcus mimed trying to get wine out of the empty skin, wringing it, shaking it, and pulling expressions that defied the average face. The performance was so well received that the hosteler implored them stay another night, but Dallan was firm.

While the guests prepared to leave, Leila played her pipe, perched cross-legged atop the blue stallion, while Liex amused some of the bystanders with sleight of hand tricks with his stones. Both were delighted when they showed off their contribution to the troupe's income, two silver coins from a kindly merchant.

"Look, Mother!" Liex shouted, running up to Riona and leaping into her arms in his excitement.

Mother. Joy welled within Riona's heart. This was no act. She was for all intent and purpose just that. She bussed the child on the cheek. "Well done, Liex." She turned to Leila and took her coin, admiring it in the light. It was imprinted in Latin, most likely from the Mediterranean. "I'll bet this will purchase something extra special for an extra special girl."

"Fynn, mount up your cousins on the dun," Finella called from the front of the wagon. "We're ready to be off."

"Come, my darling Fiona. Your steed awaits."

Riona smiled warily as she approached Marcus. The young man was perfectly wicked, in a charming sort of way. He reminded her of a cross between Bran and the legendary troublemaker Bricriu.

"Indeed, sir, there could be no more attentive husband than you," she said in a voice loud enough for the ears of the guards lingering near the gate of the outer rath. Not that they paid much heed. They were engrossed in conversation with the generous merchant.

"My joy is to see to your every need."

"My joy is to see how well *you* can swallow my sword," Kieran grumbled lowly from the travois.

Marcus lifted Riona to Bantan's golden-brown back and turned to the travois with an exaggerated mask of horror. "My stars, I don't think I've ever seen a *green* tattoo…and so ugly at that."

Riona groaned inwardly. Life was a giant stage to Marcus, but this act was not appreciated.

Constrained by circumstance, Kieran glowered. "Come take a closer look, you miming fool."

"A mime I may be, but never a fool." With that, the entertainer danced away in slow motion. Riona couldn't help but chuckle at his ridiculous antics. He did know how to pluck the strings of Kieran's patience. Hopefully they would make peace before her foster brother regained his health.

Once well away from the hostelry, Riona's tension finally uncoiled. The sun overhead washed her shoulders in warmth, relaxing yet invigorating. There was even a part of her that was enjoying the adventure. Never had Riona pictured herself acting with gleemen. The enthusiastic response from their audience would have been intoxicating if she'd not been so nervous.

It was yet another day, and once more God had taken care of them. She said as much as she blessed the ample bundle of food from the hosteler at midday.

"And thank You, Father, for sending these good people our way. Amen."

"Not *too* good," Marcus reflected aloud. "The reward was a fat one and gave Dallan and me much to consider."

Kieran stared flatly. "So why did you pass it up?"

"The reputation Lord Maille leaves in his wake isn't an endearing one." Dallan helped himself to another chunk of cheese. "So I say to myself and my good brother, if this Maille is vengeful and tight pursed, think what a thankful and good-hearted lord might pay."

"Humph." Kieran contemplated the skin containing the concoction Finella had made. As if coming to a decision, he put it aside, untouched. The curl of his lips suggested a snarl rather than words. "So you'd have a reward from me, would you?"

"I would think you'd want to reward them, Kieran," Riona spoke up, alarmed at the calculating way her foster brother moved, like a hound pushed to the edge of its tolerance in an intolerable situation.

"They'll have to take my word that they'll get what they deserve... at least until we can straighten this muddle of murder. I can offer them nothing at present."

As if to challenge them, he looked from one to the other of the men. Neither answered at first, each carefully assessing the iron bulge of Kieran's jaw. The sound of Riona's own breath was like a roaring wind to her ear in the tense quiet.

Dallan swallowed the piece of bread he'd chewed to mush in the interim and pointed to Kieran's chest. "That brooch would make a fine show of gratitude," he suggested in a matter-of-fact tone.

It was no different than if he'd asked for a loaf of bread or something as inconsequential, but the brooch of Gleannmara was hardly that. Its stones and metal were precious in their own right, but what it symbolized was even more so.

"Hah!" Kieran laughed, clearly not taking the man seriously. "Next you'll be wanting my horse as well."

Marcus shook his head. "Nay, not that one. He's too much like his master. But the clasp now, that's a fine payment." He lifted his head, as if studying the brooch. "Sapphires and gold. Sure, it'd bring a pretty price."

"You go too far, you prancing bucklet." Face darkening, Kieran struggled upright, using his sword as a crutch.

Riona shot to her feet and stood between the two men. Her foster brother's great frame looked even more so in the full drape of his brat. There was no visible sign of his earlier weakness. Braced with anger, he leaned like an oak into the storm brewing in his gaze. She seized at reason to waylay it.

"Kieran, the brooch is a small price to pay for our lives."

The warrior looked at her as if she'd lost her wits, reminding her of what she already knew. "This is the brooch of Gleannmara, woman, presented to Rowan by Queen Maire. To give it away is to toss away my heritage."

"I have jewels of my own that will bring a higher price," she said, turning to Dallan.

"Milady, chivalry stands for you and the children," the entertainer replied. "Besides, *you* are not accused of murder."

"Accused, not guilty," Kieran pointed out. "There is some foul plot afoot into which I've stumbled."

Marcus gave Riona a sympathetic look. "Alas, milady, you know what you're worth to this gent…or should I say, not worth?"

Before Marcus could sidestep Kieran's charge, the warrior held him up against an elm, pinned by the neck with one hand.

Where had his strength come from? "Kieran!" Riona latched on to his arm until her weight and Marcus's brought it down. "'Tis your foul temper that trapped you into this charge and that convicts you at every turn."

Marcus scrambled away, and Kieran spun to go after him but instead fell back against the tree. Perspiration beaded his brow, squeezed out by his effort.

"A few precious stones…hardly the worth of a lady's love," Marcus rasped.

"Hush, Marcus, or I'll choke you myself," Riona warned him. She threw her hands up in exasperation. "I don't know which of you is worse, the needler or the buffoon. Bricriu or the bull." Disgusted with both of them, Riona picked up her skirts and stormed away to where the twins played nearby.

"Marcus will meddle one time too many and never sing again." Finella approached Riona from the side of the wagon, shaking her head. "At least we know the lord of Gleannmara is much improved."

"And overspent." Riona glanced back to where Kieran refused to sit down but continued to lean against the tree. He and Marcus still eyed each other, not unlike wary dogs in a ring.

"He's young and strong," Finella remarked. "He'll come back fast. As for Marcus, it serves him right."

"What *could* he have been thinking, antagonizing my foster brother like that?"

"My husband's brother is an incurable romantic. He revels in the part of Cupid."

"Cupid! What in this world possessed him to think Kieran and I—"

Glancing at Fynn, who stalked some animal with his sling poised a distance away, Riona recalled Marcus's coming up on them locked in a tender embrace the night before. The rest of her protest faded away. How had it come to be? One moment she spoke in earnest of matters of the soul, and the next she responded to Kieran's kiss with equal fervor.

How had *any* of this come to be, she wondered in confusion.

"Are you going to marry Gleannmara?" Liex asked, glancing up from the sleight of hand trick he was teaching his sister.

"Of course not," Riona answered. "He's a godless, foul-tempered fool."

"But he can carry us on his shoulders, like father used to do." The child was serious, as if that were all the qualification required to make him happy. "And when he blows foul, we can just hide. That's what we used to do when athair got mad, 'cause we knew he loved us."

Would that it were that simple.

"I see an able, strapping man, noble of heart and unable to express what lies within it," Finella observed without invitation. "And therein lies the source of his anger, not as much at others as at himself." She stared off at where Fynn entered the forest's edge. "Where force fails, 'tis love that tames the beast."

With an ample dose of self-pity, Kieran watched the women as he rested against the rough bark of the tree. They'd kill a horse in this condition to put it out of its misery. The fever had retreated, taking the throbbing head pain with it, leaving in its place a dull ache. He'd sweated his strength away. His wounded leg gave him thunder and a limp. And all from a vicious swipe of a stable fork wielded by a hysterical wench.

Though his physical weakness plagued him, the feelings gnawing at his insides were far worse. Pride demanded the most of him. It shamed the jealousy that had reared upon seeing Marcus's familiarity with Riona and fueled indignation. His foster sister had spurned his proposal, not once, but twice. She didn't deserve jealousy. But he had every justification as a gentleman to be outraged by the impudence of a lowly gleeman toward a lady of her station. So what did Kieran gain from coming to her defense? Disdain.

He forced his breath through his lips in frustration.

"If you have half a brain in that thick head of yours, you'd go after the lady and blame love for acting the bullish buffoon." Sitting on a branch of a nearby tree, Marcus looked down at Kieran, chirping like a smug magpie.

"Leave me be, gnat." Kieran leaned on his sword and walked the distance to another tree in the opposite direction. Faith, it hurt, but at least he could move on his own without having to rely on the brothers Tit and Tat.

"You'd think she knew how you felt, wouldn't you?"

"I'd think you'd know not to press me by now."

Marcus leapt down, landing light as a cat. "Declare your love, sir."

"I did!" Kieran caught himself. "And the last person I'd discuss matters of the heart with is the likes of you. I see no wife in your court."

"An artist of story and song needs no wife. I have the tried and true words of Erin's greatest lovers at my disposal to make the ladies more than kind with their favors. But a lord of the land, who cut his teeth on steel rather than words—" Marcus tutted—"he can't beget heirs alone."

Too tired to argue, Kieran threw his free hand up as if to wave away a worrisome insect. "Why do you plague me?"

"Because I feel sorry for you." Taking care to stay out of Kieran's reach, Marcus circled around him, finger poised on his cheek as if in thought. "And I stand to gain if you really wish to show the lady that her love means more to you than…say…that brooch."

"I'd give my life for Riona but not my brooch."

"Yes, yes. The brooch will do you much honor when your bones rot beneath a cromlech."

"As much as the lady."

"How many times, do tell me good warrior, were you smitten in the head during your training?" Marcus grimaced. "Can a brooch give you an heir? Can a brooch warm your bed and heart? Can a brooch return your love? Will a brooch risk her life to free you from captivity?"

Kieran's brow shot up. "What do you know of that?"

Marcus nodded toward the spot where the women and children chatted. "Young Liex is quite a storyteller. He even makes you out to be a hero. Myself, I fail to see hero meat. I'd be challenged indeed to compose a song for the ages about a bearish brute who speaks by clanging sword and pounding fists. The women will not long to hear about you and will pity your lady."

Kieran grunted, a skeptical tilt at the corner of his mouth. What did he care what women thought of him? He was a warrior.

"You see, my friend—"

"You're no friend of mine."

"You see, my good man, for I believe you are noble of heart even if you are challenged by its matters," the jongleur said, "your training as a warrior was exemplary, but you are sadly lacking in expertise where the heart is concerned."

"I'll not stand here and listen to the drone of a gnat with a waspish tongue. Count yourself on thin grace that I haven't cut it out."

"That would really impress the lady."

Never was Kieran more tempted to tear a man apart muscle by muscle. The faint smack of truth was all that saved Marcus's light-footed hide. And it was only faint truth.

"I can have all the women I wish. Faith, they swoon in my path at fairs or in court."

"But not the woman you want." At Kieran's silence, Marcus went on. "Tell me, how did you first ask the lady to wed you?"

"I told her I was now king and needed a wife and heirs." Why was he even answering this fool?

"And she didn't fall into your arms? I'm astounded. What woman wouldn't want to take up caring for a foul-tempered man and his household, seeing to cooking and cleaning and sewing…"

"It's a wife's duty."

"And growing to monstrous proportion while carrying *your* child, not to mention spending hours, if not days, in agony giving birth. I know if I were a woman, I'd jump at the prospect," the man remarked laconically. "Oh, and then there's the caring for the child, the filthy—"

"By my mother's eyes," Kieran interrupted, "I haven't asked *you*, so stop your whining."

Marcus's gaze twinkled. He did a dancelike turn. "But that's what you asked the lady to do."

"I said no such—"

"And the second time, how did you ask her?"

Scowling, Kieran recalled the scene. "I said I made a promise to her dying brother to marry her and take care of her."

"Who wouldn't promise anything to a dying man?"

Throttling was too good for his companion. Had Kieran felt better, he'd have doled out the penance anyway. "I meant what I said. Heber was my foster brother, dearer than my own life to me."

"Of course you meant it," Marcus told him. "But promising her brother to marry her does not move a lady's heart. Not once have you mentioned love."

"I have loved Riona of Dromin all my life…since she was a toddling child. She *knows* how I feel about her. She just doesn't care. All she thinks about is her church and now those halflings." Yet her faith and compassion for the gleeman's orphans were part of what he cherished about Riona.

"If *she's* the one you'd marry, then you'd best amend your regard toward them as well." Marcus shook his head from side to side. "I don't know if you're even trainable when it comes to wooing the heart of such a lady. I can only offer my advice—"

"And the price for such advice is the brooch," Kieran cut in. "I am strides ahead of you, you greedy gnat. I can certainly tell her I love her."

"Actions carry more weight than words. If she sees you part with something she knows to be dear to you, she'll know you are in earnest."

"An earnest fool, you mean." Kieran fingered the brooch in question. "This is more than six sapphires set in gold. The gold is our Erin, beautifully shaped by a masterful hand. The dark stone is that of Gleannmara, Uí Niall mother to the six septs pledged to her. 'Twas designed by Queen Maire for her king, symbolizing the unity of Gleannmara's tribes as one people."

"I can see how much it means to you," Marcus assured him. "But it's an earthly thing. Love is spiritual. You possess the earthly thing and yet you are empty."

"You speak like a priest."

"I am a priest of the heart," Marcus declared with a sweeping bow. "The clergy are priests of the soul. Both are empty without the spirit of love."

It was food for thought, Kieran had to admit...at least to himself. He'd admit nothing to Marcus. How he missed Heber to share his innermost feelings and thoughts with, or even Bran—anyone but this greedy, self-appointed druid of love.

SEVENTEEN

The fair loomed ahead of the travelers, spread out upon a great green mound. Banners of all manner and tribe fluttered against the sky, now ablaze with the fire of the setting sun. Looking as if thatched with gold rather than straw, domes of newly erected buildings were interspersed among tents and cottars—portable dwellings made of woven wattle. Lesser in number were the shingled roofs of yew. Livestock of all kinds were carefully tended on the town's outskirts lest the law be broken against them running free and destroying the landscape.

It must have taken the groundskeepers months to prepared the land so that those attending might walk on freshly cropped green grass free of mud and wallow, Riona thought, glancing askew at the dust on her skirts. She needed a bath before even entering the grounds. She knew she'd have one before seeing the high king to appeal Kieran's case. The good burgundy dress she wore under the soiled one would do for that, even if it too was a tad worn from her service at the abbey. Before she did anything else, though, she wanted to seek out the chapel and give thanks for the safe arrival of their eclectic ensemble.

Kieran, who insisted on riding the blue Gray Macha the last half of the day, had not throttled Marcus. Clearly unhappy with the color of his warhorse and the tattoos on his face, which Finella said needed to wear off, he'd ridden in brooding silence. The twins napped peacefully, cheeks rosy with health, on the travois he dragged behind the stallion. Finella drove the cart, while Dallan, Marcus, and Fynn, who opted to lead his pony that he might walk with the jongleurs, carried on merrily in song and story beside it.

While the entertainers set up their encampment, Riona took the children to an outdoor place of worship marked by a large wooden cross. A fire was kindled near its foot that would be fed the entire duration of the event. Even at night, it would stand as an invitation to all who came.

Now it was crowded for vespers, and many of the worshipers wore the gray cloth of the clergy who were there to participate in the law-making and political sessions. Kneeling on the grass, Riona bowed her head. Leila mimicked her to perfection, but Liex and Fynn were typically restless. The larger boy elbowed the younger, making Liex gasp loudly. Heads turned, Riona's included, to see Kieran clamp a settling hand on Fynn's shoulder. The younger lad shrunk into the epitome of obedient reverence beneath the warrior's withering gaze.

Not wanting Riona to venture into the crowds alone, Kieran insisted on accompanying her. The mask painted on his face made him look all the more fierce. Her foster brother's attendance meant nothing, she realized, yet it gave her comfort. God had worked many wonders for them thus far. Paint or no, Kieran was no match for a God who called on him.

A priest with two pigeons perched peacefully on his shoulders continued to stare long after the others returned to their pious contemplation so that Riona couldn't help but return his look. Gradually, in the dimming light, the man's features became familiar. It was her uncle, Bran's father.

"Cromyn?" she mouthed silently.

With a smile, the priest nodded and turned dutifully back to his worship.

"Are they his pets?" Liex whispered, a cautious eye turned toward Kieran lest that large hand fall upon him.

"They appear to be." Riona put her finger to the young boy's lips to stay his next question.

Cromyn must have accompanied Columcille from Iona. He'd joined the revered Niall saint a few years after the battle that led to Columcille's exile. What a joy it was to see a familiar and friendly face. She looked at Kieran, who scanned the gathering with hawklike discernment, as if expecting trouble. He'd not recognized the man. Much as she wanted to share her good news, she focused on the leader of the assembly instead and added yet another thanksgiving to her growing list.

When the service closed, Riona leaped to her feet and rushed to embrace her uncle. The birds on his shoulders flapped their wings, disgruntled by her disturbance, yet they refused to give up their master.

"Dearest uncle, you are a joy to behold after all these years."

The man held her at arm's length after a long hug and marveled. "You are as lovely as ever, Riona." He glanced at the children. "And who are these fine youngsters?"

"We're her children," Liex announced proudly. "Does that make you our uncle, too?"

Before the man could answer, Kieran extended his hand. "Cromyn, it's good to see you."

Cromyn squinted in the darkness. Suddenly his face brightened with recognition. "My word, Kieran, I hardly knew you. What manner of madness have you been up to with all this?"

Cromyn pointed to the lord's face. "And you, Riona. How came you by three such fine children?"

"Faith, Father, it's a tale to rival any bard's."

"What say we retreat to more private surroundings to explain?" Kieran suggested.

"Can I look around?" Fynn asked Riona.

Riona frowned. "There are so many people here, Fynn, I…"

"The lad's fourteen, woman," Kieran objected. "He's proven himself a man with his knives and hunting. Let him go."

Riona hardly knew who was more surprised by Kieran's words, she or Fynn. The older boy looked at the warrior, clearly waiting for some sort of stipulation, but none came.

"Me, too?" Liex suggested hopefully.

The corner of Kieran's mouth tipped up. "Aye, you as well…when you are fourteen," he injected, waylaying Riona's objection. Turning to Fynn, he laid a hand on the boy's shoulder. "Keep a sharp eye."

With an eager nod, Fynn skipped away a few feet. Suddenly he let out a yelp of excitement and broke into a run. Grinning, Kieran stared after the boy until he disappeared in the throng.

"Ah, to have that much energy," he said wistfully.

"You must be exhausted," Riona said, stepping up to offer her support. "Father, will you accompany us back to our camp? We've much to share with you."

Cromyn chuckled. "I can see that well enough." He pointed to the pigeons, who'd commanded the attention of the twins. "This is Raphael and Gabriella."

"An' I'm Liex and this is my sister, Leila, but she doesn't talk to anyone except me."

Leila stretched out her arm and said something in her gibberish. Promptly, one of the pigeons abandoned Cromyn's shoulder and lighted on the child's forearm.

"So you're the one," Cromyn said matter-of-factly.

"Father?" Riona questioned at the curious comment.

"Later," her uncle promised, offering his shoulder to Kieran. "Lean on me, lad. We know of your coming."

Kieran stiffened. "Senan and Maille precede us with their lies, eh?"

Cromyn looked up at him. "Who?"

With a sigh of relief, the weary warrior answered, "Later, Father. Later."

Finella had worked her magic with a pot of porridge. It was steaming hot and ready on their return. A hot meal and brace of ale revived the lot of them as Kieran and Riona explained to Father Cromyn the dire circumstances regarding their trip to the synod. Cromyn listened, arms folded within his robe, his dark blue eyes sparkling with interest at every detail.

"From the moment Kieran escaped, God has provided a way here," Riona told him. "By all rights we should have been caught."

Kieran quarreled with the statement in his mind. Most of their fortune he attributed to Riona's influence with the brethren of the abbey, not divine intervention. Any men of good conscience would have helped. Granted, he couldn't explain Leila's warning of the approach of Maille's soldiers. She was such a strange little creature. As for the fisherman's help in providing her and her brood passage across the Liffey— or the brothers having a ready boat to take the rescued orphans to safety—that could have been simply good fortune. It was a church by a seaport. Ships sailing with the tide were hardly a miraculous event.

To hear Riona describe it, God had held her hand the entire way. God had sent the gleemen when Kieran was laid low by the fork wound. God had given Finella a knowledge of herbs. God had put the strings on Dallan's instruments. Kieran received no credit for freeing the captured orphans or anything else to date. God had done it all. It was enough to make a man's head hurt, the way she could see God's hand in everything.

How could a mortal compete with her perception of God? Not that he took half of what she said seriously, but even that was enough to make him feel helpless against whatever it was that made making Riona his wife so vital to him. Annoying as Marcus was, he was right. Whatever this compulsion, Kieran felt it was more than a promise to a dying friend. It was more than needing someone to produce an heir or manage his lodge. Crom's toes, it was obsessing him!

He leaned on a staff borrowed from the jongleurs since his sword lay hidden in the bottom of their cart. It was illegal to carry weapons at the fair, much less to quarrel. The fair's amnesty applied to all—murderers, thieves, and petty criminals—until the season was over. He should feel safe at last, should know the relief Riona did, yet he felt as if he sat on a bench of spikes. This matter of courtly love was the greatest challenge he'd ever faced, as a warrior or as a man.

Tugging at his brat, Kieran cleared his throat to draw attention to himself, but the only one around the fire who noticed was Marcus. Kieran managed a narrowing look in the gleeman's direction, portraying his displeasure.

Thus far, the priest of love's advice had been worthless. Kieran had wanted to make a grand affair of presenting Gleannmara's brooch to Dallan in appreciation for their help. That way Riona could not help but know what he'd done. But nay, Marcus insisted it was best for her to find out on her own. Kieran had stuck closer to the female than her own shadow, and she'd yet to see that his brat was now knotted rather than pinned with dignity.

"And that is why Bran is not with us," the lady explained to her uncle. "He's on his way to Gleannmara with Siony and the orphans he rescued."

Odds balls, she gave credit to everyone but him! Need he strip naked and prance about like a jackrabbit to get her attention?

Cromyn sat back in wonder. "That explains the vision I had during my fast. 'Twas of my son surrounded by children and a lovely brown-haired maid at his side. It made no sense to me, given his choice to gad about as a bard with colt's tooth enough for two men."

Kieran knew Cromyn was disappointed that Bran had not followed his footsteps into the clergy. Nobility of the church was, like that of the clans and lands, inherited. If Cromyn earned a monastery or see, it would be Bran's to take over had his son continued in his footsteps. The man's acceptance of Bran's decision earned Kieran's respect more than the man's dedication to his church.

Cromyn could have made it difficult by insisting that Bran honor his father's wishes according to the commandments, but instead he adhered to another Scripture that spoke of every man having his own talent to offer the Lord. It was sound and fair to Kieran's way of thinking. Some men were born warriors, others priests, others bards.

"Bran has the heart of a poet and too much love to waste away on song alone," Cromyn observed. "A good wife is—"

"Not Siony," Riona laughed. "Faith, I thought we'd need to separate them before they cut each other senseless with barbed words."

"Barbs are often a man's last weapon against Lady Love," the priest said.

Was everyone but him an expert on love? Impatient, Kieran struggled to his feet and stretched his arms over his head, yawning loudly. As he lowered his arms back to his sides, he drew one in so that his brat fell from his shoulders.

Riona reached over and tucked it back up in a motherly fashion. "Keep yourself covered against this dampness, Kieran, or it's back to drinking our concoction for you."

Still she did not see his sacrifice for her.

"I've been plagued with visions the entire voyage over, and now at least they are beginning to make some sense," Father Cromyn went on, picking up the conversation.

"I would keep it up," Kieran said through clenched teeth, "but without my brooch, it keeps falling."

Across the fire, Marcus went into a spasm of coughing and left the group, shaking his head in grandiloquent fashion. Miffed, Kieran didn't care what the fool did. Enough was enough.

Blanching, Riona ruffled through the folds of Kieran's brat. "Where is it? Faith, where do you think you lost it?"

"It's not lost," Kieran assured her. "I reconsidered what you said and recognized the debt I owed to these good people. So I gave it to Dallan before we broke way today anon."

"You gave them Gleannmara's brooch?" Disbelief filled her voice, but something else kindled in her gaze.

Kieran was at a loss as to what it was, but he liked the look of it. "It's just metal and stones and can be replaced. Flesh and blood cannot."

Feeling as if he were tiptoeing on thin ice, he turned to Dallan. "But if ye don't mind, I'd have it back till the end of the fair, lest I be falling over this cloak like a wee lass in her mother's skirts."

The older of the brothers reached into a pouch strung from his belt and withdrew the gold and sapphire piece. "By all means, sir. Even the commonest money lender will allow his clients the use of their pawned finery during the fair."

Riona intercepted it. With great care, she folded Kieran's brat over the width of his shoulders and ran the pin through it. Once secured to her satisfaction, she stepped back, her admiring look running up from the brooch to Kieran's face.

"I'm most pleasantly surprised, milord, that you've come to your senses."

The provocative tilt of her red lips sent heat curling somewhere in Kieran's belly, as if he'd been kicked by a silk-hoofed mule, hard and soft with the same blow. Whatever senses he had were scattered by the impact. His pulse pounded to reclaim them just as his lips staked their own claim upon those she parted in surprise.

Her breath was his, and his was hers. No wine was more heady, for all was obscured but her soft nearness. A myriad of cherished images flashed across Kieran's mind, images of the Riona he loved, laughing, praying, dancing, and sleeping. He kissed them with all an intoxicated vigor—until a bolt of pain erupted from the far reaches of his foot. With a gasp he foundered back, so bewildered that he felt her sound slap upon his cheek before he saw it coming.

"Have you lost your wits?" she accused him. "Do you think to seduce me before my uncle, a priest?"

The ice caved in and bitter cold water closed in over his head. He felt himself sinking fast beneath its surface. "No. I only sought to kiss you," he blurted out. But the damage was done.

Her eyes grew luminous wet, as though it were she that had been slapped. "Kieran, I vow, I don't know you anymore." She accused him as if her dismay were *his* fault.

"Then that makes two of us!" Stung and confounded beyond measure, Kieran turned and stalked away from the company. The agony shooting up his thigh was small in comparison to that consuming his pride.

He reeled around the cart and into its shadow, skin burning with humiliation. If he hadn't needed it for a crutch, he'd have snapped the yew crosier against the wheel or maimed himself trying. Leaning against the rough woven side, he slid to the ground.

Heavenly Father!

The cry for help formed in his beleaguered mind of its own accord. It wasn't conjured from his beating heart but from a secret place, one he'd not been to in a long time. He wasn't at home there. He didn't want to be there alone.

The soft caress of a hand against his rough-shaven cheek caught his attention. Leila stood beside him, her delicate features bathed in sympathy. He thought she and Liex had fallen asleep beneath the cart.

Without invitation, she crawled into his lap and laid her head against his shoulder, a thumb tucked in her mouth. Then, as if she knew his pain, she patted his back with her other hand, consoling. The gesture was small, but the effect was profound.

To Kieran's wonder, he knew exactly what this strange, loving creature told him. He could hear it, yet not with his ears: *I know how you feel. I, too, have lost a loved one. You may feel forsaken, but you are not. I will never leave you. You are never alone.*

Kieran drew the child closer, cradling her as if she were his last breath. Gently he rocked her and wiped away her tears—or were they his? He couldn't see in the stinging blur of the night. All he knew for certain was that this night, the warrior was a child as well—and the words he heard were not those of a little girl, but rather of a loving Father.

EIGHTEEN

The fairgrounds were immense, a veritable city of nobility and peasantry and every class in between. There were lawmakers and clergy, bards and entertainers, craftsmen and vendors, politicians and soldiers, athletes and spectators. Pushing through the throng, Riona frantically searched the sea of faces for any sign of Kieran or Leila. Both were missing when she awoke to the hawking of the bakery boys selling fresh bread from the oven wares. The amnesty of the fair insured Kieran's safety, but if Leila had wandered off—

"Milady!" Fynn hailed Riona from a stall displaying pottery and rushed toward her.

"I've searched all the stalls in the market and asked around," he told her breathlessly, "but no one's seen a small, yellow-haired girl unattended."

Riona's face fell.

"But a cloth merchant said a half-naked, face-painted warrior in naught but a loincloth with such a child perched on his shoulder purchased a length of wool just after daybreak, before his wares were even out. He paid in silver coin."

Could it be Kieran and Leila? Instinct told Riona no. He had no need for cloth and wasn't likely to haul Leila about with him, even if he had left the camp. The child was lost.

"Ye gonna punish them for leaving without asking?" Liex asked, distracted by a lady walking a small dog through the crowd. It was as blue as Gray Macha, dyed to match the lady's finery.

"I should," Riona vowed in self-righteous indignation. "But in truth, I'll be so glad to find her—" She broke off. Leila was a timid child. It wasn't like her to go off like this, especially without Liex. "Let's check back with Finella. If your sister hasn't come back, then we'll go to the hostelry and look for Kieran."

No doubt that's where Gleannmara's lord had gone, she concluded, watching as Fynn disappeared again into the crowd ahead. Kieran would want to line up his allies for a hearing with the high king. Whether he was up to it healthwise or nay, he'd want men of his own station for company, not children, gleemen, and a woman who didn't know her own mind.

The moment she'd smacked him last night, Riona wanted to take it back. He'd done a marvelous thing with his willingness to give up his brooch in gratitude for Dallan's and his company's help. She knew how much the piece meant to Kieran. Touched deeply by the gesture, she was about to burst with pride when he up and kissed her with intimate fervor before God and all their company! What could have possessed the man?

The worse of it all was that his fervor still lingered within her. Faith, it warmed her inside while the sun bearing down on the fairground did so without. Sure, it was a demon of misery, one that robbed her of proper sleep and thought. It provoked the wanton in her, for she had been indecently long in shoving him away. Yet the capitulation of his arrogant pride was deserving of some reward, was it not?

Riona halted abruptly, jerking Liex out of the way of a procession of noblemen. Her seesawing thoughts made her dizzy with dismay. Since Kieran of Gleannmara had come back into her life, her thoughts had been one tumble after another, not a one straightforward and sure.

"*There's* Leila," Fynn shouted, pointing into the thick of the retinue. "And Gleannmara, too."

Looking past soldiers in bright tunics and banner carriers, Riona spied Kieran exactly as the vendor had described him, half-naked and with a painted face. All that graced his fine body, which moved with sinewy ease at a leisurely pace, was his brat. And, Riona hoped, the loin-cloth he'd worn that day by the stream. He looked well—too well to have been as sick as he'd been. Of course, Finella said he'd rebound with his youth and vigor.

Perched on his shoulder was Leila, a laughing, golden sprite swathed in a smaller version of the same attire—no leine, just one frail, white shoulder bared and growing pink in the morning sun.

"Kieran O'Kyle Mac Niall of Gleannmara!"

The full-fledged redress—Kieran, son of Kyle, the grandfather of Niall of Gleannmara—made the bold lord falter and stop. Peering into the crowd, he spied her, and a wide grin overtook his startled expression. Like as not, he'd not been called such since his mother scolded him as a lad. With his free hand, he pointed her out to his companion, a tall strapping man as fair in his own right as Kieran. Royal purple, goldenrod, and black striped his brat, and braid adorned his leine, while gold jewelry sparkled round his neck, arms, and fingers.

"There, sire. There's the Lady Riona of Dromin," Kieran told him.

Sire? Only a provincial king outranked the monarch of a tuath. Riona took a second look at the banners. They were Dalraidi Scots. If so, then this striking figure was none other than Aidan, their new king just ordained by the sainted Columcille himself. She groaned inwardly. And her with her good dress hidden beneath her worn travel attire.

Aidan beckoned to her. "Come, milady, do not shrink into the crowd. I'd meet the brave sister of my dear comrade from Dromin and savioress of my good lord Gleannmara."

Here was the king Kieran had fought for and her brother had died for. Her feelings mixed, Riona had little choice but to approach the jewel-laden hand the Dalraida extended to her. She dipped low and kissed it. It was a warrior king's hand, strong and calloused from wielding weapons, yet blessed by the church.

"Milord," she demurred. Upon rising, she reached for Leila. "Look at you, sweetling. Where are your clothes?"

She cut Kieran a glance as if to ask him the same. None of them were fit company for a provincial king. The talk was that it would be decided at the synod who was Aidan's overlord: the Ulster king of his Irish Dalraidi cousins or the high king of Ireland himself.

"We dropped our clothes off at the laundresses row. 'Twas uncommonly damp this morning."

Kieran's wink put politics out of Riona's mind, filling it with his irascible presence instead. How could the same man be so thoughtless one moment and so tenderhearted the next? No wonder she didn't know her mind where her foster brother was concerned. He changed quicker than the weather.

Leila brushed Riona's cheek with the newly woven fabric, drawing her attention back to the new brat. "What a lovely shade of blue and green. You look like a little princess."

Blushing and smiling, Leila leaned over to reach inside Kieran's brat and draw out another fold of material, which she handed to him.

Kieran nodded toward Liex. "Go ahead, mite," he said to Leila. "You picked it out."

Leila shoved the material at her brother, who let loose a whoop of delight. He shook out the blue and green weave and then wound himself up in the fine wool. "Just like a king's!"

Aidan laughed along with the others. "Sure it is, lad. Sure it is. Your sister has fine taste."

"His is more green, and hers is more blue," Kieran told Riona. "So they can tell them apart. Mind you don't loose the clasp," he warned Liex as the lad skipped about in his kingly attire.

"So where is this blue horse of yours, Gleannmara?" Aidan spoke up. "I and my company need be on our way to session, but my man here will see him stabled properly and show your party to its quarters." He indicated a stablehand in coarse shirt and walnut-dyed trews.

"Quarters?" Riona asked in surprise.

"Aye, we'll be staying as guests of Scotia Minor's new king. Tonight, milady, you shall have a bed, not a damp stretch of ground to rest upon," Kieran promised.

A bed. La, it seemed a lifetime since she'd had such a luxury.

"And you'll join us in the hall for food and merriment," Aidan insisted. "'Tis quite a journey you've had. The shame of it is that your bardic cousin is not here to put it to verse."

Swept along by the stalwart company, Riona tried to absorb all that was taking place so quickly. Yesterday this moment seemed so far away, and now that it was here, she was determined to savor it. Safety. Hope. A real bed.

A cluster of people was gathered about the gleemen's wagon as they approached the encampment of entertainers. Most likely, Marcus was putting on a show of some sort. Unease crawled up Riona's spine, though, as she studied the audience. Mostly soldiers—grim, not laughing as though amused. With equal solemnity, Marcus and Dallan spoke to the leader of the group, who held something in his hand, as if in challenge. Her heart stilled as she recognized two of Maille's leather tunics on the soldiers standing next to the man in charge.

"Ho, what's amiss, friends?" Kieran shouted, cutting a path straight through to the forefront.

He stopped short upon seeing what it was the captain of the king's guard held in his hands. It was the sword Kieran had taken from Maille's guards the night of his escape, the one he'd hidden in the wagon, rather than surrendered to the fair authorities.

"It's against the law to bring a weapon onto the fairground," the captain of the guard told him.

"But it's part of our act," Marcus spoke up. "It's not for use as a weapon."

"And what do you do with it, *gleeman*," one of Maille's men derided, "do you play it or can you make it sing?"

"I do neither, sirrah," the younger of the brothers replied with equal disdain. He held his hands out. "Captain, if you please?"

One bushy, dark brow shooting up skeptically, the officer handed the blade to the entertainer. Half dancing, half walking, Marcus cleared a circle. "Stand back, gentlemen, lest I err and impale someone inadvertently."

Kieran started forward. "Ho, Mar—"

But Marcus tossed the sword straight up into the air. Almost as one, the group moved back another three steps, Gleannmara's lord joining them. Neatly the sword dropped back into Marcus' hand.

"Have you lost your mind?" Kieran blurted out. From the nods and asides made by the onlookers, he was not the only one who doubted Marcus's sanity. "A skewered jongleur is no jongleur at all."

His full focus on the blade shining in the sun, Marcus ignored Kieran. After balancing it in the palm of his hand, blade upright, he tossed it once more into the air, propelling it with both hands. Riona's breath was suspended in her chest as the blade somersaulted, hilt over tip over hilt, and again dropped neatly into Marcus's hand. A muffled clapping echoed around them.

"Is that all you do?" the fair captain asked, not as impressed.

Marcus smiled brightly. "I thought you'd never ask." The entertainer pulled the captain into the circle. "Now stay right here while I fetch the balls."

"For what?" the man declared.

"I intend to juggle the balls while tossing the blade back and forth to you."

"Hah!" The captain backed out of the ring, hands held up. "You *are* a fool in every sense."

"Never mind him." Finella carried a sack with the juggling balls into the ring. "I'll be glad to do the trick, but I'll expect some compensation for this unscheduled act. After all, we usually have time to prepare before attempting something so dangerous."

"Perhaps we might see it when you're scheduled to perform tomorrow," Riona suggested. Faith, neither Finella nor Marcus had juggled a broad sword. If either were hurt—

"Perhaps," Finella agreed, "but filling my husband's cap with coin might make it worth the extra danger." She cut a calculating glance at the crowd and smiled as the men dug into pouches slung from their belts. Dallan whipped off his stocking cap and walked around to collect the tribute.

These people were mad, Riona thought.

Marcus peeked into the cap when Dallan was finished and then hefted it in his hand. "Gentlemen," he chided, tutting at the anxious faces. "Would you toss a weapon like this about for such a paltry sum?" Giving them time to reconsider their contribution, he tossed the sword up and spun it on the tip of his finger. It leaned first one way, then the other. "Humph," he observed aloud. "Not the most balanced weight I've ever hoisted. Here!"

He tossed it toward the captain, who backed away, knocking aside the man beside him, but before the blade fell, Marcus caught the hilt in the palm of his hand and heaved it up on his finger again. When the hat was half again as heavy, he bowed to Finella.

"Good lady, are you ready?"

With a clean gesture, he tossed the sword, hilt first, to Finella. In turn, she threw him one ball at a time. In three quick movements, the balls rotated in their individual circles before him.

"Are you ready, sir?" Finella asked in a stage voice.

"On the count of three, milady," Marcus answered. "One…two… *three!*"

The sword flew hilt first to him. He caught it—or rather, in one movement caught it and propelled it back to her—just in time to toss a ball back into the air. Huzzahs rose loudly this time.

"Once more," Finella announced.

Marcus counted to three and again the exchange went smoothly, far more so than Riona's heartbeat. As Marcus deftly tossed the last of the balls into the sack Finella held open for him, he turned to his audience.

"Come see us at our performance tomorrow, gentlemen, and bring your ladies and purses, for tomorrow my brother and I will each toss a set of the balls while exchanging the sword between us." He grinned wickedly at Dallan. "And if he's slain, the lovely Finella shall be mine."

Finella laughed. "And if you are fatally wounded, Dallan and I shall have peace at last."

"And if Finella suffers mortally, well then, tell your daughters beware."

A laugh struggled from the tightness in Riona's chest, drowned by the uproar of the onlookers. The gleemen troupe could play an audience as well as any instrument they possessed.

Indebted for covering his reckless insistence on keeping the sword, Kieran followed Marcus to the rear of the wagon as the crowd disbursed. Riona couldn't hear exactly what was said, but they grasped arms in a manly fashion. As they broke away, however, Marcus rushed up and planted a kiss on Kieran's cheek. Before the shocked Gleannmara could react, the jongleur bounded away.

"Try that again, you trip-toed nettlewit, and yon sword will spin *you* on it's tip!"

Why Marcus delighted in plucking Gleannmara's temper was beyond Riona. But then, gleemen were known for walking on the edge of life with neither home, nor family, nor country for protection. Face mottled with embarrassment and indignation, Kieran turned to where Aidan and his men chortled with glee.

"I'd speak to these merry people about entertaining us at the Lion's Tooth, but I must be off," Aidan said. "Bring them tonight, Gleannmara." The Dalraidi king turned and nodded to Riona. "Now about that horse."

Gray Macha was of such magnificent proportion that not even his color diminished the regard of Kieran's company. Finella warned the stable hand that the dye wasn't likely to wash out, but the man left with high hopes.

Once the company from Scotia Minor departed and Kieran left to fetch the newly washed leines, Riona and the children gathered around the campfire to partake of the hot, creamy porridge Finella prepared. Fynn, who'd watched the entire scene from a bird's-eye view in a nearby tree, joined them, fingering his siblings' new cloaks in admiration.

"I been thinkin'," he said, helping himself to a cup of the hot meal. "If Dallan'll have me, I could make my way with the people. I made a handful of coin last night doin' this and that."

"Aye, you could, Fynn, but what of us? We need you." Riona was certain it never occurred to Kieran when he purchased the expensive brats for the twins that the older boy would feel slighted. He dealt with warriors, not children.

"Not if you marry Gleannmara."

"I'm here to help Kieran, Fynn, not to marry him."

"He'd never take us anyway. Leastwise not me." Fynn scraped the spoon on the wooden rim of his bowl. I don't even like him."

"I do." Liex chewed his thoughtfully. "Sometimes," he qualified. "Like when he buys me something and isn't mad."

"He just bought you something because he's stuck with us and wouldn't have you look like a ragged gleeman's whelp in front of his high and mighty friends."

"Don't you think that's harsh, lad?" Finella came around from the other side of the wagon, leaving Dallan and Marcus to chat with a few of the onlookers from the earlier performance. "To hear you talk, you think less of our kind than Kieran does."

"That's not true!" the boy declared hotly. "Maithar always said it wasn't the clothes that made the man."

"Your mother was right," Riona agreed. "It's what's in a man's heart that counts. That makes everyone here as good as a king or queen."

"So you're not going to marry him?"

The plea in Fynn's dark eyes was enough to wring her heart wrong side out. So why was she hesitating? She had no intention—

"I should think that the three of you would be plotting to convince the lady to marry him," Finella exclaimed. "He's a bit high-handed and stubborn at times, but I'm a good judge of character, and Gleannmara is a decent man for all this faults."

"I don't care how good he is, he doesn't want us."

"Then make him want you, Fynn me boy."

The elder lad sat up and eyed her warily. "Why?"

Finella leaned forward on her elbows. "Because you and these babes would have a real home, with kin to stand by you." She grimaced, thinking a moment before speaking again in a secretive tone. "I'm going to tell you somethin', lad. My father is lord of a tuath in Connaught. I ran away with Dallan, and, I'm tellin' no lie, I've loved every moment of this life with him and Marcus. But someday, our dream is to raise our babes on land of our own, maybe to own a hostelry." She waved, taking in their surroundings. "This is no life for children. I've lived both and I know."

"Have you ever thought of going home?" Riona asked gently.

Finella blinked away the wet haze that gathered in her eyes. "'Tis too late. Maithar died, and father lost the land in a feud, so I've heard."

Riona's mind raced neck to neck with her heart. "I have land in Dromin. It's near a river ford between two major sliges. If you and Dallan—"

Finella shook her head. "Don't be getting my hopes up, milady. You've not made your own nest yet." She straightened suddenly, staring past Riona.

Turning, Riona saw a man pushing a small cart toward them.

"Excuse me, good people, but I'm looking for a traveling troupe of a man by the name o' Dallan."

Finella rose and put her hands on her hips, eyeing the wares displayed in the vehicle. "Well, you've found them, sirrah. But we've no need for dry goods."

The vendor scowled. Taking off his knit hat, he scratched his shaggy head as though to clear his obvious confusion. "But the lord of Gleannmara gave me a sum for a young man's brat and sent me here for his lady or the young master himself to pick out the cloth."

Astonished, Riona turned to Fynn, who returned her look with one just as blank.

Finella took charge with her usual aplomb and slapped a hand on Fynn's shoulder. "Then bring the cart over, man, for here's the young master himself."

NINETEEN

The size of a small village and built for hospitality, the Lion's Tooth was well prepared, with both private and public accommodations for the inundation of guests. Spread over a great expanse on the well-tended green near the fairgrounds, it brimmed with the comings and goings of its wealthy guests and their retinues at the great hall and its sundry private lodges, including the extra cottars erected on its perimeter for the unusual influx of people brought in by the synod.

Servants scurried to and fro with platters of food from the massive kitchen. Boys tended additional cook fires outside, over which entire sides of venison, beef, and pork roasted. One was protected from rain by a thatched dome, where a massive mechanical spit turned at least thirty wild fowl at once, all under the watchful eyes of the cook staff.

Inside the great hall, skins and kegs of ale were distributed by serving wenches along the low tables and benches, where trencher after trencher of food continued to come in full and leave empty. Dogs growled, establishing their dominion under the tabletops for the sake of the stray cat that braved to enter, while laughter and lively conversation engaged all around.

In a new brat of variegated cloth that boasted all the colors of autumn and a bronze clasp, Fynn walked in among the bruden's revelers, strutting like a prince, his wonder-filled siblings flanking him. This was the kind of scene they may have viewed from the outside while their parents performed in a raised balcony above the floor level, but never from amid the audience itself. Riona doubted they'd even eaten at a table until coming to the abbey.

The heat of so many bodies and the lingering warmth of the late spring day was enough to rob one of breath, she thought as she looked among the revelers for Kieran. Thankfully, she'd been settled with the children in a small, private lodge assigned to the king of Gleannmara's company. They were to join her foster brother in the main hall for their meal.

Across the expanse of the hall, she spied Finella playing her harp. The clear strains of her voice and the notes of the instrument were a contrast to the raucous gaiety of the guests. Just before entering, Riona had seen Dallan and Marcus strolling through the adjoining courtyard, but they'd been too intent on earning coin to notice her.

Feeling decidedly dowdy in her good dress, which was the least worn of her two garments, Riona surreptitiously watched the ladies seemingly float about in their finery. Her limited wardrobe was all she'd needed in the past months she'd spent at Kilmare, although a lady of her station was entitled to at least three times that in size by law. But that was the Brehon Law, not God's, she reminded herself humbly. How easy it was to be distracted by earthly wants rather than needs outside the abbey.

A fair brought out the child in everyone, and she was no different from the children, who'd found a company of merchants vacating a table and were waving her over. At the same moment, she heard Kieran call out to her above the din.

"Riona!"

Seated among a group of richly bedecked peers and not the least self-conscious of his plain travel attire, the lord of Gleannmara rose and left on the table behind him the golden bracelet he wore about his forearm to reserve his place for his return. Shoving his brat behind him so that it hung more in capelike adornment of his leine than for unneeded warmth, he wove his way toward her. A comely red-haired serving maid braved the fierce but fading blue paint on his face and intercepted him. She filled the cup he carried to the brim, offering him even more with her seductive smile.

He took the flirtation in polite stride, but the fleeting glance he cast in Riona's direction betrayed his awkwardness. It secretly pleased her, even though she intended to assure him he owed her no allegiance other than that of a friend. As such she'd risked much to come to Drumceatt to help him clear his name. Riona would count on his friendship and protection in enabling her to provide a home for the

children. To ask more, even though he'd graciously given it in providing the little ones with costly brats fit for noble fosterage, was unthinkable. God's direction was to take only what was needed that there
might be enough for others.

"The bruden's master is pleased with Dallan's people, though
should an honored bard decide to entertain of his own accord, the
opportunity for such an honor would not go untaken," Kieran stipulated.

"I'm certain our gleemen are grateful for yours and Aidan's help in
placing them with this generous audience." Indeed, the performers
would make more here, where mostly scholars of music and poetry
frequented, than from their usual lot of entertaining the merchant class
and peasantry.

"I pay my debts," her foster brother reminded her. "And I am
beholden to them. Two days ago, I wondered that I'd live to see this."

"Finella has a gift with herbs," Riona agreed, "but do not overexert
yourself." She traced the faint lines of strain about his eyes with her fingers. "You look weary."

Would that she looked as fine. In a similar state, she could well
imagine her haggard appearance. God surely favored men in strain and
aging, perhaps because they didn't have enough sense to take care of
themselves. With children and men to watch over, women often didn't
have the choice.

"Wait," she called out, upon seeing the children tear into the platter
of succulent ribs that a boy about Fynn's age placed before them. "We
have much to give thanks for," she chided softly.

Drawing back greasy fingers in obedience, they licked them as they
bowed their heads. The small spot in the big room grew painfully
silent as each one waited for the other to ask the blessing. Leila giggled,
which set Liex off. Fynn, reveling in the role of young master, gave
both siblings a lofty scowl instead of his usual cuff on the head.

Her little family. Pride mingled with delight tugged at the corners of
Riona's lips as she bowed her head. "Heavenly Father, Your benevo-
lence overwhelms us. You bring us safe and sound to this place, place a
roof over our heads, clothes on our backs, food in our bellies, and

nourish our souls with Your boundless love. May all this be proclaimed in your glory. Amen."

"Amen," Liex and Fynn chimed in.

Leila bobbed her head, then looked up and grinned at Kieran.

Hastily, Riona added. "And we thank You, Lord, for Kieran's healing and for *his* protection and generosity."

"I was beginning to wonder if I'd get credit for any of our blessings," her foster brother remarked dourly. "It comes fast enough when something goes awry."

Riona gave him an understanding smile. "Aye, I'm sure God feels the same way all too often."

Instead of a quick retort, Kieran pondered her words a moment but was distracted by the mad scramble for food beside him. "Here, here," he warned. "No one is going to take it away until you've had your fill. Now take a flat of bread and put what you want to eat upon it. Don't eat from the charger."

As if to start over, Leila offered him a large roasted rib with one small bite nibbled from its middle, then primly pulled a round of bread from the stack next to the meat platter.

"You eat it," he chuckled. "I've had my fill. Fynn, my lad, keep an eye on our charges. I'll be with Aidan's company for a while and will meet you all at the lodging later."

If Fynn swelled any more with himself, he'd burst, Riona thought.

"Not much later," she reminded Kieran.

"Aye, *maithar* dearest." With a mocking bow, he danced backward like Marcus and headed to the place held by his armband.

"Hah! He called you *mother,*" Liex chortled with glee.

"When I'm grown," Fynn observed, ignoring his sibling's outburst, "I'll bet I have the ladies trailing after me like Gleannmara does." Envy burned in his dark eyes as he watched yet another serving maid try to fill the lord's already brimming cup.

"Why? Women are a nuisance," Liex objected with all the authority of his six years. "They pinch and give wet kisses. *Most* of them," he added, remembering Riona's presence. "Mothers' kisses are okay."

Riona laughed out loud. "I am much relieved, sir." Leaning over, she kissed the ruddy-cheeked lad atop the head.

The ribs were rubbed in herbs and basted in a tasty vinaigrette, so good that Riona ate more than she was accustomed to. Wild greens and parsnips, venison pastries, and puddings of every description were enough to make even her eyes widen with wonder.

"Let's not forget the alms baskets," she said at the end of the meal, feeling guilty for eating so much. Liex, who was about to toss the rest of his trencher of bread under the table to the mongrel that had already been overcome with tasty bones, dutifully put the remainder in the basket set aside for the poor. There was one at every table. Periodically, the servants replaced them when they were filled. The food would be carried out and distributed to the needy.

"We've always been on the other side of the basket," Fynn remarked, taking a moment to reflect upon his good fortune. He looked at Riona with something akin to worship. Suddenly, he yelped as Liex elbowed him in the ribs. "What, wart?" he said testily.

White showing all around the blue of his eyes, Liex pointed to the entrance. At the head of his party, Lord Maille of Kilmare walked in and casually surveyed the room. He said something to one of the maids and a few moments later, the brewy himself appeared. Kieran watched with interest from his table of comrades, but the wink he gave Riona told her he was not overly anxious.

As far as she was concerned, an enemy in their midst was like a spark on a rug. Aye, it might mean nothing at all. Then again, it could be deadly to all in the household.

The brewy shook his head as if in apology and invited the lord and his party to partake of the victuals. With a stiff nod, Maille turned toward the mass of tables and benches and walked straight to where Riona and the children sat. Riona stiffened as he approached.

"I bid you good day, milady."

"And you, sir," she said, keeping both feet planted on the floor, rather than lifting a polite knee in deference. "I wasn't aware you had friends among the Dalraidi camp."

"Rather no room, I fear," he answered, twirling one of the two forks of his beard around a manicured finger.

She tried not to make the association with a snake's tongue, but given his betrayal of justice, it was impossible. All the man needed was a lisp. Her thoughts scattered in search of a polite and truthful reply, but none that came to her qualified, which only prolonged the silent awkwardness.

"We have a fine guest house," Fynn informed him smugly.

The twins looked about to dive under the table with the mongrel they'd been feeding, but their elder brother refused to be intimidated by the lord.

The smile Maille brandished at the lad's reply put Riona to mind of a dog's raised lip. "How incredible, considering you travel with a redhand."

"Gleannmara is no murderer!" Riona protested before she could stop herself.

"The swine yearns for lavender, when all he has is mud to wallow in," Kieran injected wryly. She hadn't even seen him cross the room, yet there he stood beside her, tall and unbending as a sacred oak. "Indeed, the stench of his deceit grows old, but no less offensive."

Maille's pack of men closed ranks around him at the insult. Likewise, the men who'd been making merry at Kieran's table watched silent and poised to spring at the slightest provocation. The hush was infectious, spreading from table to table until everyone in the lodge was aware of the friction. To break the nonviolent code of the fair was to court not just disfavor but possible death. The crisp, clear notes of Finella's harp marked off the time in heavenly measure of a hellish situation.

Knowing the short wick of her foster brother's temper and the calculation of her distant relative's, Riona rose. "Gentlemen, this matter is to be settled before the high king and his brehons. Until then, it's best that each of you keep to your own camp, unless you trespass with the intention of provoking the other into breaking the law."

Kieran's brow shot up, as if the idea were preposterous. "Crom's toes, is *that* why you and your wolf pack have come here?"

Maille was unflinching at the mockery. "I assure you...and all your friends," he added for the benefit of the formidable group of Dalraidi warlords, "that I came to inquire about lodgings only and stopped to ask my cousin's child how she has fared."

"She's fared well." Kieran's flat-out remark punctuated the conclusion of, at least, Maille's alleged concern.

Maille acknowledged with a stiff nod, but the calculation in his beady gaze raced unchecked.

The spark had not gone out, of that Riona was certain. What more could the man want? What course did he have, now that the avenue of his intent had been blockaded within sight and sound of all?

"If there's nothing else, milord…" Kieran's pause affected Riona's breath as well. "But of course there is!" Kieran motioned toward the table where his comrades sat. "I would be remiss if I didn't invite you and yours to a drink with my good fellows," he bellowed in his most gregarious manner.

Insult Maille expected. This he was clearly not prepared for. "No, I…we…"

"Bring us cups, ladies," Kieran insisted, grinning like a cat with feather in its mouth.

"No," Maille countered with an impatient snap that gave the twins a start. Leila slid off her bench and buried her face in the folds of Kieran's brat. Liex sidled closer to Fynn, who was as ready to leap into action as any of Gleannmara's able allies.

The harp strings counted…one…two…three…four…

"I thank you for your hospitality, but we need to find suitable lodging for our company," Maille finished with an upturn of relief in his voice.

Fynn proved it premature. "Your lodgings are at the Boars Head, milord, where you've been these last two days. Or have ye lost your way?"

Snickers echoed throughout the room, triggering a rise of color to Maille's neck and face. He aimed a daggerlike stare at Fynn, but the boy was as intoxicated with smug bravado as Gleannmara. Riona wanted to shake them both for baiting Maille like a couple of bristling hounds with a bear. Maille was no bear. He'd never charge headlong into them. He'd lie in wait like a serpent and strike when they least expected it.

"How is it that a lowly gleeman's orphan sups with the nobles?" The words were minced with the acid of Maille's voice.

There was a short scramble of notes from the harp above before it picked up melody once more.

With a sly tug of his lips, Kieran rallied. "I invited him as my guest, no different than you."

The war of words about to erupt was more than Riona could handle alone. *Heavenly Father!* she prayed, eyes wide shut.

Maille let the insult slide. "You can dress them any way you wish, Gleannmara, but their blood's still that of a gleeman, the same as yours is a redhand whether it bears royal rings or a serf's calluses."

Kieran moved toward Maille, his broad grin all that allowed Riona her next heartbeat. Clapping the man on the back, he started walking the lord toward the door. "I bid you luck in finding that lavender, Kilmare, for you're in sore need of it."

Fynn started to make a snorting noise, but Riona seized his nose, pinching it off. "Ow!" he gasped, but further objection was silenced by her warning glare.

As the men of Kilmare made their departure without further incident, Riona gathered up the children. "Come along now. We've real beds tonight and a bath awaits."

"We can't all bathe at the same time." Fynn's practicality was sound, but his reason remained to be seen. Not that Riona couldn't guess. He wanted to remain with the men a while.

"Now *there's* an entertaining thought." Kieran's wicked whisper startled Riona from behind.

She gave him a sharp look. "Say no more, milord, for I'm annoyed with you enough as it is."

The man looked dumbstruck. "Why? Did we not send Maille scampering off with his tail tucked between his legs?"

"His tail was not between his legs, Kieran, he was gnawing on it and plotting to get even, and you with a prideful head long on tongue and short on wit." At Fynn's snicker, she nailed him as well. "And this foolish pup one bark from the same." She narrowed her gaze at the lad. "Do you think you can chase your tail and stay clear of trouble till Leila and I are done with our bathing?"

"Aye," Fynn replied, looking at the floor. Liex bobbed his head solemnly.

Satisfied, Riona gave Kieran one last piece of her mind. "You are accountable to the example you set for these children, sir. Make it a good one."

"They are not *my* brood. Besides, they need know how to stand up for themselves."

How could he be so self-absorbed? She'd so hoped his heart was changing toward the children. His flippant dismissal added sting to her reply. "Nay, but you *are* a king," she reminded him sharply, "one, it appears, who needs learn the difference between standing up for himself and openly inviting his own downfall. Good night, sir." With a defiant tilt of her chin, she spun away, herding Leila toward the door and leaving Kieran of Gleannmara to the ribbing of his companions.

The grounds outside the great hall of the bruden were aglow with soft light from strategically placed lanterns. The mingle of oil and wood smoke filled the night air with an assuring presence Riona hadn't known since leaving Kilmare. As she and Leila approached the guest house, with its own faint wisp of warm welcome hovering above the roof, one of the servants hailed them.

"The bath is ready, milady, and I've fresh stones in the hearth to reheat it."

"Thank you, lass. I'm sure it will be divine," Riona called back. Divine. Heavenly. A godsend. A blessing. A treat. A delight. The words kept on coming as she opened the plank door to the lodging and, taking the lamp off the hook beside it, stepped inside. She gasped as the light filled the interior, illuminating a terrible maleficence. The derguds had been pulled from both bed cubicles, and the stuffing from them now covered, like a snowfall of straw and feathers, the green birch leaves that were strewn on the floor. Moving in a trance of disbelief, Riona looked into each of the imdas, taking in the chaos in each portioned space.

In Kieran's sleeping chamber his belongings had been emptied from his travel sack. His bedstead was bare, save the wad of blankets and linens that had been torn from the mattress. The same was true in the imda she and the children shared. What few belongings they'd brought with them were scattered in the disarray of blankets and linens. Riona picked up a skin-covered pillow that was still intact and crushed it to her chest as she kicked her way through the tangle of bed linens and walked to the barrel-shaped tub next to the low-burning hearth. As she tested the water, she saw that it, too, was filled with debris.

Her nice warm bath. She stared down at the steaming water and did all that she could.

She started to cry.

TWENTY

A voice in the darkness echoed quietly. "Nothing, milord."

"Nothing?" Lord Maille paced in the moonlit glen, frustration and anger battling for his control. *Nothing?* He sneered at the man in the shadows. "You, sir, are a poor coward and a worse thief."

"I cannot steal what is not there, milord. Nor is it my fault that the Dalraida was a better judge of Dromin and Gleannmara's swords than our patron's henchmen."

Maille glared at the insolence. Men got a bellyful of dagger for less insolence. "So you dare muster courage from kinship?" He raised a gloved fist. "Then muster this in your yellow blood. If I am caught, I will *not* go to the gallows without company."

"If you continue to toy with Kieran, he will squash you beneath his boot like the rodent you are." The shadowy figure crossed his arms over his chest. "Has it not occurred to you that the reason you have not been charged with any crime is because Gleannmara doesn't have this evidence of your involvement?"

"Or doesn't know he has it," Maille countered sharply.

"As for me, I'll have no more of this whimsy. It's over. We all took a risk. We failed."

"It is *not* over." Maille growled the words, his lips pulled back from his teeth like those of a cornered dog. Except he was not in a corner. Not yet. "The fair provides ample opportunity for the elimination of one's enemy."

"Not by *my* hand. I'm done. I met my part of the bargain."

"And were well rewarded, just like that sniveling priest," Maille reminded the man. "'Tis *my* reward that's missing." He ground his foot into the ground as if Senan were beneath it. "I can't believe that sniveling priest let it out of his sight to begin with. All he had to do was deliver it. No blood stained his hands."

"Nay, he merely sold children into slavery. I suppose there's not enough reward in God's work."

"Tadgh took care of disposing of the abbot for him, and he's dead… drowned, according to that crone of his, at the tip of Gleannmara's sword. The child-slaver will be the new abbot, whilst I scramble to cover his bumbling." Everyone involved was clear except him. The idea gnawed at Maille, spreading its vile, green infection.

"Blood money disguised as holy water. Hah, the irony!"

The wry humor in his companion's voice grated Maille's already black humor. He'd kill the man on the spot without regret, but his accomplice had not outlived his usefulness. He would have access to Gleannmara's company that Maille could not hope for.

Meanwhile the lord's payment and connection to the plot rested in that missing vial—diamonds worth a fortune and an incriminating message with *his* name on it. This mess would never be over for the lord as long as that vial was unaccounted for. Nor was he about to let his coconspirators enjoy their fruits while he lived haunted by a condemnation that might surface today or years hence. He pointed a warning finger at his indifferent colleague.

"Stay close. You are no more finished than I."

"Let it go, Maille. Is your payment worth your life?"

"My peace of mind is."

The man in the shadows chuckled. "Then do thyself a favor and take your life now, for such as we will *never* have peace of mind."

"You know not who you deal with."

"I know him exactly. Which is why, should anything happen to me, more evidence than that in a missing vial lies waiting to expose you." The conspirator made a mock bow. "If I have no peace of mind, then neither shall you or Senan."

Maille watched his companion walk away, oblivious to the branches that snagged the chiefly folds of his new brat—as if he were untouchable. The lord's lips took on a cynical curl. Such would be his downfall. That, however, would have to wait until later. Relieving Scotia Minor of its new king and finding that vial were first on Maille's agenda. A new plan was already in place to accomplish the first. 'Twas the last that vexed the Ulster Lord most.

A bath was such a silly thing to cry over given how Riona had survived the events of the past few days, but bawl she did until Kieran ran into the shelter, demanding to know what was amiss. His eyes told him more than Riona ever could. Leila, who'd run to fetch him, hugged Riona's legs while Kieran took her into his arms. The consolation produced more tears, so that even her sniffled, "I...I'm s...sorry" was barely intelligible.

At Kieran's bellowing summons, staff soon hurried into the techleptha, filling the round, thatch-domed dwelling and working their magic on it. New derguds were brought in while the remnants of the old mattresses were swept up and carried out. Clean linens replaced new, and soon the bath was once again prepared with warm, scented water free of debris.

Now the outraged Gleannmara sat outside with some friends while Riona tried to soak away the tension and dust of their hard-pressed journey. She could hear their voices as they discussed the possibilities for the vandalism, for that was what it had been—cruel, malicious destruction. She huddled in her bath, feeling violated.

Their enemy was either searching for something or he was a madman. Given their few belongings, which were mostly carried upon their persons, the latter appeared most likely. That someone would destroy for the sake of destruction, without rhyme or reason, chilled Riona to the core. She thanked God again and again that neither she nor the children were present, lest they be disemboweled like the mattresses and pillows.

"There is a connection here," Kieran speculated grimly. "I feel it, but for my life, I cannot fathom what it is. This was amiss the very moment we spoke with Maille in the bruden."

"So he kept you occupied while his minion did this?" Aidan queried. "Think, man, have you anything of which Maille has need?"

"Aye, my life. I walked into some sort of power play involving the abbot's death and became the scapegoat."

Through the painful daze of a headache Riona tried to salvage her memory of the happenings as well, but nothing of significance emerged. She listened to the men reflect upon Kieran's enemies. Maille and who else? And why Maille? What did it matter to him who killed Fintan? Senan's zeal to find his brother's murderer was understandable, though unfounded. But Kieran, for all his pride, had many friends, for beneath his arrogance lay a good heart.

Riona recalled how tenderly he'd soothed her. His strength invited her to become lost in it and all it promised to appease. In his arms it was easy to forget his quick temper and eagerness to wage war.

"If I could but find this brigand, I'd rip off his head with my bare hands," Kieran said with chilling vehemence beyond the closed door of the sleeping house.

Riona seized the slip of scented soap she'd brought with her and lathered her hair with a vengeance, as if to wash away any inclination toward the man. Forgiveness was foreign to him. He was good and fair to those who deserved it and equally deadly to those he judged unworthy. No matter how much she was inclined toward Kieran of Gleannmara, she would not have a man who saw himself as God's equal in dealing with his fellow humankind, much less one who held that same God in contempt.

Leila was too tired to even play in the water when Riona bathed her and dressed her for bed. Her golden hair, still damp from washing, was spread upon the deerskin covered pillow and before Riona could tuck her in the little girl slept in trust that nothing and no one could harm her with Kieran of Gleannmara outside her chamber door.

The boys opted to bathe in a nearby creek and came in as Riona put more stones from the fire in the barrel to reheat the water. After checking their necks and ears with a motherly eye, Riona called Kieran to tell him his bath was waiting and tucked her squirming charges into the other bed in her knee-walled imda. Unlike their sister, they were not content to close their eyes until they'd heard a story.

"Tell us about the rich boy who had to sleep with pigs," Liex suggested.

It was one that impressed all the children. Never having had privilege, it was inconceivable to them that the prodigal son would waste it away. The boys gave poor Brother Domnall a devil of a time as to a believable reason the rich boy would do such a thing. It was simply beyond their understanding and, from his frustration, Domnall's as well. They'd driven the poor cleric into telling them some of the Celtic legends he so disdained, what with the heathen content, but the man preferred a grudging telling of fantasy to the exasperation evoked by the holier tale.

Unlike Domnall, Riona had possessed the patience to explain to the children how, no matter what social status a person was born to, there were blessings and curses. How she missed the cantankerous little brother and the rest of her holy family at the abbey. She wondered if she'd ever again know the abbey's peace and the predictability that, admittedly, sometimes drove her to distraction.

"If I were that lad, I'd have taken regular baths, studied books, and obeyed the rules to live like he did," Fynn observed. He folded his hands behind his head and stared up dreamily at the dark rafters of the building.

"I don't like soap," Liex stated emphatically. "But I used it tonight," he added at the suspicious arch of Riona's brow.

Smiling, Riona began the story. As it unfolded, so did the excitement coiled tightly in the youngsters until their eyelids began to bob, dipping lower and lower each time. There was not even enough energy left to launch the debate of what they would or wouldn't do at the end. They drifted off to sleep blessed with the assurance of the forgiveness the words were meant to impart.

"Riona?"

Kieran stood in the opening of the partitioned area, a blanket wrapped about him in deference to modesty. His wet hair dripped as he brushed it away from his face with a free hand.

"Have you more of Finella's concoction?"

Alarm shot through her. He'd not ask for the bitter brew unless his leg was worse.

"Aye, I'll fetch it," she whispered, so as not to disturb the sleeping babes. Reaching under her bed, she retrieved the skin, which thankfully hadn't been destroyed.

Kieran sat on the couch at the end of his bed as she entered his imda. She handed him the skin and knelt before him.

"Let me have a look at the wound." With authority, she moved the blanket up, exposing the shank of his leg where the nasty swipe had festered. "Hand me the lamp."

"'Tis sore, that's all." Kieran took the light from its peg and gave it to her.

It bathed his length of thigh, casting a glow on the thin, golden bristle. Soaking had removed most of the scab. The flesh had knitted with an imposing red welt, the fevers having burned away the streaks of spreading infection. Still, Riona had tended enough wounds to know infection could still rear its ugly head if it were not properly cared for.

"I'll make a salt poultice to draw out the poison," she decided aloud.

"Your touch is enough."

Riona glanced up in surprise at the huskiness in his voice. "You push your good fortune too far, Kieran, always flirting with danger."

As she rose and hung the lamp back on its peg over his head, his hands closed about her waist. He pulled her closer and nuzzled her hair, which spilled about her shoulders. His face brushed her arm, an insignificant gesture in itself, yet the effect was far from it. She stepped away as if he were flame to her kindling.

"Riona…" He rose and reached for her.

Sensing rather than looking for the blanket to fall, Riona grasped it and shoved it around him. "For decency's sake, milord, your cover—"

Then it was held, not as much by her hands as by the press of his body against hers. Her only thought to see him wrapped, Riona gathered the blanket around him, folding her arms across his back as he did the same to her. He inhaled the breath he crushed from her, sealing it between them with his lips. Unrelenting yet tender, the kiss cast an intoxicating spell that bade her sway in sweet surrender. Only her mind rebelled—and even that was halfhearted in comparison.

He brushed her cheek with his own and murmured in her ear. "This forgiveness you speak of, sweetling, will you practice it with *this* prodigal?"

Riona clenched her eyes shut as if that might shut out the confusion assaulting her. The situation with Kieran was different. He was not
her son nor she his father. He owed her no allegiance, part of her
insisted, while another paused to reconsider.

"You have never been mine to—" A tiny gasp of pleasure at the
seductive tug of her ear lobe made her stop. She pulled away before
she leaned into the contact. "Y-you've never been mine to condemn or
forgive."

Cupping her chin, Kieran turned her face back to his and peered
deeply beyond her wary gaze. Afraid he might see her wavering
defenses about to crumble, she pulled away and turned her back to
him. Cold rushed in to take the place of his warmth. She crossed her
arms against its assault.

"I have always been yours, Riona, and you mine."

His hands upon her shoulders invited her to turn back to him, to
go into his arms. She shivered involuntarily. Deep inside, his words
rang true. There was a bond between them. She'd attributed it to that
of a sibling, yet the woman only he could awaken in her knew better.
She couldn't deny it any more than she could accept it.

Riona started at the sharp knock on the door. Alarm battled with
thanksgiving as she hastened toward it. "For heaven's sake, cover yourself!" she whispered over her shoulder.

With a muffled oath, Kieran scrambled behind her as she opened
the door. It was her uncle and his birds, each claiming a shoulder for
itself.

"Uncle Cromyn...I mean, Father Cromyn." Riona prayed Kieran
was not standing mother-naked behind her out of sheer obstinacy.

"A blessed evening to you, niece," the man answered, touching his
shoulders absently. "I should have left my pets with Brother Ninian,
but I'd feel as though my head were missing without them."

Riona knew exactly what he meant, for her mind seemed to have
taken its leave without her consent. She met his benevolent smile
blankly.

"Has Kieran retired for the evening?"

Thank goodness, she thought upon realizing the lord of Gleannmara was no longer in sight. "Nay, I believe he was just readying to lie down. Is there something amiss?"

"May I come in?"

With a nervous laugh, she backed away and motioned him in. "Forgive me. This night has been trying at best. Someone ransacked our lodge and belongings while we supped. I've just gotten the children to bed. They were so wound up with the excitement and I—"

"So I heard. Ah, Kieran, there you are." Cromyn stepped past her to grasp Kieran's arm firmly. "I know you have already applied for an audience with the king, but I was able to speak to his clerk on your behalf at vespers tonight. Because of what transpired here, he is arranging for the high king to hear you in the court session after the day ordered for games and races."

"Thank God!" Riona rejoiced aloud. Reaching Drumceatt was a considerable accomplishment, but working their plight into the king's schedule of hearings was yet another, especially given the political nature of the matters to be settled at the synod.

"I'm glad to hear it. Maille is pressing me hard with his charges and now this." Kieran had pulled on his tunic and draped his brat around him. He motioned for Cromyn to take a seat on the couch at the foot of the imda. "Though that hardly gives me time to assemble a decent retinue of my own," he reflected to no one in particular.

"Given the circumstances of your arrival, I don't think it will be held against you, son."

No noble, much less a king, would embark upon travel without his own retinue of domestic and military men. *Nor would a lady,* Riona thought, painfully aware of how plain her simple shift and overdress were. But then she hardly needed a lady-in-waiting to see to her hastily assembled bag of belongings, nor one to attend to her personal appearance and needs.

"Truth, I'd best be going. Tomorrow we again argue the plight of the bards against those clerics and nobles who'd have them banished forever. The good Father of Iona himself will speak, and I wish not to miss a single one of his words."

"I will be there," Kieran promised.

Columcille was one of the few priests the lord of Gleannmara favored. Perhaps Kieran identified with Columcille's rebellion in his younger days. The young prince-turned-priest had taken up the sword to avenge a violation of sanctuary by the late High King Diarmait. With his Niall clan, the princely priest had defeated Tara's ruler. Both Riona's and Kieran's families had fought with their Niall kin.

"I think the Father hopes to pull a few of the bards teeth rather than banish them in entirety," Cromyn observed.

"Given the antagonism of the nobles who've suffered their gnashing satire and imposition on good hospitality, our poetic druids cannot go on unfettered. It is time that something be done," Kieran agreed, "but to banish them is to banish our heritage. I have all faith that if a fair decision can be made, it will come from Iona."

Such was the regard for Columcille that the church officials disregarded the mandatory punishment for his transgressions: excommunication. The kings offered him the high throne of Ireland, but he'd humbly refused it. Filled with remorse for the lives his stubborn part in the rebellion had cost, he accepted a penance to leave his beloved Ireland forever and took his faith and fervor to Scotia Minor. There, he'd ordained Aidan as the first Christian king of Scotland in the eyes of God and man. A legend in his own time, a prince schooled in the bardic tradition, and a priest of the One God Riona was certain, Columcille's defense of Ireland's historians and poets would be as fair and moving as it was eloquent.

Yet her reason for wanting to see the holy father had nothing to do with politics or bards. Her desire was of a more spiritual nature. It was reputed that Columcille's oneness with God was such that he could heal with a touch or a prayer…and that an angel of God accompanied him. If either were true, then was it not possible that he could heal Leila of the malady that had inhibited her speech upon her parents' death? Riona had to try to get the little girl close enough to Columcille to find out, despite the multitudes that flocked to him.

"I shall be there as well, with the children," she told her uncle, "for it's a rare opportunity to see and hear a person endowed with such godly grace and wisdom. In fact…" Riona hesitated, loathe to impose after Cromyn had already helped them get an audience with the high king. "Uncle, do you think it's possible to get an audience with Iona for Leila?"

The priest glanced in the imda where the child slept solemnly. "I will do what I can, Riona." His tone was not encouraging. Of course there were as many gathered here to see Columcille as the high king.

"That is all I ask," she said thankfully, rising to brush his ruddy cheek with her lips. "Good night, uncle."

As Kieran followed Cromyn out, Riona hastened into the imda where the children slept, oblivious to the grave matters to be decided on the morrow. It was another gift to sleep so soundly without thought to fear—or to matters of the heart and spirit.

She climbed into the narrow bed she shared with Leila, gently easing the spread-eagled child over against the plank partition that separated their chamber from Kieran's. Forgiveness... She settled against the soft pillow and stared at the dancing shadows cast by the single lamp outside the stall. How her own words now turned against her. She tossed over on her side as the wooden bar of the door dropped into its cradle, signaling Kieran's return. She held her breath so that she heard his when he blew out the lamp.

Darkness closed over the room, silent but for the soft pad of Kieran's footsteps and the creak of his bed as he climbed into it. His breath caught sharply, and a short oath escaped as he fell against the mattress, reminding her that she'd forgotten his poultice.

Heavenly Father, she prayed in exasperation. Given the strength of his ardor, he was in more need of a cold bath than a warm poultice. Given his words, there was a need even more pressing than the physical, one she could easily assuage if she could bring herself to do so. Never did Riona think the prodigal's story would apply to her in this particular way. There was no need to pray. She knew what she had to do. Her voice was soft in the silence.

"Kieran?"

"Aye?" His answer neither encouraged or disheartened.

She bolstered her resolve to do what she believed in, no matter how reluctant.

"I know you didn't lead Heber away to his death. He joined you of his own accord."

"That doesn't lessen the pain."

He spoke truth. Riona heard it in his voice and felt it in her heart, knifing without relent. She swallowed a sob at the picture conjured in her mind of Kieran holding her brother on a bloody battlefield. How horrible it must have been for him. How heartbreakingly horrible.

"I just wanted to say…"

"Yes?"

She placed her hand on the plank separating them, wanting to touch him, imagining that her fingers and palm were pressed to his. "I forgive you."

Silence followed as she waited to hear Kieran's voice, to know that it meant something to him, that it comforted him in some way.

She heard nothing but a slow release of breath and a small, strangled sound from his throat, as if he tried to speak but the words were too crowded to leave him.

She trailed her fingers down the wall and sighed. It was a wonder how those three words she'd released into the night could lighten the invisible weight that mercilessly crushed her heart. A wonder how the sound of Kieran's emotion carried more meaning than any words he could have uttered in response.

Three words had been enough to ease his anguish.

She nearly floated off the mattress with a relief that paved the way for one of the first restful nights she'd had in too long a time.

TWENTY-ONE

K ieran was up and gone the next morning before Riona awakened. Remembering that Columcille was to speak on behalf of the bards at the day's session, she hastily roused the children and put on the least worn of her dresses. The shabbiest served beneath as an undershift. The two would be warm with the summer temperatures closing in, but given last night's intrusion and her lack of an attendant to guard her belongings, it was necessary. With her small bag of possessions tied to her waist, she mustered her charges toward the inn.

After bracing themselves with porridge and cream, they made their way toward the hill where the session took place. The way from the Derry abbey was strewn with gifts left for the blessing of its founder. One of the pilgrims told her Columcille's entourage had already passed.

Riona's heart sank. Her inadvertent indulgence of sleeping in a real bed had caused her to miss her chance for Leila to be blessed and perhaps cured of the affliction that kept her from speaking. As she made her way with the crowd, thick with robed clerics and richly garbed nobility, Riona held tightly to the hands of the twins. Clearly wishing he were attending the fair proper rather than the synod, Fynn moped behind so that she continually had to urge him to keep up.

The session took place on an incline ablaze with the colorful banners of the notable attendees. Even if Gleannmara's blue and gold were among them, Riona would be vexed to find Kieran in the crowd. Nearby, a druidic master leaned heavily on his staff as he made his way closer, his entourage of students in his wake. They echoed a historical stanza in perfect timing as they walked, their lessons continuing even in transit.

"Dallan!" Fynn's hearty hail rose above the excited murmur of the crowd, drawing Riona's attention to where Dallan, Marcus, and Finella awaited the much-anticipated session.

"What goes on?" the boy shouted, much to the annoyance of bystanders. Riona reached for him and pinched his shoulder, eliciting a howl of surprise. "What?" he protested.

"Leash that wagging tongue or I'll pinch you again," she promised under her breath.

"Wag it while the bard of Iona speaks," Marcus warned, "and I'll cut it out and keep it in my pocket."

"You're looking well, milady," Finella said to Riona. "I take it your lord saw things returned to order?" Having performed until late, the harpist and her company had heard of the intrusion.

"Aye, very much so. And he has an audience with the high king after the games this week," Riona answered lowly. "And me looking like I've been dragged the full way here."

"You were." Finella gave her a mischievous wink. "We must go marketing when this is done and find something suitable for a king's reception. I'd rather fancy being a lady-in-waiting to one as gracious as yourself."

"I'd be honored, Finella, as a friend though, rather than your mistress."

Riona was truly touched by Finella's offer, yet she was pressed to warrant much enthusiasm for the prospect of success. There would be materials fit for a queen here, but two days was not enough time to make a dress of them. It would take a host of seamstresses working day and night to come up with something suitable.

"Look, there's Aidan, the king of the Dalraidi," Dallan said in a hush of anticipation.

Trumpets blasted and silken banners glistened in the sun as the bronzed warrior king paid respect to the high king and took a seat of honor nearby with his entourage. They were at such a distance that banners were the only way to discern who was who. The gold torques, bracelets, and brooches adorning the royal gathering were enough to blind the sun with its own reflection, and every color on God's green earth was represented in the noble display of many-folded brats. That she would walk before that same company in a few days was enough to turn Riona's knees to water. Give her the simplicity and quiet of the abbey any day rather than all this pomp and fuss.

"What of Columcille?" she asked, scanning the parade of dignitaries before them.

"He was received by Aedh first." Dallan pointed to a group of churchmen on a dais of honor. It was difficult to make out one from another, for like their secular counterparts robed in druidic white across from them, they were clustered in one body.

"I wonder if Iogenan is present?" Marcus remarked to no one in particular.

"If Aidan's brother *is* here, he's keeping his head low," Finella answered. "Imagine how it feels to be passed by on the order of an angel."

Fynn's attention was pricked. "An angel? I heard Columcille appointed Aidan."

Finella lowered her voice. "Aye, he did, but the good father's favor leaned to Aidan's brother."

"If an angel appeared to me, he'd not have to smite me to have his way."

"Angels strike people?" Liex exclaimed, saucer-eyed at Marcus's remark.

"Only when one refuses to do God's will," Riona assured the boy. "Columcille thought Iogenan the right king for Scotia Minor, but God sent an angel to the father telling him that Aidan was the divine choice. When the father of Iona hesitated, the angel struck him with a scourge that, I've heard, remains to the day."

Leila solemnly mumbled something to her youngest brother, who in turn translated. "She says Seargal would never hit anyone."

"Nay, he just wets the bed." Fynn's snicker gave way to another yelp as Riona pinched him in warning.

With her other hand, she stroked the golden head that a shamed Leila tried to bury in her skirts. If only Columcille would see the child, she knew in her heart it would help. *Heavenly Father, I cannot arrange this on my own, but if You would, show me the way to Your blessed servant for this child's sake. The scar of her loss is deep, and my love alone is not enough to heal it.*

The reception of the provincial kings was followed by that of the lesser tuath kings as Riona isolated her thoughts to prayer, but when Kieran of Gleannmara was announced, her prayful countenance turned to shock. There marched her foster brother bedecked as finely as his colleagues. Even standard bearers carried the blue and gold banners. But how? she wondered. Who? Strain as she might, she could not make out the identity of the standard bearers.

"He cuts a fine figure, milady," Finella commented in a sly aside.

His royal blue-and-gold-fringed brat billowing like full sail from a tall and mighty mast, Kieran proudly took his place among the nobles of his rank. Riona could make him out no better than the high king or Aidan, yet her mind's eye missed no detail. The rakish fall of his shoulder-length hair; his clean-shaven, angular jaw and cleft chin; those sharp, hazel eyes mirroring flecks of brown, blue, green, and gold; the undoubtedly proud yet wicked tilt of his lips...

She knew her foster brother by heart.

Suddenly, the dozens of low conversations about them stilled as though a blanket of hush had fallen over the crowd. From the midst of the church assembly, Columcille rose and took command of the scene. With a voice as clear as it was eloquent, this man with salted gold mane and high brow shaved in druidic tonsure began to speak. His strong voice rang in Riona's ear like a melody of rhythm and rhyme, as if he stood next to her. Its effect upon the crowd was as supernatural as had been reputed. Fynn and the twins stood transfixed, as did Dallan and company. Not even an infant squalled from want, for here was a message to fill every need.

The sun worked along its arch above them, marking off a time that seemed to stand still in the hearts and souls of all who listened. The Holy Spirit moved through the audience, working its spell, swelling hearts with love and pride and thanksgiving as Columcille spoke. Would the children of the One God turn out the historians who preserved their past and heritage, the same historians God Himself deemed fit to use to prepare the way for His Son's legacy? Would the people turn all away because a few abused the honor of their station?

The song echoed to the surrounding hills, a cry for the preservation of knowledge under conditions that upheld God's laws, not man's indignation.

Tears and cheers broke the loud silence following the end of Columcille's speech. People embraced each other, clergy and bard, master and servant, all in the name and glory of the One God, whose law was knowledge and therefore sacred to every heart, mind, and soul. The high king had not spoken, but clearly the decision had been made, the bards saved. Only the details remained to be worked out.

After a recess was called Riona moved with a tide of confusion as the crowd disbursed. Fynn handily disappeared into the masses along with Dallan and his company. Those who flocked to see the saintly champion of the bards made a chance encounter with him impossible. Holding on tightly to the twins' hands lest she lose them as well, Riona followed the flow headed toward the Lion's Tooth. When they arrived, Riona didn't attempt to find a table in the main hall, but left the twins with orders to remain at the guest cottage with the door bolted until she returned with some food from the huge kitchen in the back.

There would be other days of session, she consoled herself as she waited in line with the serving wenches for bread and a small round of cheese. Perhaps she would have to wait for Uncle Cromyn to arrange an audience for Leila with Columcille. Upon reaching the front of the line and speaking to the cooks' helper, Riona was given a tray to carry the food back to the children, and a young fire tender was sent along to carry a pitcher of honeyed ale for her.

Heavens, she thought, stifling a yawn as she wove through the crush of hustling guests, servants, and the menagerie of animals accompanying them about the inn yard. Would she ever catch up on her rest from her weeks' travel as a fugitive? Sure, the softness of the mattress beckoned her more than the food on her tray. Perhaps after they ate she might convince the twins to take a nap.

The door of the cottage was open when she returned, despite her orders to the contrary. Rather than rush in angrily, however, Riona stood there agape. The standards of Gleannmara flew on either side of the entrance. In the back, men wrestled with what looked like the frame of a tent. With more and more arriving by the day at the fair, the inn was obviously overrun.

"Kieran?" she called, hesitating at the doorway.

"Wait!" Liex darted out of the cottage to stop Riona from entering. "Close your eyes."

Leila was right behind him, eyes twinkling with mixed mischief and delight.

"I can't put the food down. The dogs will—"

"I'll take the food." Kieran filled the doorway, his expression as unrevealing as the children's were expressive.

He looked magnificent. No longer was he attired in his traveling clothes, but in an elegant tunic of fine linen cinched at his trim waist with a braided royal sash the same hue as his brat. The Gleannmara brooch sparkled where it held the massive folds of fabric at his shoulder. Golden arm bracelets gleamed against the tanned sinew of his forearms, matching the intricately engraved torque about his neck. He looked every inch the king he was.

"How—"

"The answer lies within, milady." He took the tray and motioned her inside the cottage.

Given the mixed signals, she hesitated a moment. On leaving the glare of the noonday sun, it took a few moments for Riona's eyes to adjust. Someone stood at the foot of Kieran's imda. As her eyes adjusted, she recognized the man.

"Colga!"

Shock kept her from saying more to her cousin. Her attention honed in on the brooch he wore—that of the Dromin chief, worn by Heber and their father before him. So it was done. Her people had chosen Colga as their new leader. Life stopped for no one.

"As glad as I am to see you, Riona, it's under a devilish shadow." Apology filled his gaze as well as his voice.

"You lost no time in claiming Heber's birthright." There was no condemnation in her voice, just resignation.

"There was none to waste." But for brown hair, rather than Heber's raven black, Colga resembled her brother a great deal. Their voices were even similar. "When the news of Gleannmara's murder charge reached us, someone needed to take control for the king."

This drew her from her melancholy. "How came it to you?"

"Brother Ninian of Kilmare sent a mounted courier straight away to Gleannmara."

Dear Brother Ninian. Surely he was one of God's earthly angels for all the help he'd been. "Kieran's rechtaire saw the lord's things packed anon, as would any steward worth his salt, and we left as soon as the issue of the Dromin chieftaincy was resolved."

Numbly, Riona nodded. "Benin is a very capable chief of the house. He runs it as if it were his own, exactly as Kieran's parents would wish."

She made no attempt to pull away as Colga seized her arms. It was hard to believe what she saw and heard anyway: "Riona, it's my fault Heber died."

"What?" Her mind began to race at the pain-filled rush of words. Bran had said as much, but for Colga to admit it to her face—

"I was vilely tricked," he went on. "I should have been guarding the rear flank with Heber, but was lured away in the fog, baited by a few, while the many swarmed down upon him from the other side of the glen. When the mist cleared, it was too late. Riona—" he gave her an earnest shake—"as God is my witness, I did not mean for Heber to die. I beg you to forgive me."

"Colga, I—"

Riona broke off, at a loss as to what to think, much less say. Never would she understand a warrior's mind, but she'd already forgiven Kieran and thusly, Colga, and all the men who'd sallied forth for the glory of battle and profit. Their hearts were good.

"Of course you're forgiven, Colga, but in truth, I have never held you accountable for Heber's death. It was just a shock to see the Dromin brooch…just a shock," she echoed weakly.

"You will have a place of honor in the Dromin chief's lodge for as long as you wish."

It was a generous offer, one Colga was under no obligation to make. The lodge went with the title, neither passed on solely from inheritance, but by election.

"I have property of my own, sir. Besides, it is your right, not mine."

"God bless you, cousin!" Colga embraced her tightly and held her in his relieved enthusiasm an undetermined time before she felt a tug on her skirt.

Riona closed her hand over Leila's as a sign for the child to wait. "And what of Bran? Have you heard from him?"

Colga shook his head. "Not until Kieran told us of him. We left as soon as Ninian's courier arrived." He added with a chuckle, "Bran the bard in a boatload of orphans. Would that I'd seen that. It must have settled on him sorely not to come to Drumceatt."

Riona remembered Bran's baleful look as the captain shoved the wickerwork boat from the shore. He and Siony would be at Gleannmara by now, and Kieran's rechtaire would take it all in his stride.

Leila tugged on her skirt again, this time earning Riona's full attention. The child pointed into the partitioned imda containing the two beds. On the boys' was a familiar trunk, laid open, but on the one she shared with Leila was a beautiful flocked shift with a sky blue over-dress embroidered with tiny-petaled flowers boasting sapphire centers. Never worn, it was as breathtaking as the last time she'd seen it—as part of the bride price wardrobe Gleannmara had brought with him to ask her hand in marriage. When she'd refused him, Kieran vowed to burn the gown, the chest, and its contents, yet here they were, carefully tended and as lovely as ever.

Good and faithful Benin thought of everything and everyone, she reflected, grateful for the steward's consideration of her as well as of his lord. The blade in Riona's throat cut many ways, reflecting the myriad emotions welling within. Pain, joy, melancholy, thanksgiving…all struggled for dominance. Leila picked up the hem of the bridal dress and rubbed it against her cheek, marveling at the softness.

"The colors pale in comparison to your eyes, milady, but this is the best attempt by man to match them."

Riona turned toward Kieran's voice, her eyes so blurred that she could not really see him. She wiped them with her sleeve in frustration, wondering that a single tear remained after last evening's debacle.

"My heartfelt thanks, milord, to both you and Benin."

It was right to step into his arms, to lay her head upon the rich fabric covering his chest. It soaked up her tears thirstily, as though made for just that purpose. She didn't resist as his arms closed around her. She fit against him as if by God's design.

"You are most welcome, lass." Pride swelled Kieran's chest beneath her cheek and infected his announcement. "I had the banns posted this morning, sweetling. We'll be wed after the hearing at the week's end."

His lips brushed the top of her head, but Riona hardly felt them. His words consumed her, not his actions. *Banns? Wed?* She couldn't believe her ears. Stepping away, she looked up at his face. He grinned like a dog chewing brambles.

"Banns," she repeated in unbelief.

He nodded, pleased beyond himself.

"Wed?"

"In less than a week, the little one will have to sleep alone," he answered wickedly.

Riona's heart did a quick pirouette in concert with the dance in his gaze, yet her nostrils flared with her growing incredulity. Shoving his hands away from her waist, she marched to the bed.

Uncertain of anything except that the lady was upset, Leila scampered out of the way as Riona snatched up the gown, wadded it in a ball and stuffed it back into the chest. Liex flinched as she slammed the lid shut.

"Colga, remove this box from my quarters this instant."

Recovering with a scowl, Kieran moved forward. "What is *this* about?"

Riona put her hand on the trunk and cocked her chin up at him in defiance. "It's about a fool who thinks he can buy a bride with a box of pretty clothes."

"'Tis a gift, not a purchase."

"A gift is it?"

He met her challenge, lowering his head so that his nose nearly touched hers. "Aye, a *gift,*" he growled lowly.

Riona refused to be daunted. "You need *banns* to give a gift?"

"Nay, I need *banns,*" he mimicked with indignation, "to marry you."

"And who says I'd do such a fool thing?" Riona's voice rose in volume as well as pitch.

Apparently a ready answer failed him. Kieran's expression went blank, as if it never occurred to him to think that she wouldn't agree. Bewilderment possessed him and his answer. "You said you forgave me."

"I said I forgave Colga, too, but I'm not going to marry him." Riona rolled her eyes toward the dark hollow of the roof overhead as anger clipped the endings off her words. "Marriage is more than postin' banns and dressin' a girl in pretties to get her into your bed, Kieran O'Kyle Mac Niall of Gleannmara. Faith, just when I think ye have a chance of bein' a reasonable man, ye play the fool like you were born to the role."

"Woman, no man can hold on to reason round the likes of a mulish lass such as yourself, with temper sharp as her tongue. *No man!*"

Kieran reached past her and picked up the trunk, hoisting it over his head.

"You don't want the dresses? Fine. You don't want me? Fine." In a black rage, he pivoted and stalked outside to a nearby fire built to warm bath water. With a curse fit for neither man nor beast, he tossed the trunk onto the smoldering coals and stomped away.

Riona's heart lurched at the sight of the flames and sparks lapping around its polished metal trappings. Why it didn't burst upon the rocks, she had no idea. With a shriek, she ran to the hearth, torn between rescue and condemnation as she shook her fist in the air.

"Well, if you won't burn with 'em," she shouted after him, "then it's a waste of a good fire!" Turning in a temper-mottled panic, she redressed her silent cousin standing among the curious onlookers who'd ventured closer to see what was amiss. "Well, don't just stand there gaping like a witless ninny; help me get this out of the bloomin' flames before it catches."

TWENTY-TWO

Kieran hadn't come back since he'd stormed off that afternoon. That evening Riona and the children attended vespers, then shared a meal in the guest cottage without him. As soon as she tucked the twins into bed, she sent Fynn out to look for him while she wallowed in remorse.

When a knock sounded on the door a while later, Riona jerked it open, half-hoping, half-dreading, that it might be Kieran. It was Cromyn. The guilt that had plagued her since her loss of temper rose sharper than ever. She dropped to her knees before the priest. "O Father, I have sinned."

"My souls!" Cromyn exclaimed, taken back at the impetuous confession. He grasped Riona gently by the shoulders and helped her to her feet. "Come, child, I can't believe it's as bad as all that."

"If I'd seen it coming, I'd have confessed aforehand," Riona said haplessly. Her eyes brimmed. Stepping aside to allow her guest entry, she wiped her eyes on her sleeve in annoyance. "I vow, a demon accompanies that man, and it possesses me whenever Gleannmara and I are near one another."

The priest's brow lifted in surprise as he coaxed each of the birds on his shoulders to respective pegs reserved for cloaks. "A demon, is it?"

"It must be true. I turn from a pious sister in Christ to a raving lunatic or worse, a wanton harlot. And I know it isn't Kieran alone." She rambled as though to convince herself. "He's a good man by the measure of most. That's why I couldn't see him hanged for a murder I know he didn't commit. Not that I wouldn't have tried to aid any man in such a circumstance, but—"

Cromyn put his finger to her lips. "Hush, child. This penitent floodtide drowns me in bewilderment." He looked about, glancing first at the imda where the twins slept and then at the Kieran's empty one.

"Have you done away with your foster brother?"

"Nay, but…ach, Father, I don't know what to think. I'm remorseful one moment and angry the next. You see, I forgave him for leading Heber off to his death. Father Fintan was right," she admitted. "Kieran didn't force Heber to go, even though it was Gleannmara's idea…and a foolish one at that." Faith, would this inner debate never end? "I know that war and battle are sometimes unavoidable, but the one that claimed Heber's life was not. Gleannmara was prosperous enough without hiring out to Aidan for reward. 'Twas all so unnecessary."

Cromyn shook his head. "The king and his men ousted pirates who've been plaguing our shipping routes, both here and in Scotia Minor," he pointed out. "Those rogues were a menace to all men. It made no difference to them who wore a cross. Only its value was of concern, not that of a human life."

"Perhaps," she conceded slowly. Marching over to the slightly charred trunk that Colga had helped her retrieve from the fire and gaining steam once more, she lifted the catch with deft fingers and opened it. "And then he gave me *this*."

She lifted out the blue dress. Holding it to her, she swung around, reveling in the rich material clutched in her fingers. "I thought it the kindest, most thoughtful gesture…perhaps done in return for helping him escape Maille's and Senan's false persecution…or in gratitude for my forgiveness regarding Heber…or simply because we were longtime friends who'd come through a difficult time together."

"A comely token of esteem to be sure," Cromyn remarked tactfully.

"But tell me, what has forgiveness to do with the acceptance of a proposal of marriage?"

The priest's bemused scowl reinforced Riona's own confusion. "Precisely my thoughts."

Cromyn held up his hand. "Wait, child. I am not certain my thoughts and yours share the same course." He took the dress from her and gently placed it back in the trunk. "Now sit down."

Riona started for the bench, then paused, remembering her manners. Kieran could befuddle her even in absentia! "Forgive me, Father. May I pour you some drink?" She rushed to the small table near the door where a flagon of ale left over from supper sat next to her untouched meal.

"Dear niece, you'd do me most service by sitting in one place and calming thyself. 'Tis like talking to a hummingbird."

Folding Riona's hand between his, Cromyn led her to the bench. She took the seat, embarrassed by her uncharacteristic behavior. Or perhaps it was not uncharacteristic at all. Not of late.

"Father, I have not put off anger, wrath, and malice as commanded by the Word, but have come to chew upon them daily since Kieran has returned. And the taste is bitter."

Would that she could swallow the things she'd said, bilious as they were, but they were out and could not be called back. Misery overwhelmed her at the thought that she'd challenged Kieran to be a good example for the little ones and then acted the worse herself.

"I know not what I do these days. I do not know this ranting shrew consumed with anger or the wanton wench who melts at the thought of his kiss. All I know is that I like neither."

"Gleannmara has kissed you?"

"Most assuredly and most thoroughly. I did not want it, yet a part of me wished it to last forever."

"The heart has its own mind, to be sure."

Her uncle's understanding smile brought Riona's tumble of thoughts to a halt. "Aye, I love Kieran, but as a foster brother, as kin—"

"Have you ever wished the kiss of kin to last forever?"

Heat from the thought of Kieran's kiss mingled with that of chagrin. "Nay, never."

"Then you do not think of Kieran as kin, child, but as a man."

"But I don't want a man!"

The words rang as false to her ear as they did her heart—the heart with a mind of its own. Dismay fell over her like a suffocating mantle.

"Father, what am I to do with a head and a heart that don't agree?"

Cromyn laughed gently. "That is a question of the ages, Riona. Consider it in prayer. That is my only suggestion. Now that you recognize the nature of your quandary, you can deal with it."

"He wants me to marry him." Riona rebelled against the idea.

"That's what the dress is for. It wasn't a gift from his heart, as I'd thought. It was part of a bride price…as if a commitment for life can be bought."

"It has been before and will be again."

"But not mine, Father. My love cannot be bought or bargained for…or pledged by someone else."

"And you think that Kieran of Gleannmara's can?"

Of course not. While decidedly more reckless, Kieran was as independent in spirit as she. He acted upon nothing in which he did not believe. But did he believe in marriage as a means to an heir or as a lifetime commitment to love come what may?

Cromyn patted Riona on the arm. "Think on it and pray, Riona. I think you have your answer already. You need to be at peace with it, and only God can give you that."

Riona rose as he turned toward the door. "Wait, Father. I've babbled like a fool without giving you a breath to say what brought you here. Has our audience with the high king been moved ahead?"

Or dare she hope that the abbot of Iona might see her? *Father, forgive me for being so self-absorbed.*

"Oh, yes, I nearly forgot." Cromyn reached into his belt and withdrew a small piece of parchment. "I was to deliver this to you…from the holy Father of Iona."

Awe numbed Riona's tongue. The Word said God wanted His children to ask the least of things, but what she had asked for was by no means small. She'd asked for a miracle. Riona glanced at Leila as she tore open the wax seal and unfolded the paper with shaking hands. The hair on her arms and neck prickled as she read the single sentence. It was written in a bold, clear hand, not unlike Iona's voice. She could almost hear his answer.

Milady, the girl child will be healed, but in God's time, not ours and by His hand, not mine.

Tears anew sprang to her eyes. How foolish she'd been to count so much on the touch or blessing of the abbot of Iona when she'd already asked the only One who could grant her wish.

"Is everything all right, child?" Cromyn's features showed his concern.

"I thought it strange when the abbot's clerk asked me to deliver this to you."

Riona looked up suddenly. "You haven't asked him about Leila? But this—" Her voice broke. She handed the missive over to her uncle, unable to speak right away.

The holy man read it and crossed his chest, murmuring in prayer.

"Everything is fine, Father." A cross between a chuckle and a sob escaped. She felt so foolish, so unworthy. "In all that has happened of late and in the excitement of seeing his holiness of Iona, I'd lost my focus as to Who was in control. I've made such a fiasco of it on my own that God sent me a…a reminder, first in you and now in this."

Riona raised up on tiptoe and gave her uncle a kiss on the cheek. "Thank you, uncle."

"I'm just a servant, child." Cromyn gathered his pets. With a ruffled flap of their wings, they settled on his shoulders. He laughed. "My friends are not used to my being about so late after vespers."

He started through the door and stopped, turning back to Riona. "If it's any consolation, Riona, know that even those such as I wrestle with decisions regarding their future. God seems to be leading me in a direction that is in conflict with the service I intended to perform for Him."

Riona put her own quandary aside. "Then perhaps I might convince you to share with me as I have with you, for you have truly been a godsend in my hour of confusion."

Cromyn shook his head. "I've a long trek back to the abbey. Suffice it to say, I may be leaving the peace and solitude of Iona for a more active role that God would have me fill."

Since his wife's death shortly after Bran was born, Cromyn, a young priest then, had dreamed of serving as one of Columcille's twelve in the isolation at Iona. It was an insulation, too, Riona thought, understanding all too well—a refuge from grief.

"You're leaving Iona? But where will you go?"

"That is for God to decide and for me to wait until His will is clear. With the changes anticipated from this summer's convention, I am to serve on the front lines."

"Would that He'd write it out as He did for Moses," she reflected in exasperation.

Cromyn's eyes twinkled as he glanced at the missive in her hand. "Sometimes He does."

Aye, Riona thought as she stared at the paper after her uncle left. Leila would be healed. She blinked away the blur of relief from her eyes and walked into the imda where the little girl slept peacefully. It appeared that she, too, would serve on a front line, as a mother and wife to God's children, both big and small.

Kneeling in the space between the two beds, she placed her hands on each of the sleeping babes, feeling the rise and fall of their small chests.

Thy will be done, Father, in Thy time. Meanwhile, I come to You with a frightful temper and stubborn will, asking that You remove them, for they are like sores upon my flesh that give me only despair. I will abandon my plan to serve Thee at the abbey to be mother to these little ones, whom death deprived of parents. But am I to provide them a father as well?

Riona stopped, struck with the answer. No, *she* wasn't. God already had—the very day she'd asked for His help. The memory of Kieran's and Bran's entrance into the abbey played upon her mind as though it were yesterday. If she'd accepted Kieran's proposal, if she'd forgiven him then, perhaps they'd not have been subjected to the tribulation of fleeing murder charges. She dropped her head until her chin lay upon her chest.

But he didn't want the children, she protested on her behalf, although it did seem that they had grown on him, especially Leila. She recalled the laughing child perched upon Kieran's wide shoulders, wearing little more than a new brat. It had given Riona hope for him until he dashed it with that careless comment in the bruden hall about the children not being his.

But, Father, what was I to think?

That Kieran was no more perfect than she. The answer slammed like a battering ram into the forefront of her defense. There was a bigger game afoot here than Riona could conceive, one that gave each of them time to adjust to each other as well as to God's intention: to provide for His innocents.

For if You are with us, who can be against us? True, evil gnawed and gnashed at them as it had the writer of the psalm, yet here they were, untouched and protected. *If You are with us, what have we to fear?* Nothing but their own disbelief.

Riona's hands fisted in shame. Looking back, it was so clear. *Forgive me Father. Help me to do the right thing.*

It began in Riona's chest, where her heart beat calmly, steadily. It poured through her veins like her life-giving blood and spread limb to limb, head to toe. She had read of it in God's Word and heard it mentioned on the lips of clergy. Indeed she'd repeated it herself. But until this moment, she had never felt it: that elusive peace that surpasses all understanding.

She rose and planted a kiss on the forehead of each of the children. Her mind was clearer than it had been in days. Instead of offering forgiveness, it was her turn to ask for it.

Her heart missed a beat as the sudden sound of running footsteps approached the cottage. She hurried to the door, cracking it open in time to see Fynn coast to a halt and smash breathless into the side of the dwelling. There was no sign of Kieran.

Disappointed, she admitted Fynn. "Did you find him?"

"He's with Aidan and his men. They just returned from Derry and are in the hall now toasting Finella's harp." The boy yawned and hung his brat carefully on one of the pegs just abandoned by Cromyn's pigeons. "Sure, this is one of the finest cloaks at the fair, for a man of my age at least." Hesitating briefly, he turned to Riona, pride replaced with a heartrending insecurity. "After today, I don't suppose there's any hope that you and Gleannmara will marry."

Riona smiled. First Cromyn, then prayer, and now this. How many messages would it take? She hugged Fynn. "Aye, lad. There's always hope. Now take off those shoes and hop into bed."

TWENTY-THREE

I 'll put my charioteer up against any," Aidan boasted. The new king of Scotia Minor clapped his wiry comrade on the back and motioned for one of the serving wenches to fill their cups. "All around," he called out.

Kieran covered his horned mug with his hand. The twitch of a smile he gave the flirtatious maid was all he could muster, despite the revelry going on around him. His wounded pride gave him enough anguish without adding a thundering head to it.

"What's this?" His royal friend waved the girl back. "It isn't like you'll be driving tomorrow. All you needs do is ride as Aengus's second."

"Unless the race turns toward the worse," the charioteer Aengus provided. "Then the horse'll need the encouragement of the hand that trained it from a weenling."

"He'll run for you quick as for me," Kieran assured Aengus. "Sure, that one's born to the wind."

Reluctantly, Kieran let the girl fill his cup. Another time he'd have been crowing like the rest at the prospect of seeing one of Gleannmara's champions race. The horses had been the tuath's pride since King Rowan brought over the first pair. Over the years that followed, the line split into solid warhorses trained to the battlefield and sleek racers for either riding or the chariot. Gray Macha was a prime example of the first. Ringbane, longer of limb and greyhound-sleek, was born to race rather than combat.

Kieran had given the yearling to Aidan as tribute to a friend rather than liege lord. Had circumstances been different, Kieran would have raced Ringbane's elder sibling at the fair. Heber would have driven as his second.

Ah, Heber. Kieran chased the melancholy thought down with ale. How was he to keep the oath he'd made to his dying friend when

Riona would have nothing to do with him? What more could he do? He'd asked. He'd taken her little brood under his wing. He'd even given her a wardrobe fit for a queen. And all she wished was that he burned with the confounded frills twice thrown in his face.

"Friend, if your face grows much longer, ye'll need a second chin to carry it. This quagmire over the murder will clear itself up. I myself will testify to your untarnished character."

"Make no mistake, sire, I am humbled by your support," Kieran affirmed with as much vigor as his heart would afford.

Aidan's offer was a considerable one. According to the law, the word of a king of Aidan's station, with so many lesser monarch's pledged to him, carried far more weight than Maille's and the bishop's. Only an abbot's testimony was equal, and if Fintan could testify, there'd be no need for a trial. While Kieran should be more concerned with the charges pending against him and the forces at work behind it all, it was Riona's rejection that spun his thoughts into a dark web, entrapping him.

"You saved my life, Kieran of Gleannmara. I shall ever be indebted." Aidan seized Kieran's arms and shook him in a manly embrace, before taking up his cup again. "And to your future bride of the Dromin, whose chief gave his life for mine."

Instinctively Kieran glanced to where Colga and some of the Dromin chiefs were involved in a game of chess. If their newly elected lord heard, he did not acknowledge. Another shadow crawled into Kieran's mind, one of doubt. He should be grateful that Colga acted so quickly on his behalf after the murder charge, bringing a lordly retinue to a fugitive. Still, whenever there was disaster, Riona's quiet cousin was not far removed.

A sixth sense bade Kieran's gaze wander beyond the Dromin men to where a single traveler sat staring back at him from a table near the door. The man quickly looked away and helped himself to more of the ale from the flagon on his table. Kieran studied him, but nothing about the man was familiar. The noble standards of hygiene and appearance were lacking. Shoddily cropped hair and an unkempt beard pegged him as a lesser lord or one new to the station his garment suggested.

It was worn, perhaps, but it had once cost a respectable sum. Perhaps he was one of the host of merchants who traveled from fair to fair. Some were richer than kings, but without the refining of a noble tutelage. Regardless, it was the first time Kieran had seen him.

"Ho, milords, for this humble servant craves an audience for his newest composition and would be honored if such esteemed souls such as yourself would indulge it."

Dismissing the man as a curiosity, Kieran turned to see Marcus bow lowly before the group.

"Is that you, my comical buffoon?" Aidan exclaimed.

The jongleur's face was not painted tonight. He carried the lute Dallan normally played, rather than his whimsical pipe and bag of tricks. "Aye, 'tis I, milord, but tonight the fool plays the bard, provided your own good master does not object."

Aidan's bard was a man twice Marcus's age with a mane of snowy hair cut away from his forehead by a skillful barber, not unlike the tonsure of Irish druid and priest. Bresal had studied with the venerated Columcille in the bardic tradition before the latter moved on to study of the church. Now, his normally solemn and contemplative demeanor softened considerably by the good ale, the elder poet waved for the younger man to proceed.

"By all means, sir, for these days my compositions lean more to recording Aidan's reign as the first Christian king of Scotia Minor than entertainment. Not that my liege is not the stuff that heroes are made of," Bresal added, lifting his cup in salute to Aidan.

"I am honored, sirrahs." Marcus strummed the lute and bowed. "Thus I shall begin this ballad with a tribute to Gleannmara, for it is his story I intend to tell."

Kieran set his cup down on the table, nearly overturning it. "My story? Faith, I have no story."

"As seen through the eyes of the children he and his lady have taken to their bosoms."

Kieran rolled his eyes toward the smoke-filled rafters of the bruden. "You are hard-pressed, Marcus, to find the matter for a poem in that, but have at it."

Marcus applied nimble fingers to the strings and began to sing.

"In cloistered abbey so serene, there lived a lady fair,
   With eyes as blue as gemstones, and raven, silken hair.
   Riona was the lady's name, an angel sent from heaven in answer
to an orphan's prayer.
   Robbed by black-robed death of their parents, three lost siblings
found their way to Kilmare,
   Where Lady Riona took them to her bosom as her own.
   Her gentle, loving manner preached to their little souls,
   Drawing them closer to heaven's way, rather than that of an
earthly road,
   Until greed came cloaked in thin disguise, to carry them away.
   In the midst of their despair, the good Gleannmara came…"

Marcus's smooth tenor and its musical accompaniment plucked at the muscles coiled in Kieran's neck and shoulders until slowly, note by note, they began to relax. It was an engaging story, romanticized almost beyond Kieran's recognition. He was hardly the answer to Riona's prayer, given her absolute refusal to consider him as husband. Yet she'd risked her life to save him. He in turn had jeopardized his life for the safety of those she loved—the homeless children.

To hear Marcus sing was to think that Kieran was a great warrior of noblest intent, as noble in heart as the lady he protected, but Kieran knew better. He'd only rescued the orphans because Riona would give him no peace otherwise. He'd had no intention of fulfilling the orphans' prayer of providing a home for them. That possibility evolved out of his determination to honor his oath.

The more Kieran listened and privately objected to the praises attributed to him, the more he came to realize just how selfish his motives for all his deeds were. They had nothing to do with the children's happiness or the lady's, as Marcus portrayed. It was all done for his honor and his glory—and that left a bilious taste in his mouth. Riona was the heroine. What she gave, she gave without any expectation of return. She was prepared to sacrifice everything for those whose needs exceeded hers. She had something Kieran envied. It made her what she was and sustained her when the world failed her.

When he failed her.

The tale grew more unrecognizable, and yet Kieran listened as though it were his penance. It stirred a bitter brew of emotions because he knew the truth behind all the noble things Marcus sang about. And when the poet closed the story with the arrival at the fair and Kieran's reunion with his friends and supporters, he was relieved. Unlike the men clamoring for a finish, he didn't want to hear what was unlikely—that he and Riona would marry, that Gleannmara would be home to the children, answering their prayers, that life would be beautiful ever after.

"Well, what do you think, milord?" Marcus asked beneath the huzzahs and cheers filling the room.

"Well done, sir!" Aidan stepped forward and clapped Marcus on the back so hard that the strings on the lute rang in protest. "And you shall drink with me the rest of this night, but first I must make room for more of the fine ale this comely wench pours." The king pinched the cheek of the serving maid, sending her into a fluster of giggles.

As Aiden swaggered toward the side entrance, Bresal approached the young man before Kieran could answer him. "Most excellent recital and composition. The rhyme and measure are impeccable. You waste your time as a fool."

"You are very generous, sir," Marcus replied.

"It was well put," Kieran offered. "I hardly knew I was so esteemed in your eyes."

"In the children's eyes," Marcus corrected with a crooked grin. "And in mine," he added, "though I've strained hard to see past your bluster and buffoonery."

"Not hard enough, I fear." Kieran glanced at Bresal. The old man hovered at Marcus's side, an expectant look on his face. "You are a good friend, Marcus, but I must bid you good-night. I'm worn from hearing of all my heroics." He clamped a firm hand on Marcus's shoulder. "Besides, I think good Bresal has more on his mind than a compliment."

"This young man may not be of bardic lineage, but he has the gift," Bresal said, affirming Kieran's suspicion. "I have not taken on students in a long while, young Marcus, but…"

"Your pardon, master," Marcus interrupted. "But I must have a short word with Gleannmara."

Kieran paused and turned upon hearing his name to see Marcus leave the aged bard.

"Milord, is something amiss with the lady?" he asked lowly.

Kieran shook his head. "Nay, good friend, if anything is amiss, 'tis with me. I am sore tired, and tomorrow is a big day for our royal friend. A good night's rest is in order."

If Riona would even let him in the cottage. Kieran refused to let the thought cloud his face. "And if Bresal's proposal isn't what you want, consider becoming the resident poet of Gleannmara. You do paint glorious with words."

Surprise took Marcus's expression, but before he could comment, Kieran turned him and steered him back to where Bresal awaited. "Now go, lad. We'll talk later."

That Bresal even hinted an interest in tutoring Marcus was an honor, for a master did not ordinarily seek out students. It was they who sought him. But that the elder teacher waited was even more tribute to Marcus's performance.

Once outside in the fresh air, Kieran slowed his step, reluctant to make his way back to the cottage. Suddenly a loud shout echoed from around the side in the direction of the fialtech. A second shout sent Kieran into a run, dagger drawn, toward the privy, for he recognized the voice as Aidan's.

The Dalraidi king leaned against a sturdy birch and pointed to the privy, but Kieran needed no direction. A light shone through the door, which lay ajar. An assassin with a lantern? Nay, a host of lanterns, for the light streaming out of the cracks was too bright for one flame. It was as absurd as it was eerie.

"What happened," Kieran asked, glancing at the bloodied hand Aidan cupped to his chest. The Dalraidi king was ashen, obviously shaken. "Faith, are you mortally wounded?"

Aidan shook his head. "Nay, he sliced my hand only. Then he—" The king stopped, stymied for words. "I canna say what happened after that. As I came out of the fialtech, the deceiver charged me with his dagger. I dodged aside, diverting the blade with my hand and shoved him into the privy. I drew my own blade and turned to face him, but he never came out."

"And the light?"

"Is why I didn't go in after him," Aidan answered, as if fearful of being overheard. "I swear it wasn't there earlier…and he, sure as I'm standing here, wasn't carrying a lantern when he attacked."

The words were no more than out when the light died. Invisible icy fingers crept up Kieran's spine and lifted the hair on his neck as he exchanged a wary look with his companion. Men ran toward them from the bruden, summoned by the same cry as Kieran.

"What goes here?" one of the soldiers demanded.

"A cowardly attack on Aidan, by the look of it," Kieran explained. That was all he could explain.

"Where is the coward?" another demanded.

Aidan jerked his head toward the door, no more anxious to open it than Kieran. Tightening his grip on his dagger, Kieran stepped forward and eased the door open. A man's leg fell out, limp as a doll's. His heart leapt to this throat, pounding so that he had to swallow, but outwardly he maintained an unruffled appearance. Someone from the rear of the group pushed forward carrying a lantern. As the light filled the small enclosure, Kieran recognized the stranger he'd studied earlier that evening.

"He must have fallen on his knife," he remarked to his royal friend, who stood stiffly while the charioteer wrapped his bleeding hand with a sash. Dagger ready, in case the man played dead, Kieran motioned to the culprit's feet. "Pull him out, lads, and we'll have a look at him."

As the body was dragged out into the open, Kieran took the lantern and held it up inside the privy. Nothing was amiss that he could see, at least now. Bewildered and not the least at ease, he handed over the light and knelt to examine the body of the would-be assassin. The stillness of death answered the inquiring press of his fingers at the man's throat.

"Roll him over," he ordered on finding no sign of the blade on the front of the corpse. The men obliged. "Hold the lamp closer, man." There was no sign of a wound much less a weapon. But a puncture could close up without much blood, especially a deep one.

"Anyone know this varlet?" Aidan inquired. Murmurs of denial echoed around them as Kieran proceeded to cut away the man's tunic from his chest. No matter how much clothing he pulled away, there was no sign of broken flesh anywhere.

"Maybe his neck broke from the fall," the king suggested, no more willing to acknowledge the strange glow they'd witnessed than Kieran.

"What happened to the light?"

Kieran jerked his head toward a young boy who'd joined the group unobtrusively. Dressed in trews and a short tunic, he was one of the lads who tended the fires for the bruden. "You saw it, too?" he asked, taken back.

The boy, very near Fynn's age, nodded. "Aye, I saw it. Big enough to light the hall, it was. But where is it now?"

Another search ensued, but there was no more explanation for the light than there was for the cause of the assassin's death.

"What kind of a murderer carries a light?" someone snorted in doubt.

"Or what kind 'o king takes one on nature's call?"

Aidan straightened, pricked by the insult. "I carried no light and neither did he," he said, pointing to the dead man. "But there *was* a light. The lad saw right, same as I and Gleannmara here."

Kieran nodded, no closer to an answer for all of his examination of the body and site than before.

"Well, his neck isn't broke, else it would roll about like a ball in a sack," another man remarked, dropping the corpse's head and wiping his hands on his tunic as if they were soiled by the contact.

"It appears milord Aidan has an otherworldly guardian."

The mere mention of *otherworld* silenced the group. There was a common belief among many that demons dwelled in the veil houses or privies—at least in those on church grounds. Men were charged to cross themselves as a blessing each time they visited such a place.

Kieran, himself a skeptic of spirits, good or bad, doubted even a demon would tolerate the stench.

Bresal addressed the king. "I would consult with the priests, but God has ordained milord Aidan as king of Scotia Minor. As such, does it not follow that God or one of His heavenly messengers would thusly protect him?"

"Then why didn't God protect his back on the battlefield where my friend died?" Kieran challenged.

"Because He'd placed men to protect His chosen one then," Bresal responded without pause. "Tonight our king was alone and unarmed save his dining dagger."

Kieran held his tongue, but his thoughts were not so easily swayed. God had used Heber to save Aidan? He neither liked the idea nor accepted it.

"We must remember that there is always a greater plan afoot than what we can see with the human eye."

Whether Kieran accepted it or not, the murmurs of wonder and speculation rose all around him. They'd witnessed a miracle. A warrior angel protected Aidan, king of the Dalraidi, because of his heavenly ordained purpose.

"Let us all pray, my liege, that you will live up to God's expectation as you have thus far. Had you not, that well could be your body lying at our feet, instead of your would-be assassin's."

Aidan nodded solemnly and crossed himself, inspiring others to do the same. Kieran followed suit out of habit and respect for his friend, uncertain if the king believed his advisor or simply humored the old man.

"Let us go back to the hall and offer our thanksgiving to the One God for His favor on a humble servant," the Dalraida announced loudly. "Will you join us, Gleannmara?"

Kieran shook his head. "I needs rest to do the Dalraidi honor tomorrow."

Aidan reached out and grasped Kieran's forearm in a hearty shake. "My friend came to my aid at first call. For that, I am also grateful."

Kieran nodded. He liked Aidan. In all Kieran had seen the man say and do, justice and humility reigned. He returned the gesture of friendship with a squeeze. "And I am grateful that neither of us had to fight the carrier of that light." Once again, the fine hair at the nape of his neck and on his arms tingled as though brushed by an unseen feather, but he attributed it to a shift in the breeze from the sea.

The body was carried away by some of Aidan's men as the crowd disbursed. Like Kieran, some elected to give up the revel for the night. He watched until the yard of the bruden was as empty as it had been before the commotion. Far from tired now, he was primed with the afterrush of the excitement. Equally strong was his desire to be alone, and he knew just the place to assuage both dispositions.

TWENTY-FOUR

The games and races drew a larger crowd than the sessions on law and order, for while bureaucracy was not everyone's passion, the competitions and sport were. Clans mustered together to form teams for hurling. Everywhere, men strutted jauntily with a camán, or hurling stick, resting on their shoulders. Some were bronze mounted in accord with the law, marking the young player as a prince's or chief's son in fosterage.

"If ye marry Gleannmara, will I have one of those?" Fynn asked, his admiring eye following one of the young gallants.

"I believe that your father must be a king or chief," Riona answered. Her heart twinged at the disappointed look on the lad's face.

If she married Gleannmara. What possibilities the idea carried Riona dared not think about lest her heart quicken and her brain turn to a stew of anxiety and anticipation. If he'd still have her, she would marry him.

"Then I'd engrave mine with the skills Father Cullen taught me."

"Now that's a fine idea." Riona said after processing Fynn's words with some effort. Heavens, her mind was a stew anyway. Kieran hadn't come back to the guest house last evening. Riona had waited, ready to concede and apologize, until sleep overtook her. That morning his bed still had not been slept in. Then at breakfast she heard of the attempt on the Scottish Aidan's life—how the assailant dropped dead in his tracks for no apparent reason. Kieran had been there but disappeared after the crowd disbursed. He was, according to one of Aidan's retinue, to participate in the race that afternoon.

A tug on her skirt brought Riona to a stop in the flow of milling attendees. Leila pointed to a vendor who had pups for sale. Unlike other merchants, this gentleman did not have to announce his goods. The eager and excited pups did all the promotion for him, yipping, growling, and providing a show for any who'd watch.

Indulging the child, she led her charges over to the small pound. The pups were cute greyhounds, all rambunctious and friendly. Next to them was another stall with wolfhound pups, all awkward legs. Liex and Leila laughed at the antics. Even Fynn allowed a smile to his lips, although he was entirely too grown up to giggle outright.

"Their sire's racing today," the vendor informed Riona.

"We're not in the market for a pup, I fear," she apologized.

"Well, now, the training is troublesome," the man answered, a twinkle lighting in his eye. "But I have something back here that would be perfect for this little lady, and it won't cost but a tittle." He reached into a small sack and drew out a sleepy kitten.

Leila's eyes widened in delight as the man handed the small ball of long, gray fur to her. The kitten yawned widely, setting the little girl off with a giggle. As she put her nose up to the kitten's, it licked her.

"'Tis the last of the litter and lonely to be sure."

Once satisfied that Leila was properly cleaned, the kitten laid its head beneath the jut of the little girl's chin in blissful contentment. Blue eyes rolled toward Riona in a plea that, although unspoken, was as loud as the man hawking pastries nearby.

"All this wee thing needs is love."

"Can we keep it, milady?" Liex implored. "It won't be much trouble, and Leila and me will give it some of our food."

"It would keep the rats down at Gleannmara," Fynn added pragmatically. "Gleannmara doesn't strike me as a man who'd keep cats just for the sake of keepin' 'em."

Riona watched Leila nuzzle the kitten. To say no would be cruel to both animal and child, not that Riona could say no. She'd always had a soft spot for kittens.

"We'll take it on one condition." Having garnered all three children's attention, she continued. "I choose the name."

A minute later they left the vendor a coin richer and a kitten poorer. Lady Gray—at least Riona thought it was a girl—rested contentedly in Leila's arms, her small neck craned as if to catch all the sights she had missed during her nap. They stopped near a slope of embroideresses while Fynn purchased a bright red ribbon for Lady

Gray with money he'd earned performing with Dallan.

At least he'd abandoned the idea of joining the traveling entertainers, Riona thought gratefully, watching him reach down to pet the kitten as they walked. He was rather taken by the respect afforded the foster son of Gleannmara. That and the brat draped from the lad's shoulders had won Kieran his favor...for now. The two had volatile tempers, each seeming to set off the other. Not that she could justly condemn either given her own behavior of late.

The racecourse was a plain surrounded by small hills that afforded the populace of the fair a good view. Next to the royal banners of the high king flew those of Aidan, the newest of the provincial monarchs obliged to Aedh. There appeared to be some sort of courtly presentation taking place, with horns heralding the arrival of prestigious persons. These in turn were presented to the high king's company. Next to the royal highness of all Erin sat the queen, robed in rose and green, and at the king's other hand, two strapping young men whom Riona took to be their sons. She rose on tiptoe, straining for a better look at the company in Aidan's court, when a voice hailed her from behind.

"Good day, cousin. Have you come to watch Gleannmara's finest race?" Colga stepped up beside her and peered in the same direction. "I myself have wagered on the Scot's chariot."

"If I were given to gamble, so would I," Riona answered without censure. "Although Gleannmara's bloodlines are likely present to some degree in all the contenders."

Kings and chiefs from all over Ireland had sought to breed their horses with Gleannmara's stock for years.

"Have you seen Kieran?" she asked, changing the subject from small talk to what weighed most on her mind.

"The last I saw of him he was working the team with Aengus. Aidan should consider himself well befriended by Kieran for such a gift. 'Twould cost him five hundred cows a head had he to pay for them."

"The king of the Scots has paid Kieran off well by his hospitality given our fugitive circumstance. Indeed, between God's good grace and Aidan's, we are well provided for."

A chorus of trumpets blasted through the collective roar of the throng, announcing the coming of the chariots on parade. Colga cleared a way for Riona and the children to where the men of Dromin had a prime spot at the edge of the track. The ground was dry despite an early morning shower, its clay surface packed hard by the keepers of the grounds.

As the chariots entered the nature-made arena, the high king and his company rose to acknowledge the salutes of the drivers and companions. Banners of every color streamed from the chariots, mingling with the drivers' brats which flowed behind like sails puffed with wind. The horses were as regally bedecked as their drivers, with enameled bridles, some embellished with silver and gold.

"Faith, some of our good lords' wives are not as well favored with ornament as their steeds," Riona commented, eyes wide. She'd committed her life to the plain confines of the abbey for so long she'd all but forgotten the lavishness of her class where fine horseflesh was concerned.

Scotia Minor's chariot passed, Kieran holding on to the rail as second to the driver. His fair hair streamed from a proud profile, clean-shaven and angular. The gold armbands and rings of his station glistened in the sun. His brat unfurled like bright blue and gold canopy held from flight by a brooch that glittered with blue fire. Without their own entry in this year's competition, the men of Dromin lifted a cheer and maintained it long after their liege lord had passed.

Kieran should have looked as sleep deprived as Riona felt, but instead of holding his fine presence against him, Riona joined the others in their cheers. At the uproar, Lady Gray burrowed under Leila's arm as if to escape, back legs scrambling for all she was worth.

"Poor dear," Riona commiserated, imagining what all this must sound like to the little animal. She helped Leila calm the trembling kitten. Remembering that it had found solace in a sack, she draped a fold of the little girl's brat over Lady Gray's head and gently held it there until she felt the animal purr.

Looking back to the track, she saw the high king rise and lift a branch to call order. Rather than tiny silver bells, which usually commanded attention at a table or in a confined meeting chamber, a trumpet sounded the call to silence. The charioteers lined up their vehicles wheel to wheel at the starting line, all eyes upon the dais where the queen now rose. She lifted a silk scarf high above her head, where it fluttered in the breeze. Horses pawed the hard-caked track and pulled impatiently at their reins.

"I've changed my mind," Fynn whispered at Riona's ear. "I'd rather race than wield a hurling stick. Why Gleannmara's horse has more gold than I've seen in my lifetime on man or beast!"

"That's King Aidan's gold," Riona reminded the mercenary-minded youth. "And remember, all the glitter in the world is no equal to a noble heart and ofttimes hides a black one."

Her last words were drowned by an explosive revel of excitement and anticipation. The scarf fluttered toward the ground, launching the horses across the starting line. So many worldly distractions for such a young and hungry mind, Riona thought, or even for a more mature one. The men of Dromin shouted and jumped up and down like leashed hounds on the trail of their prey.

There were two chariots in the lead, Kieran's Dalraidi and that of Connaught. A third Ossary vehicle hedged side to side behind them, looking for a place to pull ahead, while the others fought for the inside track to the rear. By luck of the draw, Connaught had the inside track at the outset, which meant Kieran's horse was outrunning its competitor just to keep abreast. Such was the order for the first lap.

On the next, Kieran's chariot swung wide on the turn, and Ossary madly seized at the small opening presented. Wedging in between the two in the lead, its driver veered straight for the rail like a madman. Connaught was faced with the opponent's wheels tearing into his horse or running off the course. The driver took the latter, to the cheers of the crowd, for no prize was worth the careless endangerment of a good horse.

For the first half of the last lap it looked as if Ossary was going to take the race, but at the last turn Kieran's steed seemed to take a fresh breath. The gray and white Ringbane surged forward. By the time they reached the last turn, Kieran and Aengus were in the lead. The onlookers went wild. Nearby, someone tooted a horn. The blast was deafening, giving Riona a terrible start. She placed her hand upon her rapidly beating heart and strained to see Kieran pulling a full length away from the Ossary chariot.

What made her tear her gaze from the race, she didn't know. But when she did, to her horror, she saw Leila dart out into the raceway, just beyond the finish line. Ahead of her was a panicked Lady Gray, her fur puffed and standing on end. Upon realizing the danger of being trampled by the hooves pounding their way, the kitten froze in the middle of the track. Leila caught up with the kitten and bent down to pick her up, cradling her to her chest.

Sheer panic seized Riona. Her warning shout blended in with the huzzahs raised to bring in the Dalraidi chariot. Try as she might, her feet would not budge from where she stood riveted to the ground. No one saw the child. They were all watching the thundering chariots—chariots that could not stop even if someone spied Leila.

Frozen and helpless, Riona watched the impending disaster unfold as if it were in slow motion. Leila turned, the kitten clutched to her breast, in time to see her danger, but the same horror holding Riona captive seized the child as well. The gray and white stallion from Gleannmara was less than a chariot's length from her when it veered sharply to the left, narrowly missing her.

Huzzahs turned to cries of alarm. As the chariot followed, it seemed to throw out a body. His brat flared behind him, Kieran looked as if he were flying for one still frame of time. Then he dropped from the air, knocking Leila down and covering her with his body. The Ossary charioteer had no time to change his course despite his effort. The horse missed, but one of the chariot's wheels raced over Kieran and careened precariously, nearly overturning. Behind it came Connaught's, and the same nightmare played before Riona's eyes again. Thankfully, by then the others had seen something amiss and slowed sufficiently to swerve to one side or the other of the still, dust-covered forms without striking them.

The crowd moved forward as one body. Colga and the Dromin reached them first. Riona was swallowed by the masses despite her frantic efforts to push her way through. *Dear God, spare them. Dear God, spare them. Dear God...* Her furtive prayer echoed over and over in her mind as she struggled through the heart-seizing hush, tugging, men twice her size aside.

Finally, Riona saw a small head shoot up above those surrounding her. Half-crying, half-laughing, Leila sat hoisted precariously on someone's shoulder. In her arms was the bedraggled Lady Gray, clinging with all fours to the child's clothing. Hers was the most beautiful clay-smeared face Riona had ever seen. Kieran had protected her from harm, but what of...

"Weanling, you have given me the fright of my life!"

That voice. That booming, often arrogant voice took out Riona's knees with relief. *Thank God!* She grabbed for the nearest arm until she recovered sufficiently to support her own weight. She offered thanks over and over in her mind and with her tongue. It was all she could say, even when Colga turned and ushered her into the center of the chaos.

Then she was face-to-face with the man she'd nearly lost forever. Aside from clay and dust, Kieran of Gleannmara looked positively vibrant. Sunlight danced in the cinnamon warmth of his eyes as he met her gaze. She'd always been told a man could not be beautiful, but she'd been misled. Kieran was beautiful. He was beautiful and whole and healthy—unharmed by hoof or wheel.

Except that was impossible. Riona had seen two horse-drawn chariots run him over, nearly overturning but for pure luck and the skill of the drivers. Despite her second thought, she couldn't pull away from the sweet spell spun by his gaze. Disbelieving, she ran her hand over the bronzed sinew of his arm—not a mark, abrasion, nor bruise—naught but flawless flesh.

"You should have at least warned me that fatherhood was so risky," he chided, one corner of his lips tugging in irascible fashion.

She touched it. "You're not hurt." Wonder affected her overwhelming gratitude. *God, You are so good.*

Kieran caught her hand and kissed the tips of her fingers. "Not unless I've gone to the other side. You, milady, I expect to see in heaven, but this motley band of villains—"

"What makes you think *you'd* find yourself in heaven?" one of the Dromin protested with a nervous laugh, one clearly born of terror turned to relief.

"Because my lady could be nowhere else." The huskiness in Kieran's voice raked at the fine hair on the nape of Riona's neck, as if his lips accompanied it, and his breath warmed the sensitive skin there.

She reacted to the *man*, not to her foster brother. God had spared Kieran for a purpose. He'd sent her a husband. What lay beyond, Riona had no idea. She was certain only of the one step God had shown her.

"There's not a bruise on his flesh, yet here is the mark of the wheel on Gleannmara's brat," someone commented behind Kieran. Another tugged on Gleannmara's cloak and another until he was nearly choked.

"Mercy, lads, have a care. One brush with death is enough for the day."

Riona heard the slight catch in his voice, the only sign that Kieran himself was shaken.

He lifted the garment over his head sooner than unfasten its kingly brooch and handed it over. His expression changed as they held it up and shook it out. Aside from dust, it was in perfect shape. Thunderstruck, he handed Leila over to Colga and took the garment back to examine it himself. The color beneath his tanned face drained away. He cast a perplexed look at Riona.

"I thought my stilled blood dulled my senses to the cut of the horses hooves and the slash of the wheels. Sure my heart and breath ceased the moment I saw the little one standing in harm's way. How can it be that I haven't a scratch?"

Riona shook her head. There could be only one answer. "God spared you."

Doubt arrested his features. "But why, when I've no use for Him?" An answer came, but not from Riona.

"*He* obviously has a use for *you*, Kieran of Gleannmara."

Clear as it was strong, the voice separated the throng as if by magic.

In its wake came a tall, stalwart personage robed in the coarse gray of the church. With a gaze as blue and fiery as the stones on Kieran's brooch, Columcille, the venerated Abbot of Iona stood toe-to-toe and eye-to-eye with the young lord.

TWENTY-FIVE

The rushlight flickered, the cattle fat in which it had been soaked smoking the small room in the back of the hostel. It was a black reflection of Lord Maille's humor. He didn't like being summoned by a mere clan chief whose worth was less than a quarter of Maille's herd. That the man was a coward as well made it worse. How sick he was of conspirators who failed to grasp that the rewards of ambition came at a cost: risk.

The door opened, throwing a gust of thick smoke in Maille's face. Colga, the new Dromin chief, sidled through it after glancing over his shoulder to make certain he was not seen.

"Have you heard the news?"

"Which news?" Maille stared dully at the man. This was his second meeting of the day. The first had been with that sniveling priest, Senan. The fool was wild-eyed and unreasonable—convinced it was heaven's own hand protecting Aidan, the divinely appointed king of the Scots. Even the venerated Columcille had been struck by an angel for his reluctance to support Aidan. The humbling, bruising blow made clear to the sometimes willful servant that God's will differed from his, after which Columcille crowned the new king with whole-hearted blessing. The supporters of the new king's brother should have realized their folly then. But when the plan to eliminate Aidan in Scotia Minor under the guise of attacking pirates failed, Senan said that was yet another sign that their cause was futile.

And now the hand of God was acting even more aggressively, foiling them even further. And how did Senan react? The fool wanted to confess!

"What has God done now?" the lord challenged Colga dourly. "Sent a host of warrior angels down like a cloud to stand guard over the Dalraidi?"

Maille knew the assassin he hired had been struck down with a bad heart during the attempted murder the night before, nothing more. As for Gleannmara escaping condemnation for the abbot's murder because two chariots missed running him over, that took no stretch of the imagination either to discern that it was merely good luck.

"Senan is dead."

Maille's brow arched in feigned surprise. "The bishop of Kilmare? Why, I just saw him a few hours ago." And gave the priest leave to do what he must, provided he implicated no one other than himself. His mouth twitched in satisfaction, quickly suppressed. It would not do for anyone to suspect Senan's death had been anything short of suicide.

Colga wiped the perspiration soaked hair from his forehead. The man was positively white and looked ready to heave up his gullet. "They say it was suicide."

Of course they did. Maille again quelled his pride over a job well done. No one need know that he'd read Senan's confession, an elegantly penned declaration of contrition addressed to His Holiness of Iona. The idiot thought his appeal to a fellow priest who'd fallen short of God's will himself and been forgiven would win him consideration and forgiveness as well. Maille had watched the priest drip the wax on the envelope. When he pressed his seal upon it, Maille sealed the fool's fate.

Senan never suspected that Maille had picked up the dining dagger from a tray bearing the hardly touched remains of the priest's repast. Even when Maille plunged it into his abdomen and shoved it upward into his heart, nothing but surprise had registered on Senan's face. As the priest collapsed, Maille turned him toward the desk, easing him over it and the confession. Only then was Senan done with the affair, silenced so that the questions asked regarding his confession would never be answered.

"He left a note confessing that he'd ordered the death of his half brother, Fintan, after the abbot discovered Senan's involvement in selling Irish orphans into slavery," Colga added. "In it, Kieran and Riona were absolved of any part in the crime, save being in the wrong place at the wrong time. It was a slaver named Tadgh who slit the abbot's throat."

"Selling innocent children? Assassinating his own brother?" Maille tutted. "Obviously our promise to make Senan abbot wasn't fattening his purse fast enough."

That was a wrinkle Maille had not counted on. Senan's position as messenger of the church made him the perfect courier for Iogenan's supporters. Aidan's brother would see Scotia Minor subservient to its mother province of Ulster rather than an independent kingdom. The bishop's reward was to become abbot after Fintan was eliminated by their group. Maille was furious when he'd learned how Senan panicked at the discovery of his petty part in child slavery and had Tadgh prematurely kill his brother.

"How could a man of God sell hapless children?" Colga reflected, as if the thought itself was vile.

"For a profit, I would hope." Maille smiled at Colga's shocked expression, thankful that at least he did not suffer from conscience. "The same reason you turned your back to your chief's and Aidan's would-be assassins. Don't tell me you find the brooch of Dromin worrisome?"

Colga bristled at the derision. "Men can defend themselves. Children cannot."

At least the whelp had *some* spine left, Maille observed with satisfaction. One murder a day was risky enough, although the lord was determined to do what was necessary to get his reward. He agreed with Senan that the conspiracy had failed. Those involved were already fading into oblivion, their identities at best a guess. The incompetents had received their rewards: Colga was clan chief, Senan had been a formality away from succeeding his brother. And had the fool not panicked and killed the abbot prematurely, Maille would have had his payment as well. Curse the confessing idiot!

"So Senan's killed himself. He did us all a favor. Had he lived, he might have been tempted to confess our names." Irritated, Maille leaned on one of the barrels of ale in the storeroom. "Don't tell me that you, too, are suffering from pangs of conscience?"

"No, no," his companion assured him hastily. "I'm just done with it."

Maille reached across the hogshead and clasped Colga's shirt at the neck. "You are done with this when *I* say so." With effort, Maille reined his outburst to a low growl of warning. "'Tis just you and me left, lad, and I *will* have my payment. I earned every precious jewel in that vial, curse that holy coward's cold bones!"

"It's lost," Colga croaked through the tightness of Maille's grasp. "Kieran's party does not have it."

"You haven't checked the bags they carry on their persons," the lord reminded him.

"It could be with Bran at Gleannmara."

"Senan thought he saw one of the children lurking about Fintan's quarters. It was dark, and he couldn't tell which child it was. One of those little thieves *must* have it." Maille shoved Colga away, as if the greed gnawing at him had cut through his restraint.

"So what am *I* to do? Manhandle them or steal their bags and run in front of hundreds of witnesses?"

"Befriend them, lure them off, slit their white, little throats… I don't care. Just get that vial."

Slit their white, little throats.

Colga swallowed the bile the Ulster lord's words conjured. "And if they don't have it? What then?" Never had he seen a smile so sinister as the one that spread Maille's lips. He shivered despite the warmth of the summer night.

"Sir, I leave nothing to chance. Someone is already there on my behalf, or should be by now."

Again the dark lord leaned on the barrel Colga had maneuvered behind. Even so, Maille's fetid presence overwhelmed him. The rich meal of beef and pork soured in Colga's stomach and threatened to erupt.

"Just remember, Dromin, nothing is done until I say so. No one is safe, not child, nor priest…not even you."

Colga saw Maille's fist tighten on the hilt of his knife. With a bolt of clarity, he knew from that one gesture what had happened to Bishop Senan—and what would happen to him as well if he did not do as the

Ulster lord said. He watched Maille stride past him and out the door without a backward glance. Of their own accord, Colga's fingers went to the Dromin brooch he'd coveted and finally possessed only to be consumed with a sick dread the likes of which Colga never dreamed existed in the soul of man. Maille's gesture told Colga all he should have known from the start.

God help him, he'd made a pact with the devil himself. The young chief crossed himself out of habit and then laughed. Far from amused, it was filled with irony and despair. As if God would even hear him now, much less care.

TWENTY-SIX

Milady, we should be on our way." Finella stood at the door of the guest house, apprehension overtaking her expression as Riona rose from her knees and faced her. "My stars," Finella said seeing Riona's tearstained face, "What is this?"

Riona shook her head. She'd be fine. The torrent of second thoughts that assailed her would not sway her now. She believed with all her heart that she'd made the right choice, but her mind rebelled. There were so many issues on which she and Kieran differed.

Dressed in her best costume, the gleeman's wife rushed to Riona's side, producing a handkerchief. "Hasn't anyone told you that tears will ruin the ruam on your cheeks, milady?"

"I'm not wearing any coloring," Riona answered with more impatience than she cared for. Except it was not for Finella, but for herself. "He would still turn to violence before prayer."

Both women knew what Riona referred to. In the prewedding celebration the night before, someone made a poorly worded remark about the lineage of Kieran's soon-to-be foster children, and Kieran was at the man's throat before anyone knew what he was about. His face was shot with rage in an instant, his good humor vanishing.

"Milady, do you think you are the only one who walks barefoot on nettles these last days?" Finella challenged. "Taking on not just a wife but three foundlings not even his own—and just after being absolved of life-threatening charges and a brush with death—is far more than most young men will accept before pledging their troth."

Riona shook the front of her bodice, allowing air within. Her lovely gown clung to her from perspiration, even though a soft shower had come in the early morning to cool the wedding day. She'd lain awake half the night praying, asking over and over if she was doing the right thing. Memories surfaced, one conflicting with another.

She saw Fintan expressing his doubt that she belonged at the abbey. "You are a spirited soul, Riona. Remember, even Christ did not confine Himself to one place, but went out among the peoples to share and witness His faith. To confine yourself among those who strive to be as devout as you is far easier than testing your commitment in the world beyond the safety of our walls."

A wife, lady of the house, and mother...such roles provided ample opportunity to witness and serve her God.

"Heber's dead." This from the man she was about to marry. "Would God that it were me."

Except that Riona had forgiven him. So why couldn't she forget it? Why did this memory still stir resentment toward her foster brother, the very man she was to wed? *Abba, help me!*

"It takes more courage to do what we are led to do than what we want to do," her uncle Cromyn had told her just the night before. "Follow God's lead, child."

Finella's practical tone drew her back to the conversation at hand. "I am not the most pious of souls, milady, but Gleannmara's heart has softened before my very eyes. Instead of dwelling upon himself and his wants, he's making a pained effort for your sake and the children's. It doesn't come easy to him, but he is trying. He might have remained with the Dalraidi men and celebrated till sunup but instead assisted you in the last-minute preparations. Another lord would have appointed a hireling in his stead."

The women on the seamstress's slope of the fair had just finished fitting new clothes for the children to wear for the ceremony. While Riona saw to the little ones' baths and prepared them for bed, Kieran went to collect the garments. He'd even attended vespers, kneeling with his family-to-be. He wasn't perfect, but then, neither was she. They brought out the worst in each other...and the best.

"He was the most arrogant, pompous iarball I'd ever seen when we first met." Finella smiled, fondness twinkling in her brown eyes. "But he's showed himself to be more than a beastie's hind since."

Riona laughed. It was the first time she'd laughed since waking from her troubled sleep, and it was amazingly soothing to her troubled mind. "Aye, you're right. And this is just marriage fluster. I so hate being a ninny."

A rose-cheeked Leila entered the room and tapped her foot like an impatient princess. The child didn't have to say what she was thinking: It was time to move on—not just with the wedding, but with their lives.

An hour later, Riona approached the altar in one of the older churches at the monastery on Fynn's arm. Dressed in a new saffron tunic with princely trimmings in the autumn hues of his brat, he walked like a statue barely come to life. Liex and Leila preceded them in complementary shades of bright green and blue, matched miniatures too full of excitement to contain themselves. They waved gaily at familiar faces, grinning and giggling their way down the aisle despite the stern countenance of the waiting groom.

Or was it frozen? Even Kieran's ruddy complexion could not hide the fact that the blood had fled his face and neck. His royal torque of gold looked as if it were displayed upon a sheet. Faith, he was as skittish as she! The realization was oddly comforting. Riona met his gaze and smiled. Warmth kindled in the dark amber of his eyes. She felt it spreading in herself as well—a soothing, reassuring warmth.

"'Greater love hath no man than this, that a man lay down his life for his friends,'" her uncle began. The words from the chapter of John echoed in the rafters, amplified by the natural acoustics of the building. "And it is that kind of love that brings these people here today, before God and man, to declare it. Riona of Dromin and these children risked their lives for Kieran of Gleannmara. This same Kieran has risked his own life for their sake."

Greater love had no man... Nor woman, Riona thought as Fynn solemnly presented her when asked who gives this woman.

"I require and charge you both," Father Cromyn continued, "as ye will answer at the dreadful day of judgment when the secrets of all hearts shall be disclosed, that if either of you know any impediment why ye may not be lawfully joined together in matrimony, that ye confess it."

Riona shook her head despite her thoughts. Fynn's role belonged to her father. Where the king of Scotia Minor stood next to Kieran, Heber should have been. But what was and what should be were not always the same—not for God's own Son, nor for her. The past would be resurrected in the future. For now she prayed her loved ones watched from a holy loft.

"I, Kieran O'Kyle Mac Niall of Gleannmara, do take thee Riona, to be my wedded wife, to have and to hold from this day forward, for better for worse, for richer for poorer, for fairer or fouler, in sickness and in health, to love and to cherish, till death us depart, according to God's holy ordinance; and there unto I plight thee my troth."

There could be no doubt as to the sincerity of Gleannmara's vow. He looked at and spoke to her as if to envelop her with his spirit. Such was the completeness of the embrace that her own vow echoed outside it, as though it belonged to one of the bystanders. Rings hastily purchased at the fair were exchanged in lieu of the one that had been used to frame Kieran for murder or that belonging to her father, which remained in keeping at Kilmare among the belongings Riona hastily left behind at the abbey.

Father Cromyn wrapped their joined hands with a gold-tasseled sash. "Let us pray. O Eternal God, Creator and Preserver of all mankind, Giver of all spiritual grace, the Author of everlasting life, send Thy blessing upon these Thy servants, this man and this woman, whom we bless in Thy Name; that as Isaac and Rebecca lived faithfully together, so these persons may surely perform and keep the vow and covenant betwixt them made, whereof these rings are given and received as a token and pledge, and may ever hereafter remain in perfect love and peace together, and live according to Thy laws; through Jesus Christ our Lord. Amen."

As Riona and Kieran repeated the Lord's Prayer with the gathering, she heard the small but strong voices of her children—*their* children—saying the words she'd taught them in earnest concert until the closing amen.

"And thank you for sending us parents," Fynn and Liex simultaneously inserted.

Riona glanced at them. All three siblings held hands, heads bowed.

It was hard for her to see through the tears that started somewhere in the midst of the ceremony, but as they looked up, joy spilled over their faces.

"God the Father, God the Son, God the Holy Spirit, bless, preserve, and keep you," Cromyn went on without stumbling at the improvisation. "The Lord mercifully with His favor look upon you and so fill you with all spiritual benediction and grace that ye may so live together in this life, that in the world to come ye may have life everlasting. Amen."

The priest looked up, grinning as widely as either of the youngsters. "*Nephew,* you may kiss the bride."

Thought fled Riona's mind at the prompt. She turned, toes curled within her slippers in expectation. Kieran tipped her face upward with the crook of his finger. Leaning down, he brushed her lips with a soft promise and then straightened to full height, shoulders squared. Beaming like a king's candle, he slipped his arm around her and turned to face the onlookers.

"Good friends," he announced, preempting Cromyn, "Thanks to God's good grace, I give you my lady and my life, Riona of Gleannmara."

A chorus of congratulations and huzzahs filled the chamber. Pipes gathered their wind in preparation for the couple's exit at the back of the church. Suddenly a shower of flower petals rained over them. Riona turned to see Fynn holding Leila up on his shoulders, the latter laughing as she shook the last remains from her ribboned basket. Liex scrambled to gather them up from the floor for one last toss when Kieran reached down with his spare arm and scooped him up by the waist.

"Hey!" the lad shouted, astonished as the groom tucked him under his arm and, with Riona on the other, carried Liex out backwards, Fynn and Leila bringing up the rear. Surely no stranger—nor happier—recession had ever been seen.

The journey back to the bruden didn't seem half as long as that which took Riona there. Since the brewy already entertained a king and his court, the establishment was well prepared for the wedding party and its esteemed guests. A dais had been constructed, its white silk canopy adorned with flowers and vines for the high king, Aidan,

and for the bridal couple. To the right of the entrance was Aedh's retinue and court, while the Dalraidi and Dromin dominated the benches
surrounding the low tables on the south side of the entrance.

There were too many guests for any to recline or laze normally while
they supped. Word of the extraordinary events at the race and of the
wedding that replaced a trial had spread. Each bench was filled to
capacity. Guests stood near the kegs of wine and barrels of ale where the
bruden master himself dispensed the drink. A fair *and* a wedding with
royal, clerical, and allegedly supernatural blessings was as good an event
as any Celt could want.

Toast after toast was lifted in honor of the newlyweds, while all
manner of meat, fish, and fowl circulated on trays as large as cart
wheels. Breads of all shapes, sizes, and grains were heaped on every
table along with fruits, both dried and fresh, and nuts imported from
the east. Musicians provided by the high king orchestrated the lively
conversations, inspiring many guests to tap their feet and legs without
missing a word regarding their subject of interest.

Friends both old and new, noble and common, shared the closest
tables to the newlyweds and their honorable hosts. Besides the northern Uí Niall presence—which included the high king and the
Dalraidi—a representation of their southern Niall clans was also in
attendance, including Bran Dub, the provincial king of Leinster and
overking to Gleannmara, who arrived just in time for the occasion.
Bran Dub and Aidan exchanged stories of Kieran's exploits in their service over a flagon of wine imported from Gaul.

Conspicuously absent was Baetan, the northern Niall King of
Ulster. Uninvited because of his resentment of his cousin Aedh
Ainmire and because of a stubborn insistence that the Dalraidi of
Scotia Minor owed him—not the high king—allegiance and tribute,
Baetan sulked at Tara, a would-be high king in a once-glorious court,
now cursed and abandoned. Not even Gadra and the minions Baetan
had sent to keep him abreast of the business of the fair had shown up.

For Riona's part, Maille was not missed.

Whether guilty himself or guilty by association, he'd nearly cost
her Kieran's life and possibly those of the children. Only the heavenly

Father could use evil's own redhand to point out the answer to her prayers for guidance and send the most unlikely earthly angels to their rescue, Riona thought, seeking out the gleemen in the crowded hall.

If she and Kieran had not already adopted the gleeman's orphans, Dallan and Finella probably would have. Under the fatherly eye of Dallan, Fynn and Liex participated in tumbling, but Leila held back, sitting like a petite doll beside Finella. The latter had told the child that ladies didn't tumble head over skirts, but sat like queens over their court. All Leila needed was a scepter. Instead, she held Lady Gray, who slept in regal repose on her mistress's lap.

Marcus divorced himself from the amusement that evening. Instead he was the entertained. Glued to the elbow of Aidan's bard, he listened in awe to the elder expound upon the elements of rhyme. Not a word seemed wasted on the younger man.

All told, it was a strange mix, with high king to lesser kings and cattlelords; bards of the highest order and their lowly counterparts; soldier champions of war and priestly advocates of peace. That all had gathered to honor Kieran and his bride was more than Riona could grasp. Kieran's superiors and peers toasted his character as much as his sword. Words such as *noble, loyal, fair,* and *stalwart* echoed all around her. She knew now that her own imperfections had caused her to turn a blind eye to Kieran's many good qualities and focus on a flaw. Her heart, though, had seen him as he was: a good man. Imperfect, but good.

A new arrival entered the hall flanked by two companions. The foot Riona tapped to the music stilled. How dare Lord Maille show his face! Indeed, as the Ulster lord boldly approached the head table, conversation dampened in his wake. The music played on, but the boisterous voices were now subdued to speculative whispers.

"Milord." Maille addressed Kieran, seemingly oblivious to his reception. "I have come to publicly offer my apologies and my congratulations, in that order." Maille pulled a small, drawstringed bag from his waistband and handed it to Riona's new husband.

Otherwise impassive, Kieran's brow shot up as he took it up and shook out the contents. It was the ring he'd sought the night of Fintan's murder—the one he'd intended for his future bride, that instead had nearly become his death sentence.

"The late bishop had it in his possession…part of the evidence he'd hoped to use against you," Maille explained. "Now that the man has confessed, albeit posthumously, and you are absolved both by earth and, I hear, heaven as well, I see no reason why you should not have it for your lady."

Riona shuddered. She wanted no part of it. At least, not until it was washed.

"Not *all* the redhands are absolved to my mind," Kieran observed pointedly.

Maille was unaffected by the subtle accusation. "If you refer to Tadgh, Senan's hired assassin, put your mind to rest. It seems he drowned after being run into the river at sword point."

Riona looked at Kieran sharply. They both knew the hand on the hilt of the sword. He refused to meet her gaze.

"I mourn no slaver of innocent children," Kieran disdained. "Few deserved to die more. Erin's judges were spared in that instance."

Still he refused to look at Riona as he absently toyed with the ring, the drill of his gaze riveting Maille where he stood. Was it shame she detected behind his facade of bullishness? Mayhap Finella was right. Kieran's heart was softening—not in leaps and bounds, but changing nonetheless. She placed her hand over his and gave it a reassuring squeeze, as if to say, *I am with you, beloved. I know how you feel.*

"Blood drawn from greed will return to the hand that spilled it," Father Cromyn reflected from Riona's side.

Maille gave the priest a quizzical glance. "Is that a scriptural viewpoint, Father," his voice dripped in skepticism, "or have you become a prophet?"

"Nay, milord. 'Tis my earthly one. In the end of the eternal scheme of things, God alone will judge the murderer and decide his fate," Cromyn answered. "What is judged or misjudged by us in the now will either be reinforced or rectified then."

"But earnest repentance and assuming responsibility for one's deed can change God's ultimate verdict," Riona ventured softly for Kieran's

sake. She didn't know how much he remembered of the Scripture he'd
turned from. She only wanted to remind him that all was not lost over
past mistakes. Only the future mattered to the earnest confessor.

Cromyn nodded in agreement, but Colga, sitting within earshot at
another table, lifted his goblet of ale—apparently the most recent of
many, given the slight slur of his speech. "Come now, friends, surely
there are some sinners whom even the blood of Christ cannot wash
clean." He took a healthy swallow and then peered into the remnant
wine in his cup. "Red—" he spoke to no one in particular—"looks like
blood, doesn't it, milords?"

"To a guilty eye perhaps," Kieran replied.

"Or a drunken one," Maille suggested in contempt.

Colga closed one eye and looked at the drink that threatened to
spill from the tipped vessel's edge, then switched to the other eye. With
a snort, he shoved the cup toward Maille. "Here, Ulster. Have a look
yourself."

The wine did spill this time, smack into Maille's face. With a vehement curse, he backed away and wiped his face with his sleeve.
"Contain your new chief, Gleannmara, till he learns to drink with
men."

Kieran started up from the table, but a second squeeze of Riona's
hand restrained the man, if not his tongue. "Then leave, milord, that he
might."

Instead of taking offense, Maille gave Kieran a half smile. "We've a
long journey home together, Gleannmara."

It was a simple truth, yet it reeked of threat. Senan's body was to be
returned to Kilmare. Knowing Kieran was eager to return to Gleannmara
with his bride and that Kilmare was on the way, Aedh Ainmire charged
Maille and Kieran to the task.

"I came in hopes of mending the hard feelings between us, but I
see that I speak to deaf ears."

With a stiff bow, Lord Maille turned away. He gave Colga a long,
seething look and retreated out of the hall. *Poor Colga*, Riona thought.
He still blamed himself for Heber's death. The fruit of the heath had
made his guilt worse. Her cousin's bitterness glittered like the sparks in

his father's forge in the gaze that followed Maille from the room.

The moment Ulster cleared the open door, the entire room seemed to breathe a sigh of relief. How well Riona knew that the dining daggers of the Dalraidi and Gleannmara clans might just as easily be turned to violence as to the succulent meats served in plenty all around them. Had Maille come in last night…

Riona shivered, recalling Kieran's short temper. But tonight he'd held it. Had an epiphany come to him as it had to her? Finella was right. Gleannmara was trying and succeeding, though his barbed tongue needed more pruning.

"Thank you, Kieran."

He looked at her, eyes wide, his goblet of ale poised at his lips. "Milady?"

"For taking the peaceful way rather than the violent."

"I was ready for the blackguard either way," a voice answered. "He'd have toes to match his black heart."

It belonged to no one seated at the table but came from beneath the drape of fine linen covering the food board. Kieran lifted it to expose a small, round face set in determination. Proudly, Liex held up a stone the size of a warrior's fist.

Kieran roared, not with anger but in amusement, as he dragged the boy up on the bench between him and Riona. "We've an irascible lot to redeem, milady."

"Indeed, my niece has her plate full with the four of you," Cromyn agreed. At Kieran's disgruntled expression, both he and Riona chuckled.

"Faith, I'm celebrating, and my own wife turns against me!"

Riona leaned over Liex's head and kissed Kieran on the cheek. "Never against you, Kieran. Always for you, with my love."

He rose, trapping Liex between them and pulling her into his arms as if everyone else in the room had vanished. As Kieran lowered his lips to hers, Liex reminded him in no uncertain terms that that was *not* the case.

"Hey, whaddya tryin' to do? Snuff out my breath?" His showman's blood rising to the fore, Liex beamed at the ripple of laughter he'd instigated.

Kieran backed away from Riona just enough to grasp the boy by
the sash at his waist. Lifting the lad with one arm, Kieran put him aside
on the table as if he weighed no more than a basket of bread and
returned to his original purpose: kissing his lady.

His lady.

The idea was more intoxicating than all the heath fruit in Erin.
Kieran's senses were heightened, both in the physical and spiritual
realm. While Riona's undeniable outer beauty fascinated his eye, her
inner beauty transformed his spirit. He wanted more than anything to
please her, and that meant pleasing her God. To his astonishment, it
was not nearly as burdensome a thought as he'd feared.

These last weeks with Riona had awakened more than his earthly
senses. His need for her opened his eyes to his spirit's need…for the
pained emptiness, which had hardened the wall around his heart, to be
filled. She'd never abandoned him in his time of trial, and neither had
God. He knew it now. He should have picked it up at the time, but it
took the brush with death at the race to open his eyes to the unseen
Hand that protected him and his little band of fugitives. Leila's warning
to abandon the road just before Maille's men passed…their chance
meeting of Dallan's troop of entertainers when he was wounded and
Riona needed help…

Hindsight convicted him that nothing had been left to chance. He'd
abandoned God, but God had not abandoned him. The frayed pieces
of his life suddenly came together in that simple truth, which tran-
scended place and time, for neither governed the spirit.

It did not, however, transcend the intrusion of Marcus's wry comment: "Friend Gleannmara, whilst I marvel at the power of love to
make one forget his surroundings, I'd suggest you save your energy for
later."

Snatched from the epiphany of heart and soul, Kieran reluctantly
released his bride. Marcus was right. Fire flooded Riona's porcelain features and danced in her eyes. Oh, to leap into their depths.

"Harumph."

The last remnant of love's spell snapped, as did Kieran's words.
"What *is* it, you ball-tossing nuisance?"

Marcus took a step back, as though wounded. "Indeed, milord, you were most willing to hear this ball-tossing nuisance's advice on matters of the heart, but now that you've won your love's desire, alas, you've no ear left for me."

Kieran drilled the jongleur with an impatient stare. "I am much obliged, e'en though the merit of such advice is still in question."

Dallan stepped forward. "Well said, sir. Marcus will take credit for hanging the sun if we let him."

"But that is neither here nor there," Finella added. "The fact is, we've wedding gifts for milord and his bride."

"Heavenly days," Riona exclaimed at Kieran's side. "You owe us nothing. 'Tis we who owe you for all your help when Kieran was ill."

"Milady," Finella insisted, "I've taken the liberty of packing my apron of herbs in your things."

"But that's your means of making a living," Riona protested.

"And I hope I've no need for them again," Kieran chimed in heartily.

"With that temper of yours, you'd best take them," Marcus advised, earning Kieran's good-humored scowl.

"I'm making another," Finella assured them. "It will be finished by the summer's end. Meanwhile, I've little need for it in the bruden's service. With your impetuous warrior and children about, 'tis wise to have such a collection."

Kieran frowned. Something in Finella's tone suggested she was offering more than precautionary advice. Her smile had faltered, and sobriety filled her voice. Had the woman seen something ahead that would require the use of the herbs? The men were always remarking how they yielded to Finella's notions, for they were invariably right. Kieran was about to ask, when he was distracted.

"Marcus and I wish you to keep this." Dallan reached over and tapped the brooch of Gleannmara, which held Kieran's brat in kingly fashion. "Wear it proudly, friend, for that is what you are."

Concern vanished with shock, and Kieran stood in stunned silence. When he'd given the brooch of his ancestors over to the gleemen in payment for their aid in reaching Drumceatt, it had been as though he'd given away a piece of his soul. Since then, his soul had been filled by Riona's love. Winning his bride was more important than a piece of jewelry regardless of the sentimentality attached to it. This overwhelming gratitude wasn't something he was comfortable with. Its blade wedged in his throat, cutting with both edges.

"I...you..." Words failed Kieran. He shook his head and pushed the jeweled piece away. How could he equate the brooch's sentimental value with what the gleemen had done for him? "No. This is the well-deserved payment of a debt."

"And now it is a gift," Marcus told him. "Don't insult us by refusing."

Kieran grabbed the entertainer and hugged him in a stiff, manly fashion. In turn, he thanked Dallan and Finella. Kieran's soul, once nearly empty, now spilled over with abundance. "God keep you, good friends."

TWENTY-SEVEN

It was well into the evening before Kieran and Riona were escorted to the guest cottage by their friends. As Kieran closed the door—shutting out the good wishes for health, long life, many children, and much pleasure in achieving all—Riona stared in disbelief at the nuptial bed. She was nervous enough as it was, but someone had draped it with mistletoe, enough to celebrate the Yule season rather than summer.

"Faith, someone has high expectations." Kieran slipped up behind her. "I'd like an heir, not a litter."

Riona laughed. It helped ease the apprehension that had increased with each step toward the lodge.

"You grab that side," he told her.

Riona helped him remove the garland from the headboard of the bed. He gathered it up and tossed it in a corner with a wicked curl of his lips.

"'Tis only my bride I care about this night." He walked around the bed and took her hands, lifting them to his lips. After kissing each one, he wrapped her arms around him. "Tonight we begin the loving and cherishing."

Riona expected him to lay claim to her mouth as he lowered his face to hers but instead, he pressed his forehead against hers, peering into her eyes.

"There's no need to be frightened, milady. I would never cause you harm." He backed her against the bed and, hands on her shoulders, had her sit on the freshly fluffed mattress. It protested softly beneath the crush of her weight. Her heart leaped into double time.

Again she was fooled as Kieran placed a kiss on his finger and pressed it to her lips with a husky "Stay here."

What went on in the wedding chamber had been left mostly to Riona's imagination. Even though the physical act itself sounded disgusting, she'd learned with a keen ear that men enjoyed it. And given the smile Riona's mother, Ethna, wore when her father, Murtagh, was home, Riona assumed it was possible for women to take pleasure in it, too. But Ethna of Dromin hadn't been given to talking about it like the servants, any more than had Queen Lorna, Riona's foster mother at Gleannmara. Aside from ancient love stories and romantic eloquence of the Song of Songs on the subject, Riona had been left to her own devices to discern this most confusing aspect of life.

She wiped her hands on her skirt—blue for purity—painfully aware how her new linen shift clung to her like a second skin despite the pleasant coolness of the summer evening. This night she wished she'd not been quite as devoted to purity of thought. She simply hadn't prepared to become a wife. She'd prepared to wed the church.

Anxiety gave way to impatience as she heard Kieran moving about in the other imda. What on earth was he doing? Heavenly Father, if he came in mother-naked, she'd faint. Riona had nursed men before, Kieran included, but this was different. This time Kieran was not just an extraordinary man, he was her husband.

From out of nowhere a loud hiccup—half gasp and half squeal—seized her breath. She grabbed at the sharp pain in her chest. Oh joy, this was just what she needed.

A rush of footsteps preceded Kieran into the small enclosure. "Are you ill?"

To her relief, he was still fully dressed…and carrying a basin of water. She shook her head and pointed to his burden. "What—hic—is that?"

His smile nearly overstretched the square of his jaw, he was so proud. "A foot bath," he announced. The exotic scent of the water drifted up to her nostrils as he put the basin on the floor and reached for her slippered feet. Instinct bade her draw them away—Kieran of Gleannmara knew how sensitive her feet were and had tickled her breathless too many times to count. He chuckled as he caught them, his mind obviously drifting along the same path as hers. With an irascible twinkle in his eye, he mouthed the words, "Trust me."

She'd promised to love, honor, and cherish. The trust part must have been implied.

The wary look on Riona's face brought back memories, precious ones of a time Kieran often longed for, when their parents were the responsible ones and he, Heber, and Riona were free to game and frolic with unencumbered minds. Not everything had changed though. Riona was still as sweet and innocent as she'd been then, except now she was a woman. No longer was she his playmate, but his life mate. Her childlike spirit was tempered with a wisdom beyond her years and in some respects—such as faith—beyond his.

Kieran wanted to pinch himself to be sure that this was real, that Riona was his. He wanted this night to be perfect. Marcus had reminded him that somewhere in Scripture feet washing was a sign of love. Having had more experience with the gentler sex than Kieran, the self-proclaimed Tristan thought this might impress a devout lady and put her at ease. The gleeman had sought to teach Kieran an appropriate poem to recite as well, but it sounded so ridiculous that Kieran had abandoned it—and his chortling advisor. If Marcus laughed at him, Riona surely would.

"I did—*hic*—take a bath," she reminded him as he put the slippers aside.

"This is a declaration of my love, milady."

She cocked her head to the side, clearly bemused. Kieran hid a scowl. At least she hadn't laughed. Kieran knew the game of seduction well when he dealt with a saucy wench whose appetite matched his own. But Riona's fire had not been kindled in that manner. Those sparks he had seen beyond the glow of her joy made his blood simmer.

"You know, lass," he explained, "just like one of the disciples did for his wife."

The slender, dainty feet in his hand were cold, yet at the feel of them he reacted as though he'd been scalded. With a splash, he dropped them in the water before he was tempted by the cute clench of her toes to kiss each one into relaxing. He couldn't recite his own name now, much less a poem.

"*Hic*—my skirts!" With a jerk, Riona hiked up her hem in dismay.

"And I know of no disciple's wedding in the Scripture—*hic*."

"Well, somebody washed *somebody's* feet, I know that much." Annoyance sharpened Kieran's voice. He should have known better than to listen to a fool. Marcus was a poor substitute for Heber or Bran. They'd paid far more attention to their scriptural studies.

"Jesus washed His disciples feet at the last supper," she suggested.

Her legs were the perfect match for her feet, decidedly shapely and fem—

"And Mary washed Jesus' feet and—*hic*—anointed them with spikenard. She dried them with her hair."

The base heat warming Kieran's blood deteriorated his humor by the heartbeat. "I don't mean his mother," he said, exasperated, "And I've no idea what's in this oil Finella made. But whatever and whoever was involved, they did it for love, confound it!"

He shook his wet hands. The towel. He'd left the towel in the other room.

Face burning like a cook's over a hot fire, Kieran pushed to his feet and stormed away. His plan was unraveling faster than he. He was warmer than Sheol's coals, he thought, shirking off his brat. He'd waited so long for Riona, but the time wasn't right yet. His bride's mind was fixed on his vague knowledge of Scripture and her hem instead of on her husband's love for her. The wind of his frustration hissing through his teeth, he headed for the door.

"Kie—*hic*—Kieran, where are you go—*hic*—ing?" Riona called after him.

"Soaking your feet has accomplished naught, so I'm after soaking my head!" He stepped into the night. At the corner of the cottage was a rain barrel where water was collected for the guests use. Flipping off the lid, he stuck his head in the cold water. He held his breath under the surface while his pulse pounded fit to separate his skull from his neck.

The worst of it was that it wasn't his head that needed cooling. Coming up for air, he wiped his soaked hair back from his face and took the dipper from its hook over the barrel.

"Have you lost your—*hic*—mind?" Riona asked from the door,

looking at him as if the question were merely a formality.

She was so beautiful, leaning out, her raven hair cascading like a silken mantle, framing her small, oval face and eyes a man could get lost in.

Groaning inwardly, Kieran filled the dipper and, pulling the neckline of his tunic out, he poured the contents down the front of him. "No, milady, I'm well aware of what I'm doing." He was so certain that he helped himself to another dip.

"Is this some warrior ritual?" She lifted the delicate black line of her brow skeptically. Suddenly, it dropped and wonder filled her face. "Kieran of Gleannmara! Don't be tellin' me you're nervous."

"It's not *me* standing there hiccuping like a newborn calf on sour milk."

Riona threw back her head and laughed. The mischief spanned the distance between them, drawing a smile from the bloodless press of his lips.

"'Twould make this easier if you carried a battle axe or sword, but Aedh banned decent weapons at the fair."

Pulling a straight face, Riona leaned out a little farther, and curled her finger at him with a look that ran him through like a blade fresh off the smith's fire. "Come back inside, milord, lest we both become the laughingstock of the fairground."

Kieran dropped the ladle where he stood. In three steps, he was at the door and Riona was in his arms.

"Faith, but you're wet and cold," she laughed in half-hearted protest.

He felt it as much as heard it, the vibration of her laughter against his chest. Little did she know that he felt like a simmering kettle about to lift its own lid. The height of madness to which Riona of Dromin could drive him left him breathless.

"And you're warm and I hope willing, lass, for I'm at my rope's end. I wanted this to be perfect for you, and the harder I try, the more of a fool I become."

"But such a—*hic*—lovable one." She held his face between her hands, fingers pressing gently to his temples as if to relieve the misery drumming there.

"If I frighten you, sweetling, then stop me, for—"

She silenced him with a short kiss. "You'd never hurt me. You said so, and I trust you, Kieran of Gleannmara, with my heart, my body, and my soul."

Kieran kissed her as if to explore and commit all three to his memory, not just for now, but for eternity. In that silent declaration where lips met, he endeavored to show her all that he was, all that she made him. She was his breath; he was hers. Breaking away just long enough to scoop her in his arms, he stepped inside, kicked the door shut, and carried her into the imda where he'd spent recent nights in torture. "I've learned something just now that I never dreamed," he whispered in her ear as he placed her gently on the bed.

Riona gazed up into his eyes. Reaching up, she brushed his hair over his ear, an innocent gesture with untold impact upon his crumbling defenses.

"That a heartfelt kiss will cure the hiccups, *and...*"

"And?" she prompted dreamily.

"And never leave the bathwater next to the bed." The basin was pressed against his leg where he'd stepped on its edge, and his feet were soaked by the deluge it spilled in revenge.

With a tinkling laugh, she rolled over and patted the spot on the mattress beside her. "The water we can clean in the morning. As for the hiccups—" the lazy stretch of her lips tightened his insides—"best you join me and make every effort to see they don't return."

TWENTY-EIGHT

A child's crying invaded Riona's sweet slumber. She blinked open her eyes in an attempt to separate reality and dream. The dark hollow of the thatched roof overhead was still there, as it had been since they first arrived at Drumceatt. Soft against her neck, the rumble of Kieran's snore told her that the joy and wonder of the night before had not been a heavenly dream, but real—as real as the warm sanctuary of the strong arms surrounding her. It would have been easy to close her eyes once more and revel in this newfound intimacy, but she heard the sound again.

It was more of a whimper than a cry. Riona dragged herself up on one elbow to listen more keenly, disturbing her sleeping husband.

With a grunt, he brushed her hair from his face. "What is it?"

Her own senses sharper now, Riona threw off the sheet and bounded from the bed. In a few hasty steps, she slipped her shift over her head and opened the door. The sudden invasion of morning sun blinded her momentarily before she recognized the small figure standing there.

"Leila!"

The child's face was tear streaked, her eyes swollen with dismay. Clinging to her shoulder and chewing affectionately on her mussed hair was Lady Gray.

"Darling, what is wrong?" Riona drew the little girl to her.

Brokenly, Leila told her in that unintelligible dialect the twins spoke. Meanwhile, Riona examined her dress. She didn't appear to have been molested. Still, it wasn't like her to set off on her own without her brothers, and they were nowhere in sight.

"Is she all right?" Kieran asked, drawing them both inside. He picked Leila up and hugged her. "What brings you here this hour of the morning? Did you miss me?"

A halfhearted smile touched the child's lips before she planted a kiss on Kieran's unshaven cheek. Startled and intrigued by its rough-ness, she ran a finger over it.

"That's it, isn't it? I knew it. You missed me." At that moment, Lady Gray decided Kieran's broad shoulder was fair ground. "Ach," he exclaimed, never one particularly fond of cats. He lifted the kitten away and handed it back to the girl. "Keep to your mistress, you four-legged hairball."

Leila giggled.

Riona warmed at the sight of the two. What a picture they made, the giant with the shirt he'd hastily donned hanging too far to one side and the sprite perched on one arm, their disheveled blond heads pressed together. The blessing so overwhelmed Riona that she had to blink away the happy glaze in her eyes.

Leila kept saying something and tugging at her shapeless waist, but to both Kieran and Riona's frustration, they had to wait until her broth-ers joined them later at the hall for morning meal before they under-stood what had happened.

The little girl had awakened before everyone else and decided to pay a visit to her new parents. Along the way, a man snatched the bag of her meager belongings, which she kept tucked in her sash.

Kieran growled in outrage. "I grow more tired of this place by the hour. Beneath the surface of games and court all manner of lowlife prey upon the innocent."

Riona brightened. "Do you mean it?"

She, too, had grown weary of all the pomp and people. To sleep in her own bed in her own house—in her *husband's* bed and house, she corrected with a whimsical smile—would be the answer to her prayers. She longed to go to her new home and establish a routine. If she never had another day's excitement, it would not dismay her.

Kieran leaned over and cupped her chin. "Aye, lass, more than any-thing. I want to take my wife home. To Gleannmara."

"And us," Liex reminded him, his face smeared ear-to-ear with honey and crumbs from the scone he'd demolished.

"Aye," Kieran laughed, "most certainly with our children."

Our children…to love and to cherish…I pledge thee my troth…sweet-ling…beloved wife…

Of all the words of the last twenty-four hours, Riona hardly knew which she cherished most. And she'd never forget Kieran's well-intentioned footbath. Surely no new husband tried harder or more awkwardly to impress and calm his bride.

"I was in Gleannmara only one day before leaving to find you," he told her somberly. "In truth, I haven't wanted to live there since my parents died. My foster home was more home to me. I'd lived there since I was seven or so."

Fynn looked up from scraping the last of his porridge from a bowl. "Then I'm glad we're your foster children. Otherwise you'd be sending us away." Fosterage was an accepted way of life, especially among the nobility.

Liex digested his brother's comment with a look of relief before carrying it a step further. "Does that mean if you have babies, you'll send them away when they get to be seven?"

Kieran exchanged a disconcerted look with Riona. "Well," he said, clearing his throat, "it's the custom. It keeps a prince from becoming spoiled. 'Tis part of his education, and it allies good families. I was raised by the clan champion, Riona's father. He taught me how to fight. That's how I met her and have loved her since she was a toddle-legged waif, all braids, blue eyes, and cherry cheeks."

The orphans laughed at the picture he painted.

"And I spent many years at Gleannmara with Kieran's mother," she informed them, "learning how to run a household, as well as skills with the needle."

"Tell us about Gleannmara," Fynn implored.

"Aye, please tells us," Liex chimed in. Leila nodded anxiously.

Their eager faces told more than they'd admit to or perhaps even realized. They longed for a home and a family.

Kieran rose, signaling the time to leave. There were other guests who needed the table and the benches surrounding it. Riona felt the children's disappointment. How long had it been since she had heard Kieran speak from the heart she knew to be noble and sincere? Not since his parents died, and he'd grudgingly become king at a costly consequence. And when he'd reached out to her to join him as his bride at Gleannmara, she'd rejected him. How horribly she must have hurt him, despite his façade of arrogance and indifference.

"Milady, I promise we'll talk about Gleannmara later," he assured her, obviously misinterpreting her troubled expression. "For now, let us make preparations to return with all haste so that we can show these ragmullions our new home," he added with a twinkle in his eye. "But the first order of our day is to replace Lady Leila's purse and find a suitable travel basket for that undersized mewling."

Like miniature soldiers reporting for duty, the children lined up and followed Gleannmara's king toward the door, leaving Riona to cover the flank. Her vision marred with emotion, she bumped into a hastily abandoned bench. If she were any happier, she'd need a towel hung round her neck.

The next morning, the fairground began to stir at the peep of the sun over the eastern horizon. Bells sounded from the monastery at Derry in the distance as if to ring in the day. Delicious scents of breakfast wafted in the air, blending with the smoke of the cookfires as if to hail everyone from bed to table. In the bruden yard, Gleannmara's party pulled together, preparing to depart and reluctant to say good-bye.

Finella gave each of the children a hug before coming to Riona. "A new bride's blush becomes you, milady." She blinked away a telltale tear and forced a laugh.

"I've no complaints with married life thus far," Riona answered, feeling her face grow even warmer even as she grinned.

Better to resort to humor than give in to the melancholy welling within at leaving their friends behind.

"Faith, I shall miss you and your tumbling cohorts," Riona exclaimed, embracing her newfound friend.

"'Twill only be until fall," Finella reminded her. "Then Dallan and I will show up at Gleannmara's gate, I promise." She glanced over to where the men stood with Kieran. "Indeed, I'd go now but for the handsome fee Aidan is paying us. His bard has even spoken to Marcus about going back to Scotia Minor at the convention's end as an apprentice."

"I take it that that would be a dream come true for our aspiring poet?"

Finella laughed. "A dream indeed, since noble blood is often the way of succession. The old man knows the gift when he sees it, and our Marcus does have it." She smiled at Riona. "Who'd have thought our chance meeting—"

"Godsent, not chance," Riona interrupted firmly. She had no doubt that God had indeed sent the gleemen in answer to her prayers for help.

She waved away a vendor bearing a tray of fresh-baked meat pies. They'd had their fill of porridge in the bruden hall, and a basket of food and drink had been prepared for a midday meal. By nightfall they hoped to reach another inn.

"Aye, I believe God crossed our paths," Finella agreed. She sighed. "I've long dreamt of settling down and running a brewy. That you have the land and suggested opening such a hospitality establishment was no chance. And I think God had Gleannmara in mind for you, rather than the life you had planned."

"Aye, who'd have thought it?" Riona certainly hadn't asked God to work out her problems by making her Kieran's wife. But He knew best, of that she was certain. "Our prayers are always answered, just not always in the way we expect them to be."

Finella grew suddenly solemn and hesitant. "And I believe God has given me a message for you...a warning." She seemed to think over her words carefully. "I feel foolish for saying this, but I dreamt that you desperately needed my cape of herbs. I don't know why, but I can't help but think that someone means you harm—that the dark cloud that has followed you to Drumceatt will leave with you as well."

Riona's smile faded. "Dark cloud?" But Kieran had been cleared of murder charges. They were husband and wife. The children were safe.

"It might have been the rich food at the bruden that disagreed with me," Finella added promptly. "But better forewarned just in case it wasn't indigestion. Caution is the best preventative."

The clatter of equine hooves and the creak of a wooden wheeled cart drew their attention to the approaching party on the road from

Derry. Black and red banners heralded Lord Maille's presence as boldly as the cart bemoaned its load: the wooden box carrying the remains of Bishop Senan. Driving the wagon was Father Cromyn and Brother Ninian, the late abbot's clerk and right hand at Kilmare.

"Milady!" Ninian's pious demeanor broke upon seeing Riona. "I bid you a good day a free man of God."

Finella hugged Riona a last time. "Go, and God be with you."

"And also with you," Riona answered.

She met Ninian as he climbed down from the cart. "A sad day, granted," he amended, out of puff from the exertion, "but good as well. Perfect days are reserved for the hereafter."

"It's good to see you again, friend."

Ninian's eyes twinkled. "And may I have a kiss from the bride?"

"'Tis the least I can do." Riona planted a chaste kiss on his round cheek and backed away. "We owe much to you for helping Kieran escape and warning—"

Brother Ninian put a finger to her lips, silencing her. "You owe me nothing." Lowering his voice he added, "Besides, ears are everywhere. Big ears with dark minds between them."

Instinctively Riona glanced at where Lord Maille watched her through narrowed eyes. Aye, there was a dark cloud, but a harmless one now, wasn't he? He had more the look of a poor loser than a fearsome foe at the moment. Nonetheless, she gathered the children, who'd been playing with Lady Gray.

"All right, sweetlings, mount up."

Ninian fell in beside her, his gray robe swishing with his lively step. He lifted Liex onto the pony's back after Fynn bounded up there on his own. The bounce in his voice resumed. "Indeed, milady, I have reason to believe I'm being considered for the position of bishop. While I regret the circumstances—" he glanced at the cart—"I am most humbled by the church's regard."

"May I help milady onto her steed?" Kieran said at her back.

Riona turned within the circle of his hands at her waist. With his golden locks swept back from his handsome bronzed face, he looked as though a sun god had sired him. "We're ready?"

He nodded. She hardly noticed Brother Ninian slipping away to the funeral cart or heard the abrasive hawking of the fairground vendors touting their fresh wares. When Kieran's gaze bore into hers as it did now, the world passed by unnoticed.

With ease he lifted her to Bantan's back, but not before sharing a lingering kiss. It promised more to come, and her heart danced at the prospect. She watched him fling his royal brat behind him and bound up on Gray Macha, where Leila had laid claim to her place of honor, perched on the horse like a little princess. At her waist hung the new bag Kieran had purchased for her. She fingered it as lovingly as she cradled Lady Gray's travel basket in her arm.

The steeds as well as the little pony that Bran had secured for the children were eager to be on the road after their confinement to the Dalraidi stables and crowded pasture. Dear Bran. How good it would be to be reunited with him. Riona wondered how he'd fared with Siony and the orphans. It seemed like a year ago rather than a matter of weeks that they'd parted.

Riona wrestled with Bantan to keep the small horse from breaking into a trot and passing Kieran, for well she knew his warhorse would not stand for it. A glance over her shoulder assured her that the boys were fine on the pony, which had fallen into step more readily than her mount. Flanking the small Gleannmara party was the Dromin, an all too familiar figure in their midst.

Lord Maille leaned over, bending Colga's ear. Without acknowledgment, Colga goaded his horse ahead, leaving a disgruntled Maille in his wake. Ulster's hard gaze followed her cousin as he pulled up beside the boys and then shifted to her. Riona felt as if a rain of icy daggers fell upon her, chilling her to the bone.

Instead of wavering, she held Ulster's gaze steadily, lifting one brow in question as if to demand what business he had in Gleannmara's presence. Maille's departing smile did nothing to assuage her uneasiness. "What did *he* want?" she asked her cousin.

"I wouldn't know. I wouldn't give him an audience."

Riona caught a whiff of liquor about Colga's presence and scowled. "You are chief of Dromin. Rudeness is not an option."

"I'll not linger near the man. A stench of death lingers about him like a plague."

Colga's remark was not without merit. Maille had appeared within hours of Fintan's murder. He hounded Kieran like a dark angel of vengeance out for Gleannmara's life—but his dark spirit had had to be satisfied with Senan's suicide instead.

Dark clouds, dark minds, death stench...

The words were enough to still the blood. But God had brought them safe thus far. And with that thought, another voice came to her, one that had comforted her in the darkest hours of their earlier journey. It had come from the holy well near the Liffey crossing, echoing in the night as they watched Siony approach the monastery there, yet no pilgrim had been seen singing God's reassurance. Given all that Riona had seen of God's mysterious handiwork, she no longer considered such things strange.

Father, You are my strength and my light. Of whom—and of what— should I be afraid? Of nothing! Reassured that all was in God's hands, Riona meditated upon her blessings and spoke to God also for Lady Gray.

Ahead on the prancing stallion, no amount of Leila's cooing could assuage the discomfited kitten. Riona could picture the bundle of fur huddled in its little basket, protesting for all it was worth. Her howls of protest, incredibly loud for such a tiny creature, continued to mark off the morning, but by the afternoon, she'd apparently grown contented that neither she, nor her basket would be pitched to the ground and trampled.

Instead, the creak of the cart wheel bearing Senan's casket kept cadence. Draped in a mean wool blanket, there was nothing about the casket to indicate the prestigious position the bishop once held. His suicide and the deed he confessed to had stripped him of recognition, religious or otherwise, save the presence of Father Cromyn and Brother Ninian. Perhaps that was why the wheel's whine sounded all the more mournful to Riona's ear.

No doubt a new abbot would be sent to replace dear Fintan. In the meantime, Ninian would take charge...unless Cromyn's presence in their midst was to become more than a visit to his home and family. Was her uncle to be the next abbot of Kilmare? Kieran had made travel arrangements so hastily that Riona had not had time to give it much thought. It occurred to her to drop back and ask, but with Maille riding next to the funeral cart, she decided she would wait for her answer.

It came that night at the same brewy where, during their journey to the fair, Kieran, delirious with fever, had been painted and passed off by Marcus as a sword-swallowing giant. Thankfully none of them was recognized, thanks to their regal attendance—and the absence of their more flamboyant companions. Sitting at her husband's side, Riona listened to Cromyn sharing what was transpiring between the priests at Derry and the nobility at Drumceatt.

By the end of the summer it was anticipated that each tuath was to have its own priest and bard to expand upon the spirit and mind of its children in both religious and secular schools. Cromyn had asked for and been granted appointment to Gleannmara to be close to his kin. The idea of a school in each tuath affording education to noble and common child alike, as well as a church for all at the tuath, gladdened Riona's heart and soul.

"What a shining example Erin will be for the world!" She clasped her hands together in excitement. "Truly God has brought priest, bard, and king to a glorious decision."

"Or He was as disgusted with the bards as the rest of Ireland," Kieran pointed out, ever pragmatic. "No longer will their likes extort and abuse hospitality."

Riona frowned. Kieran had come a long way toward trust in God, but he was still more rooted in earthly concepts than spiritual.

"Their wings are clipped, to be sure," Cromyn agreed, "but it is a wondrous idea." He smiled at Riona.

"Except for Marcus's wings. He's fairly flying as apprentice to Aidan's bard," Kieran remarked wryly. "And to be honest, the bards' merit as historians and teachers is worth saving. 'Tis the satirists whose bitter-sharp tongues sullied the waters for the rest of them."

Or maybe he'd come farther along than she gave him credit for, she thought, as he covered her hand with his.

"I found both church and school a trial," he admitted, "but what I've learned in both has stood me well when my sword failed. I know that now."

"I'd like to see Bran's face when he finds that Gleannmara's bard is now required to teach children as well as entertain," Colga said from across the table. Sprawled on a bench, he lazed, propped on one elbow, munching on a chunk of boiled venison. "Since our cousin gave up his notion of priestly conduct, he's been willing enough to make them, but that was the end of it."

"Aye, he has a colt's tooth as big as my fist," Kieran agreed.

Riona was torn between clamping her hands over her charges' ears and smacking both her husband and her inebriated cousin off their perches. An ever-sharp Liex gave her no time to do either.

"How does he *make* children?" the lad inquired.

"In his songs," Colga replied smoothly. "He makes them up in his songs."

Riona relaxed, amazed at the quick-witted recovery. Her relief was short-lived.

"And how did he get a colt's tooth?"

Kieran hastily jumped in to explain. "That just means that he likes the company of women a lot."

Riona scowled at the paltry attempt at redemption. Men!

"Do colts like women better than men?" She rolled her eyes at Liex in exasperation. Even little ones would worry the powder out of a scone.

"It means men are foolish," Kieran elaborated, "like young colts, when it comes to keeping the company of women," His irascible grin softened the brittle edge of Riona's humor.

"Well, *I'm* not foolish. I think girls are trouble, and I'm only six years old!" Liex crossed his arms in smug satisfaction.

Colga leaned forward with a toast to the lad, nearly spilling his freshly filled cup. "Then here's to this colt, at least, for he's wiser than the sorry lot of us, I fear."

An uncomfortable ripple of laughter circled round as he tipped his cup and took a deep drought. The excess spilled out the sides and down his chin, but the man didn't seem to notice.

Riona held her tongue behind a grimace of concern. Her cousin's drinking had markedly increased since his return to Ireland. If only she or Cromyn could help him to understand that Heber's death was not his fault but an accident. Colga said it himself—he hadn't meant to leave her brother unprotected. Indeed, Colga led his men in an attempt to protect Heber, unaware that the enemy approached her brother's troops from the other side.

She looked from Colga to Kieran. They'd matured since the day they'd ridden off, eager to test their mettle against Aidan's piratical foes. The battle had taken a toll on them both. Kieran was healing. Colga wasn't. She watched as he shoved himself upright, straightened his tunic and brat, and stumbled toward the door and out of the hall.

"Uncle, can't you talk to him?" she asked, looking over to where the door Colga swung behind him had been caught by one of Maille's black-shirted guards.

Black...dark.

A score of unpleasant memories assailed her—all associated with darkness—from Maille's threatening presence to the black moments of Finian's death and those of the brugaid. Riona's thoughts tumbled over each other till she righted alarm with reason. The black shirt meant nothing. Colga was in no danger. Both men simply heeded nature's call.

Cromyn shook his head. "He's as stubborn as his father. A good hammering with his sledge won't get his attention until he's ready to give it."

"Maybe he has reason to drink to excess," Kieran suggested grimly.

Excess of any habit was nothing to be proud of. An Irishman took pride in self-control, both in food and drink. Eating till the belt was too tight or drinking oneself into a state of foolishness was shameful.

"Bran certainly thinks he does."

Riona remembered Bran's accusation the night she'd learned of Heber's death—that cowardice, not druidic illusion, had caused Colga to flee his position as guard. She could imagine Colga's shame if that was the case. It would disgrace not only him but all of the Dromin. Yet she could not harbor resentment toward her cousin, only pity. He clearly suffered enough by his own condemnation.

"Whether he chased a fog or ran from the enemy, he's punishing himself enough for it," her husband observed beside her.

Touched by this unusual show of compassion, Riona covered his hand with hers again and squeezed it. "You make me proud to call you lord of Gleannmara." The old Kieran would have condemned Colga without hesitation. Aye, Kieran was changing, and she loved him all the more for it.

"Ah, the sins of the father are visited upon his children," Cromyn observed to no one in particular.

Liex looked at the priest. "Whaddya mean by that?"

"Colga's father, Crogher, is a fine smith, but he's always had a weakness for drink. It looks as if it's passed on to his son," Kieran explained.

Fynn took exception. "That's not fair. That's like saying if my father was a murderer—and he wasn't mind ye—that me and the twins would be murderers."

"It's not quite as literal as that," Riona said patiently. She thought back to when Father Fintan had explained it to her. "When you throw a stone into a pond, the ripples go on, sometimes beyond where we can see them, right?"

The elder boy nodded in concert with Liex, but Leila felt led to comment. Liex gave his sister a dismissing elbow to the ribs. "What do you know?"

Indignant, Leila stated her opinion again.

"What did she say, Liex?"

"She said sometimes it carries on to another lifetime…or that's what Seargal told her."

Taken aback, Cromyn crossed himself. Riona looked at the child in wonder. "Actually, Leila has a wisdom beyond her years. For indeed, we will be accountable for our misdeeds on the other side."

"You said we'd be forgiven in heaven," Fynn objected.

Cromyn regained his composure. "Forgiven, yes, but we must admit to them before God."

"You see, Fynn," Riona explained gently, "when a person does something wrong, he may never see the effects, but they do happen. Sometimes our wrongful deeds hurt our loved ones, like our children."

"Or place a burden on the entire clan, such as in the eric, or blood price" Kieran put in with a kingly observation. "When a clan member commits a sin, it's up to the entire clan to make restitution for it, be it murder, thievery…any dishonorable deed. And I've seen it for myself, that sometimes the family or the clan can be harsher on the ne'er-do-well than a hangman's noose. At least it's over and done with on the scaffold."

"Have you ever fined a man or his clan with an eric?"

Kieran nodded to the boy. "After consultation with my brehon I have."

"You ever kill somebody?" Liex asked.

Kieran paused with an awkward glance at Riona. "Aye, I have killed my share of men on the battlefield. Men who would not be stopped by the law."

"Was it exciting?"

Riona waited for Kieran's answer with bated breath. She'd so often wondered how such a good man could take another's life. Not that she was so naive as to think it never had to be done. There was self-defense at least.

"At the time," Kieran said at last. "But it plays on a man's mind later, so that he remembers only the glory and shuts away the bloody grimness of it. When you get older you'll learn that *having* to fight and *seeking* to fight aren't always the same. There's no glory or honor in fighting for the sake of fighting. It wounds more than just those on the battlefield. Like the ripples, the pain travels on and on, to loved ones and friends." He looked at Leila and smiled. "All the way to heaven."

Later that evening, Kieran's answer still played like a balm on Riona's mind. He had changed…or at least was earnestly trying. The quick-tempered warrior who fought first and questioned later seemed to be gone.

When Fynn asked her to pray with him after she'd tucked her three foundlings into beds on the crowded floor of the now dark hostel, she said another prayer of thanksgiving for God's goodness in bringing their lonely souls through evil into a warm and loving family.

She meant every word, especially when she asked that heaven sustain their family and guide Kieran as a new king, husband, and father. As she rose to a small chorus of amens, a sharp pain invaded her knee.

"What's this?" she exclaimed, feeling amid the blankets and pallets for the offending object. It was Liex's sling and pouch of stones. "Now, why isn't this in your bag?"

"A man needs to be prepared for danger," the lad told her grimly.

Riona glanced at him askance. "Well, this little man needs be prepared for sleep. Between God, your father, and me..." *Your father and me...* It sounded so strange, yet so right. "We'll keep an eye out for you," she added as she slipped into the makeshift bed beside him. The scent of the pine and straw stuffing in the pallet stirred beneath her weight.

"You'll not be needing that in here," Kieran agreed. She tucked the weapon under her pillow and mimicked Liex's grave manner. "A girl has to be prepared for danger."

Chuckling deep from within, Kieran drew her to him as though she was the most precious thing in the world to him. After a moment, he whispered against the top of her head. "I felt ill at ease when I became king of Gleannmara, but I was trained for that. Yet tonight, this new role as husband and father has overwhelmed me. There's no school for that, no champion to teach this art."

The forlorn words clenched at Riona's heart. Turning in his embrace, she looked up at his face in the blackness and framed it in her hands. "What greater champion than the Father Himself, beloved? Or what better text than that of His Word?"

Their lips touched. Riona felt his smile of acceptance as his arms snaked around her, drawing her closer. The room was filled with travelers from all walks of life. Maille and part of his retinue were a short distance away; the bulk of his soldiers were encamped outside about the funeral cart. Yet the noise of humanity faded in her ears as the smile became a kiss, and the only words she heard came straight from her husband's heart to her own. The hall was now too dark to even cast shadows, but it wasn't blackness that blinded Riona.

It was light—the light of their love.

TWENTY-NINE

The room was filled with the murmur of sleep—a lullaby in itself, with the steady, high wheeze of some and the rumbling deep snores of others, all seeming to blend into a lulling melody. Occasionally a log chewed thin by the flameless coals slipped and fell on the hearth. Sparks lifted toward the opening in the roof, briefly illuminating the pitch-blackness of the room.

Riona heard it all through the thin veil of sleep. Wrapped in Kieran's arms, she felt his heartbeat against her back and his soft breath upon her neck, an unconscious balm of his love. It was inviting enough to draw her into a deeper rest, yet she resisted. She didn't know why, and it frustrated her no end, for it had been a long day's journey—and would be again tomorrow.

But instead of sleeping, she compared her heartbeat to Kieran's. Hers was faster, perhaps because she stewed about being awake. She toyed with the slingshot. Fynn had made it for his younger brother and worked it smooth as a tabletop. No splinters here, not even in the cradle of the Y. She fiddled with the stones in the boy's bag, counting them. Ten. As she fingered the last, it worked its way out of the sack.

Riona frowned. Oh bother. She eased away from Kieran and sought to stuff it back in the pouch when a floorboard creaked unnaturally close. She blinked in the darkness. Her pulse accelerated, even as she told herself she was being ridiculous. She was overtired.

Blankets and a mattress rustled, no doubt someone turning over. Feeling foolish, she took up the sling and slipped the stone into the leather patch, laying it ready on her stomach. If Kieran woke up and found her at point with the sling, he'd laugh himself silly. Still, Riona didn't put the weapon aside. Something was not in harmony with the rest of the room. There was discord in the lullaby, and that instilled the same in her. She never slept well in hostelries or brewies, huddled with strangers—

A log broke in two pieces and pitched into the coals beneath it. A glittering display of sparks leapt toward the domed ceiling, giving definition to her surroundings. Why was Fynn awake and standing over Liex?

No, wait. It wasn't Fynn. The lad wore trews. A tunic hung over the trim legs of this shadow…this shadow of a *man* reaching for the sleeping Liex's head. Without thinking, Riona pulled back the sling and let the stone fly, just as the last of the sparks over the hearth flickered and faded into the pitch of night.

A startled yelp affirmed a hit. Scrambling of feet confirmed malintent. Those who were not stirred by the first awoke to an ungodly howl, followed by a fierce curse. Kieran bolted out of a deep sleep to his feet, shedding blankets and nearly stepping on Riona. She heard the drag of his sword, which he'd kept beside him on the floor, then the sound of other weapons being unsheathed, metal abandoning leather.

Someone had the presence of mind to light a lantern. Several people were standing at the ready, weapons of every kind brandished, their expressions ranging from half asleep to irritated to totally stupefied.

Two men scuffled near the door of the hostelry. Kieran leapt nimbly across the beds and bodies still on the floor and was upon them in an instant. He wrung the knife from the hand of the assailant and slung him to the custody of one of Maille's soldiers. Then he seized the other man and hauled him to his feet by his tunic.

"Colga!" Gleannmara frowned. "What the devil is going on?"

"I caught 'im as he run for the door," the other man shouted. Riona recognized him as a trader of small goods, coarse in speech and dress but friendly. "He tripped over me wife."

"I was just on my way out to relieve myself," Colga protested, "when someone or some*thing* bit me."

Riona felt blood rush to her face. Self-conscious she buried the sling beneath the tangle of blankets her husband had abandoned. Father in heaven, what had she done?

"Hey, that's my bag," Liex exclaimed, pointing to the sack in Colga's hand.

Colga looked at the bag as if he'd seen it for the first time. "I...I thought it was mine in the dark."

"What, do ye take a change of clothes when ye *relieve* yourself?" the trader accused, tongue in cheek.

Those awake enough to appreciate the humor laughed, but neither embarrassment nor the indignation in his voice colored Colga's face. It grew whiter by the moment. "It's none of your flumin' business how I—"

"Give the lad back his sack." Kieran leaned on the hilt of the sword he'd made ready to use, its tip balanced lightly on the floor, as though the matter were settled. The calculation and suspicion in his eyes told another tale.

Straightening his tunic, Colga reached across some of the guests who'd not risen yet and handed Liex the bag but in the process dumped the contents.

"Sorry, lad," he said, hastily jumping in to help the boy pick up the belongings.

"Well, that's that. I suggest we put the drunkard next to the door so we all can get some sleep," Lord Maille said from across the room, his gaze narrowed on the spilled contents of the bag.

The resulting laughter abruptly halted at the sound of Leila's shriek. Distraught to tears, the child held up Lady Gray's basket. The hinge of its lid had been broken—but worse, it was empty.

Assured that the unholy howl that had awakened them belonged to nothing more dangerous than an outraged kitten, helpful travelers joined in the search for Lady Gray. Colga must have stepped on the basket in his startled retreat. "Hey, what's one of my stones doing over here?" Liex said, giving Riona a disparaging look, as if to say *I can't trust you with anything.*

Guiltily, Riona handed over the sling, which the boy tucked into his sack atop the belongings Colga had helped stuff inside.

Kieran burst out laughing. "I think I know what *bit* you, Dromin."

Colga stared at Riona in disbelief.

"I'm sorry, Colga. I didn't know it was you. I just saw a shadow over the children and..." She giggled in spite of her genuine contrition.

First he was stung, then Lady Gray shrieked. Sure, the poor soul must have thought a spirit had him.

"Here's your pooka, Dromin," an Ulster guard taunted. He drew a thoroughly disgruntled Lady Gray from her hiding place in the woodpile.

"Well, I shall sleep better knowing that I'm protected by a cat and a lady with a slingshot," Maille snorted. His words evoked another ripple of merriment, but the look he gave Riona was enough to curdle blood.

Oblivious to the undercurrent, Leila ran to claim her kitten. She gave the mustached man a thank-you peck on the cheek that melted his gruff expression.

"Good as a watchdog, that one," he told her, producing a friendly, uneven display of teeth.

With the candle left lit near the door, Colga took his leave. Gradually, the guests settled back in their beds to salvage what was left of the night. Instead of going into her basket, Lady Gray snuggled contentedly against Leila. Riona tucked the children in and gave each one a kiss.

"What was Colga doing anyway?" Fynn asked after getting his motherly due.

"I think he was disoriented in the dark, like he said, and grabbed the wrong bag on his way outside."

"Who takes his bag to the privy?"

"One who has had more than his share of heath fruit," she answered. She caressed the boy's face, where manly bristle would someday replace the near invisible down of his youth. "Now get some sleep."

"Nice shot," he called after her as she climbed into the bed next to her husband.

"You may not slay giants, but you sure scared the soul out of your cousin," Kieran chuckled softly as she settled against him. He nuzzled her nose with his, voice full of mischief. "Tell me, lass, does the God who disapproves of the sword approve of the slingshot?"

Condemned already by her violent although well-intentioned act, Riona compounded her guilt. She pinched his ear soundly and then hastened to do penance with a contrite kiss.

The rise of earthworks and rooflines above the abbey's buildings took shape in the afternoon mist, pervading the landscape of the last leg of their journey from Dublin's bridge over the black ford. Riona looked forward to changing into dry clothing and a night in her old bed with her new husband. Kieran could take the chill out of a mountain stream, she thought, glancing over to where Gray Macha proudly carried his lord. The lord himself sat straight in the saddle with Liex slumped against him in the cradle of his arms.

The child had fallen asleep and nearly fallen off the pony a little earlier. Fynn caught him by the seat of the pants and shook him, but Kieran rode up and scooped the sleepy youngster up on Gray Macha's back. He'd slipped into the role of fatherhood as naturally as that of a husband. She could not pinpoint exactly when this transformation had occurred, but she thanked God for it.

Brother Domnall was in the outer rath when they rode through the gate. With a hearty hail, he ran toward them, Leila's calf trotting at his heels. What a grand reunion it was. Riona was so excited that she hardly knew which of the many brethren hugged and congratulated her. They came from within and without the rath to greet the fugitives they'd helped escape and sustained with prayer.

"This is our father," Liex, who'd come wide-awake, called out, pointing with pride to Kieran. "He married us and the lady."

Domnall's eyes twinkled as they turned to Riona. "Well, I must say, milady, that becoming a wife and mother *is* becoming." His usually stern countenance erupted in laughter at his play on words, but he quickly recovered himself, raising a reproachful finger at her. "I always said you had no place in the abbey…rambunctious as the children, you are."

He meant no offense and Riona took none. Instead, she hugged him and planted a loud kiss on his cheek. "Life would have been easier on all of us if I'd listened," she admitted.

The boisterous welcome grew subdued as Brother Ninian told his compatriots about Bishop Senan's ill fate. Riona watched their faces register shock and misgiving. Domnall and a few others showed no astonishment at all, as if they'd suspected Senan's hidden nature all along.

"He left a trail of misdeed and treachery to his end," Domnall remarked as he escorted Riona and the children to her old quarters while Kieran saw to Gray Macha. The grooms remembered the stallion from his last visit and remained shy of it.

"Milady!"

Riona stiffened as Lord Maille hailed her. The Ulster lord carried an ornate box toward them. "These are the bishop's personal things. I'm wondering where they should go."

"And you couldn't ask Ninian?" Domnall queried impatiently. "Everyone knows Ninian was Fintan's and Senan's clerk, and heaven knows you've given him enough words to write to know as much."

Maille narrowed his gaze at Domnall and then turned it on Fynn. "Then here, lad. Would you be so kind as to take this to Brother Ninian's office?"

Fynn glanced at Riona uncertainly. She nodded. "I'll put your things away."

Handing over his travel sack to her, Fynn took the large, silver-chased casket. "I'll be right back," he promised.

Maille brushed his hands together, as though ridding them of dirt. "Well then, I'll leave you to refresh yourselves before supper."

"Vespers first," Riona reminded him politely.

He nodded with a wooden smile and took his leave. She looked after him, feeling somehow vilified by the contact.

"I know it's wrong to despise someone," she began, "but—"

"Heaven's saints themselves would be hard-pressed to love that one," Domnall interrupted in the same crusty humor that had caused him to be removed from the scribes' repository and relegated to the barns. As he realized his transgression, he crossed himself.

Lips twitching, Riona did the same. She dearly loved the man, even more so since he'd been so instrumental in helping Kieran. His manner was often flawed, but his heart was pure as gold.

"Look, mind you, you bleating bother, that's not a barn," he railed at the calf that followed Leila inside the dwelling. "It thinks it's a pup, the way it follows me about. 'Tis no small wonder I haven't fallen and broken a bone."

After herding the animal out, the priest reached inside the slit in his robe and drew out a crumbling piece of scone. Instantly attentive, the calf nuzzled his hand and brushed against him. "What is to become of me?" Domnall complained. "As if I've time to mother you." He looked up at Riona suddenly. "Will you be taking the child's calf to Gleannmara on the morrow?"

The alarm on his weathered face nearly broke Riona's heart. "Perhaps you'd keep it for her, now that she has a kitten to occupy her time...unless it's too much trouble."

Domnall nodded. "Aye, I suppose I could. The journey might be a bit much on its young legs, what with how they were twisted at birth."

Riona hugged the man on impulse. Tears stung her eyes as she drew away.

"If it's going to upset you, lass—"

"No, no." She shook her head. "It's just that...that I'll miss you and Ninian and...and everyone. You were all the family I had for so long."

The brother sniffed and wiped the tickle from his nose. "With three young ones, a strappin' husband, and a home to see to, I doubt you'll be missing me or that nose-aggravating barn. I've died a thousand deaths sneezing." He rubbed his nose again for good measure. "I'll be seeing you at vespers. Try not to be late."

Riona laughed. How well Domnall knew her. In spite of her best intentions, the handbell that called the order to prayer was often already put away by the time she hurried into the chapel for evening prayers. "I will, I promise."

Leila took a short nap with Riona while the boys fell into their normal routines. When they showed up at the guest house with Kieran, she knew where all three had been. Hay clung to Kieran's and Liex's clothing, while wood shavings littered Fynn's new brat. Hurriedly, Riona and Leila brushed them to make them fit for the service.

The bell ringer was just stepping inside as the family entered the chapel for an hour of reverence. Prayers were offered for Senan. Unlike his brother, Fintan, the bishop would be interred in a burial place removed from holy ground. While the earthly placement of his remains may have been fitting, the company prayed for his soul nonetheless.

The service over, the Gleannmara guests made their way to the hall where Fintan had received Tadgh and Mebh weeks before. Riona and her family joined the brethren in the refectory, while, to Riona's relief, Ulster's company dined at its encampment in the outer rath. The way Lord Maille watched her family, as if waiting to do his worst, did nothing to aid her digestion when he was within sight.

She shook off the thought. After weeks fraught with danger and anxiety she should not be searching for more unrest but enjoying the hot porridge and bread, followed by a dish of stewed fresh and dried fruit for dessert.

Riona looked with dismay at the twins' brats, which had caught whatever their eager mouths had missed of the syrupy concoction, while Kieran and Colga talked about the morning's departure. The latter, sober since his arrival at the abbey, looked horrid.

The good meal would do him wonders, Riona thought, for despite their uncle Cromyn's efforts to keep him away from it, Colga had leaned more toward drink than food the last few days. If only her cousin would give up this demon that blackened his humor and gnawed at him. But as Father Cromyn observed, Colga was set on condemning himself more than his heavenly Father was. Until the young man came to terms with himself, there was nothing any of them could do for him. What went unsaid was the fear that her cousin might go to the same extreme as Senan.

"I tell you now, nothing in all my life will look better to me than Gleannmara on the morrow's eve," Kieran vowed with a wink for her benefit, "unless it's my wife. Take my word, man, what you need is a good woman." He clapped Colga on the back, winning a hint of a smile, nothing more.

"Good is subjective...cousin Riona excluded of course," Colga acknowledged politely. "For the most part, to believe in what is good is to open one's mind to disappointment."

"God is good, nephew," Cromyn reminded him. "And there is no subjectivity regarding His goodness. He was, He is, and He always will be good."

"For you perhaps, uncle," Colga remarked on a cryptic note. "And maybe for those who have tried to do His will. But some of us have outright crossed it."

"Like the thief on the cross?" Cromyn countered. "Son—"

The door to the reception hall burst open, cutting the priest off. Two of Maille's soldiers preceded the Ulster lord inside and stood to his flank. Maille's maleficent gaze gnawed at the room, table by table, man by man, until he spied Fynn.

"There he is. There's the thief," he proclaimed in righteous indignation.

Fynn was so taken back that his answer was no more than a blank look.

"What in the name of mischief are you up to now, Maille?" Kieran thundered, jumping to his feet so suddenly that the bench upon which he and Riona were seated nearly toppled with her on it.

"Catching a thief," Maille replied. "Where is it, lad?"

"Wh...where's what?" Fynn stammered, gaze darting from Riona to his siblings, as if they might enlighten him.

"The silver encased vial you stole from that casket." Maille marched to where Fynn sat and yanked the boy to his feet.

In less than the time it took her heartbeat to echo, Kieran took the lad back, shoving him behind him. "Touch this boy again, and I'll skin you like the weasel you are."

Maille's guards remained at the door, weapons sheathed, for Kieran's men of Dromin were on their feet. It was a rude guest who carried weapons to his host's table, so they had nothing to fight with other than will and their dining knives. Still, Maille's party was outmatched.

"You disrespect me in my own tuath?" Maille growled in toothless threat.

"I have little respect for you *anywhere,* milord, but this land is God's, not yours," Kieran told him. "The last time I yielded to your sovereignty, I was met by injustice…which is what is afoot now. On what grounds do you accuse my foster son?"

"I entrusted Senan's casket of belongings to him earlier. The vial was in the casket then."

"That's a lie!" All eyes swung to Fynn at his vehement denial. "I…I took it to the abbot's offices just like you asked. Father Clemens was with me. Just ask him. I didn't take anything out of it."

"What's this vial to you anyway?" Kieran asked. "It belongs to the church."

"Senan was long a friend of mine. I gave it to him," Maille informed them smugly. "But when I asked Brother Ninian to open the box so that I might take it back, it was missing."

"And you immediately thought young Fynn here took it." Kieran's remark was no question. It was a statement of ridicule.

"His father was a thief. It runs in the blood."

"He was not!" His dining knife brandished, Fynn lunged at Maille.

Colga caught the lad by the collar and pulled him back. "Here, boy. He toys with you like a cat with a mouse. Don't play his low game."

"'The sins of the father…'" Maille taunted. "If you're innocent, empty your sack and prove it."

"He'll empty nothing for you. If he says he doesn't have it, he doesn't," Kieran said, chin jutting in defiance.

It was a familiar stubbornness Riona recognized, unmovable. Maille might as well negotiate with a statue. Fynn assumed the same posture. Another time the imitation might have warmed her. Now all Riona felt was dread. Cold dread. Was this the darkness Finella warned about?

A fierce battle of wills between two lords of the land waged in loud silence as each assessed the other. Kieran's hands were fisted at his side, his eyes afire with warning. One of Maille's rested dangerously close to the hilt of his short sword, his demeanor black and hard as onyx. After what seemed to Riona an eternity, stone gave way to fire. Maille stepped back and conceded with a nod.

"Very well then, Gleannmara. But I'd watch these little light-fingers closely if I were you."

"Maille, your only salvation at this moment is that you stand on

God's ground. To impeach their honor is to impeach that of Gleannmara. I'd suggest you take your men and leave before I dwell overmuch upon it."

A vein bulged at Kieran's temple as he rocked on ready foot, watching as Maille led his men from the room. A collective sigh of relief erupted with the closing of the door behind them. A few of the brethren made hasty crosses.

"I suppose we should be thankful our meal is over. Elsewise, our appetites might have been ruined by the foulness of Maille's presence," Kieran quipped wryly. He made a magnanimous sweep of his arm, acknowledging his hosts and companions. "And now, good brothers and gentlemen of Dromin, my family and I bid you good night."

"I just don't like that man," Liex grumbled on the way to the stone dwelling that had been Riona's home since her mother died. "I feel like maggots are crawling on my neck when I see 'im."

Riona shuddered at the graphic description, relating too well to the feeling. "I suppose we need to pray for him, not condemn him," Riona reflected aloud, as much for herself as for Liex. "It's not up to us to judge one another." Even as she said it, she knew it was easier said than done. "Although I need God's help to pray for the likes of Maille. I'm not as strong as Jesus was when He asked that his enemies be forgiven because they knew not what they did. Think how hard that must have been."

"Maille knows what he does," Kieran grumbled. "His every move has a calculated purpose, but this time his greed has made him reckless."

"Reckless?" Riona questioned, hesitating at the oaken door for the twins to precede her. Once inside, she placed the small lamp she carried on a shelf.

"While I was grooming Gray Macha, Domnall told me that Maille's men took this place apart after we escaped, even tearing open the pillows and mattresses. Sound familiar?"

Riona eased down on the mattress beside Liex, knees taken out by Kieran's news. "You think Maille ransacked our guest house at the bruden?" What on earth was he after? Riona wondered, helping Leila out of her dress. She gave the little girl a kiss on the tip of her nose and tucked her in, sparing Lady Gray her due as well—a gentle scratch behind the ears. The kitten yawned imperiously, bored with the entire conversation.

"I'd wager Gleannmara's brooch on it," Kieran answered, fingering the royal clasp thoughtfully.

"And I my new brat," Fynn agreed.

"A silver-encased vial," Riona murmured aloud, thinking back in time. A picture came to her mind of Fintan holding up just such a vial.

"Think of it," Kieran speculated. "Our belongings were riffled through. Leila's travel sack was stolen. Colga nearly made off with Liex's sack in the dead of the night."

"But that was a drunken mistake," Riona pointed out. Knowing Colga's disdain for Maille, the two should not be mentioned in the same breath. "Still…"

"Still what?" her husband asked.

All eyes were upon her, waiting. It was probably of no consequence, but it wouldn't hurt to tell them, she decided, taking Finella's advice of caution. "Fintan showed me such a vial the night he was murdered. But it didn't come from Maille. It was holy water brought by Senan from Kildare and among the gifts to be presented to Columcille at Drumceatt."

Kieran snorted. "What need would Maille have of holy water?"

"Drinkin' the Red Sea itself wouldn't save his likes," Fynn agreed, adding with no small hint of mischief, "though it would do well to drown 'im in it."

Riona gave her foster son a reproachful look and was rewarded by an irascible grin. Now where had she seen such a face, she thought, glancing at her husband. Mayhap the boy never completely left the man.

"But as for Colga's being caught with Liex's bag," Kieran said, returning to his first line of deduction, "perhaps Colga and Maille are somehow connected." He turned abruptly to Fynn. "Hand over your sack, lad."

Fynn looked thunderstruck. "What?"

"I said let's have a look in that sack."

"Are ye accusin' me of bein' a thief?"

Riona cringed as Fynn leaped to his feet, indignant. She felt the hurt lying beneath his bravado.

Kieran shook his head. "Nay, I'm just asking to see what's in that sack."

"No!" Fynn stepped backward into the night, as if prepared to run. His hidden pain surfaced, grazing voice and features. "I thought you *trusted* me."

Kieran gave no sign that he either did or did not.

"Of course, we trust you," Riona assured the boy, hopefully for the both of them.

"What would you do in my place, lad?" Kieran challenged. "People you love have been threatened for reasons unknown. Your enemy has admitted that he believes the object of his sinister search is in that bag." He scratched his chin thoughtfully, giving Fynn time to consider his words. "Wouldn't it make sense to tell the man that the bag doesn't contain his confounded vial of holy water?"

"I did, for all the good it did," Fynn challenged. "What makes *you* different?"

"I will give my word as king of Gleannmara, on the honor of my mother and father and theirs before them."

The word of a king carried great weight in any court. While Kieran's temper was well known, his word was of equal repute. Riona glanced from one to the other, not knowing what to expect. Kieran would see what was in that bag. She knew it. Just how was up to Fynn.

Evidently Fynn came to the same conclusion. Angrily, he handed the sack over. "Take the fumin' thing," he ground out in a cracked voice, then ran out into the night, slamming the plank door against the side of the one-room dwelling.

Riona jumped up to follow him, but Kieran stopped her.

"Leave the lad to cool his hackles. I need you here." He untied the cord cinching the sack. "Let's pray we see no silver-encased vial."

"You don't have to pray," Liex volunteered from the foot of the bed, where he petted Lady Gray. "It's not in Fynn's sack." At Riona's questioning look, he explained. "I go in it all the time. I'd have found it if it was." He motioned to the bed. "Go on. Dump it. I bet I can tell you everything in it. It has a spare shirt and his old stockings with the holes in the toes, the rings Marcus gave him, his darts, a…"

Liex named every item to the last that fell from the emptied travel sack, including a scarf that belonged to the adopted daughter of the fisherman who'd helped them travel around Dublin by sea.

"*That's* why he didn't want anybody lookin' in there, I'll bet," the younger boy announced, rocking back and forth on his heels with a wide, satisfied grin. "Fynn's in love."

"Well, that's that," Riona claimed, shaking out a blanket that lay folded at the foot of the bed. "You'll most likely find Fynn in the garden behind the abbot's quarters," she suggested to Kieran. "Just look for his glowing ears. They always turn beet red when he's embarrassed."

"Why should I go after him? I'm not the one who tore out of here in a temper."

Riona motioned Liex back onto his pallet and tucked him in. "No," she conceded, without looking at her husband, "but you of all people should know how it feels to make a fool of oneself when it comes to mixing matters of the heart with a short temper. Like as not, the lad's feeling quite the fool now and could use some words of comfort."

Kieran clung to his rebellion. "*I* never got any."

She couldn't help the devilment that infected her voice. "No, but you're *accustomed* to acting the fool. This is new for the lad."

Foul humor abating, Kieran raised a warning finger at her. "I'll remember that when I return, milady."

With a tinkling laugh, Riona jerked her head meaningfully toward Leila's and Liex's pallets. "And you'd best remember our company as well."

Thwarted yet again, Kieran rolled his eyes heavenward and stepped out of the small enclosure with a frustrated sigh. "Now I know the real reason folks wait to have children after they're wed, and it has *nothing* to do with being holy."

THIRTY

The brethren heralded the new day with song, not unlike their druid predecessors, except that they sang to the Creator rather than the creation. It was a peaceful sound that lulled birds in nearby trees to sing along, not the least intimidated by the presence of Maille's encampment or the party preparing to depart at last for Gleannmara. Even Gray Macha seemed soothed by it. The stallion stood still, ears pricked, as Kieran brushed his silvery coat. No impatient stomping of the hooves or derisive snorts this morning.

In the next stall of the stable, Fynn worked on Bantan, and beyond him the twins groomed the small pony. Kieran intended that each child would have his or her own steed to care for, Leila as well. As his foster father had told him when he protested that he was a prince and above such tasks, caring for what one had made one appreciate it all the more. And when Kieran got to be king, he'd appreciate the man who took over the chore for him, which allowed him time for his royal duties. Murtagh had been a good foster father, a good example. Kieran hoped to follow in his footsteps with these three halflings.

A loud sneeze from Leila followed by a giggle made him smile. Perhaps he used the term *halfling* too liberally with the twins, slight as they were.

"Bless you, sweetling," he called to her.

She babbled something that Kieran took to be a thank-you. *Almighty God, if everything happens for a purpose or can be used by You to some good farther along the way, what possible benefit can come of Leila's affliction?*

God?

Kieran stopped running the brush along Gray Macha's shank. Had he just prayed without forethought? Faith, he'd asked the question as if His Maker were in the next stall. Cromyn said God lived in a man's heart. Riona walked and talked with Him about as Leila did her invisible friend. Until now, Kieran had thought it a bit strange. He wasn't certain of the hows and whys of God, just of His existence and loving protection.

It wasn't like Kieran to ponder such things. It made him uncomfortable, like socializing with someone he'd wronged in error, feeling guilty despite knowing he was forgiven. For now, there were other things more pressing. Tucking the quandary in the back of his mind, Kieran put aside the grooming brush.

"Bantan is fit for the lady," Fynn announced, pleased with his work. "Shall I fetch Lady Riona?"

"Nay, let the twins bring the lady. We've one last thing to do."

The boy rounded Gray Macha's flank, his face set, without emotion. The alarm in his dark eyes betrayed his true feelings. "It's done. There's no need to say a word."

Kieran disagreed. "Maille has hounded us looking for that confounded vial. I intend to let him know on my honor that none of my party has it. And I will die for that honor. He knows that."

"I wouldn't waste time on 'im."

For a moment, Kieran saw a familiar rebellion. Not long ago, he would have agreed with the lad, but he hadn't had a family to protect then. He hadn't cared what sort of example he set.

"He's wronged us. We'll give him a chance to apologize and we'll let it go…er…forgive him, I suppose. Like Cromyn said last night over supper, what good's honor in man's eyes without it in God's also?" Kieran grimaced. "You forgave me last night when I apologized. It takes a real man to forgive and forget."

"You ain't Maille."

"Ha, praise the Lord for that!"

Instead of laughing as Kieran intended, Fynn looked away, still uncomfortable with the idea. He scuffed his feet. "It sounds right, well enough, but it sure don't feel it."

Kieran clapped the boy on the shoulder, well able to relate. "Now *that* we can agree on, lad." He wanted to do what was right in God's eyes. As a Christian king, one that heaven had surely delivered of late, it was his duty. It set well with his heart but not his gut. When the two were at odds, his mind staggered in the dust of the fray. Men of war he understood. Men—and women—of peace were something of a different nature.

"He'll act like the hind end of a bull on green apples."

Kieran's step faltered with his chuckle at the image. The more he knew of Fynn, the more he liked the boy. "Aye, he'll sputter and spout, like as not, but at least we'll have done what's right."

Although Kieran walked and acted in grace, he was no fool. He took a few of the Dromin warriors with him in case Maille was bolder and madder than he thought. Fynn walked stiffly beside him as they entered the black-and-red-bannered encampment. One of the guards hastened into a tent. By the time the Gleannmara presence had everyone's attention, Lord Maille emerged, his barber trailing him.

Beard freshly trimmed into its fashionable fork, the Ulster lord made Kieran wait while his attendant helped him don his sword belt. The dagger he shoved into the top of his boot glistened, sinister in the otherwise innocent glow of the morning sun.

"So, you've found the lad out, eh?" he asked after taking one last look in the hand mirror the barber handed him and finding what he saw satisfactory.

The condemning look he gave Fynn was wasted, for the lad refused to meet the man's eye. He stood so close to Kieran staring at the campfire that Kieran could feel the heat of his slight body. An uncommon urge to take the lad under his arm took Kieran by surprise.

"I found the lad out," Kieran answered. "He had no vial in his possession, holy or otherwise. "As a precaution, we searched all our belongings, but your vial is elsewhere. I swear it by the honor of my forefathers."

"Then you are a fool."

Kieran straightened, as if the barb of the accusation prodded his back. "If you look for a fool, milord, take another look in yon mirror." He pointed to the one the barber held in his hand.

"Those little thieves have made you weak-minded." Maille grabbed Fynn by the front of his shirt, jerking him away from Kieran. Before the boy's feet touched the ground again, it was Kieran who met the

Ulster lord nose to nose, and it was Maille's feet that dangled above the earth. With the glide of metal against leather, the men of Dromin closed around them, blades out in a formidable circle that held the Ulstermen at bay.

"Will you risk war—nay, your *life*—for a trinket?" Kieran growled. "Good neighbors of Ulster," he shouted in a raised voice, "think before you use those weapons you draw. Do you wish to spill blood, possibly your own, over a vial of holy water when there is enough to drown you all in salvation three days' ride in any direction. Or over silver little enough to make your wenches ask where the rest is?"

"Put me down or I'll—"

Kieran shook his prisoner into silence. "Confound you, Maille, I'm trying to forgive you, and you're making it impossible!"

"Forgive me? For *what?*"

"For acting like the hind end of a bull on green apples, sputterin' worthless filth."

Around them laughter erupted from both factions. Kieran shook Maille again. "Now apologize, or I'll shake you breathless."

"I'll not—"

Kieran whipped the lord's head back and forth sharply three times. "I didn't hear you," he bellowed.

Maille's glare was hot enough to singe the wool of Gleannmara's brat, but his color waned by the shake. Upon realizing he was inadvertently choking the Ulster lord, Kieran loosened his hold, but only slightly.

The laughter around them died, silenced by anticipation. Hardly a shirt among them moved with breath. Behind him, Kieran heard one of the Dromin clear his throat with a pained swallow.

"I…apologize," Maille finally said in a constricted voice.

It was enough. "Then I and my son forgive you, don't we, lad?" Kieran set the man down and released his clothing. "Well?" he added, turning to Fynn.

Fynn nodded. "Aye, I suppose." From the look on his face, it might have been he who'd been half-strangled, not Maille. Kieran lifted his head, another prompt, which the boy picked up. Fynn squared his slumped shoulders and lifted his chin, as was befitting the foster son of a king.

Satisfied, Kieran clamped a hand on the lad's shoulder. "I bid you all a good day, gentlemen, and a safe journey back to your homes and families."

With that, he led the Gleannmara faction out of the camp. Ahead of him, Riona sat atop the small horse Bantan, where she'd watched the scene—how much she'd seen, Kieran had no idea, but he hoped she'd seen it all. She was a champion of forgiveness and such, and he wanted to please her. The problem was, he couldn't tell if she was pleased or not.

She should have been. Maille had fairly begged him to draw blood rather than an apology out of his scrawny neck, yet Kieran had refrained with saintly resolve.

"Good day, milady. I'd have called it glorious until I saw how you outshine it." Kieran smiled, but Riona failed to take his lead.

"Thank you, milord."

He scowled at the lack of enthusiasm behind her answer. "Is something amiss?" There was a twitch at the corner of her mouth. Whether it bode ill or fair, he had no clue.

"I'm certain you did your best."

"Indeed I—" Kieran broke off, bemused. "Best at what?" Whatever it was, given her rueful tone, it apparently wasn't good enough.

Riona glanced over at Maille's encampment, where Maille and his captain watched, their heads bent toward each other and lips moving to no obvious good. That the Gleannmara party was the subject, Kieran had no doubt. At the moment, however, it was Riona's concern that plagued him, not Maille's.

"Would milady care to share what is on her mind?"

"Your concept of forgiveness, Kieran." On that cool note, she turned her horse away and joined the main body now mounted and awaiting their king.

Faith, it was easier milking a bull! Kieran bounded up on Gray Macha's back, where Leila and the basketed Lady Gray awaited. The kitten, startled by the jolt, struggled to peep out, squeezing her furry face between the rim and the lid. Leila lifted it, basket and all, and gave her a tiny kiss on the nose and said something soothing. The creature withdrew to its comfy quarters, fear apparently abated. Raising his arm as a signal, Kieran waved the party forward.

"Good day, brothers," he called out to Domnall, Ninian, and the others who'd gathered at the gate to see them off.

"God's speed," Domnall called back, echoed simultaneously by his companions.

Gleannmara's banners flying at the forefront and the Dromin at the flank, the travelers were on their way home at last. Until now, Kieran hadn't thought of the tuath as home. He'd spent more time at Dromin, with Murtagh and his family. Then Gleannmara became his kingdom, but it had been more burden than joy, reminding him of his loss.

Now, though, that he had a wife and family he found himself anxious to settle in.

Once the abbey was out of sight, Riona spoke again, distracting him from his musings. Her words smacked of reluctant duty, as though she were loathe to address a subject that needed airing. "Kieran, forgiveness is meaningless unless the party being forgiven is earnest in his contrition. Contrition cannot be forced. It must come from within the offender."

And when the creature did give forth, the milk was sour at that. Women were hard to please, but a spiritual one was even more confounding. "Then how could I forgive my enemy, when he is in no humor to *be* forgiven, may I ask? I only tried to be a good example for the lad."

His testy words, instead of provoking her, drew a smile at last from her disapproving lips. "I know you meant well, anmchara, and for that I am grateful. You did all you could, perhaps a bit too much, in forcing Maille to apologize. 'Twas like forcing spoilt meat to be fresh, I fear."

At least on that Kieran could agree. "Aye, but I can't do penance for *his* feelings, only my own." Yet Kieran was uncertain of those as well. He'd *tried* to feel forgiving toward Maille and hoped that, in his show of grace, he'd convince himself. But the fact remained, forgiven or nay, that Maille was a dangerous snake of a man with a tongue as forked as his beard.

"And I'm proud of you for that," Riona assured him. She reached across the narrow space between them and gave his forearm a squeeze. "Sometimes that's all we can do, I suppose, try and then let the Holy Spirit do the rest."

She spoke with such certainty that Kieran refrained from a disparaging retort. Instead, he considered Riona's observation in silence. Heaven knew that but for some manner of divine intervention his own attempts to handle things would have led to the destruction of himself as well as his loved ones. Something had not failed where he had. At length, he nodded.

"Aye, milady, I'm thinking He will at that, e'en though His task is most considerable."

Riona laughed, a sound that put the birdsong to shame, infecting Kieran with a rush of joy the likes of which he'd known only of late…with her. Nothing, not even the seething visage of Lord Maille looking after them, could cloud his thoughts when that summer sound played upon him.

Kieran knew he'd not seen the last of the man, but at that moment Riona's presence bedazzled care into nonexistence.

Gleannmara.

The thick, forested clan lands between Ulster's abbey and Leinster had separated a few miles back, and now blocks of green, well-tended fields bordered by hedges and stone walls rolled before the travelers like a carpet of bounty, welcoming them home. To the west, the mist-shrouded Wicklows reigned over the skyline, and to the east and beyond was the rock-strewn coastline of the Irish Sea.

Instead of watching them with the guarded looks of the earlier tenants they'd passed, the people in the fields and along the road greeted Gleannmara's entourage with good cheer and genuine welcome. All along the way, Kieran stopped to speak and proudly present Riona as the new Lady Gleannmara. Many of the faces were familiar, for while Riona was the new lady of Gleannmara, she was not new to the tuath. Kieran's mother had taught her needlework and the domestic administration of a rath in a limited fosterage arrangement, since Ethna of Dromin was loathe to give her daughter up for the full seven years and broke convention.

Riona had missed her family at times, but she'd also gained another. Where Ethna might have pampered her daughter, the queen of Gleannmara would not, just as Murtagh would not favor Kieran in his training. Their protégés' skills were a reflection of their own, just as were their hearts. Skill begat skill. Kindness and understanding begat kindness and understanding. She wondered how the coming of priests and bards as teachers provided to each tuath would affect the fosterage tradition.

The closer Riona and the others came to Gleannmara, the less time she had to ponder such things. Remarks such as "And it's well about time, milady" and "Welcome home, milady" filled her ears and touched her heart. Faith, it *did* feel as if she was coming home—not just where she belonged, but where God intended her to be. She'd known refuge and peace at the abbey, but not this sense of belonging. Riona tried to check the emotion welling within, but when a goat cart loaded with children shot out of the blue-and-gold-bannered gate to meet them, they were a joyful blur.

"God bless ye, milord and lady," the older children running alongside the cart called out to them.

"By the stars, it's an army of gigglings," Kieran mumbled as he watched the wicker cart full of round-faced cherubs bounce toward them. Clearly, he'd all but forgotten the orphans he'd sent with Bran to Gleannmara. Reinforced by the children of the rath, they presented an impressive number.

"Where the blazes is Gleannmara's guard?" he demanded of the gatekeeper.

A shaggy-haired head popped up in the tower beside the bearded tender. "It's ridin' the border, same as always, milord," the younger of the two replied.

"And who are you, mite?"

The lad leaned out the tower window. "Don't you recognize me, milord? It's me, Naal. Siony's brother. I'm in trainin' to be a gatekeeper."

Gone was Kieran's kingly demeanor, replaced by utter confoundment as he looked at Riona. "What has that poem spoutin' cousin of yours done to me?"

Riona laughed outright, tears and all. "Exactly as you instructed him, milord. Take the orphans to Gleannmara and await your return."

"We couldn't possibly have rescued this many."

She reached across the space between Bantan and Gray Macha and touched his arm. How well she'd memorized its strength, as well as its gentleness, since becoming one with him as his wife. "Beloved, most of these are Gleannmara's own."

"Their parents have hid them well till now," her husband muttered to himself.

"Much happens when milord is away from his home for so long and pays it little heed when he is there. I'd wager your rechtaire knows them all by name…aside from the new ones," she added for the steward's benefit.

"Ach, Benin be blessed!" Kieran urged Gray Macha ahead and through the gate. "Methinks there is urgent need for some military order, not for that of a steward or a bard."

"A king's perhaps?" Riona suggested.

"Aye," he called over his shoulder. "And a host of good men and angels."

Smiling, Riona followed. Given his circumstances as a new husband, father, and lord of a ragtag band of orphans, Riona thought Kieran handled himself with relatively good grace.

Beside her, the boys were all eyes as they entered the rath.

"Look at the size of the hall," Liex gasped, pointing to a great domed roof looming beyond the stockade of the inner yard. "It's big as a king's."

"It is a king's, dolt," Fynn reminded him, adding proudly. "Our foster father's."

Thank heaven he and Kieran had mended the rift between them.

"What does that say?" The youngest boy pointed to an embroidered flag, white with a royal Chi-Rho encircled by ornate lettering.

"And reading will be the first order of the day." Kieran dismounted and handed his stallion over to the stable master, then walked back to help the lad off the pony. "It's the motto of Gleannmara, coined by King Rowan and Queen Maire a century ago. It says, 'Home to the just, enemy to the greedy and ambitious.'"

The boy mouthed the words to himself and then nodded in approval. "Sounds like a right place to live."

"You mean it? You'll teach us to read?" From the excitement in Fynn's gaze, Riona knew he would learn quickly.

"I can read already," Liex boasted, pointing to the banner. "'Home to the just, enemy to the greedy and ambitious.'"

Fynn cut a disparaging glance at him. "A bird can repeat what someone else reads, dolt."

Kieran removed Liex from Fynn's reach before the elder's intended cuff hit its mark. "But does the bird know what it means?" he asked.

With a sheepish grin, Fynn slid off the pony as Colga caught up with them, Leila and her basketed pet asleep in his arms.

"A bit of help here," he called unnecessarily, for Kieran was already headed to retrieve the sleeping little girl.

Since leaving Kilmare, Leila shared her attention between Colga and Kieran, much to the latter's bewilderment.

"Have I done something to offend the lass?" Kieran had asked Riona the first night away from the abbey as he'd watched Colga and Leila tossing a small spool back and forth for the kitten to chase.

Riona assured him that Leila had enough love for all of them. "She's special," she'd reminded her husband. "I think she knows a hurting soul when she sees one and tries to soothe it in her own small way."

The understanding that registered on Kieran's face and his thoughtful nod told Riona that Colga was not the only hurting soul Leila had ministered to with her innocent, unselfish love. And that didn't count an adoring kitten or the moon-eyed calf she'd left in Brother Domnall's care. God surely used the child, but when would He heal her?

"By my father's hammer, me brat's wet," Colga exclaimed, as Kieran lifted a sleep-dazed Leila from the man's lap. "How in time did *that* happen?"

With a laugh, Kieran wrapped Leila's brat around her and started away. "I warned you to wake her when we last stopped."

The men of Dromin teased their lord as Colga jumped off his mount and shook out his offending cloak. Not quite awake, Leila laid her head against Kieran's shoulder and cradled the basket with Lady Gray in her arms. But at the sight of the goat cart loaded with laughing children, she came instantly awake. Kieran put her down as she squirmed.

"I think you'd best see your mother before joining that lot of gigglers," he advised her.

Her mother. The two words filled Riona to overflowing with joy. As the stable lad led her faithful Bantan away, she opened her arms to receive the running child—basket and bobbing kitten and all.

"We'll change you into your old shift, and then you can play until supper."

Supper. Of course Benin would have some summer fare and there would be filling food for the staff, nothing elaborate with the lord of the tuath away. She knew exactly what to do. Lorna, Kieran's mother, had been a good teacher, though she hadn't come to her new home a bride with three strays of her own and a dozen more running amuck.

As Riona ushered her charges toward the king's lodge, her cousin Bran hailed her from the inner rath. Ignoring Kieran completely, the bard raced toward her with a sense of extreme urgency and alarm.

"Thank God you're here!" He embraced Riona so tightly, she thought he would crush her shoulders.

"I…I'm glad to see you as well, cousin. Is something—"

"It's Siony," he interrupted breathlessly. "She's having the babe."

THIRTY-ONE

A great turmoil followed Bran's announcement. Born and trained to do so, Kieran stepped into charge, taking over where Benin, his chief steward, left off. He assigned Riona to handle the birthing matters. A midwife had been sent for, but Kieran knew that his new wife having been at the abbey, which had sheltered expectant mothers and boasted its share of newborn babes, was no stranger to such affairs. Riona and Benin conspired to see that hot water and linens, as well as herbs pertinent to the mother-to-be's care, were readied. Kieran smiled. His wife was not unlike a king and captain preparing for battle.

Meanwhile, he saw to the regrouping and morale of the troops, specifically the father-to-be, for that was exactly what Bran acted like even if he was not responsible. Kieran took the wineskin Colga had nursed off and on during their journey and handed it to the Dromin's distraught cousin before they even entered the hall. Then he saw to the disbursal of the traveling party, as well as the new royal family's belongings in Benin's stead. Now Riona's things were among his in the royal lodge, while the fosterlings, who reveled and explored with the other newcomers to Gleannmara, were set up in the attendant's lodge close by.

All was well, at least to the eye, Kieran reflected in kingly silence after a fit meal of boiled venison courtesy of the tuath's fine hunters. He shifted with the twinge of discomfort from the healed wound he'd earned in arrogant folly from the child-slaver's wife. Now he knew what his father had meant when he complained that old wounds bothered him. He also understood for the first time why the men of Gleannmara pushed so hard to return home after a long journey away. Home was more than a physical place of comfort and renewal…it was a spiritual place as well, where past and present existed in harmony.

Recently scrubbed and aired of the stagnation of winter, the building's lime-washed walls and laboriously brushed and oiled columns gleamed as they had when King Rowan and Queen Maire had reigned. While the main part of the great room was filled with the song and cheers of the men accompanied by the lively pluck and puff of music, the grianán where the ladies employed their needles and wagging tongues during the day was nearly abandoned. New life occupied them, that on the brink of delivery as well as the recent influx of orphans.

The pervasive scent of smoke mingled with the tantalizing scent of the warming pots filled the great hall at Gleannmara, but rather than offending the merrymakers, it bore the welcome balm of home. There had been times when Kieran wondered if he'd live to see his home again, yet Riona had never doubted. He hoped to be worthy of this double blessing of a good wife and an ancestral home.

Seated on a white wolfskin-covered royal bench that had once belonged to his parents, Kieran stirred from his reverie. Taking up with one hand a royal branch of silver bells to garner attention, he lifted a horn with his other and shared his gratitude.

"To the good people of Gleannmara—from the lad who scrubs the pots in the kitchen to the man who tills the soil, from the cooks who prepared the meal to the hands that harvested and hunted the fare, from the milkmaid in the barns to my good and loyal steward, from the warriors who protect our homes to the prayerful who protect our souls, to my steward and Bran, who have sustained Gleannmara against an army of orphans in my absence, to my wife who sustained me, and to the One God of our ancestors, who sustains us all."

The sober words fell upon the gathering, the realization of their many blessings settling in as one by one man and woman found their goblet or cup and joined the king. Tales of Kieran and Riona's escape and deliverance from Kilmare to Drumceatt and back again had been told and had already grown in legendary proportion, for nothing pleased the ear of a Celt better than magic or miracle.

"Care of the children took no great persuasion, milord," Benin, the elderly rechtaire, assured Kieran as he lowered his cup. "There are those of us who have missed the days when you, the lady queen, and her kin ran wild about the rath, stirring all manner of mischief. More than enough volunteered to take charge of a mite or two."

Cromyn nodded in agreement. "Aye, something about the ring of children's laughter assures us that life goes on." He looked up at the ceiling where smoke from a single fire curled playfully. "I suppose that was one thing I missed at Iona. Without the occasional patter of little feet, these old ones oft have no reason to make patter of their own."

"*Occasional* is the key word there, Father," Bran put in. "Until Benin helped disburse this lot, every step sounded upon my temples sure till my head became misshapen."

"Our bard means his humor," Benin teased, "which was most foul when he and Lady Siony arrived."

"Lady?" Kieran echoed.

"You were a bit distracted by all the howling and excitement," Bran reminded him, "but Siony told us her father was a prosperous boaire in Connaught. She married beneath her station to the fisherman and was disowned."

"*Distracted* is putting it mildly," Kieran admitted. "And our would-be gatekeeper is her brother-in-law." He thought a moment. "Naal, isn't it?"

"She knows how to administer a home well enough," Benin remarked, impressed. "As well as knowing her way around a kitchen."

"She's no stranger to work, I'll give her that," Bran added, not without something more than admiration in his voice.

Kieran smiled to himself. Had the bard been lovestruck? It sounded so as he rambled on.

"Sure, Benin and I have run ourselves ragged trying to spare her, what…what with her condition."

Her condition. As if one silent command had sounded, the men at the table glanced toward the side door where women had been rushing in and out with pails of water. Kieran had seen Riona only once since she hurried off to the lodge to be with Siony. And he didn't even know if he'd recognize the girl. Brown hair, small face, plenty of spirit—that was all he recalled. He'd been selfishly caught up in his own trouble at the time.

"She never tired, not of work nor of the endless questions those ragmullions asked," Bran said, a look of wonder overtaking him. "And she's never at a loss for a smile." He smiled himself.

Aye, this was more than the admiration of old. Kieran stared at the bard, waiting for him to go on, but Bran was caught up in his enchantment, apparently forgetting the others round the table. Never had he heard Bran laud more than a buxom figure, a fair face, or a melodious voice—the shell rather than the content. But it appeared that Bran had changed—subtly, but decidedly. Kieran caught the knowing glance of Father Cromyn and Benin. Faith, but love had a fickle way with a man.

"Have you counted how many teeth she has left? Never buy a steed unless it's got good teeth." Manly mischief twisted Colga's mouth.

Bran snapped out of his stupor. "I'm speaking of a lady, not a nag! Methinks your smithy father mistook your head for his anvil and never noticed the difference."

"I've heard that love makes a man irritable, uncle," Colga said, nonplussed, to Cromyn, "but I've never seen proof till now. So tell us, cousin, will you marry her and take in this horde of parentless mites like our good king here?"

"Many of the children have been spoken for already, but Siony and I have talked about taking the rest," Bran admitted to them. A sheepish grin spread across his lips just below the ruddy glow of his cheeks.

Benin chuckled. "Aye, the poet here has a gift for singing babes to sleep. All he has to do is pick up a squawler, and it hushes like a calf on full udder."

The men enjoyed a good laugh at Bran's expense.

"What would you say, Bran, to becoming Gleannmara's bard?" Kieran asked him abruptly.

There was no time like the present to address the decisions at Drumceatt. As many looks as found their way to the door leading to the birthing chamber, they all needed the distraction. Were it Riona on the childbed instead of Siony, Kieran wasn't certain he could keep his distance, as was custom. "I already am, aren't I?" Bran said, startled from his own inner thoughts.

"I don't think Kieran has your old role in mind, son. Much is changing at synod, including the expectations of our bardic class," Cromyn told him.

Kieran and Cromyn caught Bran up on the news of how each tuath was to have its own bardic and clerical teachers.

"An education system for the mind and the soul," Bran mulled aloud.

Kieran watched the father and son as they expounded on the possibilities.

Suddenly, Colga leaped to his feet, brushing away wine a servant had spilled.

"For the love of my ancestors, man, watch what you're doin'! This is my only clean shirt!" The Dromin chief's brat and good shirt had been turned over to the rath's laundresses after Leila's incident.

The stooped servant reacted in equal horror. His wrinkled, shaven head bent, he dabbed at the stains frantically. "Saints, I'm sorry, yer lordship. 'Tis this crippled hand. I'll fetch ye a towel—"

"Here," Kieran offered, handing over a towel he'd used earlier upon finishing his meal.

His gaze met the servant's for one brief second, but never had Kieran felt such a penetrating thrust of hatred directed at him. It took him aback, robbing him of speech.

"Nis, 'tis best you keep to tending the fires and let the women see to the tables," Benin suggested sternly. "Send one back with clean linens."

As if suddenly aware of his insolent glare, the servant crumbled with humility, dropping his gaze to the floor. "As ye wish, sor. I mean no harm. 'Tis this bad 'and, ye see."

"Just go, Nis. We know it was an accident," Benin said gently. Indeed, the steward's kind manner accounted for his success, for there was not a soul at Gleannmara who would not give their utmost for the man.

"Yes, thank ye, sor. I'll see right to it."

"Never mind, I'll go with the dolt," Colga grumbled.

With a bob of his head, the servant turned without so much as a glance at Kieran before the lord had a chance to ask him what burned so hatefully behind his gaze.

"Do I know him?" Kieran asked as the foul-tempered Colga followed the bumbler off toward the kitchen. "I vow, he looked cross as a cow with milk fever."

"That look is a fixture on his face, milord, nothing more." Benin shook his head. "He came asking for food and a roof, acting as if we owed him that and more. After three days, I put him to work."

"He's a queer one to be sure," Bran put in. "Nothing much to say, and what few syllables he does mumble I'd just as soon not hear. He's as spooked by the children as I was." He laughed at himself. "And now you want me to *teach* them. Now there's a twist of fate, if ever there—"

Bran broke off upon seeing Benin's wife rush in. For a graying woman of such sturdy proportion, Ina moved so quickly that the volumes of her leine swirled behind her in an effort to keep up with her sandaled feet. Bran leaped to his feet like a spooked cat, followed by the more leisurely rise of Kieran and the others.

"Well?" The young bard's normally clear voice cracked with dryness.

Ina beamed. "Lady Siony has delivered a girl child. A healthy baby girl!"

"Wh…what of Siony? Is she well?"

"The lady and her daughter are both well and beautiful." Clasping her hands together, Ina raised her eyes ceilingward. "Praise to God for His goodness and mercy."

Cromyn made the sign of the cross, echoing the spontaneous amen that circled the table.

Kieran mimicked the priest out of habit at first and then stumbled mentally. Yes, he meant it. He *was* grateful for God's goodness and mercy, and not just for Siony. He was grateful for all God had done to bring him and his family home.

No sooner were Ina's words finished than Bran, Gleannmara's once restless and carefree bard, apparently overcome with relief, crumpled to the floor in a dead faint.

Reacting as quickly as he could, Kieran cushioned Bran's head from striking the floor with his foot and reached for his good friend. "Sure, this fatherhood is hard on a man."

THIRTY-TWO

R iona basked in the warmth of the bath Kieran had ordered drawn for her. The exhilaration of holding the new baby and watching as Bran, flanked by his father and Kieran, came in on unsteady knees lightened her heart. She'd never seen her cousin so silly over a female—especially one holding a tiny infant. Siony had him wrapped about her little finger, and Riona had no doubt that little Aine would as well.

How different things were from that dreadful night the bard and the mother-to-be had first met. Faith, they'd nipped at each other like rival pups—exactly as Riona and Kieran had done. The strange song that came to them from the holy well at the monastery played back in her mind as clearly as it had been that night. Siony had seen no one there, yet they all had heard it, like an omen...

Behold, I am the Lord, the God of all flesh; is anything too hard for Me?

Now she was married, hopelessly in love with the well-meaning man she'd once spurned, and mother to three precious children. If only Leila were healed life would be perfect. Riona glanced over to the corner of the room where the little girl, freshly bathed and in a night shift, played with her kitten.

Father, forgive me for seeming ungrateful. I am overwhelmed by Your goodness. I just love her so much that I am anxious for her healing in my time rather than in Your time. My impertinence is born of love, Father, not ingratitude. Help me to rest in Your promise, for You have never failed me yet.

A sharp knock on the lodge door jarred Riona from her prayer. Kieran called to her. "The boys are settled in the hall, and Leila's bed is ready. May I come in, milady?"

Leila hastened toward the door to open it, but Riona stopped her. "No wait, love. Kieran, give me a moment," she added in a louder voice.

She quickly abandoned the bath and toweled off. Leila helped her into her night shift and robe before Riona opened the door. Brushing her wet hair behind her shoulders, she smiled. "I fear I was lost in day-dreams and forgot the time. I need to dry Leila's hair…" She felt a kindling within her as her husband's gaze raked her over from head to toe. "And…mine."

"Give me the brush and I'll do the little one's."

Leila dug her new silver brush from the bag Kieran had purchased for her at the fair. As he sat on the edge of the large bronze bed, the little girl sidled back to him and handed it to him with a bright smile.

It was heartwarming to see the broad-shouldered warrior melt beneath the waif's spell.

"Now tell me if I pull too hard, because I'm used to combing Gray Macha's mane and tail, not a tender lass's hair."

Wondering how much more deeply in love she could fall with this man, Riona took a seat next to him and proceeded to work out the tangles in her own hair. Leila winced a few times, but all in all Kieran was astonishingly gentle, given his previous experience. He ran the brush through Leila's hair until the golden strands lifted each time he put the silver near her head.

"You didn't eat your supper," he remarked, glancing at the tray the manservant had brought by earlier.

"I was too tired," Riona confessed. "But I did eat a piece of bread with honey…and Leila drank my tea. I chose some of the elderberry wine Finella sent with us."

"Not with those horrid herbs in it, I hope?"

Riona chuckled at the face her husband pulled. "I will remind you, milord, that those *horrid herbs* saved your life."

"I thought for a while she was intent on poisoning me."

The reflection turned the corners of his mouth up in a fascinating way that begged to be kissed. Heavens, marriage had made her a wanton woman to have such thoughts while a child stood between them.

"Give me a kiss," Riona cajoled. She hugged Leila to her. "Your father is going to tuck you into your new bed tonight."

The stricken look on Leila's face made Riona's heart ache. She met

Kieran's gaze over the child's head, at a loss as to what to say. Leila and her brothers had slept near them or in the same room with them since leaving Drumceatt.

"I'm thinking if Leila and the boys show they can make out in their own cottage right next to ours, they might be big enough to have their own puppy," Kieran blurted out, clearly grasping for something to entice the child to join her brothers. "The guard's hound whelped last week, five pups at last count."

He had Leila's full attention, and judging by the look of desperation on his face, he was about to promise the entire litter to her.

Riona stepped in. "A new puppy? Now how do you think Lady Gray will like that?"

Obviously, Leila thought there'd be no problem. Nodding happily, she walked over to the bed where the kitten had settled on one of pillows and scooped it up in her arms. At her expectant pause, Kieran rose to his feet.

"So, are the ladies ready to retire?" He herded Leila toward the door. "If the pups are anything like their mother, you'll have a fine lot to pick from. She's one of the best hunters I've ever seen."

Unimpressed, Leila reached up and took Kieran's hand as he stepped outside. The gesture of complete trust was bone melting, but not as much as the backward glance Kieran gave Riona. She read the promise on his lips, underscored by that in his eyes. "I'll hasten back anon, sweetling."

"A puppy!" Liex squealed upon interpreting his sister's excited announcement. "Did ye hear that, Fynn? We're getting a puppy."

The older boy propped himself up on one elbow. "I'd have to be deaf to have missed it, dolt. What kind of pup is it?" he asked Kieran.

"A hound for hunting small game."

Kieran tucked the little girl in, making certain not to cover Lady Gray in the process. He'd learned the hard way that the kitten liked to snuggle but not be covered. As long as he'd waited to spend a night alone with his new bride, he wasn't going to risk having to chase a disgruntled furball about the cottage with three squealing youngsters.

"Now we're right next door if you need us."

LINDA WINDSOR

"I can watch after the twins," Fynn assured him. "I done it for years. Maithar and Athair performed late into the night, so I kept an eye on them."

"They were lucky to have you," Kieran answered, feeling grateful himself.

"Will you tell us a story?" Liex asked. Never had Kieran seen eyes so alert and devoid of sleep.

"I don't know children's stories...but I'll bet Fynn here does," he added quickly.

"Maithar tells the best. Is she coming to kiss us good-night?"

"She's exhausted," Kieran told Liex. "But she sends her love."

"Tell us about when you were a boy," the twin prompted. "Where did you sleep?"

"In this very lodge." It wasn't exactly true. The one he'd used had been torn down and replaced, but Kieran saw little point in going into the details. "And part of my warrior training was going to sleep when I was expected to...even without stories."

Liex digested this as Fynn fell back against his pillow, hands folded behind his head. After a moment, during which Kieran's breath waited still in his chest, the boy mimicked his brother's action. He smiled at Kieran. "I'm sorry our athair's dead, but I'm glad you're our new one."

Overwhelmed by the heartfelt compliment, Kieran started to buss the boy on the cheek, but instead Liex stuck out his hand from under the blankets. "Soldiers don't kiss," he explained.

Kieran almost felt guilty as he eased the door to the children's lodge shut. Almost. The children deserved his time and affection, but so did his bride, and it had been too long since their wedding night. As he hustled into the chief's lodge, built by his grandfather to replace the original dwelling, his anticipation grew. He'd thought his guests would never disburse for the night. Cromyn had finally excused himself, pleading exhaustion, and Kieran seized upon the same excuse, leaving Bran and Colga to drink themselves into a stupor, the first in celebration and the latter in an attempt to obliterate consciousness.

He found Riona dwarfed in the huge, bronze Roman bed, which Queen Maire reportedly brought back along with her husband nearly a

century before. All of Gleannmara's heirs had been born in it, but neither ancestors nor heirs consumed Kieran's thoughts at the moment.
The sight of his bride took them, as well as his breath, away.

Her eyes were closed, dark lashes fanned upon porcelain cheeks
blushed with youth and good health. Her raven hair cloaked her face
and shoulders, shining in the soft light of the lamp by the bed. Too
lovely to be real, and she was his.

Kieran fumbled to remove his clothes and stepped into the abandoned tub, which still smelled of her sweetness even if it had lost her
warmth. Taking up the soap, he hurriedly lathered and rinsed in an
attempt to rid himself of the long journey's grime. His eagerness to join
her was far from diminished as he toweled dry and slipped beneath the
covers.

He drew her to him, savoring her with all his senses. Stroking a
silken curl from her forehead, he brushed her lips with his. She smiled
sleepily and cuddled closer, her arm lax across him. With a sigh, she
relaxed.

"I love you, Kieran of Gleannmar…"

And to his utter dismay, sleep swallowed the remainder of her sentence, even as it consumed his exhausted bride as well.

A pained whimper of disappointment escaped his lips as he rolled
over on his back and stared, wide-awake, at the ceiling. The more
experience he had as a father, the more merit he saw to God's order of
marriage first, children second.

After what seemed to Kieran like an endless parade of reflection
over the changes in his life since he'd promised his dying friend to
marry and protect the woman in his arms, the torture of Riona's nearness subsided and a restless slumber overtook him. He was on the
bloody battlefield holding Heber in his arms, but when he looked up,
it wasn't Colga's ashen face protesting how the enemy had tricked the
rear guard, it was Maille's. It was as if Maille's wickedness had set upon
him before Kieran had ever set foot in Ulster and followed him still.
*Maille, Senan, Colga, Tadgh, and the woman—that blasted Mebh—and her
pitchfork.* Kieran winced as he tossed over on his side, turning away
from the plaguing stream of faces. Was his leg still aching, or was it just

the memory? The pain grew to an unbearable proportion, until sleep would no longer anesthetize it. Bolting upright in the bed, he felt for the wound with clammy hands.

"Kieran?" Riona mumbled groggily.

"A fiendish dream," he answered, feeling the ridge of newly healed flesh where Mebh's vengeful gash had been. An ancient warrior superstition came to his mind—one about old wounds aching whenever the one who inflicted them was near—but he dismissed it. Besides, the spot wasn't tender at all now that he was awake.

"You're damp with perspiration."

"It's warm in here, to be sure." And growing warmer. The hauntings of Kieran's past faded with the awareness of the woman beside him. The icy fingers of fear that tripped up his spine melted at her touch. "Mayhap I need another dip in the bath."

Riona caressed the side of his face and turned it toward her. "I hadn't meant to fall asleep, husband, but I am well awake now."

The suggestion in her voice was enough to set a man's blood to boiling. He gathered her in his arms and sought her lips in the darkness as though seeking his very soul. Here was goodness and mercy, seduction and passion, the fulfillment of every man's dream. Riona— *his* Riona—his bride, his friend, his wife, his lover.

The wonder of her did not completely erase the uneasiness that had plagued his sleep, but it did push it aside so that it was the last thing on his mind.

THIRTY-THREE

Riona floated in afterglow of Kieran's ardent attentions, somewhere between consciousness and the sleep that had finally claimed her husband. Time was negligible. All that mattered was his closeness, for when they were separated, it felt as if a part of her was missing. They had become one, not just in the physical sense, but in the spiritual and eternal sense as well. Visions of bliss faded in and out of sleep—until a frantic voice invaded both.

At first, Riona thought Fynn called out to her from a dreamworld, but the insistent pounding on the door sounded too close and loud to be anything but real.

"Milady…wake…God's mercy…sick…hurry!"

The impassioned plea of his tone set her into motion. With an innate motherly reaction, she shook the last remnant of sleep from her mind, convinced that whatever alarmed Fynn, it was horrible. Flinging the covers aside, she struck the floor of the lodge with her bare feet as Kieran rose opposite her.

"Wh…what…?" He reached instinctively for the sword hanging by the bed as he shook the sleep from his head, muttering beneath his breath as his feet became caught in the tangle of linens Riona had tossed aside.

"It's the children," she answered fearfully.

She slung the leine he'd hung on the back of the door at him for decency's sake and jerked at the latch. No sooner had it opened than Fynn flung himself at her. His momentum would have knocked her over but for his deathlike grasp of her arms.

"It's Leila! Come quick!" He gasped something about sickness, but Riona was already on her way to the guest lodge.

She staggered from the moonlit yard into the darkness of the building. Guided by a dreadful sound of gagging and gasping, Riona ran straight to where Kieran had tucked in the little girl earlier.

"Get a light," she called back to Fynn. The smell of the child's breath struck her. It wasn't just that of a sour stomach, it was almost sweet, as though the child had been chewing nuts.

As Leila curled in to a ball and retched again, Riona nearly went over with her. The scent was distressingly close to another familiar odor…that of the poison used in the grainery for rats.

"Liex, where has Leila been playing?" she asked, refusing to believe what her senses reported.

A whimper of an answer came from a dark corner, where the boy's bed had been placed. "Just in the yard with the other children."

"It's all right, love," Riona consoled the convulsing child. "Where in the yard? *Where*, Liex?"

"Just in the yard," the small voice insisted. "Is Leila going to die?"

Light flooded the room ahead of Kieran. Now clad in his leine, he held up the lamp. "What is it…by my father's eyes!"

Panic seized Riona's throat at the sight of Leila covered in her own sickness and looking like death's breath. She had to clear her throat twice before she could even speak. "Get me Finella's herbal blanket. I think she's been poisoned."

For the next hour, Riona tried to force the little girl to swallow a paste made of charred coals, but as soon as it went in, it came back out. Kieran sought help from some of the women, but to no avail. Their various herbal remedies would not stay in the girl's stomach long enough to help her condition. No one had seen the children anywhere near the grainery or the dairy. In fact, one of the women had watched them the entire time, taking turns so that chores could be done.

"*Think*, people, she had to have gotten the poison from some-where!" Kieran shouted in exasperation. "Check every place you can think of that a child could have gotten into. I want everyone awakened. See if anyone else is ill. As God is my witness, I will get to the meat of this matter!"

The group, save the good midwife, scattered at the thunder of Gleannmara's command. Fynn kept them in fresh water, while Riona continually bathed the child's face and tried to keep her bed as clean as possible.

Kieran at her side, Riona prayed. She called on every promise in the Word. "Father, all things are possible. Nothing is too great for You to accomplish. I cannot believe that You have brought us through so many trials to break our hearts with this. Spare this child, we beg You—" Her voice broke. She tried clearing her throat of her anguish, but Kieran took up the prayer where she left off.

"Father, I have strayed from You too long. I have just taken Your hand again. Please don't let it go. My soul cannot survive this. If a life must be taken, then take mine. I've done much to deserve death, but this child—"

Kieran's deep voice cracked with emotion. Although of late he added an earnest amen to her prayers at mealtime and vespers, this was the first time she'd heard him pray straight from his heart. He crushed Riona's hand in his own, tears pouring as freely as his words. Riona heard rather than saw them through the glaze of her own pain.

"This child," he rallied brokenly, "she's done nothing but offer love to broken hearts."

"Excuse me, milord."

Riona looked up as Ina, Benin's wife, came into the room. At least Riona thought it was Ina from her voice. Kieran had yet to lift his head. On his knees he rocked slightly, as if gathering strength to face whatever was to come. Ina was almost as ashen as Leila. She carried the supper tray Riona had barely touched earlier, her hands shaking so that the dishes rattled upon it.

"My...my supper?" Riona said, bewildered.

Ina nodded to the empty teacup and shoved the tray toward Kieran as he straightened. "Smell it, milord. 'Tis tainted, to be sure."

Face streaked and mottled with spent emotion, Kieran sniffed in obedience. Not attuned to herbs and his nose congested with grief, he shook his head, clearly unable to smell anything. Riona smelled the remnant in the bottom of the teacup and instantly recognized the sweet, nutty fragrance prevalent in Leila's faint breath. Sickness curled anew in her stomach. The tea had been intended for her, not the child.

Kieran's frustration and despair turned to outrage. "Who'd dare poison you?"

Heavenly Father, it isn't fair! It should have been me. Riona clutched Leila to her, rocking back and forth in woeful apology until it dawned on her that the child was no longer convulsing. She was too weak. Riona pressed her lips to Leila's neck. There was a pulse, but it was as faint as her breath.

Nothing Riona had been through had prepared her for this. Nothing. She'd always known the hedge of God's mercy and grace, but where was it now? She refused to accept that it wasn't there. Misery distorted her spiritual vision, as tears did the physical. *God is here!* she told herself sternly. *He is holding this child because He said He'd never leave us.* Another memory surfaced, spreading like a balm upon the black sea that threatened to engulf them. *And He promised to heal Leila.* She could read Columcille's message to her as though it were spread before her very eyes.

"Go get Father Cromyn," she whispered, wiping tears from her face.

Kieran, who held Liex in his arms, put the boy down, not out of intent but from weakness dealt by the impact of her words. "Is *that* necessary?"

"We are going to pray her through this," Riona vowed resolutely. She reached for Liex's hand and then glanced about in bewilderment. "Where is Fynn?"

"I seen him looking around with the others after he emptied his own gut, poor lad," Ina informed her. "Few menfolk can handle such as this."

"I'll find him," Kieran promised. The uncertainty on his face made Riona hurt for him. At that moment he looked, for all his manly size and presence, as lost and frightened as Liex.

"It's going to be all right, Kieran," Riona said. "God told me."

Colga leaned against the corner of the privy behind the hall, oblivious to all the activity, much less the time. His noble-hearted cousin Bran slept cradled in Gleannmara's royal chair like a newborn babe in its mother's arms, but there was no relief for the guilty. Indeed, his traitorous stomach had turned catapult, rejecting the drink he'd sought to drown his conscience in. The dull ache in his head cleared as he threw it back and stared up at the stars.

Some were bold, steady in their light. Others flickered, as if trying to hold out against the darkness for daybreak and the sun's reinforcement. He wondered bitterly which would stand firm for the sunrise and which would fade away into nothingness, despite their best efforts to survive after their one moment of glory...

Like him.

He was chief of the Dromin, yet his light was fading fast, consumed by the dark deed that had provided him the chance at leadership. Even that deed required him to do nothing, just walk away under the pretense that he suspected the enemy's approach. Without the warning Colga should have sounded, the conspirators who'd come to kill the Scots' new king had been upon Heber's rear guard before Heber knew what was coming. The mist spewed out the murderers, seemingly with as much distaste as Colga's stomach had ejected his overindulgence of Gleannmara's imported wine. Colga hadn't seen the bloodbath, but he'd heard it and seen the aftermath—every day and night since it had happened.

He inhaled deeply, filling his lungs with the summer night air. He could bear it no longer. He had to purge this guilt before it ate him alive from within. He had to speak to his uncle Cromyn, for Colga was too ashamed to speak directly to God. Heber was surely one of God's favored. Colga had seen Heber's face as he met death. 'Twas no banshee his cousin saw, given the peace that blanketed him body and soul. Heber saw God. Perhaps he even watched Colga's cruel punishment of a guilt-ridden life from one of the many stars dotting the sky.

Bracing himself with courage gained from liquor and desperation, Colga set his course toward the chapel, where Cromyn had retired for the night. It was to be his uncle's lodge until a proper dwelling was built. Blindly, he passed some of the rath's people scurrying here and there. Part of him wondered at their presence given the wee hour, but he was too intent on facing his own demons to give it a second thought.

A dim light leaked out around the perimeter of the plank door.

Good. Cromyn was still awake. Not that Colga would hesitate to awaken the man. As the new mother had been ready for her babe to see the light of day, so he was ready to give up this dark secret. He'd carried it and labored with it too long. It too deserved light—the light of confession whatever the consequence. Clammy with perspiration from his drunken weakness, Colga leaned against the thick door frame to catch his wind and overheard a familiar voice inside, as threatening and insidious as it had been the last time it afflicted his ear.

"Curse you, you sniveling little thief. Have you any idea the trouble you've caused?"

Maille? If ever there was a demon to be faced, the Ulster lord was one, but what was he doing here at Gleannmara? Hair raised on the back of Colga's neck. How had the devil gotten past the guard at the gates? "Where was it, Mebh?"

Mebh. What was that woman doing here? Colga recalled what he'd been told about the happenings at the abbey with the child slavers and later as Riona and Kieran traveled to Drumceatt. And now the slaver's wife was here with Maille? Sure, this new wind bode ill for Kieran and Riona.

"Hung round 'is scrawny neck and hid by his shirt."

"You poisoned my sister, you blackguard!"

The voice belonged to a boy, an older one given its adolescent break. Fynn? *Great God in heaven*, Colga prayed, forgetting his own shame. Flashes of Leila's smiling face, the sweet little kisses she gave so freely, the innocent trust Colga so envied, drove him further in his plea, closer to God than he'd ever venture for himself. *Not that precious little girl. Father, tell me it isn't so.*

"I poisoned no one—"

Colga didn't hear the rest of the woman's reply, for a voice sounded behind him.

"Colga, is that you?"

Grabbing blindly for the dining dagger at his waist, Colga fell against the stone-corbeled structure, as ready as his dulled senses would allow. But on recognizing Gleannmara's king in the moonlight, he put his finger to his lips with a liquor-scented *shush* and jerked his head toward the chapel.

If Maille's presence was not enough to sober Colga, the whiff he caught of his own breath was. How could something that went down so sweetly turn so foul upon him? No more had the thought taken root than Colga thought of his rise to Dromin chief. The intoxication of winning it lasted not nearly as long as the aftermath of festering guilt.

"You what?" Maille exclaimed beyond the door, jerking Colga back to the present danger as the Ulster chief swore fiercely. "I told you to keep low and look for the vial, nothing more."

"Gleannmara killed my Tadgh," the woman whined. "I wanted him to spend the rest of his life alone, without the one he loves. How was I to know the little girl would take the tea instead?" The whine came back. "I didn't mean to hurt her."

"I don't give a whit about the child, woman. 'Tis the disturbance I've no use for."

Beside him, Kieran caught his breath and fell back a step, as though the black fist of this ill wind had struck him squarely in the chest, offering no quarter.

Kieran stood, struggling to breathe. It took all his will to resist the desire that swept him…the desire to plunge through the doorway and put an end to Maille's miserable, foul existence.

Words from a conversation between the children and Father Cromyn came back to him. *Sins of the father…revisited upon his children…*

Faith, the words twisted his gut with relentless fists. Kieran was hard pressed not to tear at them with his fingers, like a madman seeking relief from his lunacy. Would Leila pay the price for Kieran's mistakes? Would she die because of the vengeance he'd stirred in another's soul?

Drawing a breath, he knew he could not give in to this agonizing remorse and undermining panic. He needed to listen with the ear of a warrior—and the soul of a saint—that God might help him form a plan.

He closed his eyes, and a fervent prayer leaped from his heart. *Father, grant me a cool head and a whole body…just one more time.*

THIRTY-FOUR

As Kieran listened—not only with his ears, but with his spirit as well—the clearer and more damning the situation became. The image of the new servant, Nis—his shaven head, crevassed and scarred...those burning coals of his eyes peering from beneath a pronounced brow—gave way to Mebh's face. He saw again her stringy, strawlike hair hiding all but her ugly fury and her determination to impale him with a hay fork.

Nis and Mebh...they were one and the same, vicious and bitter. She must have been the one to smuggle Maille into the rath.

Colga seized his arm, only now catching on to the treachery.

Kieran whispered, "'Twas no man that soaked you in wine earlier, 'twas Mebh."

Kieran shoved it away, trapped in his own agonizing revelation. Now he knew what had been wrong earlier that evening, why he hadn't felt quite as at home and at peace as he'd wanted. Even his burning wound had tried to warn him of the presence of the one who'd dealt it, but he'd been too distracted with Bran and his company to take issue with a servant's harsh glare.

Sins of the father...visited upon his children.

The haunting words impaled his heart to his soul with nails as cruel as those that had pierced Christ's own hands. Except Kieran was not the innocent Christ had been. Cold perspiration seeped through Kieran's pores till he trembled with it. *God, forgive me. God, help me.*

"He has the eldest of your boys, I think."

Fynn. Kieran's hand went instinctively to his waist where he usually carried at least a dining knife. Only then did he realize he wore nothing but his leine. He'd even left his sword by Leila's bed, where he'd knelt to pray.

Colga drew his own blade. A second, more deadly one he pulled from the top laces of his sandal and handed it to Kieran. "What'll we do?"

Kieran took it with a grateful nod, a plan forming in his mind even as he spoke. "Have you heard anything from your uncle?"

Colga shook his head. "I was coming to see him when…"

Maille spoke again inside, silencing them both. "What's this? Bring me that lamp, woman."

"If I bring ye the lamp—" Mebh's tone was testy—"I'll have to let the lad go—" She gave a small shriek. It cut through Kieran's disgust, straight to his heart with its infectious terror. He had to do something, but charging into a blind situation was a poor tactic. Perhaps by listening he might judge the whereabouts of the players in this macabre play.

"Saints be with us, it looks like blood!"

Something crashed to the stone floor.

His plan still coming together in bits and pieces from a fog of alarm, Kieran drew back to charge the door if he so much as heard a whimper out of Fynn. Instead, it was Maille who spoke.

"What manner of trickery *is* this, lad?" the man demanded.

Maille, Mebh, and Fynn—theirs were the only voices Kieran had heard, which meant Cromyn was either bound and gagged or dead. *Heavenly Father, spare us that!* As hastily as the soulful prayer shot from his preoccupied mind, Kieran's hard-hewn warrior discipline resumed. He poised, sense and soul shoulder-to-shoulder, ready to receive the sign to go into action.

"If we have to charge in blind, I'll go first. You cover my back," Kieran whispered to his companion.

Colga nodded.

"Where are my jewels?" The Ulster lord's voice rose to a feverish pitch inside. *"Where,* curse your thieving hide?"

Kieran scowled, glancing at Colga in bewilderment.

"What jewels?" Fynn answered, echoing Kieran's thoughts, in fierce rebellion. "I thought the bloomin' vial was filled with holy water. I took it for good luck."

The vial again…and the lad *had* had it.

"From a dead man's possessions?" Maille's cryptic remark only accentuated Kieran's disappointment. "A lad after my own heart."

"You have no heart," Fynn protested. "I knew I'd done wrong and tried to put it back but couldn't get the chance."

"*After* you took my diamonds, you impudent little thief. What is this, cow's blood?"

"'Tis blood money turned ta blood," Mebh wailed at a spine-raking pitch. "God's vengeance, God's vengeance!"

Kieran couldn't help the shiver that raced up his back. *Blood money turned to blood?* Beside him, Colga crossed himself. Could Mebh be some kind of witch?

Heavenly Father, give me a signal. An ill-timed assault, be it early or late, could jeopardize Fynn's safety. *And guide me straight and true, Father, for I've no concept of what I am about to charge into.*

"I know nothing of diamonds or blood, I swear!" Fynn shouted above Mebh's hysteria.

"Shut up, woman, and hold him still." Something fell over, a table perhaps, landing with a hollow thud against the stone floor. "I *will* have my reward, be it in jewels or the blood of those who took them from me."

This was it. Kieran motioned his companion clear and kicked in the door, bellowing like the northern thunder god incarnate. In the blink of a trained eye, he assessed the situation. Straight ahead of him on the altar table, a polished, golden cross amplified the fragile flame of a small candle struggling against the night draft. A sinister figure, black against the glow, poised on one knee beside a bench, which he'd obviously knocked over. Maille. And in his frozen hand was a dagger. Beyond him, bound on a cot against the wall, was Father Cromyn.

Kieran made straight for the female in man's clothing. Snarling like a vengeful beast, he knocked her to the floor and away from Fynn. Leaving her in Colga's custody, he charged like a fury that could not be stopped toward the perpetrator of all the evil that had vexed him these last weeks.

Having had a second more warning than his cohort, Maille leapt away from the table to where a wide-eyed Cromyn lay. From the folds of his cloak, he brandished a short sword in the hand opposite the dagger. With the smaller blade pressed to Cromyn's throat, he held the other ready for Kieran.

In the closeness of the vaulted walls, where the break between wall and ceiling was barely discernible, black smoke from the lone fat candle gave the man a demonic appearance. It was as if the smoke came from his long, hawkish nose and curled about the fashioned fork of his beard. Yet, it was neither weapon nor the sinister aura that stopped Kieran short. It was blood dripping from his enemy's hands. The priest was gagged and trussed like fowl, but he appeared to be unharmed.

So who was bleeding?

"Fynn, are you all right, lad?" Kieran called out, no longer trusting his senses.

"Aye," Fynn started, "but—"

"You tell that boy of yours to hand over my reward," Maille interrupted, "or I'll slit the good father's neck from ear to ear. Trust me, I had no qualm in helping Senan to the other side."

"A mad dog will turn on his own," Colga remarked from where Mebh was huddled at his feet. Indeed Maille looked like one, what with his upper lip curled in threat as if he held the advantage.

Kieran quirked a skeptical brow. "What makes you think I'll let you leave here alive if you so much as scratch the priest, redhand?" Where *had* the blood come from? Kieran dared not take his eye off the Ulster lord to search for the victim—a hapless guard perhaps. "Whose blood drips now from your fingers?"

"Blood money turned ta blood," Mebh babbled. "I seen it meself, turned ta blood, right from the bottle. Blood money."

"It's a trick, you hag!" Maille jerked the short sword to Fynn, who'd come to Kieran's side. "This thief thinks to mock me."

"You ain't worth mockin'," Fynn challenged hatefully. "I'd as soon mock a bull's—"

Kieran shushed Fynn with his free hand. "The cock that crows loudest oft lands in a cookpot before the next sunrise. Move away, boy, and hold your tongue," he ordered sternly. God willing, the boy would heed his advice on humility rather than learn it the hard way—like at the bloody end of a hay fork wielded by a madwoman.

"I'll have my reward now, boy, or the priest dies."

Kieran shook off the haunting distraction for the challenge at hand. The exact circumstances of Maille's appearance still confused him. "What reward?"

Colga moved within the periphery of Kieran's eye. "His reward for his part in the ill-fated plot to assassinate Aidan, King of Scotia Mi—"

"I know who Aidan is," Kieran cut him off sharply. "But what do *you* know of this conspiracy, Dromin?"

Even as he asked, uneasiness dragged its tingling fingers along Kieran's spine, lifting the hair on his neck. The villainous lineup of faces from his dream paraded across his mind—Maille, Senan, Tadgh, Mebh…and Colga.

Colga, who was never far away when something suspicious had happened.

Bran's words from their journey to Kilmare came to Kieran: *"'Tis that sniveling's fault."* Colga had conspired against Aidan. The realization fell upon him like an anvil upon his chest.

"Ach, Colga, tell me it isn't so!" Kieran sounded as though his very breath bore the crush of the betrayal. Aye, it was a small matter in comparison to Leila's bordering on the brink of death, but then a single thread was often the undoing of an entire garment.

Now Kieran understood Maille's assured demeanor. It was not Ulster who was surrounded by the enemy, but Kieran himself. Yet he held Colga's weapon, an inner voice noted. Had the coward given it to him to lure him inside where he could be taken without being seen?

"Go on, Dromin." Maille was a veritable spring of cynicism. "Here is your chance to belatedly confess your conscience to a lot who will not get the chance to tell of it."

Colga toyed with the dining dagger, refusing to meet Kieran's gaze. "I left Aidan's flank guard exposed to the enemy. In gratitude, they saw that the Dromin needed a new chief."

A bilious taste assaulted the back of Kieran's throat. "Your own *cousin?*"

"Aye," Dromin answered, refusing to meet his gaze.

"Unfortunately, your friend Aidan has been harder to kill than the Dromin chief. Tell me, Gleannmara—" Maille struck a cocky pose— "have *you* seen angels protecting him, or is the fact that he's still breathing simply a bad turn of fate for those of us who had seen his brother on the throne?"

"He's had many lives to be sure." After his rescue on the racecourse and what Kieran saw in the privy the night of Aidan's attempted assassination, he'd never scoff at the idea of angels again. But if they were real, then what had happened to Leila's? *Father, I want to believe.*

"Angels or nay," Colga remarked, "the conspiracy failed. Those not dead have faded into the facade of acceptance in fear that Aidan is truly heaven's choice. It's over."

Those not dead...

"Senan and Tadgh." It was no guess on Kieran's part.

"As I said before, I *helped* the good bishop repent, and I believe you saw to Tadgh's justice," Maille taunted.

"Taddy, yes, yes, Taddy's gone. No angels for him, not a one." Mebh's singsong mumblings turned to a growl. "And now I've no husband and no hair...cut it off in me grief. Poor Nis has no one. Mebh has no one." She spat in contempt. "And it's all your fault...just like 'is lordship says."

"Of that, I'm truly sorry, Mebh." Kieran's apology did little to assuage his guilt. Leila suffered for *his* arrogant pride. It had been a lark to run the cowardly Tadgh into the water. Kieran had not only judged and executed him, but he'd enjoyed it. Now it sickened him. *Father, take me, but please spare the child. 'Tis I who deserve death.*

"Maille," Kieran managed, climbing up through the misery and regret that accosted him to face the present threat. "I will hand over my weapon to you if you simply take your vial and people and leave."

"Make the lad give me my diamonds first."

Kieran glanced at Fynn. "Well, lad?"

Fynn shook his head stubbornly.

"Fynn," Kieran said impatiently, "blood begets blood. Sin begets sin, not just for ourselves, but for our loved ones. Your sister lies dying because of my sin. Yours has caused its share of travail for us all as well. Now where are the cursed diamonds?"

"I don't know!" Fynn declared. "I never looked in the vial. I thought it was holy water and kept it for luck and…"

"And," Kieran prompted as the boy dropped his gaze to the floor.

"And I was going to sell the silver case if me'n' the twins was left out on our own, like you wanted to start with."

Kieran cringed inside. Faith, was there no end to the heartache his thoughtless arrogance caused? "Ah, lad—"

"You didn't want us," Fynn blurted out angrily. "You said it over and over. We were ragmullions, thieves, cut from the same bolt as our parents—" he caught his breath—"but you changed and…well, you just changed. I'm thinkin' we all have."

"Touching as this is, I don't believe the little thief." Maille, enjoying his deranged mockery, eased up on the blade at Cromyn's throat.

The flickering, smoking candle hissed and flared brighter, capturing the sadistic glimmer of his gaze for a fleeting moment. Seizing upon the distraction, Father Cromyn threw himself off the bed and into the back of Ulster's knees, throwing the man off balance.

"Run for help, lad!" Kieran shouted, lunging for the hilt of the short sword.

He hoped the force of his charge would knock Maille over the bed. With luck, the surprise combined with the fall would knock the other blade from his hand. As they went down, he registered Colga just a shadow's breath behind him. The table holding the candle crashed against the floor at the same time. The falling lamp sent shadows leaping wildly toward the ceiling as if dispossessed of their bodies, and suddenly darkness cloaked all.

"Run for help, Fynn!" Kieran expected at any moment to feel the plunge of a blade, be it Colga's, Maille's—or perhaps both.

Grunts and curses mingled so that he knew not which was his and which belonged to his enemies. He struggled like a demon for the precious seconds it took to wring the sword from Maille's hand. As it came free, he rolled away and to his feet with long embedded training, ready for his nemesis to recover. Miraculously, Kieran was unscathed, save knocking his head upon the low slope of the ceiling over the bed.

"Cromyn?" Kieran called out in the darkness.

The answering "Here!" assured him that the priest had maneuvered out of harm's way, at least for the moment. The decision remained, though, whether to take the offensive against the unseen or wait until his eyes adjusted to the new light admitted through the door left open by Fynn's retreat for help. Prepared as he was, nothing happened. The scrambling he'd rolled away from stilled. The sounds of struggle silenced.

Frozen, Kieran strained to hear anything above his own labored breathing. It filled his nostrils with the stony dankness of a place that saw little natural light, while his pounding heart played war upon his ears.

Finally he heard Colga. "I…he's dead, I think."

"Who?" Kieran demanded warily, crouching into a ready position lest the danger be postponed and not eliminated.

"M…Maille." The other man took a deep breath and coughed, choked. "Was the least…I could do."

Carefully, Kieran rose. He still could see nothing in the square of light cast from the door save Cromyn's trussed form. Someone moved on the bed and struck the floor like a lifeless sack of grain.

Kieran's foot kicked a metal blade. In an instant, he had the short sword he'd wrested from Maille in his hand.

The only rush that followed was Kieran's own. He lit the extinguished candle from the puddle of fat still burning on the floor where it fell. Placing it high on the stone altar for the most light, he approached Cromyn to free him from the ropes that held his wrists and ankles. "Colga," he called, his vision beginning to accept the shadows in the darkness.

The Dromin chief answered with an anguished groan. "I…I think I'm…d…dying, too."

Kieran freed Cromyn and shot his attention to Colga. Blood soaked the Dromin's chest, spreading from the impaled blade of Maille's dagger. Colga had taken it in Kieran's stead.

Fynn returned then with men bearing weapons and torches. The light filled the room, robbing it of its macabre cloak of death and darkness.

Cromyn lightened it even more. "You're not dying, nephew," he announced, crossing himself in gratitude. "It appears God is not finished with you yet, though only heaven knows why."

He glanced at Kieran, their gaze kindling in mutual agreement. Colga's confession would remain between them, at least for now.

Fynn sidled up beside Kieran, staring down at Colga.

"He saved my life," Kieran told the lad, stopping the accusation he feared would come from the lad's lips. "'Tis time for prayer and forgiveness, not condemnation, wouldn't you say?"

Guilt flushed the boy's face, followed by relief when Kieran squeezed his shoulder.

Suddenly Fynn glanced around the room. "Where's Mebh?"

A quick scan sent a chill surging through Kieran's blood. The woman was gone.

THIRTY-FIVE

eila looked like a tiny, bloodless doll lying on the clean bed Riona had made for her. Faint breath and a fainter pulse was all the life left in the child, but Riona refused to stop praying. God had made her a promise, and she would hold to it to the last. At a stirring in the open doorway of the guest lodge, she looked up from her prayerful posture, expecting to see Ina and Liex returning with fresh towels and clean water. Instead, what met her eyes was a dreadful apparition.

Riona blinked as if to send it back to the dregs of perdition from whence it came, but it was still there, staring at her with unadulterated hatred, traces of spittle glistening in the furrow of its chin. Gradually, she recognized the manservant who'd delivered her supper earlier that evening.

Was this, then, the one who tried to poison her? Anger surged from the swirl of emotions in her beleaguered mind. She pointed to Leila. "Look what you've done, sir!"

"*Sor,* she calls me," the servant mimicked. "Or so ye thinks, milady." He shoved his face into the light of the lamp hanging on the wall. "Ye don't know me wi'out me 'air?"

Riona was too distracted by the kitchen knife in the man's fist to discern what he spoke of. "What—?"

"It's me...*Mebh!* The poor woman ye kept that wee babe from."

"Mebh?" Riona's eyes widened. She'd have never guessed, but then she'd not seen the woman in good light. Now that she knew, the creature's whine was familiar. 'Twas the sort that raked along the spine like a shard of ice.

"An' now look at 'er." A sob caught in the woman's voice. "A wee doll at death's door, and all because o' you and that lord o' yours."

"You were going to sell her into slavery," Riona objected, struggling from the throes of shock.

329

LINDA WINDSOR

"Not *that* little darlin'!"

Riona instinctively stepped back against Leila's bed as Mebh moved toward her, knife extended with malevolent intent.

"I lost me own girl to the yellow death," Mebh said mournfully. "I wanted this 'un for me own." She ran a finger down the dull edge of the knife, momentarily lost between past and present. Then the glaze in her eyes hardened, focusing on Riona. Her knuckles whitened about the wooden handle of the knife. "But *you* took 'er. Snatched her up from me with your high and mighty position."

Riona had thought it an act, but there was no doubt now that the woman had genuinely suffered. It was easy to commiserate. She'd felt the same when she thought she might lose the children to Tadgh and Mebh, and now her heart bled each time she looked at Leila's still form as though Mebh's knife were already wedged there.

"And then your man killed mine, same as if he took this blade and shoved it through me Taddy's heart." The knife whooshed through the air. Riona dodged to avoid its cut. Mebh smiled, what she had left of her teeth as decayed as her mental state. "Aye, that's what 'e done, milady...chased me poor Taddy with a blade like this."

She swung at Riona again, barely missing Riona's arm. Mebh's demented game would end in blood, of that Riona was certain. For now the play was satisfaction enough.

"He *poked*—" Mebh jabbed at Riona's chest, driving her back on the boys' bed—"an' 'e prodded." The point nicked Riona's rib as she rolled away and off the bed. "An' 'e took my Taddy away from me, just like I'm goin' to take ye away from 'im."

Riona scampered to her feet, but before she could run for the door, Mebh blocked her path. A pain-infused insanity contorted the woman's face as she pressed Riona up against the whitewashed wall. To so much as breathe was to force the knifepoint into the flesh just below her heart.

"I'm sorry, Mebh," Riona whispered. "I can imagine the pain you must feel losing your loved ones so needlessly." Ina would be back soon...or Kieran with the priest. Surely someone would come.

Mebh cocked her head from side to side, echoing Riona's words in a singsong voice. "I can imagine. I can imagine." She stopped abruptly and scowled. *"No one* can imagine 'ow it hurts."

"I love that child, Mebh, like you loved your daughter. And now she's—" A sob choked Riona off. She couldn't let her emotions get the best of her now. She had to remain sharp. "She's dying, Mebh, just like your little one. It already feels like that blade is in my heart. Indeed your blade would ease my pain, but—"

"But what?" Emotion crested above Mebh's suspicion. Her humor vacillated from melancholy to menace, from past to present, then back again.

Riona tried for the right moment. "But *you* were able to hold your babe until she went to the other side, weren't you? Faith, put down the knife and come with me. Hold her. Don't let Leila die alone whilst we quarrel over what can't be undone."

Mebh whimpered, glancing quickly to where Leila lay deathly still. "I wouldn'a hurt the wee lass for the world."

"I know, Mebh. But she needs to be held…and she needs our prayers because—" Riona's panicked thoughts scattered, leaving her mind blank in her desperation.

"Because what?" The knifepoint penetrated her night shift and bit into her flesh. Surely she bled.

"Because God told me He'd save her," she blurted out. "But we must pray—*all* of us. That's what I was doing when you came in. I sent Kieran for the priest. We need all the voices we can lift to save her."

"They's not comin'."

But for the knife holding her upright on its tiny point, Riona might have slumped to the floor at the news. She'd *thought* Kieran had been gone overlong. What had happened? *Heavenly Father, help us!* Riona mustered her courage to ask, "Why?"

Mebh shrugged, her gaze wandering to Leila. "Don't know, don't care no more. Left 'em in the dark, fightin' and cursin' like the devil's own."

Riona's heart felt as if it would burst with growing anxiety. It shouted *"Who?"* when her voice would not. It thundered in her ears, growing louder and louder—or was that the sound of someone running toward them? With no room for panic, she mastered her rioting emotions with the resolve of a mother whose babe faced imminent danger.

"But you do care about Leila," she reminded the woman.

"Riona!" Kieran's shout preceded his entrance into the lodge, a bloodstained sword in hand.

"Ah!" she gasped as Mebh's blade cut a little deeper.

"Stay where ye are, milord," Mebh warned, "or yer pretty wife dies to be sure."

Almost afraid to breathe, Riona looked at her husband. "Kieran, go outside and close the door."

His stricken expression told Riona that he thought her as mad as Mebh. *"What?"*

"Mebh and I need to take care of Leila," she explained. "If we don't, our little girl may die." Riona looked at Mebh, pleading. "You will hold her and help me pray? Mebh, I know God will hear us. Leila has an angel. It saved her once. We must call him back to her."

"It's true, Mebh," Kieran chimed in, seeming to sense Riona's plan. "The child fell into the path of racing chariots, and when I tried to cover her, we were both overrun. I had the tracks on my brat to show for it, but neither of us was so much as scratched. We felt nothing. Father Cromyn said Leila had her own angel."

"We must pray, Mebh. You do believe, don't you?" Riona searched the wells of grief and indecision spilling over Mebh's puffy, pockmarked cheeks. Something inside bade Riona reach for the tears and wipe them away ever so gently. "I hurt with you, Mebh. Leila is ours. Give me the knife and hold her."

"I can't lose my baby again. I can't bear it," the woman cried. She let the knife go, her round shoulders heaving in misery.

As the weapon clattered to the floor, Riona took Mebh into her arms, coaxing her over to where Leila lay. Kieran snatched up the weapon, but Riona motioned him to be still.

"If you would help us, milord, then kneel where you are and pray." In Mebh's unstable state, Riona wanted nothing to distract the woman. Mebh needed Leila as much as Riona did, for she saw her own raw anguish in the woman's tortured eyes. "God promised to hear our cries," she said, as much for her own benefit as for that of the others. "He promised to answer our prayers. He sent me a message that He would heal Leila."

"A message?" Mebh's head jerked up, doubt shadowing her despair.

Riona nodded in assurance. "Aye, I'd fetch it from my bag, but there's no time. We must do our part. She needs a mother's touch right now and a mother's prayer." Gently, she eased Leila up from the bed so that she rested in Mebh's arms. It felt as if Riona laid her own heart in the madwoman's embrace.

"Heavenly Father, hear our prayers."

"Father, hear our prayers," Mebh whispered, just syllables behind Riona.

"We beseech You with breaking hearts to save our child."

"...our child."

"...save our child," Kieran joined in from the foot of the small bed.

How Riona longed to hold his hands clasped with hers. "Send your angel back to her."

"...back to her."

"...back to her," Kieran echoed with Mebh.

"Father we are broken vessels, flawed and sinful..."

"...sinful."

"...sinful."

"We are sorry for our wrongdoings and pray that You do not visit them upon this child, that she should suffer for our sins."

Kieran repeated her words and then went on, cutting Riona off. "Father, I have been so wrong. I have caused much hurt and pain."

Mebh repeated the words after him. Her tears seemed to stream not just from her closed eyes as she rocked Leila back and forth in her arms, but from her wretched soul.

"God forgive me. Help me to start anew. Grant me the chance to give this precious little girl the family she deserves...to make it up to this broken woman and my wife for my pride, for my arrogant mistakes."

Mebh stilled, looking over Leila's head at Kieran. Riona closed her hand over the woman's gnarled, arthritic one. "We *all* need healing,

Mebh. God will heal us if we believe. He will forgive us, but we must forgive ourselves…and each other. Can you forgive to save Leila and yourself?"

"B…but blood will stain my 'ands. I know it. Maille's money turned ta blood…spilled out over his 'ands. God's vengeance, it was, and 'e curses me as well."

"Not if you are earnestly sorry for all you've done wrong," Riona explained fervently. "I promise it."

"Me 'and's curled up like this, like a sickness since my baby was took, an' me 'eart with it."

Riona took Mebh's disfigured hand and pressed it to Leila's chest.

"Heal us, Father."

The echo of her words carried more voices than those of Mebh and Kieran. There was a child's and a woman's coming from the direction of the door.

"Heal us, Father," she pleaded again, eyes tightly shut.

Again and again, she repeated the words. Again and again, there was a chorus, each time louder and louder, until her voice and those around her were the same, crying to heaven, not with their tongues, but with their souls.

Heal us, Father. Heal us, Father. Heal us, Father.

No more thought, only pleas.

Then a single, tiny voice penetrated the chant, clear and fragile as that of a newborn bird joining its first morning song in the forest.

"Maithar?"

Mother?

Riona opened her eyes, but she could see nothing. It was as if the sun itself hung on the wall instead of the dim, smoky lamp. The voice had come from the girl in Mebh's arms. Of that Riona was certain.

"Leila?" She groped in the blinding brightness until she felt a small, warm hand clasp hers in return. "Sweetling, I can't see you."

"It's Seargal, maithar. Isn't he beautiful? It's never dark when he's around. He's saying good-bye."

Kieran fairly shouted from the end of the bed, apparently as blind as Riona. "Leila? Is that you? Is it her, Riona?"

Faith, she understood every word the child spoke! But that was impossible…

No longer trusting her senses, Riona groped for Leila's face and caressed it, knowing its every feature by heart.

"I love you, Seargal!" the child called out.

Riona felt Leila's lips as they spoke, and her heart sang for joy. *With God, nothing is impossible.* "Aye, it's our darling."

"But where?" Kieran asked unsteadily. "Where is she?"

"In me arms!" Wonder struck the gravelly harshness from Mebh's voice, softening it. "The most dazzlin' spirit I ever laid eyes on passed us through, and the babe come ta life, praise the Lord! She's warm as a bun fresh from the hearth."

Other exclamations of awe penetrated the light. Mebh's words were with a mix of incredulity and fear. Then, as quickly as it appeared, the light was gone, snuffed like a brilliant flame by an unseen hand.

"Athair?" Leila called out to Kieran.

Still dazed, Riona felt him bump against her, clamoring to reach the child. "Here, sweetling. I'm here. Faith, I'm half blind, but I don't care."

His tearful laugh welled like the gladness in Riona's heart.

"Well, *I* can see," Mebh announced excitedly. "I see the most beautiful little girl ever was."

Gradually forms took shape, and the shapes had faces. The confines of the room became defined from the abrupt change of light—and then Riona saw Leila as well.

"Who are you?" Leila asked, squirming to get out of Mebh's arms.

"She's someone who loves you like a mother and prayed that you'd get well," Riona assured her, "just like your father and I."

Leila gave Mebh a smile. "Thank you, milady." The child hesitated and glanced over her shoulder at Kieran and back to the woman. "Can I go to my father now? I have something to tell him."

Mebh nodded reluctantly and let her go.

With a bright smile, Leila flung her arms about Kieran's neck. "Did you see him, Father? Seargal took off his cloak of invilla…invisda—" she wrestled with the word *invisibilty*—"Invillabillity!" she proclaimed in triumph. "Just to show himself to all of you. Now you know he's not a make-believe friend, don't you?"

"I saw 'im!" Liex exclaimed from the door. The boy scampered in and bounded up on the bed. "He was as tall and big as Athair, and his eyes were like stars...just like you said."

"Aye," Mebh agreed, still unsure of herself. "Like stars they were, and a robe the likes of which I've never seen."

For the first time, Riona saw the source of the other voices. Ina, Benin, and a host of others were crowded outside the lodge, all as stricken as she by the light. Some were still on their knees. Many were overcome with emotion.

"We saw a miracle." Riona grabbed Mebh's hand in hers. A while ago, that hand had pressed a knife into her flesh, intent on taking her life. Now a spirit flowed through them, uniting them in a warmth that went beyond the earthly. "Mebh!" Riona gasped, staring at the woman's face.

The pockmarks were gone, as was the mottled weathering of the woman's cheeks. And her eyes. They were a beautiful brown, doe-soft and bright with tears of happy delirium. Riona examined the hand she held. A rise of joy nearly choked her. Mebh's fingers were no longer swollen and twisted.

"It *was* an angel." Even the woman's voice had changed from an out-of-tune string to one that blended in harmony with the trueness of the others. "All golden and glorious to the heart's eye."

"It came in with the morning sun, like it rode on its rays." Fynn stood awkwardly at the door. Beyond him, exclamations of "miracle" and "angel" moved through the gathering like wind through wheat.

Kieran extended his other arm to the boy. "Come here, lad. This family prays together and celebrates together." Once Fynn was in the circle of Kieran's arm, Kieran turned to Leila. "So what was it Seargal had to say to me?"

Leila cupped her hands around Kieran's ear and whispered softly. Incredulity spread on his face; then he closed his eyes as if in thanks. It was some moments before he opened them again, their amber depths filled with emotion. Still, he didn't miss Mebh's motion as she pushed up from the bed and started away.

"Wait...hold her, Benin," Kieran ordered. With Leila propped on one arm and Fynn under the other, he was in no position to stop the woman.

Mebh blanched, frozen, waiting for the king to invoke his judgment on her. Outside, the people of the rath closed in around the door that they might hear and see.

"You needn't think you'll be allowed to escape Gleannmara."

Riona's heart stopped in alarm until Kieran's stern facade crumbled with a grin. "At least, not now that you're one of us."

"Milord?" The woman's face filled with confusion.

Praise God, her husband truly *was* changed. Vengeance, not this winsome forgiveness echoing in his words, would have driven the old Kieran.

"It's a new day, Mebh." His voice drove shadows of doubt and fear away like the rising sun itself. "Grace has wiped away our past as completely as the sun has cleared us of the darkness."

"Mebh was sick, too, wasn't she?" Leila's remark smacked more of observation than question. "Seargal kissed her hand, just like a man does a lady's. I didn't know he knew her."

"God bless ye, milord," Mebh fell to her knees before Kieran.

Forgiveness, thanksgiving, reverence, resounded both within and without the lodge and defied the awareness of time. At some point, Benin and Ina began to restore order. Across the rath, a clear bell from the chapel rang in the day. People left by ones and twos to prepare for what was to be the first official morning prayers, leaving only Riona's family and Mebh in the house.

"Mebh," Kieran said, relinquishing Leila to the older woman. "Will you join us at the chapel?"

Fynn pulled away. "You're going to trust her after all she did to us?"

Kieran clapped his hand on the lad's shoulder. "Son, if God forgave her enough to heal her affliction outside, how can we doubt that she isn't healed within as well?"

Riona wondered as the boy pondered Kieran's word. Could this be the same man who'd cursed God and abandoned Him at his parents' death? Wonder filled her that he, who'd begged God's forgiveness for his reckless regard for life, was the same soldier who prided himself on his ability to take it. And that she, who'd spurned him in distaste, now loved him more than life itself.

"What about me?" Fynn kicked at the stone floor of the lodge and slowly raised his eyes to meet Kieran's. Guilt still plagued his face. "I stole the vial of holy water and nearly got us all killed."

"Oh, Fynn!" Riona gasped in dismay. Kieran had placed his honor on the boy's word. He'd be furious.

Liex bounded in and across the bed. "You did? Where did you keep it?" he demanded, as if he should have been privy to the fact. "Did you taste it?"

Kieran silenced the younger lad's barrage of questions with a glance so withering that even Riona felt its frosty bite. Yet when he turned back to Fynn, his expression thawed. "Of course you're forgiven. How can a man accept forgiveness of his own sins—and I've had my share and more—" he injected with a rueful grimace—"unless he is willing to forgive those who've sinned against him? He looked over at Riona. That's the way of it, isn't it, milady?"

Riona nodded, her swelling heart trapping her words. *My soul runneth over,* she thought, as did her eyes. She wiped them on the sleeve of her shift.

"Ye gonna pardon Colga, too?" she heard Fynn ask the man who'd joined her as one in mind, body, and spirit.

"Aye, he's suffered for his mistakes like the rest of us," Kieran answered, but his gaze was fixed upon Riona.

"But who...what...?" she stammered.

Kieran checked her confusion with a reassuring brush of her lips. "Later, anmchara," he promised. Whether explanation, marital intimacy, or both was implied didn't really matter. She accepted his will, for here was a true king, a just and godly man...or at least he earnestly sought to be. God could ask for no more and neither could she, not as a woman, nor wife, nor anmchara. Her *soul mate.* Try as she might, she could not muster a queenly composure beneath his all-embracing gaze.

"Mebh..." Riona's voice faltered. She cleared it with a muster of authority. "Will you dress the children for chapel?"

"Aye, milady but—" Mebh turned anxious eyes toward Kieran.

"Yes, Mebh?"

"Is *he* still there?" The woman enunciated *he* as though she spoke of the devil himself. "And that cursed vial o' blood?"

"I'm certain Benin and Father Cromyn have seen to the removal of Maille's body."

"Maille!" Riona exclaimed. Until now, she'd not had time to consider whom Mebh madly referred to earlier when she warned Riona that Kieran and the priest were detained.

"And that cursed vial o' blood," Mebh repeated, casting a wary glance at Fynn.

Vial? "I thought it was holy water that was missing," Riona puzzled aloud.

"So help me, I *never* opened it," Fynn pledged with a shudder. "I was scared enough for having taken it." He turned to Riona as though seeking someone to believe him. "All I wanted to do was give it back, but Maille's men were always in the way. 'Twas a curse from the day I laid hands on it."

"Sin usually is, sweetling," she told him. It was the only thing she was certain of at the moment. "It gnaws at the soul like a canker that can't be stopped until we expose it to God for His healing."

"Maille *was* a canker on the shanks of mankind," Mebh observed to no one in particular. "And I weren't much better, so help me."

"But Seargal fixed your sore, Lady Mebh," Leila pointed out with a marked air of satisfaction that her friend had finally been taken seriously.

"Saints be, did ye hear what the little angel called me?" Mebh looked as though she might take flight in her euphoria. Grabbing Leila up in her arms, the woman swung her around. *"Ye're* the angel sent to me, child, when my world could grow no darker."

"And God sent Seargal to me after Maithar and Athair died because I was afraid of the dark and the boys just slept." The little girl's pout of commiseration turned to a bright smile as she pointed to Riona and Kieran. "And now I got a beautiful new mother and a big, brave father with hair just like mine."

Before her very eyes, the stern warrior king of Gleannmara melted into a besotted grin. An angel no longer lit the room, Riona realized, as affected by Leila's words as Kieran.

Love did.

THIRTY-SIX

L eaving Mebh to ready the children for the first morning prayer service, Riona leaned on Kieran's strong arm as they returned to the royal lodge. The danger had finally passed, but it had taken her strength. Judging from the weary sag of Kieran's shoulders, she was not the only one plagued by exhaustion.

If only she had the resilience of the children, she thought, as she heard Liex announce eagerly, "I wanna see the blood-filled vial."

"No you don't, dolt," Fynn answered. "Trust me."

The older boy erupted with an abrupt squeal of pain.

"That's for callin' me a dolt, dung mouth," Liex crowed.

Was it only moments ago that their lives had hung in a balance between good and evil?

Mebh's voice rose above the din. "Now git off yer big brother's back, afore I jump on your'n, ye towheaded little mite."

"Lady Gray!" Leila shrieked as only a little girl can. It was reassuring rather than spine-raking, at least to Riona, when the child ranted on quite coherently, *"Don't kick my kitten!"*

Riona hesitated at the door of the king's lodge to return to reinforce Mebh, but Kieran stopped her.

"Let Mebh handle it. Trust me, I know a good commander when I see one."

At that moment, there was a loud *whop,* followed by a collective holler from the boys.

"What was *that* for?" one demanded in a voice breaking into manhood.

"That's *my* pillow," the other cried out in accusation.

"For actin' like hooligans," Mebh answered, with all the authority of a hen settling on her nest. And then she added, prim as one pleased, "An' hooligans don't use pillows...don't deserve 'em. I know. I was married to one."

Riona giggled and stepped inside, allowing Kieran to shove the door to behind them. "I think you're right at that, milord."

The bedchamber was a shambles, blankets strewn from the bed to the door. Faith, it felt as though another full day had passed since they'd abandoned it so filled with fear just hours before. Now joy and thanksgiving brimmed. She turned and went into her husband's arms but pulled away abruptly on noticing the dampness of his leine. The bloodstains on the side jerked her beleaguered mind back to the matter of the vial and Maille. It was all a blur.

"Colga's blood," he explained before she could form which question to ask first. "He took the blade Maille intended for me. He'll be fine," he assured her. "A flesh wound."

"But how did Maille get into the rath, and…was it really blood in the vial?"

"Mebh worked for him, and, aye, it looked like blood. I hadn't the time to see. But Maille thought it contained diamonds, not holy water or blood."

"Diamonds!" Riona gasped. It was enough to make a quick wit spin, but her sleep-deprived one churned in this bog of confusion. The more she learned, the thicker it got.

"'Tis a long, long tale that goes all the way back to Scotia Minor and a plot to assassinate Aidan," Kieran assured her, stroking the side of her face with the back of his fingers. If there were diamonds among them at all, they were in Kieran's eyes. "But for now, I'd as soon put it aside and concentrate on what is right, not what went wrong."

A wise king as well, Riona thought, weariness slipping away with curiosity under her husband's sway. Hands sliding from her face to her shoulders, Kieran squeezed them, standing back as if to reassure himself that she was there, safe and sound.

He froze as her robe gapped open. Lips thinning, he tugged the front open, fully exposing her shift beneath. He stared in alarm. "You're hurt!"

Glancing down, Riona saw a tiny circle of blood where Mebh had cut her with the knife. "It's only a scratch, I'm sure."

Faith, the lot of them needed a physician more than prayers, she thought, tugging the drawstring neckline of her night shift down to the spot that coordinated with the considerable stain. To her amazement, there was no broken flesh at all—not even the scratch she suggested. But she *knew* better. She recalled the sting of the blade slashing across her flesh, pushing into it.

First Leila, then Mebh...and now me.

Kieran caught her as she swayed, overwhelmed by all that had transpired and continue to do so. "Seargal was busy."

Seargal. Leila's invisible friend. The one who'd kept the little orphan company in her lonely world. Her guardian angel, whom Leila shared as freely as she'd shared her selfless love. God's powerful healing light. God's messenger.

Kieran eased down on the edge of the bed, pulling Riona on his lap and cradling her as snugly as the wonder that held them both. Riona listened to his breath, a rhythmic and reassuring sound that marked off time in the stillness of the room. A myriad of memories from their last weeks together played across her mind. Although unseen to all eyes but Leila's, God and his messenger had been a decided presence among them all.

"What did Leila whisper to you?" Riona asked suddenly, recalling the little girl's message from her friend to Kieran. "Well?" she prompted, when Kieran failed to respond. She drew away, astonished to find his eyes swimming with emotion. Indeed, his throat was besotted with it as well, until he cleared it in a fierce effort to regain his composure.

"He answered a question I'd cried out in my wavering attempt at faith." He gave his head a shameful shake. "After all that had been done for us, I still doubted. If God had really sent an angel to protect Leila, I wanted to know where he was when she'd been poisoned."

"And?"

It was a moment before Kieran could go on. "And I was told that...that Leila had gotten sick so that we all might be healed." He grimaced. "Just like another Lamb who didn't deserve to die."

Riona went into his arms. Together they fell against the mattress, embraced not just by each other, but by the Spirit who had lived up to God's promise. For the longest of times, they shared their tears and gratitude in silence, her head nestled under his bristled chin. She heard his heart beat in concert with hers, orchestrated by an unseen, soothing hand.

As her pillow jerked with a spontaneous movement, Riona raised her head in surprise and looked into the eyes of the man she'd pledged her life and love to forever in this world and the next. She supposed they *should* be dressing for morning prayer, but he stopped her as she started to rise.

"Earlier I almost said that you wouldn't believe how God had sent me a message by an angel." With a lopsided smile that drew her toes up short, Kieran cupped her face in his hand. "But *you* of all people would." Leaning toward her, he brushed her lips with a reverence. "Because He sent you as well. As long as I live and breathe, anmchara, I will do my best to be worthy of this new beginning."

Kieran kissed her tenderly, as though she were the essence of all his blessings. A heavenly gladness brimmed between them, spilling not just from the heart of man to that of the woman given to him but from soul to soul.

Epilogue

I t was a cool, overcast day, but not even the clouded sky could dampen the spirits of the women gathered at Gleannmara's gate. Children frolicked nearby, fresh faced and bellies tight as a tick's from a hearty breakfast in the hall. They didn't seem to mind the chill at all. The twins' brats were more off than on as they helped Fynn hitch a goat to the cart for the smaller tykes visiting from Dromin.

Riona tugged her cloak about her shoulders and adjusted the brooch Kieran had had made for her. It was a miniature of his own, save the overall shape, which had been fashioned into a heart rather than a circle. Instead of the clans represented in the gemstones there was a stone for him and one for each of the children. His ruby rested in the brooch's golden cleavage. The small sapphires stood for Fynn, Liex, and Leila.

He'd jested when he gave it to her that he expected to see its entire span set in the gemstones one day, and if Riona's suspicions were correct, her husband would need to add a fourth stone in the spring.

"If you keep rubbing your belly, 'twill be no surprise," Finella whispered beside her.

At the summer's end, Marcus had set out for Scotia Minor with Aidan's company, while Finella and Dallan had come to Gleannmara as promised. Their purses fat with money earned by their talents, they'd offered Riona a tidy sum for the use of the land where they'd talked of building a bruden. She refused, proposing instead that they use it to build a proper hall. In the meantime, they could live in the abandoned rath. All she required was that it retain the name of Drumkilly, home of Gleannmara's champions and foster home to its Queen Maire.

"I can't help it. It's so hard to believe. I've not been the least sick," Riona replied.

"Best keep the herbs I gave you, just in case," her friend warned.

Siony bounced her rosy-cheeked baby girl on her hip. "Aye, I wasn't sick at all till I looked like I was carrying a calf—"

"Ach, here they come," Finella interrupted.

From the stables, a group of men led horses toward the gate. Among them were Riona's cousins and Father Cromyn. Although the man had already blessed the impending journey at morning vespers, he insisted on seeing his nephew to the gate. Recovered from the stab wound he'd intercepted for Kieran, Colga walked beside the priest, listening intently to what his mentor was saying. He'd spent his recovery with his uncle before facing the penance agreed upon by Kieran and his chiefs for his crime of treachery.

Today was the day, as new as the man whom friends and family turned out to bid farewell. Instead of craving liquor, Colga thirsted now for the Word. His exile would begin with journeying to Scotia Minor to study for the priesthood. With a letter from Cromyn to commend him, he hoped to eventually join an expedition into the unknown with the light of God's Word as Brendan and others had done.

Behind Colga and Cromyn, leading his shaggy steed Bantan, was Bran, who was not only Gleannmara's official academic master, but who also wore the Dromin brooch as its elected chief. It was agreed that since Bran had more children in house than Gleannmara, the new school would be constructed by default on the border between the royal Niall land and the O'Cuillin Dromin. Six of the rescued orphans, including Siony's Naal, were now under the bard's foster care and tutelage.

Conspicuously without a steed was Gleannmara himself. Kieran kept the others company and jested with the men, but he would remain behind this time. He would not march with the Dromin and the other clan troops breaking camp outside the outer rath, readying for their mission to put down a rebellion in Scotia Minor. Kieran's captains went in his stead to the call of the high kings of Ireland and Scotland to squash an invasion of Scottish Dalraidi soil by the Ulster king.

"And did you ever see such a fine covey of ladies," Kieran exclaimed, upon reaching them. He slipped his arm about Riona's waist and gave her a kiss. "Or a more beautiful queen?"

"Milord, you babble," she demurred, her face growing hot as the men fell in with their lord in agreement. How she loved her husband! The old Kieran would have been the first on his horse, sword raised, at the hint of a battle. But like Colga, he had changed, as if made new.

"Colga," she said, walking up to her cousin. "We shall miss you."

"And I you, milady," Colga responded. "But I shall have good company all the way to Scotia Minor," he said, nodding toward the outer rath where the troops awaited.

She'd not been very close to her youngest cousin. Bran was more her and Heber's contemporary, both in age and interest. The last months at Gleannmara had changed that as she watched a broken soul, who believed not even God could forgive him for what he'd done, mend with the nourishment of love and the work of the Holy Spirit.

"I thank God that the wolf of Tara has finally shed his sheep's clothing so that he might be dealt with," Kieran remarked wryly. "This day has been long due."

Although there'd been no tangible proof, Baetan, the Ulster king who'd hidden safely in his court at the cursed and abandoned Tara of the high kings, was undoubtedly one of the driving forces behind the failed attempt to assassinate Aidan. Maille had been no more than a pawn whose chest rose and fell with Baetan's breath.

"Thank you, Riona, for everything," Colga said, kissing her on the cheek.

She returned the gesture chastely. "God's speed. I will expect letters of wonderful tales of faraway places."

Foiled at every turn, Baetan at last showed his true colors and launched troops to force the Scottish Dalraidi to pay homage and tribute to him. So once again the high king Aedh, as obliged to protect Aidan's kingdom as Aidan was Erin's, called upon his nobles to send troops to Scotia Minor. Gleannmara's forces would be among the warriors.

"Now isn't this a twist of fate?" Bran chuckled. "He's off to become a priest *and* seek new experiences to give him tales to tell. While I, the would-be bard and ill-fitted cleric, find myself the chief he aspired to be with a wife and my own congregation of children."

"You're not complaining, are you?" Siony sidled up to her husband and gave him a beguiling glance.

"Hmm," Bran said, pretending to ponder his answer carefully. "Let me see. I could be trapped in a boat filled with quarrelsome men, heaving my insides out, or in a warm home with a good wife and smiling, red-cheeked mites." He took Aine from Siony and tossed the infant into the air. The baby girl giggled ecstatically as he caught her and hoisted her to his shoulder. "You're a lucky man, Colga."

Colga laughed along with the others, including Siony, who pinched Bran for his mischief.

"Don't forget now to give that ham and summer food to Kermod," Riona reminded the happy father as Bran swung onto Bantan's back.

Every time someone passed close to Kilmare, she sent a gift to the sympathetic farmer whom Bran had talked out of the pony for their escape from Maille. A distant cousin had been elected lord of Maille's estate, at least keeping it in Riona's maternal family.

"And I'll give him your love." Bran patted the basket of food strapped behind him.

A dozen more good-byes were said before the party was mounted and on its way. Even so, Riona stood next to Kieran, glad for his added warmth, and waved to any of the men who looked back. Everyone else had drifted away to his or her own course for the day. Dallan, Finella, and the boys juggled balls for the amusement of the stable hands and guards. Siony and Mebh tossed a ball in the rath to the older children while the smallest children bounced and squealed in the goat cart.

"There was a time I'd rather have heard pigs slaughtered than the noise of children's frolic," Kieran confessed to Riona with a wistful tip of his mouth. "It sounded much the same to me."

She snuggled under his arm as they turned and headed for the inner yard. "It's a joyous noise indeed."

"Remember the first day we arrived and the hordes of giggling that charged us?" He laughed. "Sheer horror clutched at my chest. I thought all semblance of order had gone, vanished...that poor Benin had expired, overwhelmed and overrun."

"You've grown much as a father since then."

Kieran smirked. "Aye, I've got the gist of it now."

"But you haven't mastered infants."

"Who has? The wee creatures just pass food through one end and out the other, what doesn't leak out their mouth on the intake, that is. They cry and sleep and sleep and cry at will. I sometimes think the old ones were right in thinkin' babes don't become human till they learn to walk and talk. Till then, they're as unpredictable as the Sidhe."

"Well, milord..." Riona tried hard not let her excitement bubble up through her stern countenance. "I would suggest that you apply yourself most heartily to learn what you can of the "wee creatures."

Kingly grace failing him, Kieran nearly stumbled on the smooth, well-worn yard, spooking a nearby family of ducklings. He turned Riona to face him, eyeing her warily. "Are you trying to tell me something, wife?"

"I'm just telling you that come spring, God willing, I'll need a new sapphire for my brooch."

"You're sure?" He shook her and then, catching himself, rubbed her arms as if to make up for any harm it might have caused.

Riona nodded, smiling, as she watched excitement fill her husband's gaze.

He looked about frantically and lifted his arm as if to call back the travelers who'd already disappeared in the fields beyond. With his other hand he clutched a fist of golden hair in frustration. "Faith, woman, you should have told me earlier! I'd have Bran know the school might move back to our rath yet."

"I'm having a child...not a litter," she added, remembering his observation the night they'd found their nuptial bed draped in a garland of mistletoe. "And I wanted us to be alone when I told you."

"Have you told the children?" Kieran sought out Fynn and the twins in the yard with his eager gaze. He was fit to burst with the news. Like Lady Gray about to pounce, he all but wiggled in anticipation.

"I wanted you to be the first," she told him, "once I was sure."

"So I can tell them now?"

Riona's laughter sent him scurrying off, but he stopped suddenly.

"No," he shouted back to her. "I want to tell everyone."

He climbed to the top of a dirt pile. It and the straw beside it were kept on hand to fill mud holes dug by weather and traffic.

"Hear me, Gleannmara!" he shouted, waving his arms over his head like a madman rather than a king. "I'm going to be a *father!*"

Riona saw Finella bend over in laughter. The ring Liex tossed to her flew by uncaught. Dallan tossed his aside and started toward the dancing king. From the guardhouse, men came out, approaching slowly at first. Like as not, they thought he'd lost his wits.

"I'm going to be a father!"

The alarm on the guards' faces gave way to grins. This time they understood what their king was carrying on about.

To the cheers of "Huzzah!" and the delighted titter coming from the washwomen gathered round their tubs, Kieran hopped down off the pile. He raced back to her, scattering a feeding cluster of fowl in the process.

"You are crazy as a swineherd, milord," Riona chided as he scooped her up in his arms and swung her around.

"Aye, lass, that I am!" He put her down and kissed her on the forehead. "I've been crazy since I first saw you, nothing but a wee thing like Leila." He planted another kiss on her nose. "And I grew crazier when you came back from fosterage in the first bloom of maidenhood."

He held her face between his hands and claimed her lips, lifting her spirit even higher until she had no idea whether her feet still touched the ground or danced on the clouds. All she knew was that this sweet madness of his was infectious. She still floated when he pulled away and caressed her still with his gaze.

"And if either of us goes to the other side ahead of the other," he vowed fervently, "then look for me to be dancing on the clouds, crazy as ever over you, Riona O'Cuillin."

She reached up and touched his lips. "You mean, Riona of Gleannmara."

Kieran pressed his forehead to hers. "I mean love of my life," he whispered, brushing aside her finger so that his lips met hers in a hint of a kiss. "I mean light of my heart," he went on, making with yet another gentle pass. "I mean soul of my soul."

The words came from deep within, carried to her on his breath, sealed with a completeness ordained at the beginning of time, when the Creator made man and woman to be as one.

And above them, dear hearts, the good Lord surely smiled and said, "It is good." The Fires of Gleannmara still burn like a candle in the wind with a flame that cannot be extinguished from without nor—so long as faith is its wick and love its fuel—from within. For all that, I'm pure bustin' to get on with the next tale in this tellin' of me children's illustrious and adventuresome past. Just wait till ye read about me next daughter—the willful and daring Deirdre—and the man she'll have, sure as Erin's grass is green.

But don't be putting this book aside now. If ye haven't already taken a gander at it, help yerself to me very own version of a glossary and reference. 'Tis filled with more interestin' tidbits of academic and legendary note regardin' me and mine.

Now, until we meet again, may the Almighty keep ye in the palm of His blessed hand.

Multnomah Publishers®

The publisher and author would love to hear your comments about this book. *Please contact us at:*
www.multnomah.net/riona

GLEANNMARA'S GLOSSARY/REFERENCE

Fer yer entertainment as well as enlightenment, below is a list o' tidbits regardin' me past and me people's ways, just for them what yearns for a taste o' the Salmon o' Knowledge.

adart (ey-art): a pillow o' feathers encased in deer skin.

Aedh (ed): The high king of Ireland during Riona's time. Many significant accomplishments. (See *Aidan, bard's dilemma, Baetan, Columcille, Drumceatt, to each cow its own calf.*)

aiccid (ay-sid): heir apparent to kingship or clan chief.

Aidan (ay'-dan): the first Christian king of Scotia Minor (Scotland), which earned its recognition as a full province of Ireland with homage due only to Erin's high king rather than an Ulster ruled subkingdom the likes of his Ulster Dalraidi kin's lands. (See *Baetan, Drumceatt, Columcille.*)

aire (ayre): a noble, most often in literary reference, but can refer to a free man.

Airmed's blanket (r-med): In the DeDanan legend, Airmed gathered and sorted the herbs gathered by her brother Midach, a gifted healer, after their father, the healer Diancecht, slew his son and fearing his healing powers even in death, mixed them up and scattered them all over the earth.

athair (a'-the): father.

anmchara (ahn-ca-rah): soul friend, confessor, soul mate.

ard rí (ard righ): high king.

Baetan: King of Ulster and would-be high king of Ireland and Scotland: Now here was a pompous example of bein' too big for one's trews (britches). Baetan grew in power after fightin' at Culdreime with his northern Niall cousins—High King Aedh's father, Scot King Aidan's father, and relative and saint-to-be Columcille agin the then High King Diarmait o' the opposin' clan. Baetan set up his court at Tara, which was abandoned by the high kings who came along after it was cursed out o' the sense the good Lord gave 'em, but this fool thought himself high and mightier than reality. Then, when Aedh (high king) wouldn't make their cousin Aidan (Scot king) pay homage to Baetan as the Dalraidi kin in Ulster did, this blusterin' banty rooster up and attacks Aidan's shores. (And ye think *your* family quarrels are foolish?)

Well, he failed, but what can a soul expect when they try to defeat a king divinely appointed by God Himself? Ye see, even Saint Columcille was favorin' Aidan's brother, but an angel appeared and smote the headstrong saint to make him see the light. Columcille ordained Aidan as the rightful king, and the rest is pure history. As for Baetan, his foolish greed and temper got him killed in battle not long after he was run from Scotland's shores. (See *Aidan, Columcille, Aedh*.)

Bantan (bahn'-tan): Bran's horse.

bard: a poet or historian of the druidic order; these good fellas recorded Erin's history in verse and song. Their *literary license* is what makes the separation of history and legend so difficult for today's scholars to discern. In the last half of the sixth century, the bards narrowly missed total obliteration and/or exile at the Synod of Drumceatt. Their carefree existence over, they were stripped of their political influence and their right to abuse free hospitality and compensation. The new order had no choice but to become the secular schoolmasters, earning their keep at their assigned tuath.

Interestin'ly enough, the Hebrews had no recorded history either, save in song or verse, until the Holy Scriptures. Not till the arrival of Christianity were Erin's stories recorded for posterity in cooperation with the poets and scholars. No doubt about it, the Irish of today are nearly as Hebrew as Celtic.

bards, dilemma of the: A passel o' these melody-mouthed scholars had become more trouble than they was worth, trottin' about imposing on good hospitality and payin' it back with barbed satire and curses. Sure, the nobles wanted 'em exiled, but Columcille saved them (see *Columcille*). Reform the system, says he, but to exile the bard was to exile their *knowledge*, which was sacred to every Celtic heart. It was decided that each tuath would appoint its own bards to educate its children, as well as have a priest for its spiritual education. Aye, the bards became schoolteachers, and knowledge was saved.

batagh (bah-tah): public victualer to entertain travelers and chief's soldiers; rent-free land, much like a tavern geared more to entertainment and board than bed.

blefed: plague with symptoms of yellowish palor, fever.

bóaire (bo-ayr): a self-sufficient farmer/cattleman.

Bran (brahn): raven.

brat: outer cloak or wrap; the more colors, the higher the station of its wearer.

Brehon Law: the ancient law of the Irish Celts, updated in the fifth century at a convention of druids, priests, and kings.

brewy: A name for a common inn and the innkeeper. The room and board were free, same as in any Irish home, with the land and food/cattle for travelers supplied by local landowners. This is just another fine example of Celtic hospitality.

Brichriu (brik'-ree-oo): an ancient historical satirist known for stirring up trouble.

bride price: the price paid by the groom to the bride's family for the privilege and duration of his marriage to the lady.

Quite the opposite of the dowry, wouldn't ye say? And 'twas a custom mainly Irish and connected to Erin's Hebrew roots. Goin' back to when the *Milesians* from Iberia settled in Erin, there was a shortage of women. So the *Milesians* asked the Hebrews, who'd been in Ireland since Japeth and Shem's children landed there after the Flood, if they might marry the *Hebrew* daughters. Yes, says the Hebrew elders, but only if a bride price is paid to the bride's family for the duration of the marriage. The rest was up to the groom. (Bear in mind, before Patrick, marriage was bindin' only as long as both parties agreed to it, but the custom o' payin' for the bride continued for centuries beyond.)

bruden: A much larger and higher-class hostelry or brewy, able to lodge not just individual travelers, but nobles and their entourages as well. 'Twas usually found at main crossroads and, like the brewy, 'twas free to all.

Brugaid (brew-gayd): A female innkeeper or brewy, for many a one was run by me daughters.

bulliken: a young bull

chieftancy: A chief or king was elected, no less, by the clan. To qualify, he must be knowledgeable in war, academics, and the like; of fine physical health and stature so's he can lead warriors into battle; and *usually* related to the last chief, but not necessarily. A son, brother, or paternal cousin is considered first, but should no one in that bloodline qualify, then a man from another of the clan families was picked and the line o' rule was passed to another family...leastwise till someone bigger and better took it from them.

cloak of invisibility: a legendary magical cloak, which, when donned, made the wearer invisible; believed to be used by the gods or Sidhe, and sometimes given to a mortal to use.

colt's tooth: a strong desire for the opposite gender.

Columcille (co-lum-kil-li): Patron Saint of the Scots, a.k.a. St. Columba, the Dove. A feisty Northern Niall prince, Columcille could have been a king with his bardic training, but he chose servin' the Lord instead. His blue blood and bardic tongue and his lifelong effort to remain humble endeared him to the noble, the commoner, and God's church. The church had to excommunicate the man for taking up the sword at Culdreime's battle, but he was reinstated later in consideration of his faith, devotion, and genuine contrition. Still, his remorse was such that he imposed exile upon himself from his beloved green Derry to the gray and lifeless island of Iona, off Scotland's coast.

His is yet another fine example of how the good Lord can use even a proud hothead to save souls, for Columcille took God's light to the Scots and Picts. Sure, he named and crowned the first Christian king o' the place. Later, he did come home to save the bards, decide the sovereignty of Scotland, and build the framework for public, secular, and church education in Ireland. (See *Drumceatt, Synod of,* and *to each cow its own calf* for Columcille's part in the establishment of the first copyright law. Also *Baetan* and *Aidan* for the saint's persuasion by an angel.)

crannóg: a fortified lake dwelling, usually on man-made island.

cromlech: a capstone resting on two upright pillar stones, sometimes forming a passage; usually marks a grave of someone of importance—a hero or royalty.

Cromyn (krah'-min): crooked or bent.

culcita: a quilt; also a flocked blanket or bed.

Culdreime, Battle of: What a fight, the culmination of a feud between the Northern Uí Niall (St. Columcille's kin) and the High King Diarmait in sixth-century Ireland. Even the church got into this donnybrook of a fight. See, full of himself, Diarmait invaded the sanctuary of saint-to-be Columcille's church and seized a Niall lad accused of killin' the high king's nephew in a hurling match at a fair—a mere accident in a dangerous sport by all accounts. Diarmait was defeated, and three thousand men were killed. (Have a gander at *Columcille* to see what happened to him for his hotheaded involvement. Also see *to each cow its own calf* to discover another bone the young saint-to-be had to pick with *Diarmait*.)

Dalraidi *(pl.)* (dahl'-rah-dee), **Dalraida** *(sing.)* (dahl'-rah-dah): this was an early Ulster clan; some migrated to Scotland in the fifth century, and by the sixth century, sure they ruled it and the latter half of that same period chose their first Christian king, Aidan.

cumal: female slave; a monetary unit equal to one female slave.

Dallan (dah'-lan): blind-diminutive of *dall*.

DeDana, Tuatha: See *Tuatha DeDanan.*

death of King of kings: 'Twas recorded in an early druidic historical poem about King Connor MacNessa, a kindly monarch who saw the sun black out on the day o' Christ's crucifixion. On finding out the meanin' of it from his druids, he was so overcome that he attacked the sacred grove of oak, takin' his passion out upon the trees as it were, and the exertion aggravated an old war wound, killin' the good-hearted soul. Here was another o' the legends that paved the way for the comin' o' Christianity in the fifth century.

dergud (dergu): mattress stuffed with feathers, straw, or rush (colcaid; same).

Dhagda's legendary music: In the tale of Dhagda (dahg-da), the ancient king of the mythological DeDana, and of Boann (bow-ahn), his wife a goddess of the River Boyne, the significance of music to the lives of me children is plain. The time neared when Boann was to give birth to their sons, and Dhagda was by her side. While she labored, her husband played upon his harp, crying and mourning with her in her agony. When their three boys were born, he plied the strings with notes of laughter and joy, until it was time for her to rest. For that, his fingers brought forth from the instrument lullabies, lulling her to sleep. The new mother was so moved by his music and devotion that she named their sons after it: Goltraighe (crying music), Geantraighe (laughing music), and Suiantraighe (sleeping music).

So was set the precedent of music's importance to the heart, the mind, and the soul, like hymns of joy and praise, as well as comfort to life's pain and, o' course, lullabies to lure wee ones to sleep.

Diarmait (der-mot): the high king of Ireland during Battle of Culdreime; Aedh Ainmire was the high king in this book's setting.

dillat: A cloth draped over a horse in lieu of saddle. Me children didn't use saddles early on. They bounded up on the horse, no stirrups. Indeed, the Romans marveled at skills of the Irish horsemen and employed them in Roman ranks.

dromin (dro-min): a long ridge or hill.

druid: St. Columba wrote, "My druid is Christ." Substitute *teacher* or *spiritual leader* for *druid* to catch the drift of his meaning. The sixth-century "druid" was mostly a bard, historian, poet, or musician of the highest order. Them what caused all the troubles leading to almost gettin' exiled were the black sheep o' the lot, but even God used them to prompt a new law, making the bards into secular teachers in the first public education system in the world history. (See *Drumceatt, Synod of* and *Columcille, Saint.*)

In *Maire,* me previous book o' the fifth century, the druids were not just the black-robed sacrificers reported by Julius Caesar and other foreign observers of this secretive order, but what I'd call professionals in today's—a number of an elevated Celtic learned class—spiritual leaders, teachers, lawyers, poets, bards, historians, magicians; often called magi; see *Star of Bethlehem.*

There were some o' the dark kind then, mind ye, but never was any evidence o' human sacrifice found on my shores, like across the sea. And again, God used these enlightened people to pave the way for Christianity, as illustrated in the story of Maire and Rowan's fifth-century Gleannmara.

Drumceatt, Synod of (Drum-cat): circa 574, this particular synod was perhaps the most significant of the sixth century. Called by the high king, it addressed many issues, but the most important results were as follows:

Me children established the first national secular and clerical education system for the public—a teacher and a priest to every tuath.

They saved me ancient bardic class (see *bards, dilemma of*).

They decided the major quagmire of just who was in charge o' Scotia Minor (see *Scotland—Scotia Minor, the problem with*).

Dublin (dub'-lyn): from *duibh-linn*, black pool—the color of its Liffey River due to its peat bottom.

dun: a round tower fortification.

eric: a blood price or fine; its value is based on a man's social standing.

fialtech: a privy or outhouse; the predecessor of the modern porta-potty, set apart from the main quarters for obvious reasons.

Fiana: third century Ireland's equivalent to special forces; the legendary warrior under Finn MacCool.

fine: a kindred group, a basic social unit of early Irish society.

Finella (fi'-nell-ah): fair; feminine derivative of *Fion*.

foolraide (fool-raid): foolishness; insanity.

fosterage: custom of placing children of noble families into the care of others in order to form political alliances. Like Kieran as a prince was fostered out to Murtagh, champion of the Dromin and father to Riona, for training and schooling, allying the clans of Gleannmara tuath even more. Many times, these children were closer to their foster families than to their own blood.

Fynn (fin): fair—from *Fion*.

Gadra (gier'-ah): clever—o' mind, at least, but in this story's case, not o' spirit. Now how do ye suppose Maille's sainted mother knew what a conniver he was goin' to be?

geis (gish): taboo, something forbidden; to break a geis was to invite certain death.

Gleannmara (glinn-mah-rah): glen/valley overlooking/near the sea.

gleeman: these were the entertainers of the common man as opposed to bards, like meself, who stimulate the mind as well as please the senses. They traveled about much like gypsies, often with reputations to match. Sometimes they journeyed alone, sometimes in groups, afoot or in little wagons. Among the likes were jugglers, songsters, musicians, actors, acrobats, animal trainers, and dancers.

grá (grah): term of endearment for love.

Gray Macha: the loyal steed of the Tain's warrior hero Cuchulain; Kieran's roan warhorse.

Green Martyrs (Green Saints): Like their white counterparts, these first Christian arrivals shed no blood for their faith. The good servants chose to live in the wilderness after the example of John the Baptist, which explains why so many o' the earliest churches were found in remote areas unfit for conventional habitat. No matter how far removed, their voices were heard clear to the royal courts and druidic clusters. (See *White Martyrs* for the balance o' the story.)

grianán (gri-nawn'): a solarium; a sun room (or, in me own words, a henhouse). 'Twas a favorite place for the women to gather over their needlework.

hall: the largest room or building in a fortification; used for dining, entertainment, administration, and often sleeping quarters, at least for servants.

Harp of Tara: Pictures of this harp, the likes of which were used in Tara's legendary halls, resemble Hebrew harps, like the one used by King David himself. 'Tis no small wonder, and that you'll see plainly, if ye read about the *Lia Fal* and *Hebrews in Ireland*. Sure, even our music and ancient language was similar to the Hebrews, another tie to these early roots.

heath fruit: a plant used to make beer. Scholars on ancient Ireland think this is billberry or whortleberry shrubs, rather than actual heath.

*Note: The notion of the heavy drinkin' Irish as a race came into being in recent history. After the 1400s, the company that came was enough to drive a saint to drink. Till then, 'twas beer/ales and mead/wines as common beverages. Remember, the water for the most part weren't fit to drink. Usquebaugh (pronouced roughly whus-keh-bach) is thought to be a forerunner of whiskey, imported from the Basque countries.

Hebrews in Ireland: After the Flood, descendants of Noah's sons, Japeth and Shem, settled in Ireland. Japeth's people were a reasonable lot, blendin' in with all them that came, and conquered and ruled for a while. Shem's were a worrisome lot of pirates and brigands and became known later as the Fomorians. Japeth's kin married with the Milesians and, hence, were ancestors of the dark-haired, fair-complected Irish. (See *Harp of Tara, bride price, Milesians*.)

hospitium: the guest lodge at an abbey, and nary a one could earn a five-star rating for accommodation, I assure ye.

iarball (eerball): an animal's tail or hind; the southernmost part of a creature headed north.

imda: This was a sleepin' cubicle containin' a bed or beds, especially if in a hostelry. A couch was usually fixed at the end of it, facin' the center hearth. The walls fell short of the ceilin', allowin' heat to circulate yet allow privacy.

kenning: coloring the cheeks with rouge.

Kieran (ky-ran): dark or black, more reflective of our hero's humor than his coloring.

leaba (labba): a day couch or bench, usually covered in skins for comfort.

Liex (lew): light, brightness, after the DeDana god Lugh.

Leila (lil): of obscure meaning, a popular saint's name.

Lige (lee): a testered bed with curtains hung on rings suspended from a copper rod; like as not, there were two to three person in one, lessen' it was for a king or high official.

Maille (mail'leh): from O'Malley, thought to be derived from ancient word for *chief*.

máithar (maw'-ther): mother.

Marcus (mar'-cuss): a derivative of the god of war *mart/mars* or ancient Celtic for male horse.

Maeve/Mebh (mev): intoxicating; she who makes men drunk; most popular Irish name of all time.

Midach: see Airmed's blanket.

Milesians (mi-lee'-zhuns): the ancestors of the Irish nobility who migrated from the Iberian penninsula circa 1700 B.C.

O'Cuillen (O'Cul-len): holly tree; the Anglicized version is *Cullen;* clan of Dromin (formerly Drumkilly), descendants of Maire's captains Eogan and Declan.

oratory: a private chapel.

Picts: ancient people occupying northern Britain before the Irish Dalraida (Scots).

porringer: a low bowl with a single—and usually flat and pierced—handle.

rath: a circular fortification surrounded by earthen walls; home of a warrior chief.

rechtaire: steward; chief of the house, the good noble master's right-hand man.

redhand(s): murderer.

refectory: the church's answer to the layman's great hall, where clergy dined.

* Note: The fare was meager as these good folk intended to live on as little earthly intake as possible and work their best to produce fruit as the Lord commanded, putting in six days with rest on the seventh.

Riona (ree-o-na): queenly, from *Rioghan* or *Regina.*

ruam (room): elderberries crushed for rouge.

Scotia Minor: See *Scotland.*

Scotland (Scotia Minor) **the problem with:** This became a major issue as what is today's Scotland grew. It was settled by members of the Dalraidi clan o' northern Erin, who owed tribute to the king of Ulster. But it was its own province with its own king now and declared it owed allegiance to no one save the high king of Ireland.

See: a region assigned to a bishop of the church.

Senan (sheh-nan): old; a derivative of *Sean*.

sept, subsept: clan, subclan.

setigi: a blanket, hung out and aired every day; the sheets of white linen in a noble house were embroidered.

Siany (slay-nee): health; derivative of *Slaine*.

Sidhe (sid): the magical faerie people who lived underground and in caves, possibly the remaining members of the *Tuatha DeDanans*.

slige (slee): a main road.

Star of Bethlehem: A passel o' scholars believe the wise men who followed the star to the Lord Jesus were druid astrologers. As such, the legend of the birth of the King of kings was preserved in druidic history and paved the way of Christianity to me shores in the fifth century of our sainted Patrick. Some even think this is the origin o' divine right to rule. See, Ireland was an America o' the dark ages, where Christians fled. When the Milesians married with the Hebrew daughters, the bloodline o' Christ was thought continued, and it spread into most o' the reignin' houses o' the European dynasties that came to be. Sure but God's plan is enough to set the staunchest o' souls back on their heels when it comes to light. (See *Hebrews, Milesians, bride price*.)

synod: A synod was a fairlike gathering of the provincial and tuath rulers and their entourages for the settlement of political and law issues. Vendors and entertainers flocked to provide for the attendees, which attracted others whose interest was more of a recreational nature. Games and other diversions took place when the court was not in session. These lasted for weeks due to the distances traveled to participate, so that all might put in their two cents worth prior to final decisions.

Tadgh (tad): poet, tho' our Tadgh was a poet o' lies; derivative of *Timothy*.

Tara: The glorious capital of early Ireland's five provinces in its Golden Age, until it was cursed in the sixth century under High King Diarmait (early 560s) for his lack of hospitality and disregard for God by a Christian saint. At Diarmait's death, 'twas abandoned as court of the high king. In the 570s of *Riona's* setting, King Baetan, who aspired to be high king—or at least to demand homage from Scotia Minor (Scotland)—ruled the province of Ulster from there before it was abandoned completely to rule.

tech-leptha (tek'-lep-tha): circular bed house with a conical roof apart from hall; a sleepin' lodge.

to each cow its own calf: this was the first copyright case, the result of a decision handed down by High King Diarmait to the aspiring priest and saint-to-be Columcille. Ye see, the prince-turned-priest borrowed a book of Scripture that his former teacher, Finian of Clonard, had just brought back from Rome itself. Such prizes were rare, so rare that Finian prided himself on havin' it and told his former student that he might read it only, but not copy it. Well, the temptation was too great for the young Scripture-hungry Columcille, and he copied the work. Finian found out and became so outraged that he went to the high king and demanded the copy be handed over as well. Personally, I'm thinkin' this Finian a was selfish soul, but Diarmait leaned on the precedent of the old Brehon Law and decreed *to each cow its own calf,* which was his way o' sayin', the copy belongs to the owner of the original. Needless to say, Columcille's princely pride was pricked sore, settin' him in an unholy frame o' mind where Diarmait was concerned. So when Diarmait killed Columcille's kin, Columcille was already primed for a quarrel. (See *Columcille.*)

tolg (tahl): 'Twas a noble-class bedframe built to store things in, like swords or clothes, often in yew, not unlike the hold-all furniture of today.

tonsure: a style of haircut with a section shaven; the priests' were circular with shaven center, while the druids' were shaven ear to ear across top of the head to form a high brow of intelligence; both were used in sixth century by the clergy, reflectin' the druidic roots of many of God's servants.

torque: a neck band, often made of gold or silver; many times took the place of a crown for a king or queen; its degree of elegance often indicated rank in society.

tuath (tuth [short vowel sound]): a kingdom made up of more than one sept/clan and united under one king, to whom the clan chiefs pay tribute/homage. He in turn pays homage to the province king, who pays homage to the high king.

tuatha (tuth-ah): people of a tuath, usually more than one clan/sept, all united by loyalty to tuath's king.

Tuatha DeDanan (tuth'-ah deh dah'-nahn): An early Irish learned race, who, because of their extensive knowledge of astrology, medicine, and science of the time, were thought by the common man to be gods. Folklore has them becoming the *Sidhe* (faerie people) after they were conquered by the Milesians, the fair-featured ancestors of the Irish nobility. (See *Milesians* and *Hebrews in Ireland.*)

Uliad (uh-lid): predecessor of modern Ulster; the people of the ancient province.

White Martyrs (White Saints): Peculiar to Ireland were the saints (white and green—see *Green Saints*), who did not have to shed their blood or die the horrible death of a martyr for their faith. These were a pentecostal fire-hearted lot, who sought to spread the Word with love and humility, rather than with force. Their green counterparts came first, settling in the wilderness, like hermits isolated with their Lord and faith. Their followers came to their small stone abodes evolved into monasteries and they into the white saints.

The willingness o' both to allow me children to keep all familiar and precious customs and laws that did not conflict with Scripture added to the druidic legends and prophesies regarding Christ, and the end of the druidic order as it was known paved the way for the fervent embrace of Christianity. Taking pagan holidays and rededicating all the glory and honor to God, rather than its former god or purpose, was yet another way in which they won the heart and souls of Erin's children.

These were a feisty lot, a combination of saint and warrior for Christ. They made mistakes in their zeal, just like ordinary folks, but their love for the Truth in the gospel always brought them back in line with Christ's teachings. I'm proud to boast that Erin produced more missionaries than any other country in time.

And while I'm gettin' full of meself, I might as well add that it's my children what preserved civilization and all its records, while the barbarians did their barbarian best to destroy it during the Dark Ages. Sure, they were the first publishers, so to speak. 'Twas to Erin in that Golden Age of Knowledge and the Book of Kells that nobility of continental Europe sent their children for education. Why, 'tis the subject of the whole book *How the Irish Saved Civilization* by Thomas Cahill!

Bibliography

Bardon, Jonathan. *A History of Ulster.* Belfast: Blackstaff Press Ltd., 1992. A fine account from 7000 B.C. to the present of me northeasternmost province.

Bonwick, James. *Irish Druids and Old Irish Religions.* New York: Barnes and Noble Books, 1986. If this were any more fascinatin', I couldn't stand it! Certainly an eye-opener regarding the druids of Ireland in particular. Many of these fellas got a bad rap, take Camelot's Mordred, for instance, but that's a whole 'nuther story, 'nuther place, 'nuther time.

Cahill, Thomas. *How the Irish Saved Civilization: The Untold Story of Ireland's Heroic Role from the Fall of Rome to the Rise of Medieval Europe.* New York: Doubleday, 1995. An interestin' peek at just what the world owes me children, preservin' light and knowledge in a darkening world.

Coglan, Ronan, Ida, Grehan, and P. W. Joyce. *Book of Irish First Names— First, Family & Place Names.* New York: Sterling Publishing Co. Inc., 1989. Look for the old names that described both a character and/or description, for the roots are in me history itself.

Curtis, Edmund. *A History of Ireland.* New York: Routledge, 1996. Full of historical information in a scholarly presentation, comprehensive.

Cusack, Mary Frances. *An Illustrated History of Ireland from 400 to 1800.* London: Bracken Books, 1995. *Sigh.* 'Tis hard to pick a favorite out of so many fine books, but this has to be among the best, written in an academic approach, but with true bardic flair. Like as not, me author will have to get a new copy, for this one's worn as an old swine's tooth.

Dunlevy, Mairead. *Dress in Ireland: A History.* Cork: Collins Press, 1989. A keeper o' the Art and Industrial Division in The National Museum of Ireland, the author packs these pages full o' information on fashion and tex-tiles to boot, from me early days through the turn o' the twentieth century.

Grenham, John. *Clans and Families of Ireland: The Heritage and Heraldry of Irish Clans and Families.* New Jersey: The Wellfleet Press, 1993. 'Tis a plea-sure to see just how me clans and their standards came to be, for they reflect all they stood for.

Ireland Now Media Ltd.: *Ireland Now,* http://ireland-now.com/ulstercy-cle/pronunc.htm, 2001.

Laing, Lloyd and Jennifer. *Celtic Britain and Ireland: The Myth of the Dark Ages.* New York: Barnes and Noble Books/St. Martin's Press, 1997. Ye'll never confuse "non-Roman" with "uncivilized" again.

Macalister, R. A. S. *Ancient Ireland: A Study in the Lessons of Archaeology and History.* New York: Benjamin Blom, Inc., 1972. An arrestin' plethora of early Irish information, quite scholarly in its presentation, combining the knowledge from historical record and that confirmed by archeological digs.

MacManus, Seumas. *The Story of the Irish Race*. Greenwich, Conn.: The Devin Adair Co. 1971. *Ach,* what soul with Celtic blood flowin' through their veins couldn't fall in love with this rendition of me children's story? 'Twill tickle the funny bone, move yer heart, and light yer fancy.

Mac Niocaill, Gearoíd. *Ireland Before the Vikings*. Dublin: Gill and Macmillan, 1972. We all need this kind of friend to keep us humble. 'Tis an "in yer face" account of how things were in olden times, but I got the impression that, despite himself, this learned fella had to say some wonderful things about me and me children—all of what was true, o' course. No lore philosophizin' for this one, but full of spell-bindin' facts, some flatterin' and some, left to me, best forgotten—unless ye're writin' some academic paper or whatnot.

Markhale, Jean. *Women of the Celts* (translated from French *La Femme Celte* by Editions Payot, 1972) Vermont: Inner Traditions International, 1986. An intrigin' chronicle of Celtic ladies in myth, literature, and history.

Mann, John. *Murder, Magic, and Medicine*. New York: Oxford University Press, 1992. Now I mentioned the Tuatha DeDanans were known as great healers so gifted that they were considered to possess magic powers of healing. Read as to how some of the medicine of the past—that what didn't kill folks, that is—is being used again by our modern medicine. Magic? Use that modern day brain o' yours and decide for yourself. Not only will ye be entertained, but enlightened as well.

Matthews, John. *The Bardic Source Book: Inspirational Legacy and Teachings of the Ancient Celts*. London: Wellington House, 1998. A taste o' me past in rhyme and the story o' them what composed it.

Matthews, John. *The Druid Source Book*. London: Wellington House, 1998. Here are accounts o' ancient druidism and how it has evolved throughout the centuries, with a foreword by Philip Carr-Gomm, Chief of the Order of the Bards, Ovates, and Druids.

Nairn, Richard and Miriam Crowley. *Wild Wicklow—Nature in the Garden of Ireland*. Dublin: Town House and Country House, 1998. This is the book for the armchair traveler who'd see the beauty and charm of me County Wicklow as it is today, with some hint of what it used to be in Gleannmara's day.

Ó Cróinín, Dáibhí. *Early Medieval Ireland (400–1200)*. New York: Longman Group Ltd., 1995. The man takes ye there and surrounds ye with all manner of information on what it was like to live in them times. 'Tis a veritable wealth of information and fascination.

Ó Corráin, Donnchadh and Fidelma Maguire. *Irish Names*. Dublin:

Lilliput Press, 1990. Now one can never have too many books on me children's names, for sure their use and meanin's are as varied as the shades o' green in Erin.

Scherman, Katherine. *The Flowering of Ireland: Saints, Scholars, and Kings.* New York: Barnes and Noble, 1996. Another favorite! 'Twas the most inspirational of all reads to this soul, for it's the memory of how the Pentecostal Flame kindled in the hearts of saints, scholars, and kings. Praise be, I've not been the same since. Come to think of it, neither has the rest of the world.

Smith, Charles Hamilton. *Ancient Costumes of Great Britain and Ireland from the Druids to the Tudors.* London: Bracken Books, 1989.

Smyth, Alfred P. *Celtic Leinster: Towards an Historical Geography of Early Irish Civilization A.D. 500–1600.* Dublin: Irish Academic Press, 1982.

Time-Life Books, Editors of. *What Life Was Like among the Druids and High Kings: Celtic Ireland A.D. 400–1200.* Alexandria, Virginia: Time-Life Books, 1998.

Various Authors and Topics: "How the Irish Were Saved." *Christian History* magazine 17, no. 4. In keeping with the story of Maire and of Christianity comin' to me green shores, this issue takes a look at Patrick behind the legend, the pains and pleasures of Celtic priests, and the culture clash of Celts versus the Romans. A keeper, to be sure!

Faith, I'd love to list the host of other books full of riveting fact and legend that contributed to the tellin' of Gleannmara's story, but I'm runnin' out of time and space. Since this work was started, the numbers of works on Ireland and its past have doubled and then some. Looks like the Golden Age of the Celts may not be over after all. May the good Lord take a likin' to ye, dear hearts, and keep yer eye open for me next tale, the story of Deirdre, The Fires Of Gleannmara series, Book 3, and revel in me seventh century.

Coming April 2002 from
LINDA WINDSOR
DIERDRE

Don't miss book three in the captivating
The Fires of Gleannmara series!

Deirdre stared boldly up from the ship's hold at the Saxon warrior who had captured the Mell. Blood still dripping from the long, single-edged knife hanging at his lean girded waist, he eased down to one knee and peered into the hold.

Her breath seized at the clash of their gazes, blue fire against a steel gray as hard as the hidden sword she concealed in her robe. No doubt his heart, if he had one at all, was just as cold.

She lifted her chin. "Will you stand there gaping like a village idiot, or will you help us out of this stink hole?"

His surprise transformed into a smile. "By all means, milady," he said, reaching down to help her, "do come up where my men and I might have a look at you."

He spoke the Latin of a scholar, not a brigand.

"You've nothing to fear from me…" He hesitated upon recognizing the clerical robe Deirdre had donned to hide her identity as well as her weapon. *"Sister."* Clearly, he was not convinced.

The sword strapped to her leg hampered her progress up the ladder, but that was the least of her concerns at the moment. She felt as if the stranger looked not just into her eyes, but into her very soul. She lowered them hastily but could not resist challenging his shallow reassurance.

"Is that what you said before you slaughtered Erin's sisters in God's own house?"

His cordial demeanor darkening, the Saxon growled like thunder's own god. "Neither I, Alric of Galtstead, nor my men make war upon women *anywhere.*"

As Deirdre searched her memory for either the name or the place, he tilted her face so that she could not avoid his penetrating look. "Women are for far more…pleasurable activities than war."

A rush of heat singed Deirdre's neck on its way to her face. How dare he! She was a princess, her bloodline traceable to the first kings of Ireland. He was nothing but a bloodthirsty swine. Deirdre raised her hand to slap Alric, but he seized her wrist just before it made contact with his gold-stubbled jaw.

"I see your study in Christian humility has been a waste of time."

"No more wasteful than praying for your black soul."

One of the Saxon's eyebrows shot up, arching higher than its mate.

Father Scanlan rushed to Deirdre's defense. "My colleague is new to the order. She only wears the mean garb of our church community because—"

"I clumsily dropped my belongings overboard," Deirdre finished, sparing the priest further involvement in her charade.

"Grace is sorely lacking among your more obvious charms," her captor conceded with a chuckle. "You took to yon ladder like a fool on stilts."

"Better an affliction of the limb than of the mind."

Far from stung by her sarcasm, the oaf seemed to be enjoying it. His mercurial gaze was an unsettling study of contrasts—slow, yet quick; warm, then cool; amused, then something that made Deirdre shiver involuntarily, if such intense heat could make one shiver.

At length, he made an announcement in his native language, banishing the heat she felt as she recognized two of his heathen words. She'd heard them from a family of Christian Saxons who'd sought refuge in Erin a year earlier.

"*Slave market?*" Deirdre's challenge clearly took her captors back. Her smile smacked of a satisfaction she was far from feeling. "There are some words in your sore language well known in my country. Your reputation precedes you."

"It's a shame it did not precede us on this ship." The Saxon recovered with an unsettling gravity. "Your crew wouldn't surrender until they'd spent their last breath."

"Wouldn't you prefer death's freedom to a life of slavery?"

"Life offers the chance escape from slavery, *sister*. There is no escape from the grave or urn for free man or slave."

"There's none for your heathen likes anywhere." Deirdre spat out her contempt. Anger was the only mainstay left her, for her bravado bled away by the heartbeat.

The blond giant threw back his head and laughed. "If I hope to fetch any price for you, I shall have to parade you with that tongue of yours bound securely. No man in his right mind would expose himself to its sharpness…unless he cut it out. Now *there's* an idea."

Alric scratched his chin thoughtfully, and, for one terrifying moment, his other hand moved toward the hilt of the blade at his waist. Only the faintest twitch at the corner of his mouth gave Deirdre a whit of reassurance—that and the way the sunlight cavorted in his gaze.

She ventured a breath of relief, just a brief one, for with the likes of Alric of Galtstead, it was sure to be short lived.